"We stood alone, daring Fate. We were implausible lovers from impossible worlds, defying what should be, hoping for what could be, awaiting what would be.

Victims of life's cruel machinations, we had become what we wanted, and, what we feared. . .hearts of the morning calm."

# Hearts of the Morning Calm

## An Amerasian Love Story

*by*
*Galen Kindley*

avid
press LLC

Brighton, Michigan USA

Avid Press, LLC
5470 Red Fox Drive
Brighton, MI 48114-9079
1-888-AVIDBKS
http://www.avidpress.com

for more information
www.HeartsoftheMorningCalm.com

ISBN: 1-931419-00-0

Cover photo of Susan Chin Malevitsis by Dominic Bonuccelli.
More information at www.azfoto.com.

*In memory of my Mother, Lois Kindley,*
*who loved to read and write,*
*and who*
*lovingly passed those gifts to me.*
*1920-2001*

*If thou didst ever hold me in thy heart,*
*Absent thee from felicity awhile,*
*And in this harsh world draw thy breath in pain*
*To tell my story.*

—*Hamlet,*
William Shakespeare

# FOREWORD

Since 2333 BC, long before the Western world was new,
Antiquity's name for Korea was *Chosun*...
Land of the Morning Calm.

# PART ONE
## Astoria, Oregon
## December 13, 1998

*Time it was,*
*And, what a time it was.*
*It was…*
*A time of innocence,*
*A time of confidences.*

*Long ago…it must be.*
*I have a photograph.*
*Preserve your memories;*
*They're all that's left you.*

—*Bookends Theme,*
Simon and Garfunkel

# Prologue

Despite its twenty years, his sole remaining photograph had aged gracefully. The left edge was just slightly tattered. A long ago corner-crease was nearly imperceptible. The once white border was only now turning a mature shade of ivory; even the old colors remained, New England-autumn bright. Seemingly, the remarkable snapshot was inoculated against the bacteria of time and touch.

Saunders held the picture with both hands, and again marveled at the stunning landscape. In the far background, dark, saw-toothed mountaintops sliced sharply across a cloudless horizon. Closer in, afternoon sunlight reflected from a wide river in a thousand silver sparkles. The bright water flowed slowly across the paper, finally disappearing through a narrow gap in rocky, precipitous cliffs. In the left foreground, two gigantic statues were, like the lost city of Petra, carved into the reddish-brown rock of a vertical cliff face.

Certainly, the terrain's panoramic scope, nature's magnificent touch, and man's bold artwork were on breathtaking display. Even so, the picture would never be considered a landscape. A single, powerful presence made this photograph an accidental portrait.

At the far left stood the apparently reluctant, unintended subject, a young Asian woman. Without effort, she muted and subdued her dramatic surroundings. A classically simple white blouse accentuated her short, black hair. Faded, tapered jeans emphasized her long legs. There was a supple, almost athletic look about her. She was attractive, but not striking. Yet, she was absolutely compelling.

Saunders knew the woman's commanding presence stemmed from the triple nature of her character. She possessed in full measure the gifts of strength, grace, and compassion. They radiated from her like powerful searchlights, guiding, comforting, redeeming.

Leaning his considerable bulk toward the large bedroom window, Saunders squinted and adjusted his bifocals. Gray December twilight seeped through the rain-streaked glass. Tilting the photo to catch the diluted light, he tried again to capture the woman; to find and hold her elusive, multi-stream essence. As on a hundred previous occasions, he found her unchanged. She stood facing the photographer, chin raised, head tilted, leaning against a metal railing, the sparkling river hundreds of feet below. In contrast to the nonchalant pose, her earnest expression was almost humorous. Saunders shook his head in warm bemusement; no matter the time or distance, she remained what she was, very much like her nurturing Asia; a wonderful, contradictory enigma, an elegant, intricate, delicate paradox.

With a rueful half-smile, he turned the photograph over. On the back was a promise, its faded characters carefully and methodically doled out by a steady hand. It was a melancholy pledge, sufficient to bind a wound but not stay the bleeding. Feeling like an emotional Peeping Tom, he was nonetheless compelled to read the words. The simple phrases brought her to life, illuminated her humanity; and without fail, moved him. They'd never met, but he'd all too easily fallen under her spell. Secretly, he wished the pledge were for him....

> *Remember my promise.*
> *I will hold you in my heart, <u>always</u>.*
> *You will never be far from me.*
> *We will be together.*
>                    *Y*

He thought the message was oddly mixed, and like the woman, simultaneously ambiguous and forthright. The inscription began with a command, but softly tendered. The message didn't close with "love," but love was clearly present. The promise held strong commitment and connectivity, but hauntingly...*in absentia*. Most interesting was the final, equivocally clear sentence. Did it mean "together" in some future reality, or was it tied to the preceding phrase, and meant metaphorically? No one would ever know.

Saunders gazed wistfully across his sick friend's bed and through the window at the storm-enraged breakers and the coastal gloom.

"It's really amazing. We've looked at her, thought about her, talked about her, every day for months. But, even after all that, the more I...focus on her, think I know her, the more she becomes," he hesitated, searching for a word, finally settling on, "obscure."

"Yeah, she...." A retching cough barged into Wilson's sentence, forcing him to a partial sitting position. The spasm passed. Grimacing, he eased back against the pillows.

"She was like that," he finished weakly.

Saunders nodded, leaned forward, and returned the picture to the frail man, who placed it on the nightstand between the water glass and pill jars.

The wind-driven rain tapped louder against the cold, single-pane window. In defiance, the fire popped twice; the wet wood sizzled. The scent of burning pine wandered amicably about the room. The old Oregon coast house, like most of its day, was built with a fireplace in each bedroom. When the December rains sprinted in, cold and unrelenting, from their anonymous north Pacific birth-place, a fire's warmth soothed primal fears and the firelight dispatched the demons.

Saunders picked up a woolen afghan from the scuffed oak floor, shook it open, and draped it across his knees. Settling back in the wicker chair, he looked briefly at a small, faded print of a Parisian street corner which was hanging above Wilson's brass-frame bed. He noted absently that the glass was chipped and the plain wooden frame rather nicked and in need of replacement. Though it was one of Wilson's most valued possessions, its repair, like most chores in his recent life, would probably go uncompleted. Finishing the novel had been an exhaust-ing trial. He had little energy—or now, time—for extras.

"So. Can you believe it's done?" Saunders asked, affectionately fingering the manuscript in his lap.

Wilson rolled his head listlessly toward the rain-streaked windowpane, looked out at a distorted, disturbed ocean, but didn't respond.

Saunders rubbed his chin and struggled with how to broach the next subject. They had covered this tender ground before. Wilson, the final authority on story line, consistently objected. Saunders, the vigilant editor, called it "full-circle information" and believed it was material readers would want. If Wilson could be persuaded, the novel could still be modified without postponing publication.

"Uh, Keith?" Leaning toward the bed, Saunders tapped the manuscript with two fingers. "Look-it, just one thing. We oughta rethink the Korean Air Lines stuff." He hesitated, then added softly, "You know, the double-oh-seven incident."

"Christ, Bill, not again." Wilson looked wearily at the ceiling. "I'm a sick man here. How 'bout giving me a little peace on this, huh?"

"Hey, I'm just trying to improve it, make it better. I've got a…you know, a feel for this kinda thing. I do it for a living. It's why I get paid, remember?"

Wilson closed his eyes and grunted.

Undeterred, Saunders continued. "Listen, I just think it'd give the readers closure. I guarantee they're going to want to know what happened to her. To him. It just closes the loop, that's all."

"No." Wilson raised an emasculated hand, the skin almost translucent. "Why can't you get this? It's fiction…or mostly fiction." He picked up the pho-tograph and, holding it toward Saunders, continued in a subdued, almost regret-ful tone. "I just used her as an example, a model. It's all made up, all, uh…make-believe. The people in there don't exist, not then…and certainly not now." He looked at the picture briefly, then placed it on the blanket near his side.

"Well, readers won't think so."

"Tough. Readers can think what the hell they want. It's my last book, and it's fiction. Period. Besides, that other stuff ain't germane! It happened years later, and's got nothin' to do with the story. And most important? Bill? You listening? Uh? Most important? I don't know the details. I don't want to know the details. I just plain don't want to think about it! So…no. Let it go."

Saunders sunk back in his chair, but looked up in time to catch Wilson's wicked smile.

"The only way you'll include KAL double-oh-seven is over my dead body." A convert to gallows humor, Wilson laughed loudly. The sound was bitterly sarcastic and surprisingly robust in the small, dim bedroom.

"I wish you wouldn't talk like that. Besides, you approve all the changes."

"Yeah? Well, I don't approve this one…again, and hopefully for the last time." Wilson pulled the blankets to his neck. "Always so goddamn cold anymore."

The rain slackened. The fire waned. The darkness intensified. The white ceramic table lamp, always on in Wilson's near-sleepless world, cast an unhealthy yellow glow. In the downstairs hallway, an antique wall clock slowly chimed five times, the sound muffled and weak. Saunders shifted his weight and placed both feet on the floor. The tan wicker chair squeaked loudly.

"You gotta go?"

"No." Saunders looked up quickly, ashamed he'd been thinking of an excuse to leave. He cleared his throat and said, a little too emphatically, "Not at all. You need something?"

Wilson answered softly, "Yeah, can you read me some? Just a little."

"Sure, Keith, happy to." He pause and smiled. "I'm in love with her too. What part you want to hear?"

Wilson turned toward the window. The world was quickly darkening, sharp images fading to soft edges, only the rain was audible. A silent minute passed; then two. Saunders had seen these lapses before, though they were now more frequent and their duration longer.

Finally, his voice weak from disease and encumbered with distant joy, Wilson said, "The front. Start at the beginning." Pausing, he closed his eyes. "The world was…new then, brighter, unspoiled. Things seemed…possible. The future wasn't the past. Start at the beginning."

Saunders ran his hand across the manuscript. Melancholy tried to press against him, but he pushed it aside. Wilson was correct. The beginning was bright. Possibility was reality. Opening the manuscript's maroon cover, he turned to Chapter One, smiled at what he knew was there, and began to read.…

# PART TWO

## Seoul, South Korea
## October 8, 1978

*Twenty years now,*
*Where'd they go?*
*Twenty years,*
*I don't know.*
*I sit and I wonder sometimes,*
*Where they've gone.*

*And sometimes late at night,*
*When I'm bathed in the firelight,*
*The moon comes callin' a ghostly white,*
*And I recall.*
*I recall....*

—*Like a Rock,*
Bob Seger

# One

The wide Seoul sidewalk teemed with a variety of Koreans who, like their emerging country, were a contradictory composite of the modern, the traditional, and the future. Businessmen in dark Western suits, women in Eastern silk dresses, and teenagers in plaid and gray school uniforms jostled, bumped, and pushed noisily past me as if I weren't there. A rush of sing-song Asian words swirled rapidly through the bright October afternoon, falling with an incomprehensible jangle on my Western ear. Blond, a foot taller than the surrounding crowd, and dressed in jeans and a denim shirt, my male ego felt the dull sting of an excluded expatriate, a kind of cultural trespasser, unbidden, unwanted, but impassively tolerated.

At the corner, a traffic light changed from green to yellow, slowing the crowd. The fickle light changed to red, and our babbling stream sloshed to a moving stop, pooling restlessly along the curb.

Before us, the jammed street was alive with overloaded buses, buzz-saw-noisy motorbikes, and Asia's signature vehicle, the tiny, smoke-generating, three passenger taxi. Horns blared and engines revved as the vehicles edged minutely forward, seeking even the smallest positioning advantage for the anticipated getaway.

Their restraining red light changed to green and the drivers applied full throttle. *En masse*, the vehicles burst away from the intersection, leaving a peaceful ripple of decrescendo noise and a thin curtain of acrid, hazy blue smoke. However, like the false tranquility of no-man's-land, it was a deceitful serenity. Materializing from nowhere, a flash of equally impatient taxis, motorbikes, and buses ripped loudly past in the opposite direction. Glad to be afoot, I shook my head and grinned, bemused by the always aggressive, rarely rational Asian drivers who were forever in a passionate rush to reach the next stoplight.

Through the blurry maelstrom of weaving traffic, I glanced toward the far corner where a surprising remnant of old Seoul caught my attention. A single story, Oriental style, wooden building stood in David-and-Goliath contrast to the surrounding glass and steel skyscrapers. The building's gray tiled roof swooped down and away from a peaked ridge to end gracefully in four upturned corners. Softball-sized green dragon heads snarled from beneath white, over-hanging eaves. A small, arched doorway and a pool-table-sized display window occupied most all of the red building's front.

A traditional Asian structure in 1978 Seoul seemed an impossible anachro-nism. Yet, there it was, a lost ghost from a forgotten century, standing with grace and patience next to its younger, bigger, flashier cousins. I smiled at the archi-tectural counterpoint and wondered what the little building housed, and what miracle had allowed it to escape the city's Shermanesque march to the Sea of Modernization.

The traffic squealed to a stop. The street was temporarily safe. With uncan-ny synchronization, the surrounding river of Asian faces surged into the striped crosswalk. Like unnoticed flotsam, I was carried benignly along in the backwash, across the intersection and closer to the mysterious structure.

I drifted diagonally out of the main current to stream's edge and stopped before the little building. Tilting my head, I tried to read a small sign hanging above the doorway. Impossible; just a scrambled tangle of pick-up-stick letters and jumbled Korean symbols that made no sense. I moved to the window, and in typically bold American fashion, peered inquisitively through, unconcerned about decorum or the privacy of secrets.

Beyond the glass I discovered muted lighting, accent mirrors tastefully hung on mahogany walls, and on three of four sides, polished glass counters holding pearl, gold, and silver display items. The enigmatic little building was a jewelry shop.

I leaned forward, cupped my hands against the glass and looked more close-ly. Arranged tastefully in the display window were men's and women's watches, diamond rings, and bracelets made from Korea's famous white jade. I looked fur-ther into the shop, across the emerald-green carpet to the small room's far wall. There, behind the counter, sat an Asian woman. She was alone, reading, totally absorbed in what would prove to be her beloved *Hamlet*.

I stood back from the window, surprised by an urge to step inside and browse. Hesitating, I checked my watch and sighed. Four-forty. The cusp of late. Dinner with my Army friends was at five. I had little time for, and certainly no interest in, jewelry. I shook my head in a questioning reproach; I wasn't a brows-er. Regaining my wits, I began to turn away.

The woman, unaware of my presence, arched her back in a long, feline stretch, all the while continuing to read. She relaxed and casually passed one hand through her short, styled hair. Pursing her lips, she turned the page, slow-ly, as if too rapid a movement would dislodge and scatter the words. Her move-ments were unpretentious, elegant, and inexplicably captivating. I looked at the ground, smiled, and shook my head...perhaps just a quick look. I could, it seemed, spare five minutes after all.

* * *

I opened the door. A tiny brass bell jingled. The woman looked up, expressionless, transitioning through the centuries from Hamlet's Denmark to 1978 Korea. Recognizing a customer, she placed her book on the counter, one finger marking her place, and stood. With her right hand, she smoothed the bottom of her navy blue jacket, assuring it fell neatly over a light-gray pleated skirt.

I walked toward her and noticed she was taller and thinner than the Korean bar-girls I knew, perhaps only three or four inches shorter than my five-eleven. She appeared lithe, and there was the vague impression of supple athleticism about her. Her face was more narrow and her complexion decidedly less ruddy than the saloon waitresses. Her chin was almost pointed, and she had just a trace of the classic Korean "pug nose."

She tilted her head slightly and seemed for a moment to smile, but as I got closer, I recognized the illusion. Her upper lip formed the top half of an elongated heart shape and, like the geometric French Curve it mimicked, turned the corners of her mouth slightly upward in a perfect Mona Lisa taper.

I reached the counter and concluded my very male assessment. She was appealing, almost attractive, but not beautiful. Beauty was the sole province of Western women, the much desired "round eyes." The highest praise allocated Asian women was…"attractive." Before I could pronounce further judgments, I met her gaze. Without warning, I was ensnared.

Her eyes were, of course, dark; but only as background. Shining through the darkness, they were dynamically alight, aglow with a fierce, steady fire that fueled a glimpse of her power, intensity, and intuition. She seemed to use her eyes like scientific instruments, tools to dissect, examine, and evaluate. Uncomfortably, I sensed my thoughts and secrets were being methodically dredged up and dispassionately assessed.

But there was more, and like Asia, it was subtle, a second level of meaning, a divergent but parallel existence. Asian subtlety never dealt with the event, but what the event represented. Her eyes personified this subtlety, and lying just beneath the ferocity and flames smoldered a hint of sequestered kindness and guarded tenderness.

The net effect was a confusing, conflicting, at odds set of visual clues. Was she the disinterested, scientific examiner, or the understanding and soft comforter? Perhaps she was capable of the impossible, critical compassion. In either case, she suddenly seemed more than just another Korean woman.

I remained transfixed, my assessments and judgments about her surface characteristics forgotten. She continued to watch me with exclusive intensity. The sensation was disturbing.

I cleared my throat, tugged awkwardly at my shirt collar, and with effort, broke eye contact. Still, I felt each of her unasked questions: Who was I? Where was I from? Why had I interrupted? Was I capable of coherent communication, or limited to simple noises and basic gestures?

The silence and my discomfort grew proportionally. Normally glib, I was surprised to find my vault of smooth, opening lines empty. She'd spun me akimbo. Disoriented, I glanced rapidly about for an anchor. I spotted the thin book lying innocently between us, her finger resting at the spot of interruption. A bad idea struck me; naturally, I lunged for it.

"You can't read that," I blurted.

She continued to watch me without comment.

"It's English," I added in unsolicited explanation, as if the great unwashed of Asia were incapable of mastering "The International Language."

This approach was classic military humor: rough-and-tumble, sarcastic, and delivered without the important introductory "small talk" or other obligatory Asian social courtesies. Under duress, I'd displayed my best cultural ignorance, laced up my Army boots, and trampled directly over her unseen Korean sensitivities.

The woman, however, appeared unfazed and I wondered if she'd understood what I'd said.

I tried a smile. Smiling was readily understandable, no matter the culture. She didn't smile in return, so I tried to simplify my insult.

"You speakee English?" I asked slowly in a slightly raised voice, the way Americans do when addressing foreigners.

She sighed wearily, sagged for just a moment, then canted her face upward— a posture she would wonderfully describe as "playing high-nose."

"Yes, I can read the book and I 'speakee' English. Do you?" Her confident tone was lightly indignant, but laced with indulgent humor.

"Oh." I felt the warm blush of red cheeks, but firmly seated in a deck chair on the *Titanic*, pressed on.

"Well then, prove it. Read a little…and let's just have me choose the passage," I said brightly, adding the insult of implied dishonesty to my growing list of Western blunders.

Without invitation, I took the thin red book from beneath her hand.

She raised an eyebrow.

I flipped randomly through the pages and selected a short passage. I turned the book toward her and tapped the chosen text, indicating she controlled the metaphoric dice.

Accepting the book, she lowered it to the counter with an expression of bemused disbelief. She shifted her weight to one foot and tilted her head. Apparently, this was a new game. Her manner suggested she was slowly fingering the dice. I could almost hear the ivory clicking and clacking as they rolled deliberately over one another within the boundary of her hand. Clearly, she was considering the odds, weighing risk versus return, deciding whether to pass or play.

Suddenly, she lifted the book, squinted briefly in concentration, and began to read. She did so with a charmingly smooth, lilting cadence. Her diction was almost too good, pure textbook, none of the easy melting of word upon word she would eventually call "conversational English." She read, of course, without error:

*"Laertes, was your father dear to you?*
*Or, are you like the painting of a sorrow,*
*A face without a heart?*
*Why ask you this?*
*Not that I think you did not love your father,*
*But that I know love is begun by time,*
*And that I see, in passages of proof,*
*Time weakens the spark and fire of it."*

She paused, but didn't look away from the text. Her face clouded slightly as she appeared to consider the next sentence. After a moment, she began again, slowly this time, as if emotionally measuring the words....

*"There lives within the very flame of love,*
*A kind of wick or snuff that will abate it."*

She lowered the book and looked up. Her head seemed to move in motor-drive photography freeze-frames, each picture sequentially different than the one preceding. Her gaze had lost its curious examiner quality. Apparently, she too was moved by the words' passion and touched by their timeless and universal power.

Free from the constraint of her gaze, I recovered first, cleared my throat, and spoke, breaking the spell.

"Uh.... Okay. Not bad. Not bad. Lucky guess probably." I grinned sheepishly, thinking she surely could not miss my obvious appeal and charm.

Indeed, the woman seemed to refocus and return to the small shop. However, she neither smiled nor gave any sign she'd been charmed. Yet, despite my cultural stumbles and her demeanor, I sensed she wasn't angry or insulted. She was, however, about to demonstrate her rapier-like repartee tendency.

She stooped slightly, bending gracefully at the knees. Reaching below the counter, she rummaged about in what sounded like a sack or wrapping paper.

Standing, she produced a second book, this one much thicker than the first. She opened the cover. The print was in *Hangul*, the written script of Korea. The typeface was large, surrounding illustrations of children, dogs, and cats. It looked like a child's elementary reader of the "Dick and Jane" variety.

"This book is a gift for my small sister. She would, I think, uh…permit? Yes? Permit you to see this." She handed me the book and, at last, smiled.

"So, now it is your opportunity to read the passage, yes? You," she added, pointedly twisting her embedded rapier, "may also choose this passage." In after-thought, she added casually, "With a loud voice, please." Pausing, she shook her head. "Loud voice is not correct. What is the phrase?"

"Uh, I think you mean 'out loud.' Actually, 'aloud' is best, but 'out loud' is, uh, normal."

"Yes, aloud, please."

I noted with brief interest, she chose "best."

With a satisfied smile, she leaned back against the wall, folded her arms near her waist, and with head tilted, regarded me expectantly.

Touché. Payback. I'm sure she didn't know the English slang, but clearly she knew the universal concept.

I opened the book, hesitated, and looking down as if to read, bluffed; sur-facing one of my few Shakespeare quotation fragments. I began loudly, with bravado, as would an unskilled Victorian actor, then diminished quickly in decrescendo.

"*NOW*, is the winter of our discontent, made glorious spring byeeee…sun-shine," I blurted, laughing, the correct quotation lost. The woman joined me, surrendering at last to laughter.

"This is not correct," she exclaimed, playfully snatching the book. "This is the children's book." She waved it in the air before my nose.

"Are you sure?" I sparred. We shared more laughter, crisp, clean and con-nected, with no Eastern or Western border.

"Of coors I am sure." Her emphasis was on "sure" and "course," was charm-ingly pronounced as if it were the Rocky Mountain beer.

"Also, the uh, word is 'glorious summer,' not 'spring,'" she corrected gently.

"Spring. Summer. Close enough for this test."

"Well, perhaps it is you need the more study and less examination," she sug-gested with an easy smile.

"Study. Right. I'll start this evening. But I need a teacher. Maybe you're avail-able?"

The question was not intended to be suggestive. To my Western ear it sound-ed fine, fitting nicely in the flow of give-and-take just where it should. This was how it would have developed at Sears or K-Mart back home in Alabama.

However, in a small shop in the heart of downtown Seoul, Korea, the effect was absolutely different. The idea ricocheted sharply off her Asian heritage. Her mood darkened. She withdrew. The surprising warmth between us cooled.

"Well, there are many fine language tutors for this kind of thing. You will identify one without difficulty."

The entry bell rang brightly. A Korean couple entered the shop. Seeing me, they stopped abruptly and, demonstrating that least engaging of Asian characteristics, stared.

I nodded.

They stared.

Looking back to the woman, I noticed she seemed ill at ease, so suddenly and unexpectedly trapped between two worlds.

"Sir, is there something I can show you?" she asked. Her voice had lost its lilting cadence; the question was mechanically delivered as if scripted and awkwardly read.

"Well, uh, actually no. I just happened in and, well…." I stalled, stymied by the intruding, gawking couple. "Perhaps I could just look around some?"

The woman bowed slightly. "Very well." After a moment's uncomfortable hesitation, she turned and walked to the couple.

I watched the trio with interest. There was general bowing, much smiling, several handshakes, more bows and an extended exchange of what I gathered were pleasantries. Finally, the man pointed to an article of jewelry and a three-way discussion began in earnest.

Watching this ritual, I concluded these greeting protocols were routine Asian courtesies and conventions I'd overlooked. However, displaying a gracious good nature, the woman had excused my Western manner. She seemed to understand my handicap and the game at work between us. In the shop's quiet emptiness, she had accepted the dice and played along.

But players fold; games end. More customers arrived. My five minutes had long since lapsed. She could no longer gamble. I could no longer remain.

The woman returned and with the briefest of bows, stood directly before me, hands clasped gracefully at her waist. Her previous familiarity remained in hiding. Her eyes were neutral. She was unreadable and inscrutably Asian.

"Soooo…. I better go."

The woman remained silent and immobile.

Occasionally, life moves us to places of its choice without permission or explanation. For reasons I would never understand, I fumbled in my wallet and heard myself say, "But, uh, take my card." I shrugged. "It's got my phone number. I live on the American Army base at Yongsan. Perhaps we could, uh…talk sometime? Who knows, you may even decide to become my 'tutor.'"

I tried another winning smile. No reaction. I started to hold the card out, but intuition cautioned discretion. The rules were different in Asia. I placed my card on the counter. The woman watched, but made no acknowledging comment or gesture. I hesitated, unsure what to say or do. After a moment, instinct urged I leave. This had been fun, but we were finished. I smiled, nodded, and left the shop.

* * *

Seoul's metropolitan skyline blocked most of the late October sunlight. To the west, dark clouds formed over the port city of Inchon. The afternoon had cooled considerably as it yielded to the deepening city shadows and the promise of rain. I shivered, zipped my jacket and, joining a thinner stream of passersby, walked about a quarter-mile to the perpetually bustling, open-air, Seoul City Farmer's Market. Opposite the market was a taxi stand where, surprisingly, there was no waiting line.

My tiny beige cab scurried through the capital city's noisy and frenetic traffic to the Naija Hotel, where I met fellow Army pilots for drinks and dinner. Following dessert, we enjoyed an old Abbott and Costello movie in the hotel's small theater. After the movie—and several nightcaps—exaggerated tales of aviation derring-do and our growing laughter echoed about the hotel's bar. At eleven-thirty, with some gentle management prompting, we blearily and nosily agreed to leave.

I taxied the fifteen minutes across town toward my quarters on Yongsan. The little cab's threadbare windshield wipers scraped left and right in a losing battle to clear the glass of rain. Watching the hypnotic pattern, I fell into a contented stupor; unaware of the gathering forces, unsuspecting of what they would bring, and unprepared for their lasting impact. Sadly ignorant but happily exhausted, it was a simple matter for the combined effects of fatigue, alcohol, camaraderie, and laughter to supplant dim and fading memories of a tall, anonymous Asian woman with remarkable eyes. By the morning, I had forgotten her entirely.

# Two

Korea, "The Hermit Kingdom," lies quietly between the Yellow Sea and the Sea of Japan. The tiny nation is six hundred ancient miles of beautifully rugged, mountainous peninsula. Across the Yellow Sea to the west, lies China; to the north, Manchuria, and to the east—but curling maliciously southwest toward Korea—lurks Japan.

Through the centuries, the Japanese and Koreans developed many blood-soaked animosities, the most recent concluding in 1945. At the close of World War II, the Allies evicted Japanese military forces from the peninsula. The expulsion ended a brutal thirty-five year occupation, marked by a cruel subjugation of the Korean culture and an unrelenting expropriation of Korean natural resources. Japan's departure also left Korea without a functioning government.

As a first step toward self-determination, the Allies politically divided Korea at its geographic mid-point. The Soviets administered post-war recovery plans north of the thirty-eighth parallel; America was responsible for reconstruction south of the parallel.

The Allied plan envisioned a nationwide election to establish a new government. However, due to Soviet intransigence, a national referendum was not conducted. As a result, rather than a unified country emerging, two antagonistic and philosophically divergent nations arose side by side, communist North and democratic South Korea.

In June 1950, North Korean forces crossed the thirty-eighth parallel and attacked the South, intending to force unification under communist ideology. South Korea resisted and sought United Nations assistance. The U.N. provided combat forces from sixteen countries, the largest proportion American. A bitter, three year war ensued. In July 1953, an armistice was signed. A bitter, twenty-five year peace followed. To help enforce a tense and tenuous cease-fire, American forces remained in Korea.

In the summer of 1978, I was assigned to Korea and Headquarters, Eighth U.S. Army as a helicopter instructor pilot and aviation staff officer. Eighth Army Headquarters was located on a major military installation, Yongsan compound.

Fenced and guarded, Yongsan's twenty square miles of hills, trees, office buildings and living quarters lay adjacent to Itaewon (E-tay-wahn) District, a busy
shopping area catering to American soldiers.

The Command's Aviation Office, in which I worked, was on the first floor
of a three-story brick building. I shared aviation duties and responsibilities with
my mentor and fellow instructor pilot, Hugh Stevens. Hugh was my senior in
military service by fifteen years and at forty-seven, about twenty years my elder.
He brought credibility, experience, and professionalism to the office. To me, he
brought friendship and humorously sarcastic counsel.

* * *

It was a late afternoon, at least two weeks after my long forgotten jewelry
shop encounter. I stood before a large, plastic-covered wall map of Korea marked
with aviation hazards and no-fly zones. I was inserting color-coded stick pins at
various hazard points when the phone, which seemed to ring incessantly, rang
again. I ignored it, hoping Hugh would answer, which, after needlessly clearing
his throat, he did. I half-turned toward him and grinned.

"Eighth Army Aviation, Chief Warrant Officer Stevens." Looking vacantly at
the two lockers opposite our desks, Hugh paused to listen, then said, "Uh, yeah,
it is." Another, shorter pause. "You bet he is, just a second."

Placing the mouthpiece against his shoulder, he looked across the top of his
reading glasses.

"Ohhhhh, Jaaaa-son?"

"Yes, Hugh?"

"Guess what?"

"Wouldn't even try."

"Well, it's for you, Sport. A woman."

"Christ, it's not Spiderwoman is it?"

"Nope, a Miss Lee.… Now there's a surprise."

Lee is a common Korean surname, something like the Asian version of Jones.
Inevitably, all Korean women were known as "Miss Lee" to the culturally sensi-
tive GIs—an acronym formed from "Government Issue" and slang for any
American serviceman.

I shrugged. "Who's Miss Lee?"

"How do I know? Your latest bimbo?"

I frowned, but didn't move.

After a moment, Hugh nodded impatiently toward my phone.

Raising a calming hand, I maneuvered around the file cabinets to my desk
and lifted the receiver.

"Warrant Officer Fitzgerald."

"Warrant Officer Fitzgerald? This is the same as...." She paused before continuing robotically, as if reading in dim light. "Chief Warrant Officer Jason Fitzgerald. Eighth United States Army. Instructor pilot. Yes?"

"Uh, yeah, close enough." Her appended "yes" seemed familiar.

"Very well. Good afternoon, I am Miss Lee."

I rolled my eyes. I didn't know a Miss Lee; I knew a thousand Miss Lees. I looked up, unfocused, toward the small room's only window, and repeated slowly as if greatly puzzled, "Miss Lee?"

"Yes. From the jewelry shop. Do you recall?"

Still lost, I didn't immediately respond. A small, embarrassed laugh seeped down the phone line.

"Oh, you do not recall." A playful, disappointed pout surrounded her words.

I smiled, noting her vaguely odd but delightful choice of "recall" as opposed to "remember." This certainly wasn't my favorite bar Hostess, Spiderwoman. Her vocabulary was comprised almost entirely of vulgar phrases linked with an occasional conjunction.

"Miss Lee?" I offered blankly. Then, it struck me. "Oh, Miss Lee! Yeah, yeah, right. Of course. That Miss Lee. From the jewelry shop. Yeah. Sure, I remember. You bet. Well, uh.... Hi! How are ya? This is a nice surprise. It's good to hear from you!"

It was the woman with the remarkable eyes. I sat on the edge of my desk and smiled furtively at Hugh who, taking in the episode, shook his head in playful disgust.

I was on the verge of more gratuitous drivel when Miss Lee came directly to the point.

"I am shopping near your, uh, home. Would you enjoy to meet?"

There again was that engaging, non-standard syntax. Not quite correct, not quite flawed, but enticingly different, almost exotic.

Nudged off-balance by her direct, no-nonsense approach, I stumbled. "Uh, yeah, sure, of course. When? And where?"

"Do you know the Heavenly Gate Hotel? In the Itaewon District?"

"Yeah, sure."

"Very well. In that coffee shop at five o'clock. You can do this, yes?"

"Absolutely." Then, laughing, I mimicked, "Absolutely, 'I can do this.' Heavenly Gate Hotel coffee shop. At five. I'll be there."

"Very well. Goodbye."

"Okay, great! Bye," I added to a buzzing phone line. Miss Lee was apparently not enamored of idle phone chat.

"So. Jason." Hugh uncrossed long runner's legs, smoothed his close-cropped salt-and-pepper hair and leaned back in his swivel chair. He removed his reading glasses and studied them intently.

"Miss Lee? Not original, but, methinks, new." He flicked an imaginary piece of lint from his fatigue pants, looked up at me with feigned hurt and added, "You, young lad, are holding out on me."

"Relax, Hugh, she's just a salesgirl I met downtown, nothing to get excited about, nothing to tell."

"Uh huh. I see." Hugh pulled his chair toward the desk, slipped on his glasses and looked down at an array of folders with a knowing, regretful smirk.

Unable to ignore his know-it-all attitude, I ventured, "Trust me, Hugh, this is all very innocent. I barely know the woman."

"Okay."

"Really!"

"Okay. Fine. Great. I believe you."

Hugh picked up a pen and scribbled something on the top right corner of a document. Expressionless, he appeared to have no additional comment. However, as I walked back toward the map, he volunteered distractedly, "And with any luck, that's the way it'll stay."

\* \* \*

After leaving the office, I hurried the two blocks to my living quarters, dressed in civilian clothes, and started walking toward Yongsan's main gate and beyond, to Itaewon's shopping area and The Heavenly Gate Hotel. With summer gone, the subtle, dry-leaf aroma unique to fall was in the afternoon air. The day's last warmth was draining away, encouraged in its retreat by the shadows of Yongsan's taller buildings. A southern breeze hinted at a cool evening. I slipped into my blue cotton jacket and increased my pace.

The Korean gate-guard smiled and waved through the smeared window of his two-person guard hut. I returned his greeting, passed through the gate, and turned right. The wind was noticeably stronger and I zipped my jacket. I wondered if we'd experience a classically bitter Korean winter and grinned at the GI's gift for creating disrespectful puns like "The Frozen Chosun." Frozen was clear enough, but "Chosun"? I guessed it was another name for the GIs "chosen" to be in Korea, but why the odd spelling? I vaguely remembered it was also somehow used in terms of Korea, though it made no sense in that context.

Picking a gap in the traffic between a passing, overloaded bus and an oncoming set of speeding taxis, I jogged across Itaewon's main boulevard. The hotel was just minutes away. I slowed a bit and tried to picture Miss Lee. If it weren't for those eyes, I'd be unable to pick her out of a crowd; Koreans looked alike to me.

I couldn't recall if she was attractive—unlikely, since she was Asian—so I decided I'd probably ranked her in the generously wide "Acceptable" category.

I had no trouble remembering her sharp sense of humor. Unlike most Koreans, she was willing to playfully use it in repartee with a foreign stranger. Her English was great. I wondered where she had learned to speak and, more incredibly, read it. Acceptable looks, witty, and educated; Miss Lee was clearly unlike the Korean women I knew.

What, then, was she, floating undefined about the world? Was she a new species? What rules surrounded her? Uneasily, I realized there were no rules for women like her. She was undiscovered territory and unmapped terrain. As an aviator, I liked order and predictability. Miss Lee's unknown nature troubled me; but I brushed aside the concern with a shrug. In the end, she wouldn't be so great a mystery. Though packaged differently, she was just another Korean woman.

* * *

One of the many Itaewon street vendors approached, pulled up his coat sleeve, and offered me a choice of six "Rolex" watches, each reasonably priced at "Fibe dolla, GI." I waved him away and continued walking. Reaching this Heavenly Gate didn't require passing through the biblical "eye of a needle," only a brief walk through Itaewon, almost as harrowing a task.

Beginning adjacent the Yongsan compound, Itaewon district stretched two miles eastward along both sides of a busy, four-lane boulevard. Colorful and vibrant, the district was alive with around-the-clock, beehive activity emanating from a crowded honeycomb of tiny shops and bars, both finely tuned to attract young American soldiers.

The average age of Eighth Army enlisted men was about twenty. For most of the soldiers, Korea was their first extended time away from home and familiarity. Lonely for family or girlfriends and bored by the monotony of barracks-life, the young GIs were easily lured to the exotic adventures lying just beyond the Yongsan fences.

By day, the soldiers' Itaewon escapades were lighthearted, including window shopping, haggling with street vendors, hassling the prostitutes, bolting down spicy Asian food, drinking *maekju*—potent Korean beer—kibitzing with the shop merchants, and generally finding frivolous ways to squander time and greenbacks.

In the evening, however, Itaewon's sinister nature ruled, and there was but one diversion: the GI bars. These small, dimly lit nightclubs served Americans only and featured eating, drinking, and dancing wrapped in a Western format.

However, for the young GIs, the clubs' primary attraction was women. Club women were either Hostess or Pillow Girls, each with distinctly different rules.

Hostesses were club employees who spoke fractured but understandable English, and dressed in a provocative Western fashion. They were young, somewhat attractive, not averse to physical contact, and schooled in the most effective methods of draining a soldier's wallet. Hostesses could be surreptitiously fondled, but only with strategically granted permission; usually when attempting to coax "just one more drinkee" from a sodden GI.

As a condition of employment, Hostesses were forbidden from forming relationships with the soldiers. However, in a convenient coincidence, the clubs were also home to the euphemistically named Pillow Girls, the collective title for Korean women who were either Prostitutes or Camp Followers.

Prostitutes formed the lowest of Korea's social strata. They occasionally worked from Itaewon's lesser bars, but more typically walked the streets, boldly soliciting clients and charging free-market rates. They normally spoke only enough English to cover the essentials of cost, time, location, and nature of services. Their business plan called for volume and turnover; relationships were measured in minutes.

Camp Followers existed one rung higher on the social ladder. Their business objective was a longer term, live-in relationship. The best they could hope for was one year, the normal length of a GI's Korean stay. Camp Followers spoke better English than Prostitutes and had a less "worn" air about them. Generally, they remained off the streets, cruising the bars and clubs in search of GIs willing to live with and support them.

Korean society considered Pillow Girls outcasts. Castigation was so pervasive that any Korean woman simply seen with an American soldier was presumed to be a Prostitute and subject to scorn. To avoid embarrassment and hostility, GIs and their Korean girlfriends stayed in Itaewon, a twilight area where morality was not an issue and the American dollar salved cultural trespasses.

For the GIs, Prostitutes and Camp Followers represented the total population of available Korean women; there were no other categories. The opportunity for an American serviceman to meet what my mother would have called a "nice" Korean girl simply did not exist. To the average soldier, Pillow Girls *were* "nice" Korean girls.

It was into this tangled and seedy jungle of ignorance, indifference, prejudice, and hostility that Miss Lee and I wandered. For her, the twin tigers of taboo and risk would be quick, vicious, and unmerciful. Unlike Miss Lee, however, I had no sense of jungle, no understanding of taboo, no concern for risk. I was an American, safe and untouchable. Miss Lee, like all Korean women, would have to fend for herself. Those were the rules; that's the way it worked.

# Three

The Heavenly Gate, a twenty story, Western-style hotel, was about fifteen minutes' walking distance from Yongsan. GIs know the hotel's bar as a favorite nesting spot for Korean women of questionable morals. I wondered how Miss Lee knew about this lair of lust. Perhaps she wasn't so different after all.

The doorman smiled and tipped his cap as I walked up the front steps. I shuffled through the revolving doors, entered the lobby, and crossed to the glass-walled coffee shop. Tables, covered with white cloth, were neatly aligned in four rows of six each. A center aisle divided the shop in half. Miss Lee, her hands demurely folded, was sitting in the shop's right rear corner. Seeing me, she made a small gesture of hello and smiled shyly. I waved in acknowledgement and walked toward her.

She wore a chocolate-brown silk blouse and beige wool skirt; a matching jacket was draped over the chair at her side. A gold chain hung loosely about her neck. Her short wavy hair looked like soft obsidian. She wore the lightest of makeup. She seemed relaxed, but there was that remarkable light and intensity in her dark Asian eyes. She watched me with interest.

I withdrew the chair opposite her, but didn't sit. "Hi, nice to see you again."

Motioning for me to be seated, she bowed slightly and replied, "*Annyong hashimnikka.* Hello. How nice you could come. This place is not so...."

"Crowded" occurred to me, as we were the shop's only customers. However, Miss Lee pursed her lips and looked about somewhat contemptuously as she groped for an appropriate descriptor.

" ...suitable," she continued, "but it is familiar to you?" Her voice drifted higher at sentence-end, leaving the hint of a question.

I was unsure how to respond.

*"How nice you could come"*? It was barely two hours since we'd spoken. Did she think I'd changed my mind?

*"This place"*? Did she mean Itaewon, or the Heavenly Gate, or both?

*"Not so suitable"*? For what, or whom?

*"Familiar to you"*? Did she mean I could easily find the Heavenly Gate, or was

she suggesting I was a barroom baron, constantly on an alcoholic prowl in search of willing Korean women?

Squirming slightly, I struggled to interpret, sequence, and reply. But was a response necessary? Had she asked a question or simply made a statement? Did she expect explanation or confirmation? She had spoken two sentences and I was disarmed. As in the jewelry shop, she continued to silently watch me.

As I nervously bumbled toward a rejoinder, our waitress arrived, plucking me from the quandary. I was saved, but I sensed Miss Lee had become subtly uneasy. For Heavenly Gate waitresses, GIs with Korean women were an everyday sight. They were long since oblivious to cultural taboo, scorn, or embarrassment. We ordered coffee, which was quickly poured, and our waitress off to other matters. Miss Lee stirred cream into her cup and seemed somewhat more at ease.

We began smoothly enough. In what would become a familiar pattern, she initiated the conversation in her intriguing, non-sequitur fashion.

"As you can see, I am shopping. While looking for money in my, uh...." Placing her left hand on her purse, she gestured in a wrist-rotating motion with her right hand, the thumb and index finger extended U-shaped, approximately an inch apart. It was an endearing, defining gesture. I would see it many times. She would call it, "word-searching."

"Purse?" I proposed.

"Thank you, this is the proper word. In my purse...." She slowed and drew out the word as if it were spoken for the first time and she wanted it categorized and memorized. " ...I located your card. This gave me the thought to telephone. This is acceptable?"

I realized Miss Lee had an intriguing tendency to change a declarative to an interrogative at the last moment. I'd noticed two techniques for this: appending "yes" at a statement's end, and the more subtle approach of increased voice inflection as the sentence ended. This was the case with her last statement, which, of course, was not a statement at all, but a question.

"Well, sure. I asked you to call; so you were actually obligated."

We smiled awkwardly and drifted into silence. I sipped my coffee and studied the floor. Looking up, I caught her eye. She looked quickly away. More silence. Finally, I nodded toward the packages stacked next to her.

"Looks like you've been to every store in Seoul," I teased.

"No, not all stores, just a few," she answered seriously, missing my playful sarcasm.

"Oh."

Miss Lee looked about nervously. I nodded and wondered what to say next. Eventually I tried, "Well. You've certainly more than just a few packages."

"Yes. More than a few," she replied woodenly.

"So. That's nice."

"Yes. Nice." Miss Lee cleared her throat and smiled uncomfortably.

I adjusted my chair and glanced at the ceiling. Absently, I noticed both rear corners had dangling cobwebs. Looking back to Miss Lee, I asked, "Uh, did it take you long to buy them?"

"No, not long." She fidgeted with the napkin on her lap and brushed aside imaginary crumbs from the tablecloth.

I'd been with her less than two minutes, but could feel our meeting slipping away. The surprising awkwardness was a reversal of our effortless jewelry shop banter. I wondered if it was the culture, but decided not; I didn't have this problem with Pillow Girls.

Casting about in a final effort to sustain the conversation, and exhibiting a dogged interest in her packages, I came out with the brilliantly conceived, "Uh, are they all for you?"

"All what?" she asked, nervously twisting her gold necklace.

"The packages, Miss Lee. Are all the packages for you?"

"Oh! Sorry. No. My family. Most are for my family. My brother is never shopping, so, this is my duty," she explained.

I leaped at the family angle. "How many brothers and sisters you got?" If this didn't turn the tide, I'd somehow excuse myself from this disaster, find Hugh, and line up a Pillow Girl.

Miss Lee brightened and became more animated at the mention of her family.

"There is my brother and, as you know," she glanced at me in a sly and satisfied manner, "my smaller sister. We live with my mother and father in the district of Mapo." She pronounced it "maw-poe." "We have the small rooms there. My father is old and does not now work. My mother does not work. My brother is at school during these days. I work. I am first. No, not first, how is it said?"

"Oldest?" I suggested with a smile.

"As the oldest," she continued, making no acknowledgment of the assistance, "I am responsible."

She said this without pride, anger, or remorse, just factual recitation. If she felt any of these emotions regarding her family, she did not then, nor ever, communicate them. However, it was clear in her tone and manner that she regarded her family obligations seriously.

"Responsible for what?" I probed.

"For my family's, uh...."

"Welfare?" I provided.

"Yes. Exactly. Thank you. Well-fare." She pronounced the word with two clear and distinct syllables.

"I must work until my brother leaves the university. He is now sixteen…and very silly," she lamented, sounding like any older sister, anywhere.

"Where'd you learn to speak English? Which is, by the way, quite good."

"In school and at university. I do not practice now, so, my skill is not as it was. I do wish my conversational English is soon improved."

"You also read English."

"Yes, of course," she said, drawing back in false, exaggerated offense. "Most younger people do."

The waitress cruised distractedly by, filled our cups, and left without comment.

Apparently deciding she had explained enough about her background, Miss Lee asked, "Where do you live in America?"

"I was born and raised in Ohio…."

"This is the center-west, yes?"

I smiled. "Uh, kind of—the Midwest, actually. But I live in Alabama now."

"Alabama is in the Confederate," she said flatly.

Laughing, I replied, "Well, they think so, but the rest of the country thinks of it as simply in the south." She looked at me earnestly, lost in the difference between Confederate and south.

She wasn't sidetracked long. "Your family, it is how big?"

"Well, unlike you, I have no brothers or sisters."

She sat up slightly, wonderment on her face. Her reaction stopped me. We looked at one another in surprised silence.

"No brothers or sisters?" she repeated, a lightly questioning tone in her voice. "This is sad."

"Well, I don't know about sad. I never thought about it much." I shrugged dismissively. "Just don't have any. It's no big deal," I said, feeling defensive.

"Oh, yes. Brothers and sisters are wonderful. They uh…." Word-searching. "…tie, the family together. They allow the family to continue in the uh…future, yes? They share the secrets and problems that mothers and fathers cannot know. They are laughter late in the night. They are help when you really need this. Yes, they make you angry. But no matter, they are…lifetime friends. They are important. If you have none, then you do not know this. Yes, it is sad."

"Well, good. I'm sure you're right. But I just don't have any, and there's not much can be done about it."

I tried to answer cordially, though to my ear I sounded petulant, and perhaps with good reason. Why did I have to defend this no-siblings turf? What difference did it make? Having—or not having—a brother or sister didn't seem to have affected my life much one way or the other. Clearly, however, Miss Lee had a different perspective.

I glanced uneasily through the adjacent glass wall and into the hotel lobby. I sipped my coffee and wished we could get past this family question.

Apparently sensing my discomfort, Miss Lee smiled in her uniquely engaging way and, dismissing the tension, said gently, "Well, you are correct. There is nothing to do, or not do. It is your fate to have no brothers or sisters. Tell me about your mother and father? You have these, yes?" She chuckled, pleased with her wit.

Now on guard, and somewhat aware of her feelings about family, I sensed she wouldn't like my next response either. I hesitated, trying to find the correct framework. There seemed no easy way to phrase it.

"My mother and father are divorced."

Miss Lee became serious again and after a moment said, "Duborced?"

"Dee-Vorced," I gently corrected.

She took a breath and looked toward the ceiling, as if reviewing a mental dictionary.

"Yes, this means not living in the same place together because of the disputes?"

Nodding my head, I offered the erudite, "Uh, yeah, pretty much."

"This circumstance is also sad." Miss Lee looked down at her coffee. With one hand, she smoothed nonexistent wrinkles from the white tablecloth.

"Yeah, but it happened when I was really young. I was raised exclusively—"

She looked at me questioningly, apparently unable to translate "exclusively." A second attempt produced the unwieldy, "I was raised only by my mother." Miss Lee nodded in what I hoped was understanding.

"I haven't seen my father in years. But to me, that's normal. I don't have a sense of loss. Again, it's no big deal and nothing now to be done about it. My mother's a writer. I grew up okay, I guess, and so...." My voice trailed off; I shrugged, unsure how to finish.

Miss Lee stepped in and continued smoothly. "We do not have this kind of thing so much in Korea. Many marriages are chosen, set, by the parents. The couple does not, cannot, de-vorce," she said, careful to use the "V" sound. After a short pause, she added, "We have the different family histories."

"Yeah. Different."

We sat silently, discomfort an unwelcome visitor at the table. This was not the clumsiness of our earlier "first date" conversation, but the awkwardness of my dysfunctional family disturbing and disrupting our harmony.

But, as I would learn, Miss Lee, blessed with the gifts of intuition, charm, and graciousness, could identify and soothe any difficulty. Moreover, she could summon these gifts at will and manifest them in any form. On this occasion, she simply smiled slightly, lowered and tilted her head, catching my eye, and like a playful, soft wind, gracefully changed direction.

"You are in the Army, yes?"

I brightened. "Yeah, the Army."

"You like this?"

"Oh…it's okay."

"Why this is? In Korea, the Army is not the so, uh…pleasant job."

"Well, it's sort of the same in the States."

Miss Lee looked at me quizzically, my semi-confirmation defying her logic. To clarify, I decided to start somewhat from the beginning. I leaned back in my chair and tried again.

"Yes, it's like that in the States also, but, I got kinda trapped."

"Trapped?"

"Uh, yeah. Trapped. You know, no choice."

"Umm. Choice." Miss Lee nodded somberly. "Yes, I know this kind of thing."

Feeling I was missing something, I continued slowly, "Anyway, I started college at Ohio State, but was more interested in parties and football than academics. So, my grades suffered…were bad. I never got them back up and, well.…" I squirmed. "I got kicked out of school."

"'Kicked out of school?' This means the asking not to return, yes?"

"'Not to return.' This is exactly correct," I laughed. "To make it worse, this was during the Vietnam War, so I had two choices; get drafted or join voluntarily. Neither was an especially appealing alternative, but volunteering had the advantage of job-choice. So, I joined."

"What job did you choose?" she asked, seemingly fascinated by my undistinguished and failed history.

"I chose flying. Helicopters. I'm an instructor."

"Really?" She sat up and smiled brightly. "In January, I will try for the new job that is also flying. Once each year, KAL.…" She paused, and with an inquisitive sideways glance asked, "Do you know KAL?"

"Uh, you mean the airline?"

"Yes, it is the major letters for Korean Air Lines."

"Letters? Oh, uh…an acronym."

"Um. Once each year, KAL accepts new students for the flight attendant school. I will complete this application. There is also with this the examination and interview."

I whistled. "That's pretty brave isn't it?"

"Brave?"

"Well, yeah, I mean aviation's a dangerous job, not like working at a jewelry shop."

She shrugged. "Not so brave. Anyway, fate will take care of this kind of thing."

"You think so?"

"Of course, do not you?"

"Well, I never thought about it much. I guess I believe a little more in planning, preparation, and training. How long's the training?"

"The training is six months," she answered with enthusiasm.

"Is it here, in Seoul?"

"Yes, at Kimpo. This is the Seoul *konghang*, uh, how do you say...the airport," she added proudly.

"What kinds of things do you get tested on? Is there a special study course, or do you just take the exam and hope for Fate to do the rest?"

Miss Lee allowed my "Fate" sarcasm to pass without comment, but she did explain the KAL testing and interview procedures and her plans to prepare for both. We also spoke of other, less serious, getting-to-know-you things.

The early evening slipped steadily around us. We found a sweet rhythm. Our discussion was punctuated by her frequent, quiet laughter, the give-and-take flowed easily. I happily admit to falling under the spell of her diction, syntax, cadence, smile, and abundant charm. Listening to her, being with her, was a unique and agreeable comfort.

Near the end of our visit, I suggested and she agreed to meet at the Heavenly Gate again on Saturday. We planned strolling, shopping, and of course, her favorite—and rapidly becoming mine—more "conversational English."

As we prepared to leave, Miss Lee smiled wryly and said, "I have a small gift. This first-meeting gift is a tradition in my country. This is perhaps your first culture lesson?" Her voice again rose slightly.

I decided she'd asked a question, but before I could answer, she turned quickly to her bundles and produced a wrapped package measuring about eight by fourteen inches.

"It is for you," she said, placing it on the table before me. "I hope you like it."

"But I have no gift for you," I said, with growing embarrassment.

"Of course. You do not know this culture, uh...habit. I think there are many culture things you do not know. Do not be concerned with this. I am not."

"Gosh, I...I don't know what to say."

"There is nothing to say or not to say. This is not so great a gift, just a small one."

Still, I hesitated. Realizing I need a nudge, she edged the package further toward me, saying, "Just smile and say thank you. That will be your gift."

"Okay." I smiled, pleased at her elegantly simple solution. "Thank you very much, Miss Lee."

She nodded slightly.

Surprised and pleased, I took the package, untied the string and removed the wrapping. Beneath the brown paper was a simple, wood-framed impressionist print of what looked like a Parisian street corner. Red and blue umbrellas covered tables in front of several small bistros. Artists with easels lined a tree-shaded square. Tourists milled about.

"This is Paris…the Place du Tertre…in Montmartre." Miss Lee pointed to a large white dome in the background. "There, in the uh, away part? This building? This is the Sacré Coeur. These things are on the Right Bank," she volunteered knowledgeably. Then, as if stating a preordained divine right, added, "I will visit there."

"Yes," I said, feigning recognition, "it is Montmartre."

In point of fact, I didn't know Montmartre from K-Mart. Further, I had no idea what a "Right Bank" might be. I speculated that for every right bank, there was probably a wrong bank. As an aviator, I knew aircraft banked when turning. I had money in a bank. Snow was piled into banks. I donated to a blood bank. Billiards had bank shots. Information was stored in a databank, and there were people on whom I could bank. However, none of those seemed to fit. Of course, the obvious and logical Left Bank never occurred, though I wouldn't have known what it was in any event. To preserve my dignity and ego, I simply continued the benign deception.

"It's very nice, thank you, Miss Lee. I'll hang it in my bedroom."

"You will not dispose this away?" she teased.

"No, of course not!" Warming to the game, I said, "I'll tell you what. No matter where I go from now on, I'll always hang this in my bedroom. It'll be the first thing I put on the wall, and the last thing I take down, always. I promise."

"Very well. One day, when you are President of Alabama, I will visit. I will look for this, uh, poor gift."

I smiled at her cross-wired civics reference. "And you'll find it. It'll be there, really."

We were suddenly serious and quiet a moment, both perhaps surprised by such an easily offered and readily accepted lifetime promise.

Barging past the lull, I brightened and added with youthful enthusiasm, "Hey, I'll go to Paris too! We could meet there!"

Miss Lee nodded and looked away, past my shoulder.

Eventually, we would travel to Paris.

Eventually, we would climb the "Mountain of Martyrs."

Eventually, we would light votive candles in "Sacred Heart" Cathedral.

Eventually…but never together.

Her "poor gift"? The colorful Place du Tertre? As I promised Miss Lee that chilly October evening, the print hangs faithfully above my bed, its colors faded, the frame nicked, the glass chipped. Yet, twenty years distant, it is defiantly bright with covenant, warm with memory, and patient for reunion.

# Four

Quickly, Miss Lee was gone, swept away in a tiny Seoul taxi. I watched the little blue car vanish into the crisp Korean twilight. In her wake, floating phosphorescent, was a surprising, cold emptiness. I shivered and pulled on my jacket.

Rising to fill the void of her departure, Itaewon's malignant presence seeped relentlessly around me. As the district's sinister power took form, Miss Lee's gracious essence ebbed. I tucked her rewrapped gift securely under my arm. The frame and glass were a reassurance that she'd really been there; a concrete connection to a very different woman.

She was the antithesis of the Pillow Girls Hugh and I knew. She could speak complete English sentences, none of which contained American slang, vulgarities, or GI-unique expletives. She knew nothing of the American military. She didn't smoke, spit, or chew gum. She hadn't adopted an American pseudonym. She didn't brood, but laughed frequently. She worked during daylight, at a salaried job. Her pay was not in cash, placed discreetly on the nightstand, but by check, deposited in a Korean bank.

Miss Lee even looked different. Her clothing was tasteful. Her cosmetics were lightly applied. Her eyes were reflective, bright…and dangerous. Her voice was bright and lilting. She didn't shuffle slowly about, carrying some unmentionable burden on stooped shoulders, but walked quickly, head up, a bounce in her step.

But most remarkably, she seemed blessed with a rare and wonderful gift. Nestled in the warmth of her nature, Miss Lee sheltered a compassionate graciousness. Her presence and manner could soothe and comfort. Endearingly, she appeared completely unaware of this power, though she'd exercised it expertly and without reservation during our discussion.

Looking down toward the curb, I shook my head in wonderment. I'd never considered that women like Miss Lee existed. Korean women always seemed somehow, well…unworthy. They were Pillow Girls! By definition, they were to be used and discarded. They weren't actual, feeling creatures. They were prototype people, uncommunicative stereotypes. They weren't alive and vibrant like Miss Lee. They didn't have families and hopes and plans and dreams. Was it possible I was so wrong? Had I missed so much? I sighed and massaged my temples with both hands.

Turning away from the Heavenly Gate, I began walking through Itaewon. As nightfall matured, the little district experienced its daily transformation. Emphasis was no longer on shopping. Now, the nightlife fun-seekers haunted the streets and bars. They were apparitions, materializing with the darkness, and like Hamlet's ghost, *"Doom'd for a certain term to walk the night."* Sadly, these specters seemed not to understand their fate. Worse, with no avenging Prince to set free their souls, they were bereft of redemption.

I shuddered at the thought of eternity in Itaewon. If nothing else, the experience would assault the senses. A painful cacophony of Western music spilled loudly across doorway thresholds. The brightly illuminated bar marquees were garishly multicolored. Gregarious street-walkers prowled "Hooker Hill," aggressively grabbing GIs and pushing up close where the combined stench of cheap perfume, cigarette smoke, and inadequate hygiene was overwhelming.

I elbowed eternity in Itaewon aside and hurried toward the American compound at Yongsan. I was anxious to find Hugh, relay the events of my meeting, and get his reaction. Finding Hugh after duty hours meant finding The Statue nightclub. Since our earliest visits there, we'd wondered about the club's unusual name. We assumed it was somehow connected with the twenty foot tall statue in the traffic roundabout situated directly in front of the club.

We asked Mr. Yun, a Korean civilian who worked at Eighth Army Headquarters, about the old bronze statue. He explained it depicted Admiral Yi Sun Shin, Korea's most honored historical figure. Mr. Yun suggested Hugh and I visit the Seoul National War Memorial Museum, which happily, was not far from Yongsan. There, he said, we could learn not only about the Admiral and see one of his inventions, the *Kobukson*, or Turtle Warship; but we could also see a history of all major military actions in Korea dating back thousands of years. The soldier in us was attracted to this suggestion; so we followed Mr. Yun's advice.

During our museum visit, we learned Admiral Yi defeated Korea's ancient nemesis and tormentor, the Japanese, on several occasions in the late 1500's. Admiral Yi's primary weapon in subjugating a numerically superior Japanese navy was the one-hundred foot long Turtle Boats. The Japanese, in their larger, more cumbersome warships, were easily outmaneuvered, isolated, and defeated.

Interestingly, the museum had an actual, full-scale Turtle Boat replica on display. The boat's unique name was descriptive. A lightweight, spiked, turtle-like armor shell completely covered the boat's crew area. The shell dissuaded boarders and shielded against arrows, cannonballs, and gunfire. Most Turtle Boats were powered by one or two main sails. Twenty oars, ten per side manned in

Roman-galley fashion, provided for quick attack and escape.

The warship's most striking feature was a figure of a huge head carved into and rising above its bow. The museum guidebook said it was, naturally enough, a turtle head. To me, it looked more like a dragon's head. Turtle or dragon, there was little debate that it was both ugly and functional. Admiral Yi's sailors lit smoky sulfur fires in the beast's open mouth. This had the double effect of psychological warfare and the more practical effect of masking the ship's maneuver and movement.

Hugh found it especially intriguing that, again according to our book, Admiral Yi, a master of naval strategy and an apparently prolific writer, was required reading for the Korean Military and all Korean school children. Leaving the museum, we passed by a ping-pong-table-sized painting of the Admiral dying romantically, as legend dictates heroes should; with honor, in combat, during the last battle of the 1598 war.

Armed with our museum knowledge, we had a new respect for the old bronze statue, posing fiercely and ignored absolutely, in the middle of the frenzied and maniacal Itaewon traffic. As military men, Hugh and I found a bond with Admiral Yi, and were somewhat uncomfortable that our favorite nightspot traded so lightly on this slice of hallowed Korean history.

We tried to mitigate the sin. Hugh observed that The Statue could have been named The Turtle, or worse yet, Yi's Joint. I noted that The Statue was less frenzied than most clubs, its music sedately played and at a volume allowing conversation. Hugh added that "our" Hostesses were softer and less jaded than most he'd seen, and The Statue's Pillow Girls were most certainly a cut above average. We contorted and massaged these pathetic attributes until they sounded not just respectful, but laudable. Perhaps Admiral Yi would have understood.

# Five

The October wind blew up chilly and damp from south of Seoul, rolled across the Han River, drove through Yongsan, and with a moan, pushed down Itaewon's main boulevard. Scraps of paper danced and twirled along the narrow sidewalks. Funneled between buildings, the wind's velocity and chilling power were magnified. I pulled my jacket collar up further around my neck and hunched my shoulders.

Through the darkness, at the edge of Itaewon's glitzy lights, I saw the ever-vigilant, never-cold Admiral Yi, standing tall and bronze. The Admiral marked the boundary between Yongsan and Itaewon districts, and more importantly for thirsty, women-hungry soldiers, the entry to The Statue.

The club was located below ground level, beneath a large tailor shop. A long, narrow staircase led from the sidewalk directly to the table and dancing area. I had just started down the steep, dimly-lit stairwell when Elton John and Kiki Dee's "Don't Go Breakin' My Heart" drifted up to greet me.

The harshness of the upper landing's single dangling light bulb receded as I continued down into semi-darkness. Ahead, muted multi-colored light seeped through a curtained, arched doorway. The music grew louder. The last stair-step ended on a dark and empty dance floor. I stepped through the curtains. The Statue smell of greasy fried foods and cigarette smoke wrapped around me, a living thing, familiar but unpleasant.

I glanced about, looking for Hugh. Wall-to-wall, the club was about the length of a tennis court and not quite twice as wide. Beyond the wooden dance floor were four rows of circular tables. Hostesses had to be nimble maneuvering between the cramped table area and the bar, which stretched along the entire wall to the right of the entryway.

Opposite me, past the last row of tables, were booths; three against the back wall, six on the longer wall to my left. The booths had comfortable bench seating, the padding covered in dark green plastic.

It was still early; only a few tables were occupied. I spotted Hugh ensconced in his favorite corner booth, regaling two Pillow Girls. A gaggle of unoccupied

Hostesses congregated at the bar, chattering merrily in Korean. Nevertheless, I was quickly noticed.

Two Hostesses descended on and greeted me with loud, exaggerated ceremony and faux goodwill. I was recognized as Hugh's friend, and arm-in-arm with the Hostesses, whisked to his booth and seated with great fuss. Hugh, rather bluntly, dismissed his Pillow Girls. Five dollars each soothed their feelings.

"So, lad, how'd it go?"

Before I could respond, a loud, approaching female voice rasped in mock anger, "Hey, GI! Where you be no bullshit? Hugh here hour! Where you be, fucka?"

I resisted the urge to duck the flying shards of broken profanity, even as the assault continued.

"Play buttafly some otha club, huh? Lucky Seben Club, maybe? Huh? I know. It Miss Choe club, huh? Miss Choe hab big tits, I know. I know you like. You no hab bullshit me, GI."

This unrelenting hurricane of cracked and vulgar "English" was courtesy of my regular Hostess, Miss Pak, better known—to all but her—as Spiderwoman. Her name's origin is unclear, but legend holds it reflects her clinging, physically aggressive manner, her squat and stocky physique, and her stinging, spider-bite tongue.

Spiderwoman was typical of the Hostesses. She wasn't a Pillow Girl, but simply a creature from life's harder side attempting to make a living hustling drinks to lonely, female-starved GIs. For each drink she sold—one for her "guest," one for her—she received a small percentage. In addition, she received a token salary. Tips were her principal source of income.

Spiderwoman's limited English skills were cobbled together from her combined exposure to American Forces radio and television, American soldiers, and "lessons" from the other Hostesses. She communicated by stringing together common English phrases she'd laboriously memorized. During "conversation," she inserted these fragments at appropriate dialogue points. Given her limitations, Spiderwoman had to control the discussion, keeping to familiar and predictable topics. Families, girlfriends, the Army, Korea, alcohol, food, money, sex, cigarettes, and the Itaewon clubs were within her comfort range. When outside this range, or unsure what to say, Spiderwoman simply swore…adroitly. On the whole, it was a successful formula.

Spiderwoman's schooling ended about fifteen years earlier, around age ten, when she was forced to find work to support her family. Her five brothers and sisters also worked at various trades requiring little, if any, training or skill. Her family members lived communally, pooling resources. The family bond is strong across all classes of Korean society.

Spiderwoman, like all the Hostesses, had "regular" guests. The Hostess select-ed her guests, not the reverse. She expected them to visit nightly and spend gen-erously. In return, Spiderwoman made her guests laugh, listened to and sympa-thized with their problems, danced with them, touched them emotionally and physically, and allowed them to touch her. Thanks to my friendship with Hugh, I had instant credibility and was adopted on my first Statue visit six months ear-lier as a Spiderwoman regular.

It was not unusual for two or more guests to visit simultaneously. When this occurred, Spiderwoman simply rotated between tables. While at one table, she kept a surreptitious eye on her other guests, alert for signs they were becoming bored—or worse, on the verge of leaving. When necessary, she'd excuse herself, visit the appropriate table and work her magic, keeping the drinks and "conver-sation" flowing. She had an uncanny ability to remember her verbal location in several concurrent, similar discussions.

The GIs, of course, knew this Hostess-and-guest system was crazy; but all the players accepted the rules. No one tried to reinvent the game. No one got angry or jealous. Hostesses, GIs, and Pillow Girls all survived and coexisted by prac-ticing that oldest of Army adages, "Cooperate and Graduate." In this case, grad-uation was a ticket home for the GIs and survival for the women.

Spiderwoman jostled me as she settled into the booth, an inch, perhaps, sep-arating us.

"I know you buttafly, goddamn-it."

"Hey, I—"

"Don't even try bullshit me." She waived a dismissive hand. The inch disap-peared as she pressed her breast against my upper arm. I pretended not to notice.

"Miss Pak, lighten up! I had to work late, for crying out loud. You really think I butterfly you," I said, slipping into pidgin English and defending my honor with a lie.

"You betta believe it, no bullshit."

Loosely interpreted, this portmanteau phrase was fractured military-slang for: "Sure, I think you were unfaithful, of course." Spiderwoman's paranoia was well-founded. The GIs were infamous for having several "favorite" clubs, each with a dedicated Hostess.

"Miss Pak! Man, I'm hurt. How long I come here, huh? I say June. June I come here now. Six months. Huh? I neba go otha clubs, neba. You know. I don't care Miss Choe's, uh…body-parts. Anyway, you got all my money already, sweetheart. How I go otha club? Huh? How I do?"

Miss Choe, her bra size, my infidelity, competing nightclubs, and all other topics were forgiven and forgotten at my mention of the universal balm, money.

"Well," Spiderwoman replied in a lowered voice, "you America Offica. You

got much money. You neba run out. Don't bullshit me." These final four syllables were accompanied by four finger-jabs to my chest.

This was a familiar theme. The Hostesses were quick to determine a soldier's
rank. They knew the higher the soldier's pay-grade, the larger the paycheck.
Officers, like Hugh and I, were deemed akin to Midas. For a Korean woman to
marry an American officer was the ultimate: a sixty-four thousand dollar nirvana
jackpot, a ticket to the land of milk and honey. Such marriages were as common
as unicorns.

"Well, neba mind, I here now."

"Yea, you here now."

Placing her hand on my thigh, she slowly flexed her fingers in a painfully suggestive manner. I refused to flinch. She smiled and leaned further against me.

"But you got no drink, baby," she cooed, successfully and cleverly turning the
encounter to business. Extending her lower lip in an exaggerated pout, she
added, "Wha happen you? You Cheap Charlie now?"

Her grip on my leg steadily increased, her long "combat fingernails" pressing
painfully into my flesh.

"No, just waiting you ask," I pidgined merrily in response, refusing to show
pain. Spiderwoman smiled and released her grip. I had gained face.

"Okay!" she said suddenly, rubbing her hands together with relish, all trans-
gressions forgiven in the dollar's healing shadow. "You beer or bourbon Coke?"

"Wellllll…better make it bourbon and Coke."

"Okay!" As she swayed sexily away, she tossed over her shoulder the inclusive,
"Me, too." It was how the game was played.

We watched Spiderwoman swagger toward the bar. Hugh shuddered and
mumbled, "Wrap those legs around me, please." He sighed wistfully, "Don't cha
just know she'd break my back, but still, what a way to go."

"At ease, Hugh. You're too old for that perky stuff. Besides, it's not your back
she'd be breakin'."

Hugh guffawed, regained his composure, and continued. "Yeah, probably.
But leave an old-timer his dreams, will ya?"

Finishing the last of his beer, Hugh wiped the back of his hand across his lips
in a satisfied manner and asked rhetorically, "So, where were we? Oh, yeah.
How'd it go with you and Miss whatzit?"

"Well, a lot different than this, that's for sure," I said, nodding in the general direction of the Hostesses, tables, and dance floor.

"Different good or different bad?"

"Good."

"And?"

"And what?"

"Come on, Jason. Don't be cute, you know you wanna tell. Let's have some detail, some fact, the nitty-gritty. Don't make me pull it out of you. I'm too old for that. I'd be dead 'fore we got to the good stuff."

"There is no 'good stuff' in the sense you mean, Hugh."

"Gee, too bad."

Miss Pak returned with our drinks when another of her regular guests arrived.

"Hey, I be back. You stay here," she commanded, "bullshit Hugh."

Without waiting for a reply, she bolted down her drink like it was water, turned, and bubbled to the doorway. There, with great, put-upon "anger," she greeted a tall blond man with a familiar refrain: "Hey, GI! Where you be?" Starting a new circle, Spiderwoman complained about the late hour and his much lamented absence.

Turning back to Hugh, I recited my "Miss Lee Adventure" in short-form. He listened intently, his interest growing with the detail.

"You mean she's been to college?" he asked with disbelief, apparently considering Korean women and college mutually exclusive.

"Yeah, that's what she said. Actually, she said 'at University.' I guess that means college. I don't know if she graduated, but at least she attended."

"And you believe her." He said it matter-of-factly, always the skeptic.

"Oh, you bet. She's got a great command of English. It's very different, though. Not wrong, just different, intriguing."

"Different English?"

"Well, it's kind of hard to explain," I said slowly, trying and failing to find an example rather than an explanation. "It's really nice listening to her. Different, but...nice."

"Nice? Nice, different, English? 'Fraid that's beyond me."

"Come on, Hugh, you know, pleasant, easy, almost musical."

Hugh rolled his eyes.

"For example, I guess Korean and English have different inflection patterns, 'cause she uses voice inflections in places a native English speaker wouldn't. Again, it's not wrong, it's just something you don't normally hear. The effect is really charming."

"Charming inflections mixed with nice, musical English," Hugh said sardonically. "Well, that certainly clears it up. Guess you had to be there, huh?"

"Not if you have the even slightest bit of imagination."

"Sorry, old Hugh's a little short on frills like imagination. Got any specifics? Any will do, I'm not picky."

"Okay." I thought a moment. "She uses non-standard words and phrases, and puts them in non-standard places. I remember she said something like, 'I found your card in my purse.' Except that's not the word-sequence she used. She reversed the phrases, so it came out like, 'In my purse I found your card.' And she sounds almost, uh…formal sometimes. She asked if it was 'acceptable' rather than 'okay' or 'all right,' that she'd telephoned. Oh, and she doesn't use contractions much; or maybe at all. 'It is' instead of 'it's,' 'do not' rather than 'don't,' you know, that sort of thing. Mix in the inflection thing and the total effect is, well, charming. Clearly, though, she's had schooling. I told you, she read Shakespeare better than some of the kids in my English Lit class, for sure; better than me for that matter."

"Better than the wannabe writer? What an admission."

"Well, maybe not better," I said with a grin. "She *is* Korean."

"Well, if she's going to apply at KAL, her English better be good. That part's sure different. Quite a change from what we're used to, lad."

"I don't know, Jason." Hugh shook his head warily. "Spiderwoman's more your speed, and a lot less complicated, I might add. Besides, the 'Spiderwoman Rules' are already in place. You know what to expect, how to react, 'when to hold 'em and when to fold 'em.' All the GIs that came before have played the game and left a map of how to get safely home. Now you want to rewrite the rules. Navigate off the course. Play with some bimbo who's outside the lines, who doesn't fit in our world. How smart is that?" Hugh paused for another sip of beer. He slumped a bit, and wrinkled his brow.

"I gotta tell ya, Jason, this Miss Lee sounds like more trouble than she's worth. Can't you just find a nice Pillow Girl? Look around, man, joint's full of 'em. Had two when you got here! This gal, on the other hand?" He shook his head again. "Hmmm, not so sure. She smacks of uncharted and dangerous water. You know, like on treasure maps: 'Arrrr, Matey, here be dragons.'" Hugh gestured dramatically with his arm in an arc-like motion, apparently trying to simulate a pirate map's printed banner.

Smiling at his nautical accent, I started to respond. "But she's better than a Pillow Girl. She—"

"Whoa, partner. Hold on. Let's just define 'better.' If she's half, no, a quarter of what you say, I guarantee she ain't goin' to bed with you. Korean men prize virginity…so long as it's not theirs, of course. So, she ain't going to give hers up for a GI…supposing she has it to surrender, that is. You'll just get frustrated. That don't sound better to me." Cupping his hands around his mouth, Hugh called out faintly as if he were several blocks distant, "Jason. Wake up. Five bucks is all you really need." With this, he leaned against the side of the booth and gave way to rolling laughter.

"Goin' to bed is not the issue, Hugh," I objected, just a little irritated.

"Oh, yeah. Right. Sorry. Saint Jason, I forgot." This witticism brought on a second wave of laughter.

"It's not! I wanna meet a woman that can think. One I can talk to. I'm tired of 'Where you be, GI asshole,' and 'Buy drinky for Dinky, GI.' So, if she's more trouble than a Pillow Girl, it's because she's worth more. If she's different, that's great. I hope she is. In either case, she's better."

Hugh calmed and rested his chin in his hand, but said nothing.

"And as far as outside the lines is concerned, well, maybe, maybe not. Miss Lee's unusual to us, but probably pretty normal by 'real' Korean standards. The problem is…our frame of reference is Spiderwoman. See, we've got it backwards, Hugh. Spiderwoman's the exception," I said earnestly. "It's Spiderwoman who's outside the lines, not Miss Lee. I'm just doing something…a little different, that's all."

"I guess." Hugh shrugged in resignation. "No matter, still sounds too good for you. It'll end badly. I'm tellin' you, get a nice Pillow Girl and settle in for the duration, Hot-Rod."

"No thanks," I held up my hand, palm toward Hugh, "at least for now. I think I'll try my luck with Miss Lee for a while. Probably nothing much will come of it. But hey, can't be any worse off than I am now. What's the worst could happen? We go out a couple of times, have a few laughs, she shows me some 'real Korean stuff,'" I made quotation marks in the air with the fingers of both hands, "I pretend to understand, soak up some culture, and who knows? Hey, she is a woman. I'm not, after all, without charm and good looks. If nothing happens," I shrugged, "then she's an interesting diversion. No big deal. What's the harm? I'm not going to hurt her…and she damn sure can't hurt me."

Hugh sighed. "Okay." Apparently he'd given up trying to convince me I was on my way to Relationship Hell. "You going to see her again?"

"Absolutely. Saturday, about three. Window shopping." I smiled. "Or, as she called it, 'eye shopping,' in Itaewon. Maybe a bite to eat."

"Itaewon?" Hugh repeated in surprise.

"Yeah, if that's okay with you?" I replied defensively.

"Well, if she's as upper-crust as you say, I'm surprised she'd come to Itaewon the first time, much less a second."

"Look at it this way," I responded, ticking off what seemed to me logically sound points. "Where's a better place for us to hide? GIs with Korean women are commonplace in Itaewon. We're practically invisible. None of her friends will see her here. And besides, where in polite Korean society could we go?"

Hugh nodded halfheartedly. "I guess."

"Now what?"

"Well, no offense, but again, what's this apparently high-class Korean gal doing hanging around with you, a blond, blue-eyed GI from Ohio? You know that kind of thing doesn't happen. Gotta be a problem here of some kind."

"Man, what a skeptic. Look, in the first place, she's not 'hanging around with a GI.' I've seen her exactly twice, for Christ's sake; once was business she couldn't avoid, the other, just now. Saturday is shopping and dining in full public view. That pattern hardly constitutes 'hanging around'; it doesn't even constitute a pattern.

"Second, I think she's just an educated, modern woman, probably bored, who doesn't like the traditional role she's supposed to play with Korean men. You know, subservient, two steps behind, speak when spoken to, all that. Trust me, her nature has an abundance of sass." Remembering the rapier, I added with a smile, "No, not abundance, what's the next level up? No, better make that two levels up. Anyway, she's got plenty of fire. She'd probably be, has been, in big trouble with Korean men. She doesn't strike me as the subservient type.

"And finally, I think she's just naturally curious about a different culture and happened to stumble across me." I spread my arms wide. "The ultimate different culture." I grinned stupidly.

"Sounds like you got it figured out." Hugh leaned back in the booth, rubbing his chin. "Well, could be. Let's hope you're right."

"Sure I'm—"

"Hey! GI!" From across the room, our nearly empty drink glasses attracted Spiderwoman's radar-attention. She sauntered seductively toward our table, her sharp, piercing voice violating the intervening distance. "Hey. You asshole ready 'notha round?"

As it turned out, we were ready for several more rounds. Hugh and I lingered, casually burning the night, eating a Korean-style dinner, sharing some laughter, listening to the music, bantering with the Hostesses, buying enough drinks to keep out of Spiderwoman's web, and swapping "war stories" in one-upmanship fashion. Finally, Curfew, an unnecessary but vigorously enforced Korean law that required everyone, Koreans and Americans alike, to be off the streets between midnight and four a.m., began to press us. At 11:50, in high good spirits, Hugh and I surrendered the sins of The Statue for the sanctity of Yongsan.

# Six

Saturday arrived dressed in a cold, November rain. It was nearly four when I met Miss Lee in the Heavenly Gate coffee shop. Today, however, the shop was filled with a variety of rain-refugees and all the tables were occupied. Improvising, we ordered coffee and found our way to the lobby where we sat in an out-of-the-way corner adjacent to a bushy fern.

While the weather curtailed Itaewon's normal buzz of activity, Miss Lee and I sipped our drinks and chatted casually. Eventually, the confining showers became an inviting drizzle, drawing the District's characters from underneath umbrellas, awnings, doorways and shops. Shortly, the rain abated. We slipped into our jackets and left the Heavenly Gate. We stopped on the landing between the revolving doors and the front steps. I turned to her with a question, but fell silent.

For the first time, I noticed Miss Lee's simple beauty. She did little to cultivate her appearance; tasteful but nondescript clothing, the briefest of makeup, no perfume. Only her always-in-place, styled hair hinted at time spent before a mirror. Yet, her attractiveness was certainly there, hiding in full view. But its understated nature was shy and could be easily missed, like a small gesture, an imperceptible whisper, a stolen glance.

I stared a little too long, and Miss Lee blushed. Watching her open and guileless expression, I had the strong intuition she was unaware of her attractiveness.

"So, anywhere in particular you'd like to go?" I asked.

She deferred. "Well, what is it you wish to purchase?"

"Nothing. What about you?"

"No, nothing."

"Yeah, after all those packages from your last trip, I don't imagine you'd need anything," I teased. No reaction. The Package Subject seemed worthy of avoidance.

We looked blankly at one another. An anonymous stream of people flowed past, separating before and rejoining behind us, like water around a river's protruding stone. We stood silent and ignored in the crowd's current. I raised my eyebrows in a "what now?" gesture.

In response, Miss Lee began to smile, slowly, embarrassment surfacing on her face. Her grin was infectious and I began to smile. Her smile grew larger. I continued to grin and shook my head. Her smile now lay on laughter's doorstep. She bit her lower lip and looked away, willing the door closed.

"Well, for crying out loud, we gotta go somewhere!"

Miss Lee finally gave way to giggles. "There is no need for the crying. It is only shopping, or with more precisely, not shopping."

"I don't mean crying, crying. I mean—"

"Yes, yes, I know, this is in my idiom book," she advised, wiping a laughter-tear from the corner of one eye. A thought seemed to strike her and she said quickly, "We shall do an idiom!"

"An idiom?"

"Yes, we shall start walking to 'see which way the wind blows.' Fate will take us to the correct place. This will work, yes?"

"Uh, kinda."

"What is 'kinda?'"

"Well, it means almost."

"Why almost?"

"Because. Look it, I hate to complicate things, but we still have to choose. Left or right?"

Miss Lee tossed me an exasperated glance. "Please, do not make this the 'horns of a de-ly-mna.'"

"Dilemma?"

"Exactly so."

Without further discussion, she grabbed a small piece of my sleeve with her graceful fingers. With me firmly in tow, she turned and started down the steps, the tall, tailored, assured Korean woman leading the blond, blue-jeaned Westerner. Upon reaching the sidewalk, the wind, and Fate, turned us left.

We strolled past the usual assortment of GI-oriented shops, but Miss Lee showed no interest in these. Presently, near Itaewon's boundary, we wandered into a large store, complete with a second story. The store's size was unusual, as most GI shops were small-one room affairs and locally owned. This was more on the order of a Western-style department store.

The store's primary offering seemed to be clothing. We browsed through the shirts, blouses, slacks, dresses, shoes, and as Miss Lee was quick to verbally point out, purses. Upstairs, we found something that captured her attention: ski wear. The Asian Winter Games were soon to begin and Korea's national ski team was, for the first time, competitive. The public was captivated. Ski posters and ski items were everywhere.

Not surprisingly, the store had ski wear prominently and abundantly displayed. There were multi-colored outfits, two piece outfits, one piece outfits, cutting edge styles, traditional styles, even some portly styles. We ambled through the traditional section.

"Can you play the skiing?" Miss Lee asked casually.

"That would probably be a good way to describe it," I bantered.

"Really? I can play somewhat," she said, missing my sarcasm. "The snow near here is not so suitable, but on the east coast are mountains like Soraksan, uh, the Snow Capped Mountain, and Kumgangsan, the Diamond Mountain. These places are very high and the snow is perfect. But also, there are problems."

"Problems? What kind?" I asked, fingering a red ski jacket.

"Well, Kumgangsan is in the North Korea."

"Yeah, that's a problem all right. Scratch Kumgwhatever. What about the other place?"

"Soraksan is in the south. Its ski place is Dragon Valley. Only…the Japanese tourists are there. That is not so comfortable."

"What's the problem?" I inquired offhandedly.

Miss Lee looked at me as if I had recently landed from another world; which, after a fashion, I had. She quickly softened, apparently remembering my cultural handicap.

"Well," she began with a weary sigh, "this story has many uh…parts. But for now, well…." She shrugged. "They do not act so kind to us. And we do not like them so much."

Not grasping her "for now" hint, and following my Western instincts, I innocently pressed the issue. "Why? What's wrong with the Japanese?"

Miss Lee's eyes flashed. Passing over Japanese sins once was all she could manage.

"Well, we shall only discuss recent things, like the Japan's thirty-five years in my country!" she began sarcastically. "And, of course, the cultural stealing! The taking of our, uh, nature? No, natural goods. The using Korean women. The War. And also other events."

I winced. "Oh. Uh, sorry. I didn't realize there was a problem."

"Yes, there is the very big problem. They treated us badly for many years. They said we could not speak our language and could not use our Korean names. They tried to kill Chosun and make us like the low servants. How do you say? What is the word, please?"

"Uh, slaves?" I suggested uncomfortably.

"Yes, the slaves. Your country knows of this kind of thing, I think." Having bloodied me with a closing barb, Miss Lee took a deep breath, sighed, and looked back to the ski wear.

Her slave reference stung. It was unfair to lump America's slave-keeping past in with Japanese atrocities, but then, I was privileged, white, and middle-class. Miss Lee, a person of color and apparent moderate means from a not fully developed country, held a different perspective.

Seeing no point—or logical way—to defend or explain an evil, and understanding I had opened the wrong door, I belatedly tried to close it.

"Do you like any of the outfits?" I asked, transparently trying to change the subject.

"Yes, of course," she answered without warmth.

"Uh, which ones?" I persisted, attempting to guide us out of the cold.

Certainly not fooled, but graciously allowing me to escape, Miss Lee sighed and returned to our previous pleasant path. "These traditional kind are more like me, I think."

"I'm not so sure," I mumbled.

"Uh?" she ventured questioningly, looking briefly away from the garments.

"I'm not sure I like those new styles either," I said more loudly. Then, without thought or consideration for implication or impact, I blurted, "Hey, let's you and I go skiing!"

She looked deliberately away from the ski outfit in her hand and at me as if astonished. It reminded me of my jewelry shop blunder when I suggested she could be my tutor.

She looked at me for some time, eyes piercing, her penetrating gaze turned up to full intensity and wrapped firmly around my heart. I felt that discomforting sensation again and smiled weakly. I had, only moments before, displayed my ignorance of Korean history; now, this snafu.

Looking back to the ski outfits, Miss Lee absently adjusted the garments, evenly spacing the hangers, each with about an inch of separation. She shook her head, and with disappointment and disapproval in her voice, said slowly, "This is not the good idea."

"Oh. Yeah." Realizing I'd suggested an overnight trip, I continued uncomfortably, "Uh, guess not. Sorry."

"This is enough shopping," she announced.

Miss Lee turned toward me, straightened her shoulders and said seriously, "Let us walk, please. I can explain. You can talk. I will listen. Perhaps in this way you will understand, and I can capture your uh…true heart."

# Seven

At the Heavenly Gate, I had eagerly volunteered to drive Miss Lee home in my car—a 1965 Green Mercury Comet sarcastically dubbed the "Rocket." She initially declined, but I pressed the issue and she relented. As we strolled through the early evening drizzle toward Yongsan, Miss Lee discussed the weather, the crazy Seoul traffic, her jewelry shop job, and other innocent non-subjects. I concluded she was either composing what needed to be said, or was not yet ready to discuss my "true heart."

The drizzle eased to a heavy mist that cast a blanket of tiny, bright water droplets over the things it touched. The mist transitioned to a drifting fog. Seeping from the narrow Asian alleys and tangled dark back streets, it floated free-form onto the main thoroughfare, wrapping uninvited about stationary objects.

Twilight encroached. Wedging between daylight and dark, its damp November cold caressed us, slipping past the protection of jackets and gloves. Daylight gone, wind barred, the air damp and cold, there was little doubt...we were in the gloaming. I loved this melancholy, fine-line border that was neither daylight nor darkness, but a swiftly passing buffer, an implied warning, the last opportunity to embrace sanctuary and defend against the consuming night.

Itaewon, electric with its daily transition to evil, watched us pass, begrudging our escape to Yongsan. The sidewalks were nearly empty in this pre-evening shift from shopping to night-life. Underfoot, brown and yellow leaves were firmly pasted to wet concrete. The damp streets shimmered brightly, brought to life by the headlights of oncoming traffic. The "whoosh" of fast tires on wet asphalt hung momentarily in the chilly air, died, and was resurrected seconds later in the wake of another passing vehicle.

There was a lull in the traffic. We scurried across the boulevard and turned right toward the main Yongsan gate. Miss Lee volunteered that this would be her first visit to a "soldier fort." She seemed to consider it an exotic adventure. The Korean gate-guard recognized me and waved us through without ID card or other hassles. I caught disdain and a knowing smirk as he eyed Miss Lee. She ignored his leer, but I sensed her discomfort.

Yongsan's rolling hills were dotted with office buildings, motor pool mainte-nance areas, recreation fields, clubs for both enlisted men and officers, craft shops, a movie theater, post exchange, hospital, gymnasium, and living quarters. We walked the short distance to my billets and the waiting Rocket.

The single-story building was about the length and width of four mobile homes placed end-to-end. The design was simple: A hallway divided the build-ing in half lengthwise. At the center, on one side of the hall, was a TV and lounge area; directly opposite, a communal shower room with toilets. The remainder of the building was divided into eight sets of single occupant rooms.

Parked proudly in front of my quarters was the old green Mercury. Most GIs didn't own cars. Seventy percent or more of Eighth Army's soldiers were sta-tioned in the countryside just south of the line dividing North from South Korea. This "Tactical Zone" was the area where combat would likely occur in the event of a North Korean invasion. Life in the Tac Zone was Spartan and disci-plined. Troops trained for combat daily, lived close to their weapons, and enjoyed few amenities. Automobile ownership was prohibited.

Outside the Tac Zone, a number of commonsense barriers limited car own-ership. The American military and Korean civil licensing process was cumber-some and complex. Insurance for driving in Asia was expensive. Gasoline was rationed and triple the stateside price, while bus transportation was readily avail-able and cost a quarter. Taxis were commonplace and the fare inexpensive. Lastly, everything a soldier could want, except Pillow Girls, was located within walking distance on the compound. For the average GI, owning a car was either prohibited, expensive, unnecessary, or all three.

However, when I arrived in Korea, the man I replaced, one "Jersey" Joe Richter, owned the Rocket. Proving P.T. Barnum's dictum, I was easily con-vinced that my Korean tour would be a disaster without the Rocket. I could scarcely believe my good fortune that rescue from an auto-less year would cost only five hundred dollars! Ownership papers later disclosed Jersey Joe's purchase price as three hundred dollars. Grimacing, and much wiser, I determined my replacement would gladly pay six.

Turning toward Miss Lee, I placed my hand on the trunk and made intro-ductions. I enthusiastically stressed the Rocket's two known virtues: It would start, and—as a bonus—the heater worked. Unfailingly gracious, Miss Lee was impressed, overlooking the tattered interior, empty pop cans on the floor, news-papers scattered across the back seat, multiple rust spots, mismatched paint, and the obvious front fender dent. Nodding approvingly, she allowed that the car had "character." I beamed like a new father.

Despite the darkness, it was not quite six. I had the sense we hadn't yet examined, and certainly not captured, my "true heart." With much yet to do, and in truth not wanting to let her go, I invited Miss Lee inside the billets and out of the quixotic weather, which again had turned to drizzle.

We stood on the grass between the sidewalk and the Rocket in a sort of neutral area, no commitments, no expectations, all options before us. Perhaps she wanted to tarry. Perhaps her curiosity prevailed. Perhaps she was still finding my heart. Whatever her motivation, she finally smiled and agreed to a "small" visit.

We walked up four or five steps to the building's front door and entered the TV lounge. The small room was, as usual, filled with most of the building's occupants. They were watching the old reruns it seemed the American Forces Television Network favored. Our entry disrupted a *Batman* episode. In unison, my friends looked toward us, staring blankly.

Miss Lee gaped as she surveyed my friends and the landscape. Empty potato chip bags and beer cans were scattered across a coffee table. Other unidentifiable, but presumed food remnants lay on the couch and carpet. Absently, I wondered if we'd just missed a food-fight.

"Hi guys." I gave a semi-wave and nodded. "This is Miss Lee," I continued brightly, proud of a woman who was neither Prostitute nor Camp Follower.

Various forms of halfhearted greetings and grunts emanated from around the lounge. Then, more blank and silent staring as they fell into a collective torpor. I was momentarily surprised by the lack of enthusiasm. Then, I realized that for this group, Miss Lee was nothing special, just another Itaewon Pillow Girl. To underscore their disinterested disrespect, someone belched. No one laughed. No one offered an apology. I thought it best to complete the introductions quickly and escape.

"Uh, Miss Lee, the guys." I rattled off their names. She stared. Clearly, she'd not expected to encounter six unshaven, beer-drinking men, lounging about in ragged attire with their feet propped on furniture.

"Wanna beer?" asked Al, my hallway neighbor.

"Uh, gee, 'preciate it, but, uh, we'll pass."

Wiping his fingers across the front of his dirty, unattractively tight-fitting T-shirt, Al picked up a ripped potato chip bag from the floor, jammed some chips in his mouth, and holding out the bag, tried his best to share.

"Chips?" he mumbled, his mouth full.

"You know...Al...uh, we just ate so, no. Uh, no thanks."

"Oh."

Nodding toward the TV, he swallowed visibly and observed, "*Batman*'s on."

"Yeah, I see."

Al turned to a stubble-faced man with his legs stretched across the couch.

"Donnie, slide over. Make a hole for Jas and uh, Miss What's-Her-Face."

"No! Donnie. No thanks, bud. We're just passing through. Can't stay. See you guys later. Enjoy."

Al shrugged. There were more grunts and an in-unison attention shift back to *Batman*.

Miss Lee, beginning to recover herself, bowed slightly. Too late. We were no longer an afterthought. I grabbed her sleeve and we quickly left the lounge. We walked the length of the hallway to my rooms, the last door on the left. I unlocked the door, swung it open, reached inside, flipped on the light switch and grandly bowed, bidding Miss Lee enter.

Each of my two rooms was about twelve by fifteen feet. The entry room served as the living area. Its decor was functional U.S. Army: two chairs, a lamp table, and a desk. Through a doorway to our right, the bedroom, with furnishings you'd expect as well as a sink, mirror, and a small closet. Both rooms were painted an unattractive lime-green. The floors were perpetually cold, and covered by squares of alternating green and gray linoleum tile.

As I hung up our jackets, Miss Lee asked, "Those men, they are always there?"

"Yeah," I shrugged, "mostly, I guess."

"This is not acceptable."

"What? What's wrong?"

"Well," she intertwined and twisted her fingers, "you and I come to these rooms. Alone," she added with emphasis. "We are here for some time. Then, we go again. It yields a poor image. This is not allowable."

I looked at her innocently, though I understood what she meant.

"You can imagine very well what they think," she added with a soft scowl.

"Oh, come on, Miss Lee, those guys couldn't care less about us or what we do."

"Well, this is probably correct, but it is not permitted."

Wrapping her arms about herself as if chilled, she turned and wandered toward the desk, then pivoted quickly to face me.

"Also, these people?" She shook her head. "It is like...like...looked on by...TV lizards," she blurted, coining my all-time favorite "Miss Lee phrase." "Only the head moves, the eyes wide, staring at me or the TV, no speaking, only the eating, food is all places. What kind of people do this? What kind of life this is?" She shuddered.

Envisioning Al, firmly planted in his rocker, wearing a lizard's head and slowly swishing a huge, reptilian tail brought a smile and laughter.

Miss Lee looked at me seriously. "There is not laughing in this circumstance," she stated flatly.

Anxious to please, I said, "Okay, okay, I'm sorry. But I...I don't think they care about anything except food and the TV. They're good guys, really. They just miss their families, don't understand Korea, are bored, and mostly, just want to go home." Raising both hands, palms toward her, I added quickly, "But if you'd be more comfortable, we can use the side door," secretly pleased at her implied future visits.

She brightened. "There is another passage?"

"Yeah," I nodded to my left. "At the end of the hallway, ten feet from my door. We can use it without anyone seeing us. It's how I usually come in."

"This is good," she said with a relieved smile. Then, as if sharing an important confidence, she lowered her voice, leaned toward me, and for the first time, touched me, placing the palm of her hand lightly on my chest. "This will be our Secret Way," she said in a near whisper.

So, the side door adjacent to my rooms became what Miss Lee called, our "Secret Way," as in, "We will use the Secret Way." I was never sure if she employed this phrase as a place or a methodology. She was always, like the poetry she loved, wonderfully ambiguous.

# Eight

Sitting atop my dresser was a multi-component stereo system. It immediately captured Miss Lee's attention and drew her to it. As would become our pattern, she led; I followed. She loved music, and her taste varied widely, including Beethoven; Elton John; Don Williams; Fleetwood Mac; Willie Nelson; Crosby, Stills, Nash and Young; Mozart; Simon and Garfunkel; Kristofferson; Hank, Jr.; Merle Haggard; The Beatles; and McCartney's Wings.

She selected a Don Williams tape from my cassette collection and watched intently as I showed her how to operate the system. Nodding, she added an occasional "umm" in that low, relaxed way I would so frequently hear. I guessed it was verbal shorthand for "I understand" or "okay." Given its informal nature, I hopefully concluded she only used it under comfortable circumstances.

Her inquisitive nature was fascinated with the stereo's complexity, and she quickly learned the effect of the set's dials and buttons. She set the balance, tone, bass, treble and adjusted the volume.

With no chairs in this room, we used the bed as an oversized couch. We sat at opposite ends, propped against pillows. The cassette recorder rewound to the beginning and began to play. Williams' deep, warm voice drifted plaintively across the room.

*Some broken hearts never mend.*
*Some memories never end.*
*Some tears will never dry.*
*My love for you will never die.*

"Tears that do not dry." She sighed. "This is a very sad, but true thought." After a moment, somber and reflective, she said, "Sadness is the only real feeling."

"What do you mean?"

"Well, of all the feelings, I think we know sad most frequently. We see loss and disappointment more than, uh…victory. Also, it is most pure and deepest. I think we keep it the longest. Happiness does not stay fresh, it fades to…neutral. Anger is the same. Sadness…" She moved her head slowly left and right. "…sadness never leaves. It is a deep and lasting cut. It is with us always. Sometimes hidden, and always, we look away, yes? But it is there, alive, but in shadow."

She spoke as if she could actually see sadness, furtively lurking in her heart's shadowy corners. Miss Lee's streak of hidden pathos was powerful and unexpected. I wondered if melancholy was simply her nature and universally present in the way she saw the world, or if her connection with sadness had been established by a specific event and was more pointed than broad.

Pulling both knees to her chest in that limber, feminine way men can't, she wrapped her arms gracefully about them, loosed a small sigh, and rested her head against the wall. The music continued to wash over us. We sat introspectively for several minutes.

At last, she stretched her long legs before her and, taking me by surprise, playfully tossed her pillow at me.

"So," she said with a smile, "you want to play the skiing." New subject, new mood. The woman was proving mercurial.

"Uh, well, yeah," I said staggering, my mental gears jamming as I tried to catch up. "But I got the impression it was a bad idea."

"As you know very well, nearly the far coast, at Yongpyong, there is the Dragon Valley. This is the only acceptable ski place. This is not near Seoul. This is the overnight trip. Normally, people take a bus on one day, early, play ski, stay at night, and return the next evening. There are several companies that conduct this kind of tour."

"Okay," I said, feeling my way slowly, looking for the hooks, determined to not screw up again.

"Now," she continued, apparently satisfied with my reticence, "there are problems with your idea. First, you are *oeguk saram*, uh, the foreigner. I am not."

Unaccountably, she smiled brightly at this observation. "This foreign and native idea is not good here. This is especially true, because with your short yellow hair, you are clearly not Asian and clearly American Army. We like the American Army, but the soldiers are not always polite, and use the Korean women. So, if people see the American soldier and Korean woman, then, well…you know very well what they think. The Korean guard had this thought on his face. But this is a problem for me only."

I looked at the floor and waited, unsure where she was headed. She seemed to be verbally sorting out the issues as she discussed the proposal's elements. It appeared she didn't need my input.

"Another point," she acknowledged with a deep sigh, "is my family. To do this, I would have to invent the story of some kind. I could never say, 'Oh,

Mother, I am going to the mountains with an American soldier for two days. See you when I return.'" She closed her eyes and shuddered. "Oh, my mother and father would…." She didn't finish; casting the idea of parental knowledge in tangible word-form seemed too frightening.

Again, I felt a comment would be inappropriate.

She looked at me with kindly irritation, pointed her finger and lectured, "If you were the Korean person, this question would not be asked. This question is the insult. This is why I had the, uh, quiet reaction before. But then I thought, 'Oh, he is not Korean. He does not understand.' Of course, you are a man. This is a different, but old question in any country."

"Miss Lee, I was afraid of something like this. Look, I didn't mean anything suggestive." She looked at me quizzically.

I tried, "I didn't mean anything insulting or bad against your culture, or you as a woman." She seemed to grasp this.

"It's just, you know, I don't understand much about your culture. I'm gonna make mistakes. It was only an idea that jumped out before I thought about it. Let's pretend I didn't bring it up," I suggested, backpedaling to the nearest neutral corner and hoping I had extricated myself from the linguistic and cultural snags.

Miss Lee remained silent and regarded me seriously with those examining eyes. I felt she was looking past my skin with that penetrating gaze she seemed to turn on and off at will. I was floating, immersed in an uncomfortable, in-the-balance feeling. A long moment passed before she spoke.

"I think you have a kind, honest heart. I think your heart can be trusted. With you, it is difficult to know because of the language and culture things." She continued with an expression of disbelief, "I have never spoken with an American so much, and never so…privately about such things before. I am surprised by this. I do not know you for so long a time, but I think these things are true. I do not know if these things are good."

Pausing, she pursed her lips and expelled a little puff of air as if perplexed, or even displeased.

"I think you are different in a way I cannot define. But I know your, uh, rhythm, yes? And mine? Somehow, even if we are from the opposite places, still, they seem to be the same kind of…thing, the same kind of music."

I didn't understand what she meant. "That's good, right?" I asked hopefully.

My question was sincerely offered; I had no agenda except understanding. Still, I must have appeared earnestly serious or comedic in some form, because her head rolled back and she laughed loudly. It was a guffaw. Always conscious of deportment, even in private, I never saw her laugh that way again. Quickly embarrassed, she placed her hand over her mouth, capturing the tiny explosion.

She recovered to a warm smile. Dropping her hand in her lap, she tilted her head to one side and hesitated a moment.

"Yes, of course, 'that is good,'" she said, her face soft with tenderness. "I think this is my precise point. Your different way?" she echoed, recalling her earlier comment. "Perhaps, it is, you are innocent."

# Nine

With Miss Lee navigating, I drove the Rocket through Seoul's evening drizzle to the quiet Mapo District, a mostly lower-middle class residential suburb, north of the Han river and about fifteen minutes' driving time west of Yongsan. She directed us to Yang Kang Kil, a two-lane street wide enough to allow parking on both sides. Trees lined the sidewalk, their bare branches overhanging the curb. This evening, as would prove characteristic, the street was quiet. There was little traffic, pedestrian or motorized.

She indicated I should park near the base of a hill. A concrete pathway ran the length of the slope and led to a maze of small, garden-walled, one story apartments. Miss Lee said her home was about halfway up the path on the left.

I pulled to the curb and shut down the engine. A streetlight's dim, yellowish lamp light fell into the Rocket, softly illuminating the front seat. The evening's damp, dusky gray had imperceptibly become night's wet darkness. I watched in fascination as tiny rain dots coalesced on the windscreen, then raced down the glass in tearful streaks, blurring the world beyond.

"This day was the enjoyable experience."

"Yes, Miss Lee, it was."

We fell silent. I was unsure how to proceed. She had not ruled out the ski trip, but I certainly wasn't going to raise that issue again. Perhaps I should ask her to dinner, or a movie? That seemed safe and would be the standard "next step" in Alabama. Of course, Alabama was seventy-five hundred literal, and millions of cultural, miles distant. I continued to vacillate. Perhaps she didn't want to see me again. But instinct told me otherwise.

She cut through my indecision, announcing, "I will telephone you again."

"Okay, great!" I said, rescued and relieved.

"I am not sure exactly when, but not so long."

"Okay."

"Do you still wish to play skiing?"

"Uh, well, I...."

Grinning wickedly and apparently enjoying my discomfort, she made a quick thrust and parry. "It is a difficult question?"

"Miss Lee," I said with a broad smile, "you are evil."

This observation pleased her greatly. "Yes, this is correct," she responded, tilting her head.

"Well, sure, I'd like to go, but what about all the problems?"

"I will consider them."

I had no idea what she meant, but was happy with where we were on the issue, so I said, "Okay," and counted myself lucky.

"Very well, good night." She turned to find the door handle.

"I'll walk you up."

She looked up quickly, astonishment on her face. "You cannot be serious? My neighbors and family are there."

"Oh," I said, remembering the cultural taboos and, for the first time in my life, feeling uncomfortably second class.

Softening, she said somewhat formally as if reciting from her English phrase book, "Perhaps at some future time, but not now, thank you."

"Okay, sorry."

She looked again for the door handle.

"Uh, one more thing before you go."

Turning back to me with a patient smirk, she said, "Yessss?" I sensed she enjoyed prolonging our goodbye.

"Look, I don't want to call you 'Miss Lee.' It's like you are my teacher or something. What's your first name?"

She considered me a moment and shook her head slowly, a smile coming to her lips. She looked through the windscreen and said with a sigh, "You are not Korean."

"Whaaaaat?" I playfully exclaimed. "What now? I just wanna know your name, for cryin' out loud."

"We do not use familiar names so quickly," she chastened.

"Oh." I rubbed my eyes, frustrated and shortstopped by yet another culture trap.

Miss Lee watched me a moment, then in a patient, explanatory tone said, "First, you must know about our names. We have three. Lee is my family name, and unlike in the West, it is placed first. My next name is for my generation, Kwang." She pronounced it with a "long A," ah. "The final name is mine, Young. Lee Kwang Young. Each name is more familiar than the one before, yes? It is an honor to use the more familiar kind of name. This is not so in the West, I think."

"Yeah, we do it differently," I acknowledged, embarrassed I'd gaffed again.

Miss Lee didn't let me fall. "Well, in a way, you are correct. This is west Korea. And so, we can make the rules we please, yes? Call me Kwang Young."

"Okay! Great. Kwang Young. I like it. Thanks." I flashed a happy grin, pleased she'd allowed me to weasel some Western intimacy between us.

"You're welcome, Mr. Fitzgerald," she said, a slight emphasis on "Mr." Apparently, she wanted the same first name courtesy extended to her, but was "too Asian" to ask.

With a playful seated bow, I said, "Please, call me Jason."

"Jason." She said it just once, as if trying it on for size. "Very well. Now I must go!" Emphasis on "must." "My parents will much worry already," she confided.

She stepped out of the car, turned, stooped, and through the open door said, "Thank you for the pleasant afternoon. I will telephone you...." Then, with a warm smile, added, "Jason."

# Ten

The following week passed without contact from Kwang Young. Hugh and I shuffled papers, conducted a meeting for the Command's instructor pilots, briefed the Colonel about a proposed regulation change, and, of course, flew missions. These were typical activities and I enjoyed them all. Evenings were spent with Hugh and Spiderwoman at The Statue, pursuing our normal miscreant behaviors; again, typical. Structurally, organizationally, my life was little changed.

However, as the days fell aside, I thought more, not less, about Kwang Young and her promise to telephone. I found this emotional distraction disturbing and tried with little success to focus on other things. It was Friday, near close of business, and still, no phone call. I was now thinking only of Kwang Young and getting anxious I'd miss her call, or worse, that there'd be no call.

Her home, like most Korean homes, had no phone, so I couldn't call her. I didn't know which of the many small Mapo apartments was hers, so an in-person visit was neither practical nor possible. I could go to the jewelry shop, but somehow that didn't seem appropriate. She said she would telephone. Protocol dictated I should relax and let that happen, or not happen. But relaxation was difficult to find.

Instead, I dreamed up wild scenarios that explained her failure to call. Perhaps she had lost both my office and quarters phone numbers. Perhaps her parents had found the numbers and destroyed them. Perhaps she had been trying desperately to reach me but was turned away by the gate guards. I seized upon this last plot as most likely. I considered going to each of the ten Yongsan access gates to ask if a somewhat tall, somewhat attractive, very witty and exceedingly charming Korean woman had recently been about inquiring after a dashingly handsome aviator.

Hugh pulled open a squeaky file cabinet drawer and brought me back to reality. Angrily, I wadded up a draft document on which I was supposedly working and tossed it in the trash. I passed my hand through my hair. Why was I so concerned? "The Rules" were clear: Korean women would do anything to "catch a GI." My situation was getting uncomfortably close to the other way around.

This Kwang Young business had inverted normalcy. She was just an Asian woman. Itaewon was full of them. Just walk over and pick one. Simple. Hugh was right, Spiderwoman was a lot less complicated and considerably less trouble. To hell with it; I didn't need this.

"Jason, where are the performance charts Bell Helicopter sent us?" Hugh was across the office, his arms buried in the top drawer of a file cabinet.

"Huh?"

"Performance charts. You know, aviation data, stuff like: fuel flow, climb rate, max range, glide ratios, that kinda thing. They got little lines, and tables, and crap like that on 'em. Performance charts? Remember? You work with 'em every day. Where are the new ones?"

"Christ, Hugh, I don't know. Goddamn Private Bond 'filed' them; who knows where the hell they are. Probably in the 'I wanna go home' folder, it's all the little bastard whines about," I snapped.

"Little testy are we?" Hugh looked over the top of his glasses and smiled.

"What testy? I don't know where the hell the charts are, and I'm sick and tired of Bond's screw-ups. If the little whiner was competent it would be one thing, but...." I trailed off, shaking my head, too frustrated to finish.

"If Miss Lee had telephoned, do you suppose Bond would be a little more tolerable?" Hugh asked, patience in his voice.

I expelled a deep breath, slumped in my chair and tossed my pencil on the desk. "Yeah, probably." A slow smile came to my face. "But not very goddamn much," I added, laughing.

"Well, today's what, Friday? If she doesn't call, what say you and I make a Thunder Run on Itaewon tonight? Hit, oh, five clubs, minimum. End up at the Statue in Spiderwoman's tender embrace. And, to help snap you out of it, I'll let you buy."

"Nah, I'll have a bite and maybe a drink, but I'll pass on the rest; my heart's just not in it."

"Phew. Passing on a Thunder Run? You are sick. You know, it's a payday Friday; all the little Pillow Girls will be out thick as thieves, brand new weekly certifications on their VD cards and acting verrrry friendly."

"Thieves is right. And their VD cards are as good as their last customer. No thanks, I'll grab a fast, early bite, but that's it."

"Okay." Hugh shrugged and turned back to the file cabinet. "I'll still let you buy. It's just the kinda guy I am."

Promptly at five o'clock, the Installation's cannon fired. Its loud report could be heard across Yongsan. All the soldiers out-of-doors came to an immediate stop, turned in the direction of the flag—even if they couldn't see it—and saluted. A loudspeaker system carried the sound of a bugler playing "Retreat." The flag was lowered and the business day officially finished.

"Ah, the martini bell." Hugh always called the cannon's echo "the martini bell." It was a predictable comfort; something I could always rely on.

He began to gather and organize his paperwork in preparation to leave. Turning to me, hat in hand, he said, "So, see you at The Statue in what, hour and a half?"

"Yeah, six thirty. Sounds good. See you there."

"Right." Heading for the door, Hugh called back across his shoulder, "Bring money!"

"Yeah, yeah."

I lingered, hoping the phone might still ring. I arranged my desktop, putting the various project folders in order for Monday morning. I straightened and organized the bulletin board. I wiped the grease-pencil marks off the plastic-covered aviation map. I even emptied Hugh's ashtray. Still, no call. Clearly, a ringing phone and housekeeping were not linked. Giving up, I trudged to the doorway, plucked my hat from the adjacent rack, turned off the lights, locked the office door, ambled slowly down the long hallway, and left the building.

It was a short five minutes to my quarters. I managed to cover the distance in double that time, kicking any pebble whose misfortune placed it in my path. Entering through the side door, I smiled regretfully, remembering it as Kwang Young's "Secret Way."

I crossed to my room and noticed a scrap of paper thumb-tacked to my door. The note on it read: "Miss Lee called. Will call again. Ain't love grand!?! Al."

The lounge telephone rang.

\* \* \*

Yes!! I knew she'd call! Never doubted it a minute. Completely devoid of dignity, I ran down the hallway to the lounge, overshooting the doorway as I tried to stop. No Lizards. Still too early. I snatched the receiver from its cradle.

"Hello! Mr. Fitzgerald."

"Jason, have you been doing the exercise?"

Another no preamble, non-sequitur opening. "Huh?" I shook my head, thinking it must be the culture.

"Well, you have, uh…large breath. Is it from the exercise? Are you well?"

"Uh, no, Kwang Young. That is, yes, yes, I am well. And no, I haven't been exercising, I just ran to pick up the phone and—"

"Oh, is it correct?" she cooed. I could hear the pleased smile in her voice.

Realizing I had disclosed too much, I lied. "Yeah, I uh, just came in and the phone was ringing. You know, uh, I wanted to catch it before it stopped, that's all."

"How fortunate, there were actually only two rings, and then…you." A playful quality bounced about her voice. She knew.

"Imagine that."

"Did you receive my message?"

This was too much; she was toying with me. I cleverly evaded with a non-answer, "Did you leave a message?"

Rather than respond, perhaps out of mercy as she had clearly won the point, she jumped, quicksilver, to the next subject. "Would you prefer to meet tomorrow?"

"Yeah, that'd be okay," I answered, trying not to sound too enthusiastic.

"Perhaps we could go to the country in your Rock-ette. There is an interesting place in Korean history I know and would like to share this with you. You would like to do this, yes?"

"Sure, you bet."

"Very well. Please meet me under my hill at eleven a.m."

"Okay, I'll be there." I smiled, thinking of the image and her clarifying "a.m."

"Very well, goodbye."

Throughout our relationship, she referred to the bottom, or base, of her Mapo hill as "under my hill." Intrigued by her word choice and pleased by her imagery, I couldn't bring myself to correct her idiom, and so our rendezvous point became "under my hill."

# Eleven

Protective mountains, sharply peaked, guard Seoul on three of four sides. Through a narrow gap in the eastern sentinel, some thirty miles distant, flows the Han River. The Han continues westward from the mountains to the capital, partitioning the ancient city. Kwang Young guided us out of the city and toward the Han River Gap, following an old and increasingly narrow road that roughly paralleled the river.

As Seoul fell farther behind, the road began to climb and narrow. Still later, the road started to weave, gracefully curling about large stone pillars. It wasn't difficult to imagine the ancient road builders seeking the line of least topographical resistance as they labored deeper and higher into the increasingly rocky, red clay mountains.

Fall was in temporary retreat, driven briefly away by an unexpected November appearance of "glorious summer." Exactly seven days prior, the rain was cold, piercing, foreboding. Today, the sky was crystalline blue, visibility unrestricted, the temperature almost balmy. Despite the fifteen hundred foot elevation gain, it seemed warmer than an hour before in Seoul. Perhaps it was a temperature inversion, perhaps it was the effect of a high-noon sky, perhaps it was just good fortune. Whatever the cause, the weather kissed and gentled us. We were very much at ease.

Kwang Young said our destination was an ancient memorial at the Han River Gap. As the Rocket labored higher into the mountains and closer to the Gap, she told me the Legend of the Seoul Warriors.

In antiquity, a fierce and war-like tribe of barbarians from beyond the mountains to the east, planned to attack and conquer what is now the city of Seoul. Their purpose was to pillage the bountiful markets, plunder the city's treasury, kill the children, sell the women into bondage, and make slaves of the men.

However, spies from the tiny imperial city discovered the plot. They learned the attackers would be waterborne, approaching Seoul on the Han. They couldn't discover the timing of the attack, but knew it would be soon. Seoul city elders, unwilling to wait passively until the city was besieged, chose to strike first. A small army of Seoul's bravest warriors was quickly organized and dispatched toward the Han River Gap.

Following the steep and winding road we now traveled, the warriors half-ran, half-marched day and night for nearly two days in a desperate attempt to reach the tactically important Gap before the barbarians. Once there, they planned to rest, devise a detailed surprise-attack strategy, and lie in wait for the unsuspecting barbarians.

On the afternoon of the second day, the exhausted warriors reached the Gap's overlooking bluffs. But there was no time for rest, and little time for a plan. About a mile upriver, slowly drifting around a bend, were the watercraft carrying the barbarian attack force. A plan was hastily concocted.

The warriors would divide into two groups. The first group, archers, would remain atop the bluffs and provide archery support for the second group, hand-to-hand fighters, the foot-soldiers. This second group, in accordance with the hurriedly prepared plan, would descend the Gap's steep and treacherous cliffs to the river's edge, some five hundred feet below. Once there, leveraging the combined elements of surprise with the support of the archers above, the warriors would engage and destroy the numerically superior barbarian attack force. It was a desperate and unpopular plan. Various warriors pointed out flaws and suggested improvements. However, with the barbarians nearly at the Gap, debate was not encouraged. The plan would have to be executed, flawed or not. On this day, the people of Seoul would survive or not, trusting in their warriors' individual courage and initiative.

The plan began badly with the warriors' late arrival. Now, the situation worsened. Though they moved as quickly as possible, the Seoul foot-soldiers reached the waters of the narrow Gap just minutes before the barbarians. The element of surprise was lost. Terrible, bloody fighting ensued. Compounding the problem, the warriors were outnumbered at least four to one. But, with archery support, the small Seoul army managed an initial standoff. However, twenty minutes after the attack began, the supporting archers expended their supply of arrows.

Almost immediately, the battle turned in favor of the barbarians. In desperation, the archers began descending the steep, jagged cliffs in an attempt to aid their overwhelmed comrades below. However, the leading group of archers, now about halfway down the cliff face, could see the tedious descent would take too long. The battle would be lost, the imperial city razed; its helpless families, slaughtered.

The situation was critical. But these were Seoul's most elite warriors; defeat was unthinkable. They had courage, they understood honor; it was now time for sacrifice. To extend the battle and allow the archers still on the bluffs above to climb safely down to the river's edge, the leading group of two hundred descending warriors, in an act of sacrificial heroism, hurled themselves from the cliff face to the water, boats, and barbarians waiting below.

Many warriors were killed by the jump. Some struck the cliff face as they fell; others broke backs and necks as they awkwardly struck the water with devastating velocity; some drowned, pulled underwater by the weight of their battle armor. Many that survived the jump, exhausted from the long march and fumbling helplessly in the current, were beheaded or mortally maimed by the mercilessly barbarians. However, a few archers survived and, joining the original foot-soldiers again, incredibly, brought the terrible battle to a standoff.

Gradually, the remaining archers successfully descended the cliffs and joined the bloody pandemonium which had now spread to both sides of the river. The battle raged for two hours. By late afternoon, through courage, tenacity, and sacrifice, the warriors had prevailed. Tragically, the small army of martyrs was decimated; only a handful remained alive. But Seoul, its government, treasures, and families were saved.

As a memorial, the grateful people of Seoul carved two giant, one hundred foot tall warriors, an Archer and a Foot-Soldier, into the reddish rock of the Gap's vertical cliff face. A plaque at the base of the monument read:

*From antiquity to infinity,*
*these warrior spirits guard*
*the Eastern approach to Seoul*
*at the Han River Gap.*

Kwang Young said it was a sacred place of honor and heroism.

We stood aside the giant warrior statues in the tourist area, a cantilevered steel platform extending from the cliff face over the Han River.

"It's a tragic story, Kwang Young."

"Yes." Then, with more surprising pathos, "It is also, I think, a beautiful story. A few men with honor against many bad men. The cause almost hopeless. So, because of how they died and why they died, protecting the people of Seoul, the warriors that day became, uh, like brothers. The people of Seoul, then and now, also are brothers, family, with them. We remember and honor them, even today. We will never forget."

"Is this a true story?" I asked surprised, thinking it only a legend.

"The story is so old, no one knows for certain. I want it to be so. And you see very well the large, uh...forms. These, I think, would not be here without some truth." She paused and looked up, squinting into the past-zenith sun at the gigantic, weathered carvings.

"But Jason, is it so important, truth or not truth?" She looked directly at me.

"This is Western, technical thinking. This kind of thing is not yes or no, black or white, true or incorrect. It is not an examination. No. It is the idea, the heart, the feeling of...."

She paused, fist clenched at her breast, word searching, not academically, but with real passion. Her lips were pursed in an almost painful expression as she struggled to find an English word.

"Sacrifice?" I suggested reluctantly, like a hesitant school child in a crowded classroom.

She nodded slowly, as if considering the word and its fit into her sense of sentence and concept. Looking up again to the statues, she said, "Yes. Sacrifice is correct for English. There is a Korean word, but it does not translate. Sacrifice for country. Sacrifice for family. Sacrifice for ideas. These things...not technology things, are most important." She looked away from the statues for the last time and again, directly at me.

"This idea, sacrifice, this kind of feeling we have for one another and our country describes the Korean people. It is something you must understand to know us. To really know me."

I nodded in understanding and agreement, swallowing hard. I looked up again, but with new respect at the two ancient, silent guardians, the sacrifice they represented—real or imagined—spanning the millennia, and very much alive.

* * *

I was never clear about the technique used to sculpt the guardians. I guessed the ancient artisans were suspended by rope from the bluffs above. This seemed the logical approach, but I didn't want to surface the question or the hypothesis as both were close cousins of the much disdained "need-to-know Western technology." However, no matter the ancients' approach, the Korean Tourist Bureau facilitated modern visitors by cutting steps into the stone adjacent to the figures. The steep stairway led to a steel observation platform extending from the cliff face and supported by bracing sunk deep into the rock.

We were standing on the visitor's platform, the Han sparkling silver in the sunlight hundreds of feet below. Kwang Young had suggested I bring a camera, and I'd taken several photos: four or five of the warriors, one looking straight down at the Han, one facing east toward the river's origin, and another in the opposite direction, toward Seoul.

I was finishing a series of shots that were supposed to be a continuous east-west panorama of the far mountains. Kwang Young lounged against the railing to my left. Resting her chin in her right hand, she quietly watched me with patient disinterest.

"How 'bout I take your picture?" I asked, squinting through the view find-
er.

"No. This is too, uh…pretty for people." She was somber, apparently still
under the warriors' spell.

"Oh, come on. It's a great background. You can see clear to the those jagged
mountains, must be forty miles or more."

"This land and sky is better without me."

Turning up the charm I tried, "Well, that depends on who's doing the looking. Come on, just one shot."

Kwang Young waved a dismissive hand and briefly shook her head in disagreement. "People in this kind of photo is the mistake, I think."

"Okay, let's compromise. I'll put you on the side and center on the mountains?"

She shrugged and sighed, clearly not much taken with the idea, but unwilling to protest further. Reluctantly, she turned toward me, more erect but unen-
thusiastically propped on her left elbow. I thought I'd better get this done quickly. Backpedaling about fifteen feet, I placed her in the far left corner of the
viewfinder, set the aperture, focused, rejected the urge to ask for a smile, and
snapped the picture.

"Okay. That's it; simple and painless. You ready to go?"

Allowing a trace of a smile, she nodded.

We left the viewing deck and made our way up the stone stairway. Kwang
Young, tall, graceful, and athletic, climbed steadily. As we ascended, exertion
took effect and her sober intensity began to burn away. She chattered loqua-
ciously about all manner of things, none of which—fortunately—seemed philosophical. However, I remained attentive. I could be called upon for comment or
observation at any time. Like an eager-to-please puppy, I wanted to be ready.

The steep, reddish-brown stairway was narrow. I climbed behind and slightly to Kwang Young's right. I stayed close because it was difficult to hear her. She
was facing away from me and beginning to breathe more heavily. To complicate
matters, an aggressive wind swept away words and phrases; I could hear only
sentence fragments.

We'd climbed about halfway to the top when, glancing over her left shoulder
to emphasize a point, Kwang Young released the hand rail and gestured. The
combined actions caused her to lose equilibrium. She slipped and staggered. Her
left arm flailed as she tried to regain balance. She reeled backward, twisting and
falling toward me.

Because I was close, had forward momentum, and outweighed her by at least
sixty pounds, I easily checked her fall. She grasped my upper arm with surprising strength. Her eyes wide, face drained of color, she looked at me, speechless

and frightened. I imagine she suffered from the effects of the very real four hundred foot vertical distance to the river below and the fresh, powerful image of falling, martyred warriors.

"It's okay, pal, I got you," I said quietly, my right arm at her waist, my left hand holding her forearm.

Still frightened, she turned fully and placed both arms around my neck in a surprisingly tight embrace. She pressed her body against mine. Exertion and fear's sudden burst of adrenaline drove her heart rate to its maximum; with my arms around her, I felt her warm body pulse. I enjoyed the embrace and her dependence very much.

But, quickly, I was ashamed. Of course I wanted to hold her, but this trickery was artificial and cheap. She had physically touched me only once, and that spontaneously, the week before in my quarters. Weaseling the familiar form of first names from her was one thing, but this, this was manipulative and tawdry.

Over my shoulder, Kwang Young spoke fear-purging, rapid-fire Korean. I patted her back lightly, trying to reassure her.

"You're okay, pal, you're okay," I said as calmly as possible. "No harm, no damage, no danger. I've got you."

She expelled a large breath and relaxed slightly. Regaining my conscience, I released her. Calming rapidly and close to composure, she slowly took her arms from my neck.

Leaning back, she looked at me in her deeply piercing fashion. No comment, no expression, just those fierce, penetrating eyes that seemed to flash directly to my heart, push aside the masking façade and read uncensored intent. I felt naked, defenseless.

Surely, she had seen my stolen, illicit gratification. I had used her fright; exploited it for my pleasure. I was deeply ashamed. I looked down at the rock steps, feeling like a despoiler and wishing to be anywhere but the sacred, honored cliff face of the Han River Gap. Kwang Young remained silent. I rubbed my palms on my jeans, shifted my weight, and looked up.

I had misread her. It would not be the last time. She wore an easy and relaxed expression, tenderness on her face, her fright fully gone. She placed her right hand lightly on my chest, near my heart and sighed deeply, almost plaintively. Her touch was warm and electric. I immediately felt connected to her in a surprisingly profound and bonded way.

Kwang Young looked over my shoulder, past the Han, past the opposite cliff face, past the distant, ragged mountains and into the cloudless blue sky. She was momentarily elsewhere. When she returned, she slowly took her hand from my chest. Clasping both hands gracefully together below her waist, she made a slight bow and, to my great surprise, gave me the priceless, sweet gift of willing intimacy.

"Please, Jason, you, may call me Young."

* * *

The Rocket carried us safely from the mountains to the foothills where night waited. The thieving sun, long since escaped, had stolen the day's warmth. It was again November, clear and cold. During our last descending turn, Seoul, brightly lit and sparkling, burst into view. It hung before us, a luminescent diamond suspended against black velvet. Inadvertently, I slowed the Rocket.

The ancient capital was simultaneously compact and sprawling, nine million people within its boundary. With night's darkness cast over it, Seoul was especially impressive. Its lights, so intense and massed near the city-center, thinned as they spread concentrically toward the surrounding mountains. Splashing up the protective mountain bases, the lights became scattered, shimmering white pin-points tapering to abrupt, vertical black.

To the south, the Han River was a wide, black ribbon, dousing the city lights and dividing Seoul into its familiar two unequal sections. The Han's bridges, thin, weakly glowing strips, bisected the ribbon, joining the city's northern and southern halves. In the Rocket's dark quiet we sensed the magic, felt the majesty. We were privileged observers, silent guests at the King's court.

We continued descending. Mountains became foothills, then simply higher terrain. Losing the outlying high ground to urban sprawl, the spell evaporated and we melted commonplace into the edges of Seoul's Saturday night traffic. In self-defense, we darted, weaved and zipped our way through the motorized craziness to Mapo. At last, we turned onto Yang Kang kil and parked at the base of Young's hill. I shut down the engine. We sat quietly, savoring our day's final moments.

"Young," I began, still charged by her legitimately granted intimacy, "today was…." I hesitated, shaking my head. I sensed something dear and rare had passed between us. However, I couldn't identify the vaguely familiar emotion. Finally, I tried the inadequate, "…remarkable."

She looked at me through the Rocket's darkness. "Yes." There was a long pause. She nodded slowly. "The water here is warm and clear." After a moment, she glanced at me and added enigmatically, "And restless."

"Restless?"

"Umm." She glancing down at her clasped hands, the palms open, facing up, fingers entwined. Looking up at me she said tenderly, "But mostly, very warm and clear. Restless water does not last."

"Yes," I said, having absolutely no idea what she meant, but with the emotional wine at work in my head, too wonderfully languid to care.

Young always seemed at least one step beyond me, and maddeningly, that step was normally on another plane. Being near her was so different in so many ways, all of them confusing, complex, wonderful, and above all, contradictory.

She was paradox and counterpoint personified. She was simultaneously, but without conflict, clear but ambiguous; linear yet hyperbolic; slow and mercurial; joyful but melancholy; strangely exotic and comfortably familiar; excruciatingly shy yet excitingly passionate; guilelessly open but mysteriously obscure; quietly reserved and garrulously electric.

She was Mozart and Elvis. She was melodic Tchaikovsky played jarringly by Little Richard. She was a conundrum. She was easily understood. She was an experience unlike any other. She was an unrecognizably volatile and dangerous hybrid of East and West.

Sitting in the quiet Korean darkness, Young's comfortable, gracious presence draped warmly and tangibly about me, I began to understand why she seemed so confusing and contradictory. Initially, it didn't seem possible. It was so totally unanticipated. But as my sense of surprise grew, so too did my sense of certainty. The unexpected, unplanned, and unwanted had occurred. Without trying and without warning, I had fallen in love with Miss Lee Kwang Young.

# Twelve

The night of our return from the Han River Gap, Young, in her direct, matter-of-fact way, said it would be at least ten days before she could telephone. Unhappy with so long a separation, I pressed her lightly, hinting we could see one another the following Saturday. But she was evasive, saying only it was time to leave the jewelry shop and begin preparations for the KAL examinations, though they were some eight weeks distant.

Vaguely uncomfortable with this explanation, but unwilling to challenge her, I reluctantly accepted the delay. However, I arranged a specific date, time, and place for her to telephone. We agreed she'd phone me at my quarters in two weeks, a Saturday, at ten o'clock.

This specific approach comforted me greatly. Certainly, it fit my planner personality. But more important, there'd be no more pins and needles. No more biting off Private Bond's head for every imagined transgression. No more sprints down the hallway to fall on my sword, or more accurately, Young's rapier. Nothing but two Youngless weeks.

The first week passed slowly, but eventually brought Saturday morning, which found me at breakfast in Yongsan's Eighth Army Officer's Club. The military club system provides a convenient setting for both social and professional activities while promoting morale and *esprit*. Generally, the clubs are open daily, serve inexpensive meals, and sponsor entertainment such as pool, card games, movies, bingo, stage shows, bands and dances. The clubs are especially effective overseas where they're an island of Americana in an ocean of things foreign.

It was about ten past seven. Not surprisingly, the club's large dining room was almost empty. Aside from mine, only two of the fifty or so cloth-covered tables were occupied. Near the twenty foot floor-to-ceiling windows—which ran along the entire west wall—sat three "round-eye" women. They were leaning forward toward one another, exchanging hushed dialogue. Occasionally, laughter and giggles interrupted their discussion. The women seemed absorbed in some fascinating, secret topic. Their hair was worn short, "above-the-collar," in the women's military fashion. I assumed they were American nurses from the

Yongsan "Evac" hospital.

At the other table sat a group of four silent, scruffy, almost unkempt men. In contrast to the perky women, the men slouched in their chairs and stared vacantly, sure signs of too much Friday night Itaewon "fun." I wondered abstractly if they realized it was Saturday morning. With their long hair and sideburns, I guessed these zombies were civilian contractors, specialists hired by the Army to conduct some one-time task not normally within the military purview.

There was a small commotion at the dining room entrance. At least five of the club's Korean waiters were fussing about a tall, lean man. Colonel Zane Barth was the Eighth Army Aviation Officer, and as with all senior officers, drew the waiter's obsequious attention. I smiled as the Colonel, always self-effacing, raised both hands and waved them left and right, trying to dismiss the unsolicited and unwelcome attention. However, he was outnumbered and respectfully ignored by the chattering, Lilliputian waiters.

Colonel Barth was high on my credibility list. He was a no-nonsense commander who emphasized performance and results over fluff and pomp. He wasn't a "yes-man" and didn't countenance them on his staff. He was well known for both his common sense and tough fairness. Most importantly, he always supported his soldiers, and they loved him for it. He was also a reasonably fair pilot who tried to stay proficient and knowledgeable—something rare for senior officers. Hugh and I were his staff officers for aviation standardization, Eighth Army's instructor pilots. He liked and respected Hugh and, I believed, me as well. We certainly admired and respected him.

Seeing me, the Colonel smiled and gave an abbreviated mock salute. He politely tried to brush the waiters aside, indicating he would sit at my table. The waiters quickly grasped his intent, but wouldn't be cast off. Doggedly, three of the group, one on each side, one leading the way, proudly escorted him across the room. The lead waiter withdrew a chair from the table and, with a huge grin, indicated the Colonel should sit.

Rising as he approached the table, I said, "Morning, sir."

The Colonel quickly waved me to my seat, a grunt dismissing the military courtesy. Accepting the offered chair, he shook his head and, providing an instant flashback to Kwang Young, said without greeting or preamble, "Gosh, how do ya keep that bunch at bay?"

"Don't know, sir." I shrugged. "Price you pay for being a big shot, I guess."

"Big shot?" He grinned broadly at the needle. "That's a laugh. What would happen if an actual important person showed up, for God's sake?" He flipped open his red and white linen napkin and draped it across his lap. "And good morning to you, also. You're up early for a Saturday. And you look sober! No way for a young aviator to behave. What's up?"

"Hmm, nothin' much, sir," I said, adjusting my chair. "Just lying about. A rare day off. I get so few of them, and I'm worked so hard during the week, I want to enjoy every opportunity to relax." I smiled slyly. Colonel Barth knew what Hugh and I did or didn't do. We were far from overburdened.

A master at this respectful sarcasm game, the Colonel smoothed his dark hair and replied, "That so? You know, it's funny, I ran into Hugh Stevens yesterday."

"Oh?"

"Yeah. You remember Hugh? Tall guy, just a bit of a drawl, drives helicopters?"

"Unfortunately, yes."

"Hmm. Well, anyway, Hugh asked for more help in your office."

"Really?"

"Yep."

"Didn't say why, by chance, did he?" I inquired, playing "straight man."

"Well, it's funny you should ask, 'cause I asked that very question."

"And his answer?"

The Colonel mimicked Hugh, "'Well, sir, it's Fitzgerald. He's a worthless shit, and does less than nothing. That clown needs to be fired, or shot, or both! Uh, not to put too fine a point on it, sir.'" The Colonel's imitation was exactly right and we laughed loudly. The nurses and contractors looked our way. We ignored them.

"Well, sir, if Hugh says it's so, then it must be. I can only say in my defense that he does outrank me, and you know what they say about rank?"

"It has its privileges?"

"True, but not what I was thinking."

"Uh, it's always right?"

"Again, true, but again, not what I had in mind."

"Okay, I give."

"I was thinking more along the lines of, 'He's got more rank than brains.'"

The Colonel laughed. "I'll have to remember that next time I talk to the General."

The fawning waiters returned and hovered solicitously over Colonel Barth, serving his usual breakfast. With the obligatory but much important rough-and-tumble banter retired, we were free to move on.

"Why up so early today, sir, and all dressed up to boot?" The Colonel was wearing his formal green uniform with tie in lieu of his normal flight suit, Army fatigues, or more typically for a Saturday morning, civilian clothes.

"Well, I assure you, I'd prefer to be in my jammies, tucked up next to Mrs. Barth. Unfortunately, there's a court-martial matter today; I'm on the board." He shrugged and shook his head regretfully.

"Oh," I said, not sure whether to pursue the issue.

"Yeah, it's one of those Korean women/GI situations."

I shrunk in my chair.

"One soldier caught his girlfriend with another GI and things got ugly. All three ended up in the hospital. Now the local Korean authorities are involved. It's a mess. Just a mess. I hate this kinda thing. Seems like we have more of 'em all the time."

"Sounds badly done by the GIs, sir," I offered lamely.

"Well, they're both young enlisted guys. Classic profiles for that age and rank; no experience, no education, no judgment, nothing to lose, no sense of consequence. The woman's your basic Pillow Girl, trying to line up her next boyfriend." The Colonel shook his head. "You can just about write the script by looking at the characters."

He sipped his coffee and continued. "We gotta command and staff meeting next week. I think the General's going to discuss a new policy of 'aggressively discouraging' contact between Korean women and the soldiers. We just see too many problems and too few benefits. What's more, this is not an isolated incident. It's getting out of hand. Everyone's getting fed up, especially the locals. You know how sensitive they are about Korean women and soldiers. And it's just getting worse."

"Yes, sir."

My heart rate accelerated. I didn't know what "aggressively discouraging" meant, but for an officer, especially an officer on the Eighth Army Staff, a policy or "suggestion" from the General was a de-facto order. You did whatever The Man said, period. No questions, no equivocations, no exceptions.

The Colonel sighed in a perplexed, resigned way. "I understand a soldier's need for women. Also, I understand if his job performance doesn't suffer, then the command is on damn thin ice mucking around in a soldier's private life or bedroom."

He shook his head and continued with increasing passion. "But this is the goddamn U.S. Army, last time I checked. We do have a mission here. This is 'Freedom's Frontier.' The war's just cold, not over. This isn't a lonely hearts club of some kind. The American taxpayers didn't send these guys here to wine, dine, and screw the locals. I don't know where all this is headed, but we may be in for some sharp changes. I know the General Staff is damn fed-up. Needless to say, I'm not happy about getting gee-gawed up on a Saturday morning and sorting out this kinda tragedy."

Sensing my best comment was no comment, I simply said, "Yes, sir."

The Colonel was accustomed to the stock, military phrase and took no note of my reticence. He looked at me, smiled lightly, and slapped my shoulder.

"Can I get off the soapbox now, or do you need more abuse?"

I laughed with what I hoped sounded like camaraderie but made no specific response. It didn't seem to matter.

"You've been scarce lately, Jason, what's new?" This wasn't pro-forma verbiage. To his credit, Colonel Barth was genuinely interested in his soldiers' welfare. He frequently stopped by the various staff sections simply to chat and be accessible.

"Well, sir...." I swallowed hard and hoped to give a respectfully flip and humorous answer that included time-consuming activities, but excluded the truth. "Not much really, just reading a bit, little TV, the standard stuff." Then, incredibly, I added, "And writing the girl back home."

Christ! Where did that reference originate? Perhaps a Freudian reaction to our just completed discussion? Perhaps—no, certainly—just plain stupidity. I cringed inwardly, hoping we would move to another subject. There was no "girl back home." God, what was I thinking? Could it get any worse?

"Yeah?" said the Colonel with a smile. "Tell me about her."

I was fully up to my lower lip in dangerous, dangerous water. I was about to lie to the Eighth Army Aviation Officer, my Commander, and a man I liked and respected. I wanted to press the rewind button and start again. Instead, feeling like a liar and Judas, I improvised, remolding Young in American form.

"Uh, her name is Dawn." I blurted. Then added weakly, "She's pretty."

"Of course." The Colonel nodded and gestured in a rolling motion with his fork for me to get beyond the obvious and provide some detail.

"Uh, yes sir. And, uh, she has dark hair. She's bright and charming." Now beginning to roll, I continued with increased enthusiasm. "She's interesting, and maddening, and fun to be near, and mysterious, and clever, and she makes me laugh, and she laughs at my jokes and I enjoy being around her."

"God, soldier, it sounds like you're in love." Colonel Barth flashed a teasing smile and lightly punched my arm. "Be careful; next thing, you'll be getting married." He laughed loudly, leaving the impression of sad experience.

"Uh, yes, sir. Careful. I'll remember that." The Colonel glanced at me oddly, but only for a second.

"Well, she sounds terrific, Jason. Congratulations." Looking back to his plate, he pushed some egg onto his fork and added darkly, almost in an aside, "You can be damn glad she's not Korean."

# Thirteen

I passed the following week in misery. There was no word of an Eighth Army policy change regarding fraternization with Korean women. I telephoned my contacts in the Headquarters' Administrative section; those bean-counters were the first to know everything, particularly if it was bad news. They had heard nothing. I humbled myself and asked Private Bond, the whiner, to dig around for information with his enlisted contacts. Again, nothing. I couldn't just waltz into the Colonel's office and ask for an update on the "Korean women/GI situation," as he had so elegantly phrased it at our Saturday breakfast. It was as if the issue had spontaneously disappeared. So, true to my misanthropic nature, I concluded silence was a bad sign and waited for the always cloudy sky to fall.

Compounding my misery, I worried about loving Young, though I hadn't spoken the "L" word aloud. Still, I was surprised by my deep attraction for her. I had never, never imagined falling in love with a Korean woman. Never. The idea was simply not in my universe of potential occurrences. If I were honest, perhaps I'd admit I'd never loved anyone. But a Korean? It was just inconceivable. Nonetheless....

I tried to come to grips with what loving Young might mean and—as if I had the power to choose—if I should love her. Was this affair good or bad?

Obviously, there were cultural differences. But these didn't seem so great. In fact, we shared many similarities. She was certainly more Western than Asian. She loved Western music. She dressed in the Western fashion. She read Western authors and liked American movies. She could tolerate Western food. Her English, already polished, would only improve. We hadn't talked about religion, but I had no spiritual ties or preference, so that—in the Army vernacular—was a non-problem. Yes, I'd stumbled a time or two, but that was early on. Graciously understanding my handicap, she had given me the benefit of the doubt. We'd recovered. So, it wasn't as if we were tiptoeing through a field of cultural land mines. All that seemed good.

On a personal level, we were cementing that most enduring and important of relationships; we were becoming best friends. From the outset, we seemed to have a good and strong intrinsic connectivity. We were comfortable in one another's company. We laughed at the same things. Time spent together didn't drag. She made everything a pleasant adventure. She was interested in my current and past activities and asked specific questions, listening intently to the answers. She put me at ease. If I was grumpy, five minutes with her seemed to set everything right. These things seemed to fit nicely in the "Good" category.

But surely, there was a downside? Nothing surfaced. Determined to find balance, I looked a little deeper...and thought of her parents. I wasn't clear about Young's role with them and what authority they exercised over her. However, there would certainly be the stress of first time separation. Of course, they would require financial support and perhaps—no, most certainly—personal visits as time passed, or if they became ill, or if other unforeseen problems occurred. I wondered what impact would these issues have on me, Young, and our relationship. This parents business wasn't really good, but didn't fall cleanly into Bad territory either.

I tried to think of other problems. Prejudice quickly came to mind. Young might not be well received in "The World." Alabama had many—mostly—broadminded and tolerant citizens. However, there were also a few "red-neck" holdovers from an older, uglier era. Clearly, Young wasn't a blond, blue-eyed, Southern belle from Mobile. She would stand out in any Western crowd. Positively so, in my view. But would she be given the opportunity to display her many fine qualities, or simply dismissed as a "gook war bride," or another "Korean whore" who'd tricked a GI into marriage? Remembering the Lizards' reaction, I wondered if my friends saw her as just an upper-class Pillow Girl. What of the other side of the coin; how would she react to prejudice? This issue couldn't be dressed up as positive.

My dark side arose and spun me about. What about children? They'd be half-castes; not accepted by either race. Could I really look into their semi-slanted little eyes and be proud they were mine? I was ashamed of the question, but it wouldn't disappear.

My enthusiasm was melting in the heat of rising concern and doubt. Perhaps I was just infatuated. Young was clearly charming, and so very different than the Pillow Girls. Could it be I was simply lonely for intelligent female companionship? Maybe I was getting way ahead here. We had only known one another for a matter of weeks. We hadn't even kissed. Now I'm thinking love? Back in the States? Children? Where had these ideas come from? I liked her now, isolated and cut off from the "real world," but how would I feel when I got home and we were tossed in with my normal, real society? How many Buddhist temples were within driving distance of Fort Rucker, Alabama? Was it possible Young's difference and charm could become more burden than blessing? Things were speeding out of control. This train had to slow down. What had I gotten into?

I recalled Hugh's sage counsel, something brief and pointedly cruel, like, "It'll end badly. Get a Pillow Girl and settle in." Apparently I, to quote Oscar Wilde, "always pass on good advice."

# Fourteen

It was not quite ten a.m., but Al and the Lizards were camped in their usual lounge spots, tethered to their chairs and velcroed to the TV. A ball game played the week before blared from the television. Due to the twelve hour time difference between Korea and America, real-time or live events were rarely shown. Typically, the event was taped and mailed to Seoul for replay the following Saturday and also on Sunday. Most always the outcome of these games was known before they were broadcast. Little matter; the Lizards had been known to watch the same game, in its entirety, on both days. Sometimes they wagered on the game's outcome…on both days. The docile Lizards could be sardonic.

Today was the much-anticipated Saturday of Young's promised call. Today, at least until she called, I too was a Lizard, watching TV and waiting by the phone.

Al, a beer balanced on his generous stomach, belched and said, "What the hell's the name of the guy playin' third?"

"Eddie Johnston," mumbled Lizard Frank, jamming a handful of popcorn into his mouth.

"Yeah, that's right, Johnston. Didn't he break an ankle last week?"

"Yep."

"What I thought. Shit, guess we're lucky to see games played in this century."

Lizard Donnie was distracted. "Wanna shut up, or I'll tell who wins."

Al responded with a smirk. "I know who wins, Donnie, for Christ's sake. I just wanna see if they can do it again." This witticism generated much loud and prolonged laughter. Lizard humor is obtuse.

The telephone rang. Leaning casually against the doorjamb, almost hovering over the phone, I smiled but didn't move. The phone rang again.

"Somebody answer the goddamn phone," said Donnie, without looking away from the TV.

It rang a third time. Donnie, in exasperation, propped himself on one arm and started to turn. Before he could complain, I picked up the handset.

"BOQ, Mr. Fitzgerald speaking." I sounded calm and dispassionate.

A teasing voice carried through the ear piece, "Hello Mr. Fitzgerald speaking. This is Kwang Young speaking."

I didn't want to sound too lovesick with the Lizards about, so I turned away from the group and scraped off as much of the sugar in my voice as I could.

"Hi pal, how are you?

"Fine, thank you very much. And you, please?" Her response had that odd phrase-book quality I'd previously noticed.

"Good. But I've missed you."

"Is it correct?" she asked, sounding pleased.

"Yes, it is correct," I mimicked with light sarcasm.

Then, so like her, she came directly to the point. "Would you prefer to meet today? This is possible, yes?"

"Absolutely."

"Very well, then. Under my hill in one hour."

"Yes, ma'am, one hour. I'll be there."

# Fifteen

When I arrived, Young was waiting, hands in pockets, leaning against one of the large trees that flanked the hill's concrete pathway. She wore faded jeans—pressed—and a loosely fitting black sweatshirt with "University of Cincinnati" in red and white block-print letters that arched across her chest. The single word "Bearcats" was embroidered in white script at the midriff. She carried no purse, as was her habit with jeans, but instead, a small wallet which, oddly, she always kept in her front pocket. I noticed her hair was somewhat longer. She looked tired, but smiled broadly upon catching sight of the Rocket.

She was in the car quickly. Young, like most Koreans, shied from public affection. She wasn't comfortable openly holding hands or embracing. The anathema, Public Kissing, would simply never occur to her. Consistent with her nature, she opened the car door, sat down, and smiled in her disarming fashion.

"Hello. It is nice to see you today," she said, each syllable clipped, distinct, and sounding as if she had just learned the phrase.

"Hello, Young. It's nice to see you as well," I responded affectionately.

Within the privacy of the Rocket, I reached across the front seat and squeezed her hand. She seemed both pleased and embarrassed, but didn't resist; indeed, she squeezed lightly in return. Then, apparently self-conscious of the instant warmth between us, she recalled her hand.

"Very well, we may go now."

"'Very well, we may go now' where?" I bantered in that teasing, mimicking style we'd adopted.

"You may follow my directions," she said playfully, looking through the front windscreen, shoulders hunched, hands on either side of her knees as she leaned on the seat's front edge.

Young directed us south, across the Han, past the city limits, and finally onto the Seoul-Pusan turnpike. The turnpike was a six lane freeway identical to any American interstate, and totally dissimilar to the ancient, winding road we had traveled only two weeks before. The smooth, modern Seoul-Pusan was welcome medicine for the Rocket's creaking suspension and we moved comfortably south through the hazy, chilly November Saturday.

"Okay, now, can you tell me where we're goin'?"

"Yes, to the Korean Folk Village. This is a special place I want to show you. The Village is nearby Suwon. It is some distance from Seoul. It will take a little time to reach this destination."

"Oh. Well, I've got gas."

"You are sick?" she asked, looking at me with concern.

I laughed loudly.

Her looked of concern changed to mild surprise, then irritation, then hurt. "Is there humor in this situation? I am not correct in some way? If so, it is polite to laugh?" Frustrated and embarrassed, she asked sarcastically, "This is an Alabama custom?" She blushed, seemingly ill at ease by what she may have said, or missed, and probably by her reaction.

"No, no, Young. Wait." Seeing I had unintentionally cut her, I quickly lost my smile. "You didn't understand. I'm sorry. I wasn't laughing at you, it was.... I don't know. It was a mistake. I apologize. It wasn't mean laughter. Don't be angry, please."

I found her reaction odd. She was seldom out of sorts. This was one of the rare times she was impatient or angry. In response to my apology, she grunted, folded her arms across her chest and looked out her side window. She stared at the passing Korean rice paddies, brown, dry, and brittle with the late fall. The adjacent small country huts showed the dark gray smoke of *ondol* charcoal heaters drifting from chimneys.

Not having faced this situation with her before, and having previously misread her, I chose to say nothing. She understood I was sorry. My clear apology lay on the seat between us. When she wanted to pick it up, she would. I hoped silence was the correct tactic.

After a few minutes, she turned toward me and in that gracious way she wore so naturally, bowed slightly, and said, "I was rude. *Mian hamnida*. I'm sorry."

"No, pal, I'm sorry. You were fine. Don't worry about it. Let's just start again, okay? The car has plenty of gasoline and I feel fine. There, better?"

She nodded but remained somber. Still looking toward but not at me, she said, "Before we, uh, know each other more, I must tell you about something."

This didn't sound good, and began to explain the weariness on her face and her unusually short temper. In anticipation of what her "something" might be, my pulse accelerated. My experience with preambles that began with phrases like "we need to talk" told me there was danger, or heartbreak, or some similar unpleasantness ahead. Sharpening my sense of danger was Young's propensity to begin discussions totally without preamble. If she found it necessary to begin slowly, it could only mean trouble.

"Oh?" I responded cautiously.

"Yes," she replied, now clearly uncomfortable.

"Okay." I expelled some quickly accumulated tension with a large breath, and braced for whatever might be next. "What is it?"

Regretfully, I was rewarded with a return to her direct manner. "I have the Korean boyfriend," she said flatly.

I was crushed. Why didn't I see this coming? Of course she would have boyfriends, for all the obvious reasons. Damn! I had her married off, speaking perfect English and living in the States without ever thinking she might be romantically involved with someone of her own culture. What the hell was wrong with me? I should have anticipated this. I never slowed the damn train. Goddamn it! Serves me right.

"So, that's where you've been for two weeks?" I snapped coldly.

"Yes, some of the time."

"Well, Christ, don't sugarcoat it, Young."

"I do not understand."

"Never mind."

The silence and tension were palpable. I was hurt, scared, jealous, disappointed and angry. I wanted to kick the dashboard and slap the steering wheel, all the while cursing madly. But instead I sat stoically.

I had no claim on her. I'd not said anything about my feelings for her. Likewise, she'd made no commitment to me. Beyond her poetic and obscure "water" remark from a couple of weeks before, she'd not said her feelings toward me were particularly affectionate. It stuck me that my reaction, and to a degree hers, was inappropriate, given the surface circumstances. Still, various negative emotions ran through me.

We said nothing for several minutes, she fidgeting, me immobile. The Korean countryside hurried by unnoticed. Slowly, I began to cool and gather my wits. Did her disclosure mean she felt drawn to me? No. More likely, it was a way of building a wall between us. Obviously, she wanted to make sure I didn't get too close.

Perhaps she sensed I was moving toward her romantically and recognized it as folly. A boyfriend would certainly derail me. I thought it would be best to simply ask what this was all about. I'd use her approach and be direct. See how she liked it.

"Well, Young, what does this mean?" The irrational anger and sting was almost gone from my voice, but burned brightly in my heart.

Witty and nimble, I'd rarely seen Young lacking a response, but now she hesitated, looking down at her shoes. "Well…well, it means I have made a not so comfortable circumstance." She hesitated again. Looking at me, she said brusquely, almost as if the thought annoyed her, "You know very well I like you."

I did not know this "very well," but was not at all displeased by the idea.

Young looked away. "I like him as well." She omitted his name, depersonalizing him, wandering about in the abstract, salving the sting. "You are a mystery…and different. It is very difficult to read you about several points. There are many things we do not understand about one another. This is not so with…my other friend. I understand him very well. But he is not like you in some important way that I cannot explain."

I nodded in semi-understanding. It seemed she did care about me. If she were wall-building, she'd have gently let me down and explained how great her relationship with Mr. Korea was, and why a Korean-American liaison was doomed to failure and just a bad idea all-around.

Greatly mollified, and somewhat dazed at the unexpected reversal, I asked as evenly as I could, "What should we do about this?"

"This is Western thinking, Jason." She smiled with understanding and patience. "What we will 'do' is what is set out for us. It is Fate. We follow where our path leads. The power to do, or not do, is not with us."

"Fate," I said flatly, having never seriously considered the concept, though I recalled she'd mentioned it at our Heavenly Gate Hotel meeting. Something like, it was my fate to not have siblings, and Fate would protect her while flying. I'd paid little attention at the time.

"Yes, you know very well what this means," she replied, apparently a little miffed at my tone. "Our course is set, we simply follow. It is very, uh, relaxing actually. There is no looking for the next action. The next action will find you."

"I'm not so sure I agree with that. I think you control your future through the things you do, the actions you take, or don't take. What I do today, defines what happens tomorrow. I control my future, it doesn't control me."

Silence. Obviously, she didn't understand. Perhaps an example would clarify. "For example, if you don't study for your KAL exams, you won't do well. You won't pass the test. You won't be accepted for training. The opposite's also true. This clearly has nothing to do with Fate. Your action, or inaction, drives a predictable result."

Good example, relevant, brief, and absolutely clear. I was quite pleased. Of course, I was dealing with Kwang Young, and of course, she had an immediate rejoinder.

"In a way, you are correct; what we do makes a difference, but only on the, uh, first level of thinking."

Ouch, did she just call me shallow? I smiled inwardly, waiting for the rest. This would be good.

"You see, in this example, if it is my fate to be accepted at KAL, then I will study and learn. I will find the correct books. I will choose the correct lessons. They will be easily remembered. I will pass the examination. The question is, is it my fate to be with KAL? If so, then these study things will happen, if not," she shrugged, "they won't. I am just a tool for Fate. Fate gives me the opportunity to do what it commands. I do not change Fate, I just, uh, exercise Fate," she said, finishing brightly, apparently happy with "exercise." "It is not so difficult, really. Do you understand?"

"Yeah, I understand, I just don't agree. Isn't that all a little too easy, too convenient? If "X" happens, that was Fate, if "Y" happens, well, that, too, was Fate? Where's the logic in that? Sounds more like…convenience."

"This is the basic problem." She smiled indulgently. "In the West, the question is always, 'How does this work?' 'What is the logic for to solve the problem?' For building the rocket planes, this is good and necessary thinking. For living every day, this is, well…foolish."

"Oh, really?" I snorted, more than a little indignant. "This 'foolishness' has given us history's highest standard of living. America leads the world—including Korea, I might add—in just about everything."

Young nodded. "Well, yes, but this is not important."

"Well, if you lived in a mud hut without electricity, or telephones, or televisions, or cars, it would damn sure be important."

"No, probably less so. And, please, Korea had the civilization when Europe lived in caves…and long before there was the America."

I was becoming exasperated. "Okay, just for argument's sake, let's say logic and problem-solving and modern conveniences aren't important. So what is important? How do you ensure a better future?"

"This is difficult to answer. But your question shows the difference between East and West."

"Well, humor me, please, and try."

"In Asia, we do not try to control things, to make them work as we want," she said, passing over my sarcasm. "We think this control is foolish. Here, the idea is waiting, patience, accepting. We know Fate works in its way, and time, and uh, manner. It cannot be hurried; it cannot be twisted to some different destination. Events, things, the future, will find their place as they should, as they are set to do."

"And what's that got to do with problem-solving?"

Young looked at me with surprise. "Everything. We do not try to find answers for all problems. Fate gives these answers. Our role is to wait, do our best, follow the right paths, and accept. We will consider what the problems mean and how they will change us. But we wait for the answer. Sometimes it is years to see, but the answer always comes. When it comes, we accept and continue."

"Crazy," I said in polite disapproval. "What if you don't like the answer?"

"More Western thinking. There is no like or not like. The answer is only, well, the answer. It cannot be changed; it cannot be turned; it is not good or bad, like or not like. It is…the way of things. We cannot change the, uh, how do you say, nonchangeable, yes?"

I shook my head. "I guess."

I understood about two percent of what she'd said and disagreed with that. We were clearly at a philosophical Promontory Point, but unlike the railroad builders, we were staring at one another across a considerable chasm. For Young, passive acceptance of the future made perfect sense. She seemed to believe that problems and circumstances arrived at her doorstep with a pre-designated solution or end that would, in its own good time, mysteriously surface. Efforts at changing or controlling events were wasted. As a lifelong problem solver, I refused to believe that logic-based solutions were suddenly irrelevant, replaced by patience and some Asian version of what sounded a lot like luck.

I rubbed the back of my neck, frustrated, wondering where to go next and how to get there. Suddenly, it occurred to me I had somehow been diverted to "rocket planes," mud huts, and some kind of weird predestination. Had Young intentionally steered me here? I almost smiled at the thought. Almost. What I really wanted to know was what was to be done about her goddamn boyfriend! A slow learner, and very Western, I again tried the logical, problem solving approach.

"So, what are you going to do about this boyfriend 'circumstance'?"

Young smiled patiently, having just answered this same question in plural form. "I will 'do' what Fate says," she answered, emphasis on "do."

Accepting I would dredge up nothing concrete from her, but responding to my psychological needs and drives, I said, "Look, I don't know where we're headed, if anywhere."

She looked at me quizzically, clearly unable to translate. Normally, I enjoyed cleaning up these little word-spills, but I didn't want to get distracted. I felt I was already behind on debate points and the thought of her Korean boyfriend relit my anger. I continued with intensity.

"But I'll tell you what I'm gonna do. I'm gonna proceed as if it's only you and me. I can't control your 'other friend.'" Sarcasm was again in my voice at the mention of her euphemism. "I can't control you. I can't control how, or what, you feel. But I can damn sure control what I do, say, and think. Therefore, I don't know who this guy is or your history with him, and please, I don't wanna know. But he'd better look out, 'cause while he's using 'Fate,'" I said with derision, "I will be using the arrows of charm." I flashed my best Tom Sawyer grin.

Young smiled broadly and, shaking her head, allowed her chin to drop rapidly to her chest in a gesture of surrender, as if she, the wise and all-powerful giant, had been inexplicably captured by an army of tiny, indefatigable, persistent idiots. Presently, she looked up and smiled.

"Yes, Jason, you have charm.... It is your fate."

# Sixteen

The Folk Village was enlightening and enjoyable. Designed to showcase Korea's cultural past, the village is best described to Americans as an Asian version of Colonial Williamsburg, only from a much older era. The village depicted the already ancient Korean culture, society, and daily life from the Yi Dynasty, which began about one hundred years before Columbus discovered the New World.

The village was comprised of about two hundred twenty-five buildings built in the style typical of shops and homes as they appeared in the first half of the millennium. The shops featured artisans skilled in the old crafts of pottery, papermaking, basketry, calligraphy, and the spinning of silk from cocoons. There were also fortunetellers, seamstresses, carpenters, and blacksmiths; just about every trade imaginable for the period was represented.

The shops were fully functional and actually produced and sold the craft featured. The men and women who worked at various trades and crafts also lived in the replica homes and shops. Tourists were free to wander about as they pleased. The buildings and people were living examples of life in Korea five hundred years earlier. Young was quick to point out the buildings were not mud-huts.

On a larger scale, both to preserve the culture and to entertain the tourists, the villagers assembled daily to reenact important cultural ceremonies, just as they would have originally been conducted. Young said many of the festivals and events reenacted were still observed.

We came upon a crowd of people watching a woman standing on a simple rope swing. The crowd cheered as the woman swung higher and higher.

"What's going on?"

"This is one of the *Tan-O* Day games. It is a holiday honored particularly by the country people. It is a day to make sure the good…collecting of…. How do you say the cutting of wheat and the taking of rice?"

"Harvest?" I guessed.

"Har-Vest," she tried, the word obviously new to her. Again, two distinct syllables.

"Yeah, I think that's right. Just, kind of make it one word, Harvest. I gotta teach you to slur."

"Harvest," she said quickly. Shaking her head, she smiled with exasperation.

"The 'R' is a difficult sound to make. The slurring will make this easier?"

"Uh, yeah. But you said it right, and you got the 'V' sound too, that's good." She waved her hand dismissively, apparently a bit embarrassed.

"The celebration is interesting in how it happens on a special day every year. In the moon calendar, uh, no…lunar calendar," she said, pleased to have found the correct word, "the day is always on the fiveth day—"

"Fifth," I corrected.

Young exhaled deeply, and with her characteristic dogged determination, started again. "The celebration is always on the fifth day, of the fifth month, of the lunar calendar. This is in June. On *Tan-O* day, there was no work. There was a festival and games. For men, it is *ssirum*, the uh, how is it said? Body fighting?"

"Wrestling?" I suggested.

She shrugged, not much interested in men's fighting games.

"For women, the game is this swinging competition." The crowd cheered again, and Young raised her voice. "To win, you must stand on the rope and try to be the one with the highest, uh, elevation? The champion wins a small gold ring, yes? Of course, there is also the music, as you can hear. They played dancing and had the theater for…." She hesitated, unsure of a word. "The small cloth forms?" Speaking a single Korean word, she raised her hand above her head and wiggled her long, elegant fingers. "What is the English for this?"

Mystified, I said, "Pal, I'm sorry, I don't know what you mean."

"Umm, I can show you, come."

She led and I followed as she looked about the village in vain. Finally, she stopped a Korean man who listened to her and, typically Korean, stared at me. Still looking at me, the man replied and gestured over his right shoulder. In response, Young bowed slightly. He did the same.

Pulling me by the sleeve, she hurried toward a large round building tucked away near the fence. Approaching, we could hear children's laughter spilling through the arched doorway and across the threshold. We entered and stood in the back.

The building had a single, circular room filled with about fifty people, mostly children, seated on benches or standing around the curved walls. In the front was a ten foot high wall extending the width of the room. Centered on the wall was a rectangular opening about the size of a living room picture window.

"Here, these forms," she gestured toward the front wall, her eyes bright with enthusiasm. "How do you say these things? How are they called?"

"Princess, these are puppets."

"Puppets," she repeated, careful to slur the syllables. It was very endearing.

We watched the show. Language wasn't a barrier; we all laughed at the same times.

Strolling away from the theater, a group of children burst past, chattering and laughing. One little boy bumped Young. He stopped and bowed. Young also bowed. There was a brief exchange of dialogue after which he turned and, chasing after his friends, vanished.

"You'd never get an American kid to even slow down, much less bow."

"Why?"

"Oh, I don't know. I think we're a lot less formal maybe. And bowing is just something we don't do." I laughed. "Maybe we're too proud to bow."

"It has nothing to do with proud. Actually, it is a kind of respect and communication. There are many, many different kinds of ways to bow…and to return the bow, yes? Normally, the younger person bows first with the greeting. The other person also makes the bow and answers. The bigger the bow, the greater the respect. It is not humiliation like in the West. It is simply polite."

"Yeah, I'm sure, but it's something we just don't do."

"There are many difference between Seoul and Alabama. Do you know the polite way to give something to another person?"

"Uh, not the way you're talking about, I'm sure."

"To show respect, especially to an older or higher person, use only the right hand. The left hand is put here." She pointed between her elbow and wrist. "Or at this part," she said, gesturing toward her elbow. "The very great respect is to use both hands together. Of course, the correct bow and greeting is added also."

"Phew, compound cultural requirements," I whined. "This is tough."

"Uh? I don't understand." She place inflection emphasis charmingly on "don't," in a rare use of a contraction.

"I just mean things here, in Korea, are different in ways that aren't always clear. It'd be hard for me to understand…ever, probably. I'm not sure I could do some Asian things, or would want to…like bowing. I know it's not humiliation, but still, it just wouldn't feel right. I don't think I could do it."

Young looked at the ground, hands in her pockets, and considered my observation for some time. Slowly swinging the toe of her sneaker in a small arc across the sandy soil, she nodded her head.

"I understand this. This kind of thing is also, I think, true for Alabama…and me."

# Seventeen

The daylight faded. November twilight settled across the Suwon valley, coloring the mountains various shades of mauve, erasing the rice paddies, and tossing winter's chill over the landscape. The Rocket provided refuge and rescue. The heater's warmth filled the car. The headlights opened the road before us. We slipped anonymously though the late evening dusk, the Seoul-Pusan our silent, concrete guide. A large, blue "Interstate" sign rushed past. Its white script lettering, printed in Hangul and English, read: "Seoul 43 KM."

"Do you still wish to play skiing?"

I nearly drove into the ditch. "I thought you'd forgotten about that."

"Why should I forget? It was your honest question."

"Well, you hadn't mentioned it for a while, and there were so many problems that, I don't know, I just thought it was dead."

"Yes, well, it is alive," she said, in her matter-of-fact way.

"Well, sure. Again, though, what about the problems of foreign and native, my 'true heart,' your parents, all of that?" Then, adding as an afterthought and not without sarcasm, "Not to mention 'Mr. Korea.'"

"I have considered these things for some time." she began, ignoring my boyfriend reference. "As you know, we have visited the public places with other Koreans there. They stare, but it is not so bad as I imagined. I need to test this further to know for certain." Lifting her chin, she added with exactly the right amount of self-assured arrogance. "Actually, it may be I do not care.

"Concerning your heart?" She paused, tilted her head, and looked at me with a sly smile. "It is wicked, and evil, like the witch in 'Snow White.' I cannot change this kind of...low character, so I don't care about that, either."

We laughed, but after a moment, Young became serious. She looked for some time through the Rocket's side window. Sensing she had more to say, I remained silent.

"My mother and father are not so simple a matter." She looked forward again and frowned slightly. "The idea of respect and obedience to the parents is very, very important in Korea. Normally, there is the strongest respect between the most old son and the father. In the country, where the farm work is hard and long, daughters are not so important because they cannot help like the son.

"We, of course, live in the city. But also in my family, there is the different circumstance. As you know very well, my father is old and does not now work. I am the most old child. Also, I, not my brother, work and keep the family...welfare." She used the slurred word form she'd learned at the Heavenly Gate Hotel. "Because of this situation, I have the greater freedom than most daughters. Of course, I love and honor my parents and will only do as they ask. However, because of our family circumstance, they do not always ask me to do as they wish. It is a great honor, this freedom, especially for the daughter."

Young drew a deep breath and, looking at the car floor, continued, "I will ask my mother if I may go to Dragon Valley with friends for the overnight trip to play skiing. I will tell her this is a last party before the KAL study begins. She will tell my father. If I hear nothing more, then I have the permission. If they ask me questions I must answer with a lie, or they do not want me to go, then I will not go. This is the compromise between truth and lie, freedom and obedience."

I was unsure how, or whether, to comment. This was obviously a difficult place for her. It was clear she didn't relish the idea of deceiving her parents. However, she had proposed an elegant solution. Young couldn't acquiesce with her parent's wishes forever; she was the "breadwinner"; she was twenty-three, an adult, and more West than East. At least, I thought so.

However, this approach did address her Eastern nature; allowing her parents the final right of refusal. Technically, it wasn't an outright lie, though she was seriously stretching the truth. The destination was Dragon Valley. She would ski. I was a "friend." However, there was only me, not her story's plural from, and the clear implication was her "friends" were female Koreans. Nonetheless, if she wanted to make the trip, and apparently she did, it seemed a workable, Solomon-like solution.

She looked up from the floor and directly at me. "Thoughts on this?" she asked seriously.

I smiled, surprised by her semi-slang. She hadn't learned the phrase from me. She sounded very much like a college professor asking the class its collective opinion of some eclectic theory.

My response was equally academic, and pure inspiration. It pleased her Asian nature greatly. "Well, Young, let's just see what Fate allows."

# Eighteen

I returned to the office from the Yongsan Heliport about two o'clock on Wednesday afternoon. I'd spent the day flying with the 128th Assault Helicopter unit. We had conducted an air mobile training exercise just south of the Buffer Zone, a half-mile wide no-man's land on either side of the line dividing North from South Korea.

As I put away my flight gear, Hugh, watching with a smirk from his desk, asked, "So, Bubba, how'd it go?" Without waiting for a response, and flashing more of his famous "wit," he continued. "You're back alive, apparently, so it must have been successful."

"Yeah, no thanks to Captain Ellis," I replied, fumbling in my locker with flight helmet and survival vest. "Goddamn, do they give these guys check rides out of flight school any more, or what?" I waved my arm dramatically in large, irregular patterns in imitation of the disparaged Captain Ellis's flight skills. "All over the goddamn sky."

Air mobile operations featured multi-helicopter formations. Each aircraft carried troops. The idea was to simultaneously land the soldiers in roughly the same area so they could disembark, form up as an effective fighting unit, and do whatever infantry people do once safely on the ground.

Tactically, the helicopter formations are flown "loose" while en route to the drop-off point, with no specific spacing or distance. Loose could be defined as up to a quarter mile separation between aircraft. However, from the initial assault rally point to the landing zone, the formations of eight or so aircraft were generally flown "tight," each helicopter tucked up a few feet from the one preceding it, and twenty feet or so from another helicopter, to the left or right. Tight formations had everyone flying in a slot. Naturally, the steadier the pilot, the steadier the aircraft, the easier to "fly off of."

Newly qualified aviators took some time to learn formation flying skills. I was fortunate to have learned formation techniques quickly, flying every day, six hours a day in Vietnam. Captain Ellis, the new Administrative Staff Officer, was only two months removed from flight school. He flew two hours at a time, once per week—maybe. Obviously, but not surprisingly, he was in need of practice.

Hugh placed both hands alongside his temples and closed his eyes. I couldn't help smiling; there was going to be more wit, and no doubt I would be its target.

"Waaaait," he said slowly, drawing the word out. "Wait…I see…myself! And…and…. Yes! You! The intrepid Jason Fitzgerald, natural born aviator."

I shook my head and leaned against the locker with a smile.

"We're sitting in The Statue. It's late. The joint's nearly empty. You've had several drinks…of the not-so-soft variety. What? Yes, uh huh, uh huh, a confession! Let me replay it. Poor old Hugh's memory banks aren't what they were, but I'll try: 'Hugh, my first month outta flight school, I flew so poorly my boss asked if I had a problem with depth perception.'" Hugh opened one eye, looked at me, and said, "Is yes? Or is no?"

"You know, Hugh, I'm not so sure about your comedic skills, but you make a terrific asshole."

Hugh dropped his hands and shrugged. "Must be yes."

I grunted, plopped into the chair behind my desk and reached for the overflowing in-box.

"Didn't forget the three o'clock staff meeting, did ya?"

"No. Any idea what's on the agenda?" I asked apprehensively.

"Not really. The usual stuff, I guess, been a couple months since we had one." He shrugged. "We're due."

"Yeah."

"Relax, bud. I just don't see how the Command can dictate a soldier's off-duty activities." Hugh knew I was concerned about the much-dreaded but still-rumored policy change toward "Korean Nationals." The grapevine had even dreamed up a new acronym: KN.

"I hope you're right. The Colonel hinted at that, something about being on thin ice in a soldier's bedroom."

"Well, he's right. Colonel Barth's a smart guy; he's not going to do anything dumb."

"Yeah, well, it ain't him. It's the General, or worse, the General's staff; those boot-licking yes-men are always trying to curry favor at the expense of regular guys."

"Jason, don't make it a problem before it's a problem. We don't even know if it's on the agenda, for Christ's sake."

Three o'clock found the entire staff, about thirty people, gathered in the command's large conference room, listening to the Colonel. Thus far, it was the standard fare. He'd droned on for about thirty minutes, addressing various points ranging from maintaining our military appearance to improving our response time to the units we supported. Nothing about policy changes.

"Okay, that brings us to the last item."

I perked up. Perhaps I'd get out of here safely after all.

"There's been a lot of discussion at the General Staff level about the Command's increased problems between GIs and KN's."

I sunk in my chair. Hugh kicked my foot and I sat up.

"You all know the problems I'm referring to."

There was a mixture of snickering, smirks, and shuffling feet. The Colonel ignored these reactions.

"The General's Staff has looked at this issue from about every perspective, including legal. At first, there was a sense that we should institute some kind of outright ban on...." Colonel Barth groped for a politely descriptive word. "On...'inappropriate' contact between GIs and Koreans. Specifically, Korean women. However, this approach was abandoned for several reasons I won't go into here."

This sentence cheered me considerably. The next did not.

"But within a few days, the 'Old Man' will publish a policy letter addressing GIs and Korean Nationals. There will be a lot of polite talk in it. Let me shuck that part away and give you the proverbial bottom line, loud and clear, and my take on it."

He paused, took a sip of water and continued. "The command will not tolerate, I will not tolerate, any problem, of any kind, from any soldier, in the area of...Korean-American, uh, relations. If such a problem arises, from any source, for any reason, the soldier will be court-martialed and sent directly back to the States at the earliest possible opportunity."

He looked around the room. No snickering, smirks or shuffling. Satisfied the point was understood, he continued, "Is that clear?" His voice rose with the expectation of a response.

In unison, and loudly, the soldiers, including myself and Hugh, responded, "Yes, sir!"

"Gentlemen, I hope so. There will be no exceptions. Do not test me on this. If it has the General's attention, it damn sure has mine. And if it has mine," he smiled benignly and lowered his voice, "I just know it has yours."

There was a smattering of polite laughter.

As Hugh and I returned to our office, I asked, "Problems? Wonder what the hell he means by 'problems'? That could be anything from a nickel-dime speeding ticket with a KN in your car to, well, something worse."

"I don't know, Jason, but didn't he say any problem of any kind? That's awfully narrow territory; close to one strike and you're out. A court-martial for an officer is the end of his career, period."

"Yeah," I said, still uncomfortably foggy about what might constitute a "problem." I liked things in neat, compact boxes. But I sure wasn't going to the Colonel to say: "Oh, by the way, sir, I lied to you the other day. My girlfriend is actually Korean after all, imagine that. Oh, and did I mention I'm taking her to Dragon Valley? Overnight, of course. Naturally, we're lying to her parents about this, as it's certainly against their wishes. And, just to spice matters up a bit, she has a Korean boyfriend who probably would not be too pleased if he knew what was up. Does any of this qualify as a 'problem'?"

"Hey, Jason, look at it this way. Contact with Korean women isn't banned, you just gotta be careful to not screw up. Like, say...lying about it to the Colonel."

"Thanks, Hugh."

# Nineteen

"Young, this was a great idea, pal."

"Yes, it is pleasant here and the day is fortunate. The, uh, sky is blue. We can, I hope, see the distant places."

It was early December, and chilly, but not cold. The morning sunlight was unfiltered and warming. We wore lightweight jackets, but not hats or gloves. Young suggested we visit Nam San (South Mountain) Park and its seven hundred foot tall Seoul Tower. From the tower, we'd watch the city awaken.

The tower's original purpose was to broadcast TV signals, which it still did. However, it had become a tourist attraction notable for its rotating restaurant and breathtaking Seoul panorama. The tower's height and Nam San Mountain combined for an elevation of about fifteen hundred feet above the city. With clear weather, we'd be able to see not only all of Seoul, but perhaps as far as the coast, some fifty miles distant.

Strolling along the park's narrow pathway toward the tower, I noticed sections of what looked like an earthen barrier. I looked closer. It appeared man-made, perhaps a wall. The sections ran along the crest of a ridgeline, disappeared, then reappeared. This pattern repeated randomly. The wall was thick, perhaps five feet or so, and easily twice that height. It looked old and weathered, what must have been formerly sharp angles were worn and rounded.

"Young, what's that, uh, wall-looking thing?"

She smiled and with gentle sarcasm, dipped her head slightly and said, "A wall."

I dropped my chin to my chest in what had become our common expression of defeated exasperation. Looking up again, I said in measured tones, "Okay. What kind of wall? For what? To keep something in? To keep something out? To mark a boundary? To protect something? What?"

"Well, all of those things, really. It is part of the Seoul City wall from old times."

"How old?"

Young rolled her head fully back and looked at the sky. With playful frustration, she said, "Jason, if I knew we would meet? I would have been the more diligent student. You have many questions."

"Yeah. I know. How old?"

"I do not know exactly, maybe since about, oh, fourteen hundred or so, I imagine. Before Alabama, for certain."

"Hey, watch it. Alabama's plenty old, if that's the measure for quality. And the only stone wall we ever needed was Jackson, but that's a different story."

She looked at me with furrowed brow, completely lost. Whenever I needed a cheap and easy victory, or in this case, revenge, I could always draw on American History 101.

"Anyway, what was the wall for?" I asked before she could gather her wits and puncture my hollow win. "What did it do?"

"Well, mostly in those days it was to protect the city, yes? This is part of a wall that made a, uh, circle around Seoul." She gestured, her hands forming a dinner plate shape. "In the wall, there were gates, nine or ten I think. You see some of these gates still today. South Gate, Namdaemun, is probably the most famous in the downtown. Also, there is still the Tongdaemun, East Gate, with the large international shopping area. This place is near my jewelry shop where we met."

"Yeah, I've been there. Went to the outdoor part the day we met, as a matter of fact."

We repositioned to a wall remnant and tourist reader board. Young skimmed the information. "Oh, yes, I remember. This wall part has an interesting thing about it. In the old days, the country people, uh, talked, to the capitol using, uh…I don't know the English."

I shrugged. She smiled and motioned in circles with her hand, frustrated.

"Oh, uh, fire piles?"

"Bonfires?" I suggested.

She shrugged.

"Gotta be. Go ahead."

"Each section of the country chose several mountaintops, the last one visible from here. Each mountain had five places for fire on it. The number of fires means more or less trouble in that part of the country. If only one fire, everything was fine, only normal problems. The more fire? Then the more serious problems. In these cases, messengers from the country would bring the story to Seoul."

"In Seoul, the king could see this mountaintop and the city wall from his palace. So, this was chosen as the place to relay to the king the kind of trouble, or not trouble, in the country. Here, on this part, the wall would have the same number of fires as the fire keepers saw on the country people's mountaintops."

"Uhmp. Sounds awkward. Did it work?"

"I suppose; they did it this way about four hundred years."

"Oh. I guess it did work."

We moved on, past the old guardian wall to the new gondola cable-car for the ride to the top of the tower. It was just after eight and before the crowds. We stepped into the car and were whisked to the tower's top. There, we very much enjoyed the quiet and lonely emptiness. The tourist area housed shops and restaurants, while the observation deck offered a three hundred and sixty degree panorama of the city and its protective mountains.

With nearly unlimited visibility, the view was, as we'd hoped, spectacular. The port city of Inchon, perhaps fifty miles to the west, was outlined on the horizon. About ten miles to the south, the high-rise apartments and the great, domed National Assembly Building on Yoi-do Island were easily visible. To the east, the Han River Gap with its ancient Lord Protectorates created a narrow break in Seoul's mountain crescent.

The steep northern mountains, peaked and jagged, seemed very near in the sharp clarity of the morning's sunlight. They pushed close-up, crowding the city, nudging it ever south. Inside this encompassing pocket lay Seoul, deceptively quiet, its intense activity masked by the height.

I leaned against the railing and took a deep breath of the cool air. A light, silent breeze drifted passed my collar. I closed my eyes and felt the sun's weak morning warmth.

"The mornings here always seem so…well, so…peaceful. No, peaceful isn't right. Maybe slow is better. The morning just kinda creeps…."

Young looked quizzically away from the sharply etched horizon. I backed up and tried, "The morning just walks up slowly, silently, from behind. I mean, the sun never arrives suddenly, but somehow, you look up and there it is, early morning's pearl-gray, turned mid-morning's blue. In Alabama, the morning is there quickly, suddenly. Sun, blue sky, heat, everything at once. This is different. Maybe it's my imagination."

"No," Young said quietly. "You are correct. This situation has always been the case here, from the beginning. In ancient times, two thousand years before Christ, Korea had another name. You hear it still today, Chosun."

"Yeah, I've heard it before. You've used it."

"Yes. It means, Land of the Morning Calm."

"Oh? That's pretty. Kind of poetic, huh? I didn't know it actually meant any-thing."

"It is difficult to explain. It is more than the words. This means a special way we feel about our country, the culture, the people. It means something very strong, special, uh…not changing, forever." She raised her hands to chest height and held them together, fingers entwined "It means a uh, locking-together since five thousand years."

We looked at one another across her clasped hands. Her eyes were bright and intense. Finally, she opened her hands and looked wistfully at them. After a moment, she folded her arms at her waist as if chilled, though we stood in direct sunshine. She glanced at me, her expression sadly pensive. I smiled. She turned away, toward the ancient, beckoning Korean landscape. I felt awkward, as if I'd missed something, some…hint or message. Identifying female nuance was not my strongest characteristic. We fell into silence.

Eventually, we began to amble about the circular platform, Young on the outside of the walkway, adjacent to the railing. At the south side of the tower, we stopped and lingered a while. Young pointed out various distant landmarks. I pretended to see them. I suggested refreshments, and we lounged in the Tower Tea House at least an hour, ordering expensive hot tea and *yakbap*, sticky, sweet, rice cakes. Eventually, the inevitable crowd began to arrive, then thicken noisily. We elected to leave, agreeing we'd captured the best of the morning.

We strolled down a tree-lined path toward our indispensable and faithful green Rocket. As the cool morning melted, activity within the park and along its pathways increased. Koreans, it seemed, loved the outdoors. It followed that with Seoul so densely populated, the few available "green spaces" would draw crowds. The warming December day lured Korean families and couples to the park grounds, where they wandered the quiet pathways and queued up to ride the tower cable-car.

Walking along the park's narrow, paved paths, mostly against the flow of oncoming Koreans, we garnered stares by the bushel. It was understandable, really; the attractive, well dressed, composed, rather tall, almost elegant Korean woman, and the out-of-place, almost frumpy, blond Westerner.

I began to wonder why, beyond the obvious, Young had selected this public and busy place to visit. While we hadn't previously hidden, we had never before been in quite so open and crowded a pure Korean forum. In Yongsan and Itaewon, we were invisible. The Han River Gap tourist area was deserted. The Korean Folk Village was overrun with foreigners of every kind. Here, there were many, many Koreans, but I was the only Westerner. It was impossible not to notice me, and consequently us, as we were obviously together. I began to formulate a theory.

"Young, is this a test?"

She looked at me with a smile, as if caught at some nefarious act, her only defense, charm. "I'm sorry, I don't understand."

"Come on, pal. You understand 'very well,'" I said, emphasizing one of her favorite phrases.

She shrugged and a smile grew on her face.

"Yes! I knew it."

"What?"

"This is a test, isn't it? To—to see if these people bother you. You know, staring and all that. Or somethin' like that, right?"

"Well, not completely, but yes, there is that kind of thing." Quickly, she lifted her chin in that softly proud, aloof, self-assured manner she could adopt and added, "Of course, I don't care, but still, it is also nice to be comfortable, yes?"

"And?"

"And?" she repeated, playfully exasperated.

"How do you feel? What's the result?" I asked, again the pestering puppy.

She swatted me lightly with a rolled up verbal newspaper. First, there was something whispered, but incomprehensible in Korean. Then, her voice louder but still low, she leaned toward me.

"Must you know everything? If you can assist in some way, I will, uh, 'advice you.'"

I loved her malapropisms.

"You embarrass me with this…this kind of questions." A smile appeared at the corner of her mouth.

I used my best you'll-be-sorry tone of voice. "Ooooh-kay." I paused, then added, "But I think you need my help, you know, to make this a really good test."

To Young's abject horror, and before she could question or stop me, I started to skip alongside and in a circle around her. My nonsense generated significant and serious onlooker stares, many with gaping as an added bonus. This was great fun, shocking the always publicly reserved Koreans! Of course, Young, little Miss Prim-and-Proper-Public-Deportment, was mortified, scandalized. She stopped and put both hands over her face, shaking her head rapidly left and right. I thought for a moment she might actually cry.

"Stop it!" She dropped her hands. "Stop, or I will go in the other way!" she hissed, gesturing back up the pathway toward the Tower.

"Okay, okay, sorry," I said, greatly enjoying myself and falling in step beside her as she began to walk with increasing speed, apparently in an attempt to escape our gaping witnesses. As the stream of people parted to let us pass, I addressed the crowd in general.

"'Scuse us. 'Scuse us. Coming through." Nodding to the group as a whole and no one in particular, I tossed in, "Show's over."

More aghast gaping.

Young continued along the path, head high, looking neither left nor right. After a short time, torn between humor and irritation, she whispered intensely,

"You have much to learn about the public acts in Korea…and probably everywhere. You can very well imagine why people think the foreigners are barbarians." She shuddered, as if having placed her hand, unsuspecting, in some gelatinous goop.

"Yep," I said, very flip and satisfied, "I can very well imagine indeed, missy. In fact, I kinda favor being a barbarian. Perhaps I could teach you some barbarian skills. No extra charge," I added, hands raised, palms outward, stupid grin firmly in place.

"I think," she said with patience, accepting my playful idiocy, "it is supposed to be the opposite teaching."

Enjoying our repartee immensely, I was about to deliver another thrust when I stopped, literally.

Reacting to me, Young also stopped, looking at me warily, apparently ready for another attack of my insanity. Instead, I took her arm and led her off the path and under a nearby tree.

"What? What is the trouble now?" she asked, looking about nervously, ready to fall into embarrassment's arms yet again.

"Young, does this mean what I think?"

Looking back to me, she smiled in an I-wondered-if-you'd-figure-it-out kind of way.

"Well," she answered coyly, fingering her gold chain. "This depends on what it is you 'think.'"

"Very cute, Young."

She smirked, but said nothing.

"I 'think' this test would only be necessary if you'd spoken with your parents. Did you speak with your mother about Dragon Valley?"

"Yes."

"When?"

"When we returned from Suwon, the Folk Village, as I said."

"What did she say?"

"Nothing."

"Nothing? What about your father?"

"No, nothing."

"So you—we, can go?"

Smiling, Young turned away from me and stepped gracefully toward the pathway. Then, as if the much discussed and agonized-over trip had been neither a problem nor in question, she looked back over her shoulder and said, "Of course."

# Twenty

Looming protectively on Korea's northeastern coast are the rugged Taebaek, or Great White Mountains. The Taebaeks are majestic, filled with endless narrow ravines, hidden canyons, rocky, pencil-point mountaintops, and long, thin waterfalls that cascade into meandering streams. Below the frost line, densely growing firs and hemlocks remain green the year round, while broadleaf trees set the autumn hillsides aflame in wandering streaks of yellow, red, and orange. The area's remote, primeval character adds a sense of mystery to its natural beauty.

The Taebaeks are home to the Dragon Valley Resort Complex, a multi-recreational, four season vacation area tucked into the sharply creased terrain south of Mt. Soraksan National Park. With multiple chair lifts, groomed trails, abundant powder, and supplemental snow-making machines, Dragon Valley attracts skiers from throughout Asia. Resort lodging includes a deluxe, Western style hotel, and a less expensive hostel. Young and I were booked into the hostel.

Young coordinated the trip details with a local excursion and tour company. Transportation to and from Dragon Valley would be by a Trailways-type bus which ran daily, making scheduled stops around Seoul. Surprisingly, one stop was the American Military installation at Yongsan Compound. It was from this location that Young and I, along with three GIs, and an American couple—probably a doctor and a nurse—boarded the bus. We six Americans were the only Westerners.

We embarked and were greeted with the expected silent staring from our fellow passengers. Young continued to chat merrily about any number of topics as, and after, we boarded. Interestingly, though not ever specifically mentioning it, she seemed to have reached a kind of peace with this obvious curiosity. When encountering the frank stares of her fellow Koreans, she became oblivious, or uncaring, or both.

Young's relaxed erasure of the surrounding curiosity was quite remarkable. Displaying neither hostility nor embarrassment, she simply and effortlessly ignored the onlookers. Her tactic was to focus intently on me, alternating between talking animatedly and listening carefully. Her attention was commanding, and basking in its warmth, I felt as if she and I were wonderfully alone, no matter the circumstance. Her power to perform this warm and lovely magic never ebbed.

Yongsan was the final ski-bus pick-up stop; so, at about seven a.m., on 1978's last Saturday before Christmas—some eight incredible weeks after having read flawlessly from Shakespeare to satisfy the challenge of a foreign stranger, ignoring centuries-old cultural taboos, circumventing her beloved parents, and ultimately, trusting my "true heart"—Miss Lee Kwang Young and I departed for Dragon Valley.

* * *

Young was a late sleeper. To catch the seven a.m. Ski Express, she was forced to rise well before her normal seven-thirty. Not surprisingly, once the bus joined the freeway, her conversation slowed and she quickly fell victim to the hypnotic drone of big wheels humming across concrete pavement. She yawned, much to her embarrassment, curled her long legs beneath her in that feline way only women can, and settled in comfortably.

After a moment she leaned close, murmured something in Korean and—to my pleased amazement—placed her head on my shoulder and drifted away to find sleep. This spontaneous intimacy was without precedent and totally unexpected. Her willing connectivity and simple affection were powerfully bonding. The threads of unexpected pleasures weave memory's purest fabric. That quick and singular moment was newly spun silk.

As Young slept, seemingly without worry or care, I wondered again about the issues before us. As we became more entangled and serious, so too did our problems. Worse yet, they seemed to proliferate insidiously. Worried and fretful, I tried to identify and organize our concerns into some sort of meaningful whole, the first, very Western, problem-solving step.

I closed my eyes and thought about her family. They were truly dependent on her. Aside from a tiny government pension, Young was her family's only means of support. As her parents aged and after her brother enrolled in college, the family's financial needs would certainly grow. How would these needs be met?

Family obedience was also a concern. True to her culture, Young was unwilling to disobey or defy her mother and father. Most certainly, they were unaware she was dating a foreigner. How would she respond if told we could no longer see one another? On a larger scale, her parents would never agree to the idea that she would leave Korea.

Developing on the border of my awareness was a different, unanticipated problem. As our relationship matured, I could hear her Asian voice more clearly. It was faint and surreptitious, and I wondered if she could hear it. I was only now learning to listen, but below her Western exterior was a soft whisper, the language unmistakably Korean. Was she really more West than East? At the Han River Gap, her clear understanding of sacrifice reflected Asian perspectives. She was obviously proud of the Asian customs and traditions preserved at the Korean Folk Village. At the Seoul Tower, her description of Chosun and what it meant was powerfully Korean. Of course, her Asian willingness to surrender to Fate's will complicated the issues and frustrated me. How would this Eastern melody influence her feelings and, ultimately, her actions?

Perplexed by the issues, and wondering if I had fallen victim to my over-analysis tendency, I involuntarily wriggled, jostling Young. She didn't wake, but moving in sympathy, placed her right hand on my inner thigh. I recalled Spiderwoman's similar but totally different touch. I smiled, imagining Young's horrified reaction if she could see herself in such a publicly intimate posture with anyone, much less a "barbarian." I pulled the ski jacket she used as a blanket over her forearm, moving her discretely within propriety's boundary.

The bus slowed and with a small jolt, downshifted. We exited the freeway and turned onto a two-lane secondary road. The terrain here was much steeper; the hills drew steadily closer to the bus. A big plow drove slowly past, pushing snow to the roadside in jagged, dirty, waist-high piles. In contrast, higher up the mountain, the snow sparkled bright white in the sun, and where drifted, cast a vague, aqua-blue shadow.

Young's makeshift blanket slipped slightly. I caught the movement in the window glass, a hard, cold canvas framed in chrome. On it, in reflection, were the three subjects: Korea, Young, and me. Jarringly, the picture was dominated by the severe, intransigent Asian landscape, boldly immortal in sharp, vivid oils. Against this background, gossamer and ephemeral, were Young and me, a superimposed afterthought in pale and fading watercolor.

It took a moment, but I realized someone was missing from the portrait; Young's euphemistically described "other friend." Would he be a problem? Would he play on her sympathy for him? Would he belittle me as a Western barbarian? Would he be combative and angry? Would he be moved to confrontation? I cringed, remembering the Colonel's words: any problem, of any kind, from any soldier, no exceptions, court-martialed, sent home. I guessed street fighting with a Korean National was well within the Colonel's definition of "any problem." The unknown nature of Young's boyfriend meant I was placing my career in jeopardy. I'd not previously considered this perspective.

I rubbed my temples in weary frustration. It would take time to iron out these issues and, as if we needed more challenges, now time was becoming a problem. My tour would end in June. I could try to extend my stay, but the command had recently disapproved almost all extension requests. Still, if I could get the Colonel's endorsement, I might be an exception. It made sense: specialized job, save on relocation expenses, the Colonel's recommendation. Then again, the Army never seemed to take the common sense approach to anything; instead, tending to adopt a one-size-fits-all solution to almost every problem. No, better not count on the Army for rescue.

I turned over and revisited these issues during the morning's bus ride. It was becoming distressingly clear that Young and I were wandering about a field of gorgeous but thorny nettles. I wondered what we could do to avoid the promise of pain hiding just beneath the enticing petals. Reluctantly, I remembered Young's lesson on Fate. "The power to do, or not do, does not lie with us." It was beginning to look as if she was correct.

The morning grew older; the winding mountain road narrowed, and the snow restricted it to little more than one lane. We'd long ago lost the predictable, sweet road-rhythm of the freeway. The engine and transmission noise was clearly noticeable as the bus fought and labored up the increasingly steep terrain.

After a time, Young awoke. I had never seen her do this. It was a new and pleasant intimacy. She surfaced slowly, rolling her head left to right in a slow, circular motion. She hunched her shoulders and extended both arms, hands clasped, palms outward, in a long, cat-like stretch. The jacket fell from her lap. She put both hands momentarily to her face, in a combination of rubbing away sleep and masking a yawn. She ran her right hand quickly through her black, tousled hair. Lastly, she looked at me, blankly, then self-consciously, then flatly.

"What are you thinking?" she asked in her characteristically direct way.

"Nothing," I protested defensively.

"Nothing?" A smirk came to her face. "I think this is not the total correct response."

"Must you know everything?" I responded, paraphrasing her Nam-San Park question.

She grunted and managed a small grin. Looking to her right, then quickly back to me, she complained, child-like, "*Paega kop'umnida.*"

"Uh?"

"I'm hungry." With eyes wide, she asked, "Do we have food?"

"No, princess," I said, my heart filling with emotion for her innocence, "we don't."

Mumbling in Korean, she pinched me, the act apparently staving her appetite.

I whined in mock pain.

She made no comment or expression of sympathy, but leaned away from me and into the aisle. Waving her left hand at me dismissively, she looked back and said brightly, "It does not matter. See?" Gesturing to the front, she continued excitedly, "We are nearly there."

# Twenty-One

The bus stopped in front of Dragon Valley's Western-style hotel. We were greeted by a woman dressed in a blue ski suit who boarded the bus and, using its loudspeaker system, explained the check-in and baggage procedures. Of course, the information was in Korean. For all I knew, she could have said we had inadvertently wandered into North Korea and upon leaving the bus would be braced against the nearest wall and, unfortunately, shot. So sorry. Young, however, remained calm. Accordingly, I concluded there would be no executions.

Instructions completed, we disembarked. Once outside, the passengers formed two groups. Young explained one group would identify baggage and ski equipment as bound for either the Hostel or the Hotel. The second group would see to the check-in details. The Americans traveling with us were confused, and asked what had been said. I waited for Young to explain, but surprisingly, she remained silent. Instead, she looked at me, expecting I would relay her instructions. I found her reticence with the other Americans discomforting. Nonetheless, I quickly summarized the procedure.

Young tasked me with baggage identification duties, saying she would deal with the front desk and check-in. The bags and ski equipment were unloaded and placed in one of two piles. One pile was for bellhop service into the hotel, the second placed directly on a small trailer towed by a Snow Cat for transport to the hostel. Our bus companions were apparently veterans at this arrival procedure business; by the time Young returned with our room keys, all the baggage was identified, segregated, and ready for transport.

Pre-trip arrangements called for us to stay in the hostel, which was considerably less expensive than the hotel. Less expensive inevitably means something less. In this case, the something was privacy. Young was assigned a room with two other women, I, a room with three Korean men. This communal approach was typical for Korean hostels. We divided into our respective groups and began the trek toward our lodging, snow crunching coldly underfoot, our breath visible in the crisp mountain air.

Young and I found our rooms, unpacked, changed into our ski clothing and met in the dining area where we assuaged her hunger, and now thirst as well. It was almost one o'clock when we made our way across the snow to the ski rental hut.

Except for the attendant, a young Korean man of about eighteen or nineteen, the rental shop was empty. Against the wall to our left hung at least seventy-five skis of every length. The opposite wall had shelves holding probably fifty pairs of ski boots. Against the back wall were propped ski poles in ascending order of length, shortest beginning on the left. After much discussion in Korean and general hurly-burly, Young settled on appropriately sized boots, poles, and skis. It was my turn to be fitted.

"What is your normal size ski?" Young asked, as always a willing translator.

"Don't have a normal size."

She looked at me blankly, as if trying to translate but unable to make sense of the result. Assuming she had missed a key word or phrase in either question formulation or answer translation, she tried again.

"I'm sorry. What is the size," she added the gesture of length to her question, "this way, of your normal ski?"

I really admired her ability to reframe the question so even a moron could understand. But understanding was not the issue. I had never in my life worn, touched, or been within ten miles of snow skis.

"Princess, I don't have a 'normal ski'; I have never skied before."

The rental attendant apparently spoke no English, but looked on from behind the counter with an expression of eager helpfulness. On Young's face, there was dawning comprehension. She surely must have translated twice, checking to ensure she had not made an error.

"You said you knew how to play skiing," she said, with growing amazement.

"Well, not exactly," I evaded. "When you asked with that phrase, 'play skiing'? I said that would be a good way to describe it."

This "clarification" didn't help. She was lost in logic and linguistics. Becoming frustrated, she waved both hands quickly left and right at chest level.

"I'm sorry, I do not understand. Do you know how to play skiing?"

Clearly, the time for hiding and obfuscation was past. The time for lumps had arrived. I looked bravely over her head to the far wall.

"No."

"No" was readily translated, and without error. At first, only silence, then, aimed directly at me, rapid-fire Korean. Her tone was initially anger, then irritation and finally, incredulity. The rental attendant asked something. Young turned and exchanged incomprehensible, laser-speed dialogue with him, complete with arm waving. At one point, her voice assumed the sing-song pitch of someone sarcastically repeating another person's statements. He, in turn, began to smile and then laugh, shaking his head.

Slowly, the last of Young's irritation fell away as she leaned momentarily in exasperation against the rental counter. She glanced out the frosty window and gathered herself, as if facing a large but solvable problem.

"Very well," she said, looking back toward me with purpose, "we shall start in scratch."

"From scratch." My idiom correction was rewarded with another pinch, this time considerably more intense.

"Ingrate," I mumbled, rubbing my arm.

She ignored my comment.

For the next ten minutes, Young and the rental attendant fussed over me, measuring, gawking and asking me to hold various items of ski paraphernalia. In the end, I left the rental area with all the equipment I would need to prove I could not "play skiing."

# Twenty-Two

Young, graced with a natural athleticism she never really seemed to recognize, was actually a more than adequate skier. Optimistically believing I'd be able to unravel the mysteries of alpine skiing in an hour or less, she took me to the beginner's area, the euphemistically named "bunny hill." There, we joined a host of super-coordinated, fearless children and a few awkward, terrified adults. The laughing children were generally zipping down the gentle slope in a somewhat controlled fashion. The grim adults were not so much alpine as supine, ski tips pointed at the sky and flopping about like beached fish.

Young patiently explained and demonstrated the basics of snow-plow, stopping, and how to get up after a fall. I developed quick and enviable proficiency in the get up procedure. After some time, it became apparent that my maximized learning curve fell short of the skill required for steeper terrain. Mildly frustrated, Young chastised me for misleading statements. I pled guilty, and in defense, tried to look appealingly contrite. She accepted my *mea culpa*. I suggested she ride the chair lift up the mountain to get in some "real" skiing while I remained on the bunny hill to "practice."

She was, at first, unwilling to leave me. However, I convinced her I'd be fine. Where would I go with the handicap of six foot skis strapped to my feet? What harm could befall me surrounded by fifteen hyperactive children? If anything, the kids were in danger of being mashed by a huge, out-of-control barbarian. Reluctantly, she agreed and made her way to the nearest chair lift, turning back just before joining the queue and waving cheerfully. Then, she disappeared, her green ski suit melting in to the colorful lineup of shuffling skiers. I turned my attention back to avoiding what seemed like two million darting, screaming children.

As will happen in the mountains, particularly late in December, the sun disappeared early. Some of the ski runs were lighted, but Young, still inexplicably worried about me, made her way back to the bunny slope while the sky was still five o'clock gray. I was easy to find: the only adult, covered with snow, rigidly erect, moving robotically down the slight incline at tortoise speed…and obviously irritated at my lack of progress.

Young came neatly and professionally to a stop beside me, spraying snow from the heels of her skis. She leaned on one of her poles and inquired brightly, "So, you are prepared for the higher places?"

"The only higher places I want to go are courtesy of Jim Beam."

"Who is Jim Beam? He is here?" she asked, looking about.

"Princess, Jim Beam is an old friend of mine, and yes, I'm sure he's here. After this experience, he and I are going to have a long talk. As my advisor, he'll be very helpful."

"Oh."

I sensed this news had hurt her, as if she were my confidante in things-ski, and this Jim Beam person had come surprisingly and quickly between us.

"No, princess, I'm just kidding, it's kind of an old Army joke. Don't worry about it, there is no Jim Beam."

"Oh," she said again, looking at me as if she had missed something, but intuitively understanding it was best left alone.

"Shall we go?" she asked brightly.

"Yeah, pal, that sounds like a very good idea."

We removed our skis and propped them over our shoulders, looking every bit like old alpine professionals. We lumbered, in that Frankenstein way ski boots force, back to the hostel. We stored our gear in the Ski Room, skis propped against the wall, pole straps slung over tips, and boots hung from large pegs extending from the wall at a forty-five degree angle. We parted company, going first to our rooms, then to the public but segregated baths.

We met an hour later in the hostel lobby. We hurried through the cold night air to the hotel and enjoyed a Korean-style dinner. Young, of course, dealt with the waiter and ordered our meal of meat, rice and vegetables. In a departure from Western restaurants, the waiter brought a utensil that looked very much like a large inverted metal bowl sitting in a flat, oversized lid. As it turned out, this item was the stove.

The inverted "bowl" was the heated frying surface. A small gas line led from the bowl to an outlet built into the wall adjacent to the table. The waiter plugged in the line and lit the burner. The burner sat in the "lid," which was also used to collect cooking residue run-off. It was an odd looking setup.

We were given strips of raw, seasoned meat on a platter. The rice and vegetables were brought to the table already cooked and in covered bowls. Young actually cooked the meat strips to our preference right there at the table. This procedure was a first for me and I was initially skeptical, but it all went smoothly. The dinner was spicy and warming after the cold afternoon on the snow, or in my case, in the snow.

After dinner, we drifted to the dimly-lit hotel lounge and listened to a very good piano, bass, and drum trio play soft and quiet jazz. I was keenly aware this world was miles and miles from Hugh, Spiderwoman, and The Statue. A few couples were dancing, but Young and I did not then, nor ever, dance. I was never sure why. For my part, I was never comfortable dancing; egotistically self-conscious, I suppose. For Young, I can only guess, but embracing in full view of total strangers came dangerously close to the dreaded Public Displays of Affection from which she shied so aggressively.

Dancing that night didn't seem wrong, but without Young's customary leadership, without her suggesting it, it just didn't happen. My relationship with Kwang Young had many paths leading many places, virtually none were regrets. Oddly, never dancing with her was an unredressable regret. It was such a simple thing. The most ill-matched, failed couples do it. We were magic, but I let it slip away.

We sat at a small, secluded table near the back of the nearly-empty lounge and talked quietly. The slow, dusty ballads of Louis Armstrong, Dinah Washington, and Nat King Cole flowing warmly over and around us.

"Young?"

"Umm."

"Today. On the bus?

"Yes?"

"I was thinking."

"I know."

"I…uh…I…believe I like you very much, princess."

"Yes, I know this is true."

"No, I mean, I like you *very* much."

"Yes, I know very well what you mean. I also…like you…very much."

"Is this a problem?"

"Oh, Jason.…"

She looked away, through the large picture window, frost gathering at its corners. The closer ski runs and the base area were illuminated. The halogen lights created a pink tinge on the snow. The chair lifts continued to glide silently up and down the hill, willing, tireless servants of the few hardy souls still about on the slopes. After a moment, Young looked back to me.

"You are asking, so you know this is not a simple answer. We are not the, um, standard kind of couple. This is perhaps a little of what makes us exciting. Of course, anything not standard is the problem and brings the attention."

"Yeah, I guess. You know, Young, this all hurts in a way it shouldn't. I don't know why."

"Umm. Well, perhaps it is because we cannot see where is our future. We cannot draw the future we want, then walk to it. It is not like a map, predictable with comfort. There are many questions before us. Many questions."

"Yeah." I sighed. "Well, these questions and the unknown trouble me. We don't seem to have any answers or control. I don't know. It's confusing. I not only hurt, but I'm also afraid. It's stupid, I know, but…princess, these things make me sad. What's going on here? I'm not supposed to feel like this."

Surprising me, as she so easily could, Young leaned toward me and took my hand in both of hers. She paused a moment, looking down at our joined hands. She ran her fingertips lightly across my palm. Her essence was manifest in her touch, warm, gentle, compassionate. She looked directly at me, eyes wide and earnest. She squeezed my palm lightly.

"Jason, perhaps we should not consider these things too much, or too, uh, deep. Perhaps, it is we are just given a gift. We do not know if we can keep this gift. Perhaps, we should simply enjoy it. If this gift will stay with us, then this worry and tears will not matter. If we must return the gift…then, there will be time for all our tears. Like the song, they may never dry. But for now, perhaps we should accept the gift without question, as is polite. Do not worry with the questions and control. As you know very well, the next action will find us."

I shook my head in understanding, but sadness and fear ran in parallel paths across my heart. Sensing this, Young surprised me yet again. Perhaps it was the quiet, bluesy music, or the dim and undefined lighting, or her sense of my sudden need for comfort; whatever the catalyst, she leaned closer, the distance between us nearly gone. She placed the back of her fingers on my cheek. Compassion, like a soothing balm, flowed from her. She closed her eyes. Her fingertips moved to my lips. She traced them, as if reading Braille. I had the sudden insight she was finding my "true heart."

I closed the remaining distance between us. The warmth of her breath lay on my lips. I kissed her lightly and found unbelievable softness, the connectivity of shared loving, and the ancient excitement of intimacy.

A small sound escaped her. Placing her hand on my upper arm, she clutched my shirt sleeve. After a moment, she leaned back slightly, took a deep breath, and looked at me, seriously, appraisingly. She leaned forward and kissed me, briefly this time, seemingly taking a second sample, verifying her reaction to the first. To my surprise, she smiled in an odd, almost knowing way I had not before seen.

Suddenly, the quiet music ended, recalling us to the lounge. Young sat back quickly while looking self-consciously about.

I grinned at her reaction.

Catching my smile, she lightly kicked my shin in retribution and said with a stern smirk, "Jason, kissing is not for the public places. People here can see the nice Korean girl kiss the barbarian! Oh, this is too much. You have made the bad influence against me."

"Yes, dear, it's true, I am 'the bad influence against you.'"

She moved back to a respectable distance in the booth.

"Well, I know now you are the, uh, dangerous kind of thing. Now I will have to maintain up my, how do you say, soldiers?"

"Guard, princess. You'll have to keep up your guard. But are your guards stronger than the barbarians?"

"Hmm. Perhaps…perhaps not."

# Twenty-Three

We left the lounge about midnight, walked quickly across the cold hotel parking lot, slipped unnoticed between the giant, sleeping buses and through a side door, into the hostel's quiet and dimly-lit hallway. We said goodnight at her door—where I stole another kiss. She acted shocked, playfully pinched my arm, and disappeared into her room.

I did not fall immediately to sleep that night, but picked through the remnants of my troubled bus wanderings yet again. They seemed more dangerous now, amplified by Young's intimacy. However, when sleep did come, it brought the soft blanket of her increasing affection and wrapped it snugly about me. With her metaphorically near, I slept soundly.

We arose late the next morning, but it was of little matter. The bus to Seoul was scheduled to depart at five o'clock. The day was ours to harvest as we liked. We met in the hostel common area and walked to the hotel. There, a breakfast of yogurt, thick bread, thinly-sliced meats and cheddar cheese was served continental-style. Young drank hot chocolate and expressed amazement about what she considered the excessive amount of cream and sugar I used in my coffee.

After breakfast, we elected to forego the slopes, lounging instead near the large river-rock fireplace, nibbling on Christmas sweets, finding many small pleasures in one another, and weaving our fabric. The previous night's somber tone had somehow vanished. We didn't talk further of differences, or problems, or Fate, or gifts, or tears, or guards. Rather, we returned to our easy and upbeat playful banter.

As a hands-on problem solver, I wasn't in agreement with Young's *laissez-faire* approach to our relationship. However, it was certainly more comfortable than worrying and searching for answers that seemed oddly tearful, elusive at best, or more frighteningly, simply not to exist at all. Following her lead, and wanting to believe the best would befall us, I, at least for the moment, surrendered to Fate and turned away from our shadow of troubles.

When the first of the morning's skiers returned for lunch, Young suggested we try the slopes, as they would be less crowded. We collected the ski gear and made our way back to the groomed snow. Unlike our arrival, the day was overcast, the temperature considerably colder, and snow seemed in the air. Young said skiing in a snowfall was romantic, but miserable. Actually, she called it "disgusting," but we agreed what she really meant was closer to miserable.

In deference to my self-esteem, we avoided the bunny slope. The children's quick learning and youthful coordination had pricked my dignity. To soothe my pride, we found a section of gently sloping, deserted terrain at the base of an inactive ski lift where both my ego and backside could be bruised without embarrassment. Young again demonstrated the basics, encouraged me, and at my urging, left for the mysterious terrain at the end of the ski lifts and her exotic world of high-alpine adventures. In her absence, I side-stepped up and snowplowed down my private bunny hill, dignity intact.

The new practice area didn't improve my technique. The ski boots were too tight, my fingers were cold and my legs ached. After an hour or so of snowplow, I concluded my case was hopeless and, taking off my skis, clumped to the ski rental hut. The attendant recognized me, smiled broadly and said something in Korean. Clueless as to what he might want, and realizing how dependent I had become on Young to save me from predicaments like this, I smiled mightily, greeted him with the standard phrases she had taught me, and using only my right hand, held out my ski equipment. My canned phrases seemed to satisfy the occasion.

I again thought of Spiderwoman, this time with new respect. In the matter of foreign language mastery, she had the greater skill. It was a thought that gave me unexpected pause, and I wondered in what other areas I had shortchanged her and Koreans in general through stereotype, prejudice, and ignorance.

The attendant took my equipment, bowed, and spoke more incomprehensible Korean. Incredibly, I also bowed. I smiled broadly, and wondered what Hugh would say about my Asian behavior. I remembered Young's injunction that bowing was not humiliation "like in the West," but simply a form of politeness. I was big on politeness, so I bowed again, deeper this time. The attendant did the same. I returned his bow, and he again mine. The situation was bordering on a Three Stooges vaudeville routine. When my turn again arrived, I unilaterally changed the rules. Nodding, I smiled, waved goodbye, turned and escaped through the doorway.

I stepped into the icy mountain air. It was snowing. The mountaintops were obscured in grayish-white clouds and fog. I scanned the slopes for a descending green ski suit. Nothing. I returned to my room, cleaned up, packed, and carried my bag to the hostel common area. I drank the free coffee and waited for Young. After about twenty minutes, she came though the front double-doors, snow on her green and white cap, her nose and cheeks blushed with red. She looked alive, vibrant, and very appealing. The sight of her sent a warm surge through me.

As usual, she came directly to the point. "You did not stay at the rabbit hill so long."

"No, princess, it was hopeless and I was cold, so...."

"Well, if you had been more forthcoming—" A new word, I noted. "—you would have been able to play skiing on the higher ground with me." There was just a touch of disdainful, you-got-what-you-deserved floating in her voice.

She pulled off her cap; snow fell to the floor. She shook her head; light bounced brightly from her short, obsidian hair. She motioned toward the mountain.

"It is nice there, and the snow is beginning. It is pleasant to watch," she wrinkled her nose, "but not so comfortable to be in, so," she flashed a winning smile, "I looked for you."

"And I for you. Did you return your skis?"

"Yes, and the rent man said you were polite, and used high Korean when you spoke."

"Well, I guess. I just said the things you taught me and did a lot of bowing."

She smiled rather broadly at this. I gathered she was pleased her pupil remembered the tongue-twisting phrases and was not afraid to bow.

"You are an adequate student, Mr. Fitzgerald."

I gave a sweeping, Three-Musketeers bow, and doffing an imaginary feathered cap, replied, "I owe it all to you."

"No extra charge," she said, holding up her hands, palms outward, now her turn to mimic my phrase and gesture from Nam San Park.

We laughed at our silliness; reveled in our comfort.

"Kiddo, you better get ready to catch the bus, okay?"

With childlike disappointment, she replied, "Okay." Then, with instant enthusiasm, eyes bright, she added, "But this has been great fun! I wish we could remain longer. Your skill would improve. You could go up on the mountain."

I nodded. "Perhaps we can come again before spring."

"Yes, perhaps we can," she added hopefully.

We never returned to Dragon Valley.

# Twenty-Four

The trip to Seoul took the better part of six hours. A combination of snowy weather, darkness, and icy, single-lane roads added an additional two hours' transit time. We slept on and off for most of the trip. The Yongsan sentries waved our bus through the compound gates about forty-five minutes before curfew. I would need to move with alacrity to gather our bags, transfer them to the Rocket, drive Young to Mapo, and return to Yongsan prior to midnight. Good fortune seemed with us; after ten minutes, we'd unloaded, transferred, reloaded, and were ready to go. God bless my lucky Irish ancestry, we were going to make it.

Packing the last of the bags, a nagging worry surfaced. The night was absolutely frigid. Would the Rocket, silent for three days, start? It had never let me down before. Young settled into the passenger seat. I walked to the driver's side, opened the door, and dropped behind the wheel. The plastic seat-cover immediately split, fracturing from my weight and the cold. Inauspicious. I kissed the key, placed it in the ignition, winked at Young, crossed my fingers, and held my breath. My Celtic shaman tricks didn't conjure a spark. Repeated efforts, identical results. The cold-soaked engine did not, would not, start.

I ran through the options, crossing them off checklist-style.

No Rocket.

No Lizard car.

Too far to walk.

Too late for taxis.

Too late for Buses.

Clearly, Young would not get home. We were marooned, curfew victims.

Reluctantly, we stepped out of the car and into the blustery night. I kicked the Rocket, mumbled and swore, irritated that my carefully devised plans were thwarted. I apologized for the car, the weather, and the inconvenience. In contrast, Young was not upset. She shrugged, and in her fatalistic Asian way, accepted both the present and the future. We made our chilly way to my quarters.

I insisted she sleep in my bed. I would sleep on the floor. I rooted around on my hands and knees in the bottom of the closet, looking for extra sleeping gear. Rummaging through my chest of drawers, Young turned to me with an oversized T-shirt in hand.

"I will use this for sleeping clothes, yes? I may change there?"

Looking out from the closet, I discovered "there" was the second of my two rooms.

"Yeah, but you'd better lock the door," I teased wolfishly.

She made no acknowledging comment, but turned and moved to the door. Stopping, she looked directly at me, catching my attention. Without expression, but with great show, she pressed the door's lock button. Then, leaving the door open, stepped into the adjacent room. Her sense of words and humor were a wicked rapier-thrust to my chest. She had done exactly as instructed. She knew I was a toothless wolf.

I heard a quiet rustle as she undressed. I occupied myself by preparing my sleeping arrangements. They were simple: an Army sleeping bag for warmth, an L.L. Bean high-density foam pad for cushion, one pillow. More than adequate.

Returning, Young walked to the bed and with arms folded, watched skeptically as I arranged my sleeping items on the floor. I tried not to notice the shapely curve of her long, athletic legs, highlighted by the mid-thigh T-shirt.

"You know," I said profoundly, "a gentleman never exploits a lady's circumstance for his advantage. This is a southern custom."

"Is it correct?" she replied coyly, raising one eyebrow.

"Yes," I said, playfully mimicking her syntax, "it is 'correct.'" Now, do you need anything more before we turn in?"

"Turn in?" she repeated inquisitively.

"Yeah, it means uh, go to bed."

"Ahhh," she cooed in a decrescendo, followed by some quick-time Korean, spoken below comprehension threshold.

"This is a colloquialism?"

I'd learned to successfully distinguish statement from question about four of ten times. I would never master this skill. I elected to treat her latest as an inquiry and responded with exaggerated but gentle weariness.

"Yes, dear, it is a colloquialism."

There was more quietly light mumbling, presumably about English language vagaries.

"No, nothing more. I will 'turnin.'"

She moved with feline grace, slipping fluidly between the bed sheets. Propping herself on an elbow, she turned to regard me. After a moment of watching me fidget, she said, "You are finished?"

"Yes."

"And your sleeping clothes?"

"What about 'em?"

"What will they be?"

Embarrassed, I evaded, "What they always are."

Terrier-like, she pursued me, teeth embedded in my leg.

"Which is?"

"Look, Young, did I bug...." Recognizing the syntactical dangers of "bug," I paused, word-searching, finally selecting the inelegant, "trouble you about your 'sleeping clothes'?"

"No." She extended her lower lip slightly in mock hurt.

"Okay, then." After a second, I provided the elucidative, "I ordinarily sleep in my underwear, and will do so again tonight...after we turn out the light. Thank you very much."

Before she could respond, I switched off the overhead light. External, ambient light seeped into the room. I climbed into the sleeping bag. My modesty preserved, I pulled off my jeans and T-shirt. She was quiet for only a moment.

"Jason?"

I turned and looked up at her through the semi-darkness.

"Huh?"

"We can start this, yes?" She gestured toward a candle on the nightstand.

"Sure. Matches are in the drawer."

She fumbled briefly about. Then, simultaneously, the acrid smell of a struck match and a flare of light. A moment later, the candle's wick submitted, igniting. The flames joined, their combined lights boldly shining. A triumphal birth. But it was bravado. The match, high intensity and short-lived, burned out. Immediately, the candlelight sagged, nearly overcome by the weight of darkness.

We lay quietly, our senses adjusting to the night. Through the room's diminished light crept frail, nocturnal sounds, faded creatures granted life by the twilight underworld of magnifying darkness and half-sleep.

Lost street traffic.

Wind, rubbing cat-like against the building's corner.

Water, quietly astir in the bath area.

The furnace's warm, oily breath.

Faint music leisurely strolling the hallway.

The night sounds exercised a gentle comfort, disconnecting the present and nudging me toward surrender. Slumber, like fall's last leaf, twirled to me in a slow-motion, decelerating spiral. Time regressed in that Neverland way just before sleep. Drifting away, Peter's ageless, distant voice called faintly: "Second star to the right, straight on 'til morning."

Then, Young's voice, quite clear and in a not-before-heard timbre.

"Jason?"

"Um?"

"You should sleep here." It was unmistakably a statement.

Suddenly, I was fully awake; slumber, night sounds, Neverland, and Peter Pan vaporized.

"Well, uh, I, I don't know if that's a good idea, Young."

Always the pragmatist, she replied, "The floor is hard and cold. The morning is not near. Do not be foolish." She drew back the blankets and patted the bed beside her. In that lovely, lilting way, she said simply, "Come here."

"*Come here.*" Two words. Request and command. Present and future. The foggy path, clearly lit. As always, I did as she asked.

Our candle's flame shaped and moved its delicate shadow randomly: larger, smaller, left, right. The pattern never repeating. Young lay at my side, her skin, always beautifully warm, was now more so, washed in candlelight. I touched her forearm. Looked in her eyes. Tried to measure her mood. Impossible; she was an enigma, caught between East and West.

She looked away briefly, distance on her face, sighed lightly; then, moving closer, rested her head on my chest. Her hand lay on my breast, close to her cheek, palm down, fingers slightly curved, a gentle crescent. My touch moved languidly across her back and shoulders. I felt her body ease, relax. There was perfect stillness in the Korean night. Time conquered consciousness. Seconds? Minutes? Her patient, ancient, Eastern nature could have waited endlessly. But the uneasy boy from western Ohio could not.

"Young, I love you very much. I hope you know this. I think we're on a path that will make this clear. Are you comfortable here? Are…are you sure about this?"

She didn't immediately respond, but the silence was smooth and easy. Without looking at me, but moving her fingers lightly back and forth across my chest, she addressed the point directly in her singular and familiar way, without preamble, disarming me and the issue.

"I love you, Jason. I know this since the Han River Warriors. But most important, I know very well you love me. We have found a different, um, rare place." She sighed. "Our path is the one set for us. We do not know where it will lead. But it is the one chosen for us. I accept this. So, yes, I am comfortable."

She paused a moment, then continued slowly, pathos in her voice.

"Only…I want to capture this time…photograph this, this feeling. We must hold this memory. Perhaps, it must last a lifetime. There are many questions. We do not know what Fate will choose, or when."

Her foresight was powerfully and painfully correct. She'd cut cleanly through the present to find the future. As usual, she was a vanguard at our life's leading edge. She felt. She knew. She understood.

Slowly, I mussed her hair, a wonderfully confused ebony mass. Lightly, I traced circles on her cheek. After some time, she lifted her head and smiled in that small, endearing way, unique to her. She seemed centered, at peace. For the moment, her conflicts were resolved, our cultures reconciled. She kissed me. Quiet electricity, crisp and stirring.

Young slipped from her shirt and lay her head against the pillow, her black hair in stark contrast against the white linen. Gracefully, with imperceptible downward pressure, she placed her right hand against my neck.

I responded, moving closer, our bodies in full contact; her breasts warm, soft, supple against me.

Temporarily hidden, deep from life's arctic and evil heart, we were warmly aware only of one another. Nothing else alive. Troubles revoked. Concerns cancelled. The world suspended. The future now. We were completely, innocently, totally absorbed. A kind of tearful selflessness. Tenderly, we loved one another.

\* \* \*

Morning sunlight struggled through the frosted single-pane window, was filtered by the tattered yellow curtain, and drifted genially across the bed, covering us with a new day. Beside me, Young stirred. Her eyes flickered and closed. A drowsy semi-smile crossed her lips. Her arm lay draped across my chest; she hugged me fleetingly. I closed my eyes and lightly pressed her hand.

We were committed. Our path was set. We stood alone, daring Fate. We were implausible lovers from impossible worlds, defying what should be, hoping for what could be, awaiting what would be.

Victims of life's cruel machinations, we had become what we wanted and, what we feared…hearts of the morning calm.

# PART THREE

*When the night has come,*
*And the land is dark,*
*And the moon is the only light we'll see.*
*No, I won't be afraid,*
*Oh, I won't be afraid,*
*Just as long as you stand...*
*stand by me.*

—*Stand By Me,*
Ben E. King

# Twenty-Five

Young began to study for her KAL examinations on New Year's Day, 1979. The exams consisted of written tests and a combination interview/oral exam. Testing was scheduled for two days during the last week in January. The written exams would be administered on the first day, the oral interview the day following.

The written exams were wide-ranging, covering Eastern and Western history and culture, social graces—East and West—geography, and of course, the international language, English. The oral—administered only upon successful completion of the written exams—consisted of three parts: responses to a series of "standard" interview questions; follow-up quizzing from the written exams; and recitation of KAL flight phraseology in English and Korean.

The examination process was understandably rigorous. KAL flight attendant positions were competitive and highly prized. Only one of every ten applicants passed the initial screening to become an examination candidate. Only one of every twenty examination candidates was accepted for training.

Having successfully passed the screening criteria, and knowing the statistical mountain only got steeper, Young studied hard, or as she charmingly phrased it one snowy afternoon, "diligently." While she didn't seem unduly concerned—having surrendered to Fate—she was, in that maddening Eastern/Western combination sandwich way of hers, practical enough to acknowledge the benefits of hard work.

During this "study month," as she called it, we saw one another only on Saturday and Sunday, and only for a few hours, usually from mid-afternoon until the late evening, perhaps seven or eight o'clock. Even then, she quizzed me about English grammar and usage. I was somewhat apprehensive about my answers as my forte, conversational military English spiced with vulgarities and slang, would most certainly not be on the examination.

It was a difficult, stressful time for us. Our newly discovered world of emotional and physical intimacy was artificially truncated by real world demands. But, as Young pointed out, "We must make the sacrifice for all good things.

Easily won is poorly appreciated." This dictum struck me as part Korean culture, part folklore, part Poor Richard's Almanac. She, however, seemed to think it true, and as was increasingly becoming my habit, I happily agreed.

The weather had turned cold and occasionally bitter, a blustery Korean winter in full maturity. I remembered the disrespectful GI reference to the "Frozen Chosun." I fully understood the meaning of Chosun and was subliminally concerned that its power was slipping between Young and I, though I had no concrete examples.

In deference to the weather, we spent most of our limited time together on "indoor" activities, such as watching American movies at the Yongsan theater. Young always marveled at the number of people killed in the first five minutes of any Clint Eastwood movie. Another indoor pastime she loved was assembling jigsaw puzzles; the more pieces and more complicated the picture, the better the little show-off liked it. She was quite good at this, and we spent hours on the floor of my room, sitting on cushions, piecing together puzzles and chattering away the time.

Other winter activities included dinners at a favorite Korean restaurant near her home in Mapo, short drives around Seoul in the Rocket, and, probably our mutual favorite, lounging in my room, creating some of our favorite memories. While the wind howled and snow drifted, we were cozy, tucked under blankets, practicing KAL phrases, listening to music of every kind to meet her eclectic tastes, and quietly holding one another, whispering our soul's secrets, napping, and, of course, loving one another.

We were never concerned with what specific activities lay before us and rarely planned anything in advance. Simply being together was enough; the rest seemed to somehow work itself out. We became more dependent on one another, our lives and emotions more integrated, more wonderfully tangled and ensnared. We fell further in love and became absolute and unshakable best friends. We liked one another greatly.

It was the last weekend before exams. We were practicing KAL phrases in my quarters. Young sat at the head of the bed, a pillow behind her back, legs crossed "Indian fashion." I sat at the opposite end, propped on pillows, back against the wall, legs perpendicular to the bed. In my lap was the KAL study guide containing fifteen required Flight Attendant phrases.

"So, there can be no more than two errors. Watch the words carefully, please. Stop me if there is the omission."

Grinning at her choice of "omission," I replied, "Got it."

Clearing her throat, she began quoting the KAL phrase book from memory. "Good afternoon, ladies and gentlemen. On behalf of Captain X and First Officer Y, welcome aboard KAL Flight 454 from Seoul to Pusan. I am Miss Lee, your flight attendant for our thirty-minute trip to Pusan International. Please note the instruction card in your seat-back pocket. On it, you will find a diagram of the airplane's emergency exits. Please take a moment to familiarize yourself with this card and to locate the exit nearest you. Our flight altitude—"

"Hold it, hold it."

"There cannot be the omission," she responded with flat, humorless certainty.

"Well, princess, you've made two errors. You told me—"

"Yes, yes, I know, stop after two."

"So, you wanna know these, or what?"

She rolled her eyes in frustration and buried her face in her hands. Without looking up, she said, "Yes." The word sounding muffled as it struggled through her fingers.

"Well, they were small, pal. It should be the 'emergency' instruction card. You left out 'emergency.' And this is really small, but you said to watch carefully."

She sagged a bit and half closed her eyes, but remained silent.

"You said the 'airplane's' emergency exits? Actually, it's 'aircraft's' emergency exits. Sorry," I added in a small voice.

She dropped her hands to the bed, amazement on her face. Her head fell back against the pillow. She rattled through some quick Korean, fortuitously aimed at the ceiling. She looked at me in bewilderment.

"And what is the distinguishing thing between airplane and aircraft? It is the same, yes?"

"Well, no actually, but the difference is so small that it's silly. The important thing is that the book says aircraft, so don't fight it, just remember aircraft and we'll all be happy."

"Enough." In exasperation, she held up both hands, palms toward me. "Enough. Aircraft? Airplane?" She shook her head. "Enough for now."

"Good," I said, flashing a wicked smile. Tossing the KAL phrase book to the floor, I began to crawl toward her from my perch at the foot of the bed.

Young unfolded her legs, placed her right foot on my shoulder and pushed with just enough resistance to hold me back.

"Enough means enough in all things, Mr. Fitzgerald." She smiled coyly, then quoted from her KAL phrase book again. "May I have your attention? Please note the Captain has illuminated the seatbelts sign. Kindly return to your seat and fasten your belt." She wore a giant aren't-I-clever smile.

Disappointed, I sank back to my end of the bed, but began massaging her foot and ankle...hopefully.

"Young, how do you feel about your exams? Think you're ready?"

She looked at me and, for the first time, I was struck by the fatigue in her face.

"Yes, I think I have studied as well as I can. I think I have studied the correct things. The English grammar and memory of the phrases is difficult, but you have been very helpful. Some girls must hire the tutor for this."

I cringed, realizing a professional tutor was a good idea. I would have paid for it gladly. Why the hell was she mentioning this only now, with the exams just three days away? Christ, if something I taught her screwed this up, I'd never forgive myself. At this late date, we'd just have to see what happened on Wednesday. I tried to boost her spirits.

"Well, I think your English has always been great. And your memory work has been good, really. I don't think you'll have any problem with that aspect. Even if you make an error, you'll still be better than the others."

"Umm, thank you, Jason. I could not have studied so much without your help," she said warmly. "You make me want to do well. I want you to be proud of me. It is difficult to explain, but I want to do well for you."

"Maybe you're just in love, Young."

"Yes, dear, I am in love."

We were silent for a few moments, one of the many comfortable and easy times that seemed so frequently to find, cloak, and gentle us. I looked up at her and winked in a conspiratorial "it'll-be-okay" way.

She smiled, pulled her foot from my massaging hands and hooked it behind my arm. She hesitated for a moment, then pulled me gently toward her.

# Twenty-Six

For me, Wednesday was a routine work day. For Young, it was The Big Day: KAL Exam Day. Her interview, if her test scores merited, would be Thursday. Candidates accepted for flight attendant training would be posted Friday in the KAL administrative building, a modern high-rise in downtown Seoul. I sat at my Yongsan desk and imagined her there now, working through the various exam sections. She said each exam was administered in its own test booklet—five subjects, five booklets. One exam was graded while the next was administered.

Young and I had never much discussed her academic skills, but I found her a fast learner, quick to grasp a point, and—usually to my chagrin—witty. Was she a good test-taker? I guessed we'd find out. She agreed to telephone after the exams. I'd pick her up and no matter how the day had gone, we'd go to dinner.

I reached across my desk and again adjusted the phone perhaps an inch, angling it more toward me. The motion caught Hugh's eye.

"Move that phone one more time, just once more, and I'm gonna make you stand in the hall," he said without looking away from his paperwork.

"Hugh!" I whined. "Come on, give me a break, will ya? I'm nervous."

"Shit, I guess. How many times you fritzed with that phone today? A hundred? Drivin' me nuts."

"Yeah, well, I can't help it."

"Look, she's gonna do okay. Besides, any worry on your part ain't gonna help, so just let it go. What happens, happens. It'll be okay."

"Damn, you sound like Young, for Christ's sake. You a Fate believer, too?"

"I don't know about Fate, but I do know you can't help her by moving the goddamn phone through every angle in the Euclidean universe. And it's buggin' me to death, so quit it."

"Okay, okay," I said, moving the phone one final time.

"You know, Spiderwoman was askin' after you."

"What'd you tell her?"

"I told her you had a Korean girlfriend."

"How'd she react?"

Hugh shrugged. "Not surprised. She said she thought you were lonely. That's an interesting comment, isn't it? I didn't think Spiderwoman noticed anything but empty drink glasses."

"Hey, I'm not lonely. I'm in love!"

Hugh, older and worn, smirked and shook his head slowly in sarcastic understanding. "Good," he said without enthusiasm.

The office door opened and Colonel Barth walked in. Hugh and I stood behind our desks.

"Hey, guys." He waved us to our seats in his unassuming, easy way. We remained standing.

"Afternoon, sir," we parroted in unison.

"Just dropped by to see if you picked a day for our standardization meeting."

"Well, sir," Hugh replied, "it looks like it's either the third or sixth, whichever fits your schedule best."

The Colonel shrugged. "Not sure. I'll check and let you know, probably the sixth, but let me get back to you."

"No problem, sir."

"Jason, I need to visit the One Seventeenth Assault Company next week. How about you and I get an aircraft and fly up there for, hmm, probably most of the day? Say, oh, next Thursday. No, sorry, Thursday won't work. Better make it Friday."

Before I could respond, the telephone rang. Nothing unusual about this; the phone rang constantly in our office. But this call could be very different. We'd not concocted a plan for talking to Young with the Colonel standing two feet away. We were momentarily frozen. Another ring. Colonel Barth looked at us and then to the phone, which rang for the third time. Hugh recovered first, picking up handset.

"Eighth Army Aviation, Warrant Officer Stevens." He paused to listen. "Sure, stand by just a second. Jason, for you, uh, about that KAL question you had." He handed me the phone.

Colonel Barth perked up immediately and said with concern, "We got a problem with KAL?" As the Eighth Army Aviation Officer he would be directly involved with any Korean civilian/U.S. Army aviation problems. It was a politically sensitive area, and one on which the Colonel spent considerable time and energy.

"No, sir!" Hugh and I blurted in unison.

The Colonel looked surprised by our simultaneous reaction.

"Uh, Jason had a question concerning the, uh, increased KAL traffic into Kimpo and if the new low-level helicopter transition routes we have south of the airport are working out okay," Hugh ad-libbed.

"Oh."

There was an awkward silence as the three of us stood around my desk looking expectantly at one another, I with the phone on my shoulder, Hugh nervously twirling a pencil and rocking slightly on the balls of his feet, the Colonel with hands in pockets.

After a moment, sensing we were for some reason waiting on him, the Colonel slapped his stomach with both hands, as if having just eaten a filling meal, and said, "Well…Jason…uh, let me know about Friday, will ya?"

"No problem, sir. I'm available. You say when; I'll be there."

"Good, good."

He turned to leave the office. Upon reaching the door, he turned back.

"Hugh, I'll advise you about the meeting date."

Hugh nodded and smiled. I scratched my head and adjusted the phone which was still pressed against my shoulder. Colonel Barth looked at me oddly, but said nothing and closed the door behind him.

"Shit, Hugh," I hissed, "soon as I get off the phone, I'm gonna goddamn kill you."

Hugh started to reply in defense, but I waved him to silence.

"Young!"

"Yes."

"How did it go?"

"Well, can you also drive me on Thursday? I will have the interview test that day."

# Twenty-Seven

Friday was crisp and clear, with a cloudless blue sky. I drove Young to, or more accurately near, the KAL high-rise building. I had to park a block or so away, as she couldn't risk being seen by anyone from KAL in the presence of a foreigner. It seemed the stakes on this issue had risen from mere social stigma to loss of potential livelihood.

Her exams had gone well enough to qualify for the Thursday interview. Young said the interview panel consisted of three men and two women. Each asked questions in turn. Occasionally, one member would follow up a point raised by another panelist. The process had taken less than an hour and had gone well.

A happy victim of her charm, I understood why. Knowing her bright and easy manner, her gift for saying just the right thing, and her guileless and winning smile, I was surprised they hadn't offered her a vice-presidency on the spot. However, I was probably biased. More impartial heads would make the evaluation, and today we'd learn if she was accepted for flight training.

"Okay, princess, I'll wait here."

I'd never seen Young nervous before. She wasn't exceedingly so, but her manner was clearly different, serious, almost tense.

"Very well." But still, she lingered.

"The results are posted, aren't they?"

"Yes."

"You did well, right?"

"Yes."

"Well, get goin'," I urged. "Let's find out. It'll be okay."

"You know, it is comfortable to sit here and not know. This way, I haven't disappointed myself, or you, or my parents. I have not succeeded, but also, I have not lost. There is no cut, no bleeding."

This morose thinking was unusual for her, and I began to worry she hadn't done as well as she'd originally thought. I tried to think of something supportive to say, but nothing even semi-brilliant surfaced. Instead, I reached over and patted her knee.

"Hey, Young? What happened to Fate and all that? Remember, the next action finds you. Relax. Accept. Etcetera. Huh? What about all that stuff?"

She said nothing for a moment, but rested her elbow on the door's open window, her hand on her forehead.

"Yes," she said, looking blankly out the window. "I know very well what you mean, but discussing Fate in, uh, academic is like talking in school. Now, I must meet and accept Fate. School and life are different."

I was growing increasingly concerned; this just wasn't like her.

"Well, princess, you'll have to find out sometime. But kiddo, it doesn't matter. It's not life and death. I'll love you regardless. So will your parents and family. Okay?" I rubbed her knee with increasing pressure. "Now, go on, sweetheart. Go check the list and let's go celebrate, no matter what. Go on."

The verbal and tactile encouragement seemed to stir her. She took a deep breath through her open window. It looked as if she were at last unstuck. She smiled at me in her small and endearing way, opened the car door, stepped out, closed the door behind her, and without looking back, melted into the flowing crowd making its hurried way along the Seoul sidewalk.

My heart ached for her; she'd studied so…"diligently." Clearly, passing these exams was a major hurdle. Short of working in theater or television, this KAL job was the most prestigious a Korean woman could have. Most women didn't work outside the home. Those that did, didn't hold professional positions. Most working women were waitresses, or sales persons, or cooks, or maids, or seamstresses, or Pillow Girls.

In Korea, men, for literally centuries, had dominated the workforce and the society. In most all things, and certainly in the workplace, women served at men's pleasure or not at all. KAL, born in the latter half of the 1960's, was a bit more liberal. To a degree, women working at KAL could achieve and advance based on merit.

I waited in the Rocket, slumped behind the wheel. The early spring sunlight radiated through the windscreen, warming the car. Five minutes passed. Ten. Then, nearly fifteen. I wondered nervously what the delay was. She only had to walk one city block and check a list! Her name would be on it, or it wouldn't.

As an aviator, I did what came naturally: I began to figure ETR, Estimated Time of Return. The building was one block and a streetlight away. Two minutes to get there, tops. Let's say the list was on one of the upper floors. Okay, another two minutes to catch and ride the elevator. Four minutes. Let's say there was a crowd at the bulletin board. Another minute to get to the list. Five minutes. Thirty seconds to find—or, God forbid—not find your name. Five and a half minutes. Then, the reverse procedure. Down the elevator, seven and a half….

My math was interrupted by a light knocking on the Rocket's trunk. I sat up and looked around. It was a Seoul city policeman. I swore and wondered what I'd done. Would I be arrested and arraigned on charges of being a barbarian? I'd have to plead guilty. The Colonel's warning flashed though my mind. I swore silently.

The policeman moved to the driver's door. I rolled the window down and used my best Korean greeting on him. He looked mildly surprised, presumably to find an apparent Korean speaking Westerner in downtown Seoul. I added a semi-bow as best I could from the behind the wheel.

He spoke firmly in Korean.

I had no idea what he said.

Trying to recall Young's lessons, I said what I hoped was, "I'm sorry, sir, I don't understand." To hedge my poor Korean, I also made a gesture indicating I didn't understand.

He leaned down and placed his forearms on the window frame, looking inside the car. I noticed he, like most of the Seoul policemen, wore white gloves. His manner wasn't hostile, but clearly, he wanted to communicate something. He spoke again, slowly, enunciating precisely, fooled perhaps by my stock phrases into thinking I actually spoke Korean. At mid-sentence, he looked briefly past my shoulder. He may as well have been speaking a dead language from one of the lost tribes of Israel. I simply had no idea what he was saying. I began to gesture helplessly.

Emanating from the passenger's window, a soft, lilting voice said, "He says you are in a not-parking area, and must move or he is required to give the small piece of paper."

I turned quickly. There, leaning through the passenger window, a box full of KAL material in her arms and a huge smile on her face, was Kwang Young.

# Twenty-Eight

Young spoke quietly, and what sounded like charmingly, to the policeman who grunted and walked away. She slipped into the Rocket and I drove her home, waiting in the car while she took some time to relay the favorable KAL results to her parents, change clothes, and make her way back down the hill. I told her we could go to the best restaurant in Korea to celebrate, but she said no. She just wanted to stop at her favorite neighborhood café, pick up something to go, and return to my quarters. Young was a "homebody," and for us, that meant my rooms at Yongsan.

The aroma of spicy Korean food filled the car. Young slouched and rolled her head back against the car seat. Closing her eyes, she smiled. I was very happy for her. Today's events were a huge leap forward; she seemed poised to experience some significant changes. We exchanged minimal conversation. The pressure and stress were gone, and it seemed right to silently savor the victory.

We lounged on the floor of my quarters, finishing the last of the hot and spicy foods. Young said it was polite to make slurping noises to show the food was tasty. I tried this with my usual idiotic enthusiasm and was appropriately admonished.

"So, what's next?"

"You mean with KAL?" she asked, licking sauce from her finger.

"No, silly, with the fight against world hunger. Of course, KAL. When does training begin?"

Young laughed. "Uh, in about two weeks. At Kimpo. There are fifty girls in my class. We will divide into two parts. The school will be about three months."

"You excited?" I asked with a knowing grin.

"Yes, very," she began enthusiastically. "It will be a wonderful opportunity to work and see the world, and for salary, all at once. KAL has the flights to Paris, London, Honolulu and Los Angles, yes? These are the international routes," she added knowledgeably in case I might mistake them for Korean cities or Seoul suburbs. "At first, though, I will begin within the Korea and," she wrinkled her nose, "Japan."

We fell silent a while, still basking in the warmth of her success. I was beginning to see a potential problem and after a moment or two, said, "Young, have you thought any more about us?"

"Uh?" She looked up in surprise, eyes wide, face open and questioning, fingers endearingly messy with sauce.

"Well, what's going to happen to us? We talked about this a little in Dragon Valley, but there've been, uh, some changes since then," I said, looking at her hungrily.

She blushed. "Well, yes, I have considered these things. I'm afraid I do not know anymore. Of course, I love you. But I loved you at Dragon Valley and could not say. One thing is different, I spoke with my mother about you."

This bombshell got my immediate attention. A major event, and she casually dropped it into the conversation, like crushed crackers into hot soup.

"Christ, are you serious? When?"

"Oh, some time now." In Young's Asian world, "some time" could cover five minutes or five years.

I stammered. "Why? How? Why didn't you tell me? Why'd you do it?"

"Well, I must do this sometime, and well...my mother is also a woman, Jason."

Wiping my hands on a napkin, I nodded, acknowledging the obvious. "Yeah, so?"

"Oh, Jason, do not be so surprised. Women...know things. We have the, uh, how do you say...inspiration."

"Huh?"

"You have heard this. It is in my phrase book, and it is true. Women's inspiration, we know things."

"Princess, women are inspired, no disagreement there, but I think you mean 'intuition,' women's intuition."

"Yes, well, it is the same, do not quabble over the small points."

Working a mental crossword puzzle furiously, I was torn between squabble and quibble. I chose the latter. "You mean quibble?"

"Exactly so, do not do this."

"No, never."

She shot me a combo glance of suspicion and frustration. I smiled inspirationally.

"Well, my mother asked about my Korean boyfriend. She had not seen him in some time. At first, I told her it was because of the KAL study, but she did not think that was all. So, I said yes, I no longer see him."

"Well, good. Mr. Korea is dethroned. Long live me."

Feeling smug, I took another bite of the Texas-chili-hot Korean *kimchee*.

Young's mood, however, seemed to dip slightly. She bit her lower lip and crossed her legs, absentmindedly bouncing her foot. Noting the nervous mannerisms, I concluded there was more information lurking in her emotional bushes.

"Is it over, then? With him?"

"Yes. I think so."

"How'd it happen?"

"Must we speak of this now?"

"Well, uh, why not?"

"It is not the happy kind of thing. This is why not," she responded testily. "Perhaps later is better."

"Princess, it's like you said about your mom. I gotta find out sometime. Come on, what's going on? This is important. I don't know this stuff unless you tell me."

She paused quite a while, either deciding or organizing, or both. I'd seen her this way before and knew it was best to simply grab my Asian patience and wait. We sat silently for some time.

"I was thinking about what to do with him; how to talk to him about us. But I did not find the good solution. So, I waited more. But it was too long, because one day not so long ago, he saw us under my hill."

This was a revelation. I whistled briefly. I'd not very smartly ignored the possibility he'd accidentally meet us at Young's pathway. We were lucky he'd not approached and become belligerent. All I needed was a knock-down, drag-out fistfight with a Korean man over a Korean woman. God, the Colonel'd get in a fit. Two GIs fighting over a Korean was bad enough, but a Korean and an American military officer slugging it out on the streets of Seoul pushed beyond the unthinkable.

Young sighed and continued. "He waited. When you departed and I went up the hill, he followed and spoke very angry. We had the loud discussion on the pathway. It was not so pleasant."

"What'd he say?"

Young pursed her lips and looked at the ceiling. "It is difficult to explain all the small points in English." She looked about at nothing in particular, then down at her hands.

"There are mainly two things. He could not understand why I would go with someone else. We are together for some time now, and he did not understand what was wrong. He asked many times what did he do wrong."

"What'd you say?"

She looked up quickly and gestured with her arms bent, palms up in a kind of frustrated shrug. "I said the truth. He did nothing wrong. He is doing only what he can do. It is not right or wrong. But I was interested in you more."

"Yes!" I exclaimed. "That shoulda done it. The bastard." I was enjoying the apparent victory, and my prehistoric male ego was on sad display.

"Yes, exactly so. 'That did it,'" she echoed. "Then, he was…how do you say when hurt by the broken electric things?"

"Broken electric things? Ummm…shocked?" I guessed.

"Um, yes, shocked. This is the second point. He was shocked I was with the American barbarian."

Young's barbarian references were never offensive, but somehow "cute," like her unique English. However, her boyfriend's demeaning characterizations were another matter. I was immediately irritated.

"Barbarian? Well, he's a.…" I managed to stop my retaliatory insult. However, to my horror, the incipient word on my lips was "gook."

More ashamed than angry, I wondered what Young's reaction to the racial slur would have been. After all, she too was a "gook." Was that how I saw her? When the veneer was stripped away, was that how I really felt? When all the moonbeams and roses were spent; when her English was no longer "cute"; after our first—or fiftieth—fight, would I still be able to stifle the slur? I shuddered, but Young, wrapped up in relating her story, seemed to notice neither my sentence fragment nor shame, and continued with sadness.

"He said we were the mistake. He said I would be regretful. The culture was too different. My family would not permit this. He asked, what I was doing? What was my plan? What kind of thought I had? Where was I going with this thought? I had no answer. I think I have no plan, only Fate."

I started to interrupt and comment, but she raised her hand and stopped me. I guessed she wanted to get through her recitation as quickly as possible.

"He told me I must not see you again; even once more. If I did, he would not be my boyfriend, even when you were gone and I was alone."

"What does that mean, 'alone'?"

"He said you would leave me. He said the Americans always go home. Always. You would be the same. I would be alone. Then, any Korean man who knew of you? Well, they would not have me. I would always be alone. He said it was almost too late. I was nearly, uh…dirty now, and if I did not stop, I would never be clean again."

I was in a quick fury. Perhaps he'd struck just a little too close to the truth. I secretly harbored a fear that she'd be left alone. Perhaps the thought of anyone, much less a spurned boyfriend, mistreating Young rankled me. Whatever the cause, I erupted.

"That prick! Well, we're not gonna stop, and we're not gonna be done, and you're not gonna be alone, so he doesn't have to fucking worry about it! Particularly as it's none of his goddamn business. Shit! And what's this 'dirty' comment about? What the hell does he mean by that? What an asshole! What'd you ever see in this clown? The guy's damn arrogant, ain't he? What the hell makes him think you'd want him? He's the one getting dumped, for Christ's sake."

"Uh?"

"Oh, uh, dumped…getting rid of him. You're getting rid of him, not the other way 'round."

"Oh."

Young's weak affirmation stirred my attention.

"You *were*," I said with emphasis, "gonna dump him, right?"

She looked away, rubbing her eyes. After a moment, she sighed and said, "Jason, this too is difficult. We have been together for some time. You do not want to hear this, but as I said before, I liked him as well. I think I wanted you both. I know I cannot do this. I know I cannot have you both. But I did not want to choose. He made me do it. I chose you. But still, it hurts to see him go. I am sorry, but this is the case."

"Well, that ringing endorsement makes me feel a whole helluva lot better." I sat back and folded my arms, stung. "Thanks…I think."

"I do not understand clearly, but I know your meaning. I am sorry. I do love you, Jason. I do. Do not be hurt. This kind of thing is not simple. But I am afraid he could be correct. I have thought of this before and said nothing. It was my secret. Jason, I could be left with nothing. Not you. Not him. No one. No chance for anyone. This kind of alone is frightening."

She was, as usual, correct. More kindly, I said, "Yeah, princess, I know." I sat up, reached over and took her hand. For one of the few times in our relationship, I led us out of darkness.

"Look. He's gone. Right?"

"Yes, he is gone," she admitted half-heartedly.

I struggled not to hear the regret in her voice. "Okay. Then let's not worry about him. It's over. Finished. Done. Can't be changed. Let's look forward. We got problems that aren't resolved…and they need our attention. Right?"

"Yes, we have the problems."

"You bet we do," I confirmed almost proudly. "So, let's worry about the ones we face now and can control, or try to control. Like, what lies in our future. What can we do to answer that question? Will we be together? Can you come to Alabama? If so, when? If so, what's to be done about your family? Stuff like that. Not to mention, you gotta concentrate on your KAL training. So, there's lot's to be done. Let's get moving toward the future and not worry about the past."

She gave a great sigh. "Very well."

"Okay. Good. So, you told your mother about him. That's good. But that's all you had to say. You didn't have to say anything about me?"

"My mother knows, Jason. She knows I am different. Sometimes home late, gone all day. I don't know, I am just different; she understands this and asked me if there was someone else? I said yes. We talked about you."

"Was she angry?"

"No, my mother would never be angry. She was troubled, but not angry."

"Troubled in what way?" I said, afraid we were going to finally face "The Parents Problem."

"Well, in the ways you could very well imagine and we have discussed before."

"Can you be a little more specific?"

"Well," she expelled a large breath through pursed lips, "you are a foreigner; this is the problem enough. But then, of course, you are also the American soldier. This is worse. You know very well these kinds of things."

"What about your father? Does he know?"

"I do not think so. My mother will speak with him about this soon. It is wrong to not say this kind of information to him. Perhaps she will do this today, because of the good KAL news."

This strategy was simultaneously comforting and depressing. It was good to know that Young's mother wouldn't run screaming, in tears to her husband, wailing that a foreign barbarian had ruined their daughter. I thought of the Colonel's admonition again. On the other hand, it was unsettling to recognize that a strategy was necessary at all.

"Young, perhaps I should meet your parents. I mean, I'm going to have to meet them sometime. You know how charming I am. I could prove I'm not a barbarian."

She shuddered, remembering, I'm sure, Nam San Park and the thousand other acts of public idiocy I had conjured in our time together.

"Yes, you will have to meet them. But perhaps we should give my father a chance to think about the concept first. Also, we need to plan the correct kind of meeting. This first meeting is very important. We must have a small gift, as you know. We must plan what to say, and how. You must learn some culture things to show you know and appreciate Chosun. We need to do all these things before we do this meeting."

"Yeah, and I'll be on my best behavior."

"This is not so great a promise," she said with sarcasm.

We cleaned up the dinner paraphernalia. After much vacillation, Young chose Merle Haggard for the stereo and adjusted the volume. We lay on the bed, facing one another, my left leg draped over both her legs at the knee, my left hand resting on her hip. She lay with hands together, not clasped, but one on top of the other, at her breast. She rested her head in the crook of my right arm. We were very close, inches apart, and—as we so often did—spoke in whispers. Merle's slow, sad songs washed over us, low-tide fashion. We talked and giggled quietly for some time. It was a warm place.

After a bit, Young placed the index finger of her right hand on my cheek, moved it in an arc across to my lips, paused, and then to my chin. Her dark eyes were liquid and earnest.

"Jason, what will become of us?"

"Princess, that seems a question we can't answer, try not ask, but keeps surfacing. I don't know. I know I love you. I know you love me. We'll work something out. But time's getting short. It's already February. I'm supposed to leave in June."

"Yes, June. It seems far distant. It seems nearly here. Remember, we met in October?" After a moment, she added, "It's the same distance from October to now, as now to June, yes?"

"God, don't put it that way," I groaned.

She moved closer, her head on my chest. I smelled the clean, fresh, shampoo aroma of her hair. Without forethought, I asked a most natural question.

"Would you like to go to the States?"

She moved her head slightly in a questioning tilt.

Deciding the question was too ambiguous, I said what I actually meant.

"Will you marry me?"

I wasn't at all surprised by the question, though it was the first time I'd ever spoken those words, in that sequence. I loved her dearly. She loved me. We were best friends. I wanted to be with her. Marriage was the right choice.

She was silent for some time. Then, spontaneously, she kissed me—softly. Her touch was warm, moist, velvet. There was the accompanying aroma and taste of spicy Asian foods.

"Jason, these are difficult, difficult choices. As you can imagine, I have thought about these items before. Sometimes they seem possible. Sometimes...not." She sighed deeply. "We are becoming, are now nearly...one heart, one river...the water pure. How can I let you go? I cannot. I will not." She closed her eyes momentarily, as if enduring some small pain.

"But, while today's KAL news is wonderful, it is also troubling. It is another large reason to stay in Korea. How would my family survive without me? I cannot abandon them. I cannot." She lay her head on my chest. Her fingers tightened almost painfully around my forearm.

I was very frightened.

In the late afternoon's dusty stillness, Merle's sad voice brought us a song's final, slow lines:

*"There's a million good daydreams to dream on,*
*But, you are…my favorite memory of all."*
"Young, promise me. Promise we won't become a memory."

Indistinct voices drifted toward us from far down the hallway and into the silence. Young raised her head, and more lightly than I imagined possible, kissed my cheek. Placing her lips next to my ear, in a small voice, tight with fear, choked with emotion, she whispered, "I promise."

On the day of her greatest happiness, Young began, softly, to cry.

# Twenty-Nine

A week had passed since Young's KAL exams. It was Friday and I was scheduled to fly to the 117th Aviation Company with Colonel Barth. As was my custom when flying with the Colonel, I'd arrived at the Yongsan Heliport Operations Office well before takeoff time. The Colonel was always busy with administrative and command matters. As a consequence, he was habitually late for any appointment, including flying.

To ensure we made our takeoff time, I completed the many before-flight tasks pilots normally share. Because it was Colonel Barth, I was glad to do them. I'd finished the helicopter's "walk around" pre-flight inspection, filled out a flight plan showing our intended route of flight and time en route, and was listening to the last of a weather briefing.

"So, Mr. Fitzgerald. Uh, it looks like you'll have Visual Flight Rules at takeoff for your proposed departure time. It'll continue VFR along your route of flight with steadily improving ceilings and visibility after about 0900 hours. For your 0945 arrival at the One Seventeenth, you can expect much the same as Yongsan. cloud bases at eleven hundred feet overcast, four miles visibility, with light rain and ground fog. Minimum forecast altimeter we'll call, oh, say, 29.87. Brief is valid until 0930. My initials, November Mike." Sergeant Newsom scribbled what I took to be his initials at the bottom of the form, looked up and asked, "Questions, sir?"

"Nope. Looks pretty straightforward. Thanks, Sergeant Newsom."

"You bet, sir, no problem. Once you get airborne, we'd 'preciate a PIREP on 32.30 Fox Mike. Particularly on the segment between the Han River bridges and the One Seventeenth; there's just no other way to gather weather info in that area unless the pilots report it."

"Okay, partner, will do."

"You flying with Colonel Barth?"

"Yeah, he's gotta do some kind of award business and other command stuff up there. We were gonna be gone most of the day; looks like we'll be back by one or two at the latest. We'll update weather before we leave."

"Sounds good, but I think it's just gonna improve throughout the day, so should be no problem." Sergeant Newsom slid the weather briefing form across the desk. "Have a good flight, sir."

"Roger that, thanks."

I attached the completed weather briefing to the flight plan, crossed the small office to the operations counter and gave the paperwork to the Dispatcher for filing with the Flight Operations Center, or FOC. The dispatcher would telephone FOC with the details of our flight gleaned from documents I gave him. After takeoff, we'd use the aircraft radios to contact FOC, who'd flight-follow with us until our arrival at the One Seventeenth. Once we were "landing assured," we'd close the first leg of the flight plan, leaving the return leg "on file" for activation upon departure. Should we encounter any problems en route, FOC would notify other aircraft in our vicinity, and initiate an appropriate ground response. Ninety-nine percent of all flights were uneventful; however, if something did go wrong, the flight-following system provided a simple and effective safety net.

The Operations Office door opened and a harried Colonel Barth stepped into the aircrew waiting area. "Hey, Jason, sorry I'm late," he said sheepishly. "Nothin' new though, huh? I ever been on time?"

"No problem, sir. Got the weather. We're filed. Aircraft's pre-flighted. Crew's briefed. We're ready to go."

"Great. Remind me to double your pay, will ya?"

"Only double, sir? Well, expect nothing and you'll never be disappointed, I guess."

The Colonel grinned and put his hand on my shoulder. "My point exactly, Jason."

"Gee, thanks, sir."

We made our way to the helicopter, reviewing last-minute emergency procedures and other crew briefing items. Our crew chief, Specialist Randy Coons, was waiting at the aircraft. He stowed our non-essential gear and helped us into our survival vests. We climbed in the cockpit, put on our flight helmets and gloves, and strapped in. I turned on the battery switch and checked the intercom system that allowed conversation despite the engine and rotor blade noise. Using the checklist, we started the engine, and "ran it up" to full power.

When the systems checks were completed, I "worked the radios," calling the heliport tower for taxi and takeoff instructions. The Colonel repositioned the aircraft to the departure pad. Since he could escape office duties to fly only two or three times a month, I let him do almost all of the actual flying. As an instructor pilot, I was designated as the Pilot-in-Command. Though the Colonel outranked me, our positions were reversed when we flew. Army aviation protocol required the instructor be in charge of operating the aircraft and responsible for successful mission completion, regardless of rank.

Once we'd established a hover over the takeoff pad, completed a "go-no-go" engine power-check, and the Before Takeoff checklist, I contacted the tower for departure clearance, using the radio call sign reflected on our flight plan.

"Yongsan Tower, Freedom Eagle Six."

"Freedom Eagle Six, Yongsan."

"Roger, sir, Freedom Eagle Six ready for departure."

"Freedom Eagle Six, wind one six zero at five, caution CH-47 crossing extended centerline, low level, two miles. Cleared for takeoff."

"Roger, we got him. Freedom Eagle Six on the go. Please pass our off-time to FOC."

"Roger, Six, will do. Safe flight."

The colonel placed slight forward pressure on the cyclic control stick, increased power, and quickly we were airborne.

"Any change in the departure procedures or routes, Jason?"

"No, sir. Continue straight ahead to the Han, then a left turn, follow the river to the third bridge, then left along the highway to the North. I'll call clear with tower and 'up' with FOC."

The Colonel's question was important. All aviators flying in Korea, civilian and military, foreign and domestic, were aware of the "Papa-73" Prohibited Area around Seoul. The Presidential residence is near the city's center. Because of the short flight time from North Korea to Seoul, the government had established a wide, prohibited flight area around the palace. Its numerical designation was seventy-three. Hence, "P" or the phonetic "Papa"—for prohibited—seventy-three.

Over the years, the area had gradually expanded and, of course, Eighth Army had added a buffer area of its own. Now, the prohibited area included virtually the entire city and its suburbs.

The prohibited area's basic rule was simple enough: flight inside Papa-73 was prohibited. No exceptions. Should an aircraft wander into the prohibited area, the Government's demonstrated policy was to shoot very accurate anti-aircraft missiles first and ask questions later. Knowing exactly where the safe transit route lay was important.

Our flight proceeded uneventfully, proving the old aviation cliché that flying was "hours and hours of boredom punctuated by seconds of stark terror." We had cleared the departure route and Papa-73 by about ten minutes when the Colonel looked across the cockpit and tossed me an unexpected question.

"Jason, what's on your mind?"

"What do you mean, sir?"

"Well, we've been airborne about—what, twenty minutes?—and you've not asked me one emergency procedure, aircraft operation limitation, or regulation question. I actually studied last night, knowing your history of making my life miserable whenever we fly. But...nothing. So, you've either given up on me—not like you to give up on anything—or, there's somethin' on your mind." As an afterthought, he added, "Or you're ill."

"Uh, no, sir, not ill."

"Yeah, I didn't think so. Seriously, anything up? Or anything up you want to talk about?" This was vintage Colonel Barth—intuitive, concerned, solicitous.

"Well, sir, I guess there is something."

The Colonel made no reply, but continued to fly, looking through his flight helmet's clear visor to the front and occasionally the window to his right. I gathered he would allow me to get to this the way I wanted. I used Young's direct approach.

"I want to extend my tour and stay in Korea another year if possible, sir."

Colonel Barth rubbed his jaw and pulled at the skin under his chin before responding.

"Jason, you know there's nothing I'd rather have than both you and Hugh here for the rest of my tour and even overlap to my replacement. I'm losin' Hugh in May, and you in June. The new Commander arrives in July. In terms of continuity and historical memory, that's a problem. As far as I'm concerned, you guys do a great job in the Standards Shop. You'll be hard to replace. And I'd like you both to extend, though Hugh's made it clear he's goin' home."

I looked away, silent and embarrassed.

"No, I mean it. That's not gratuitous, throw-away dialogue. I think you know I don't deal in that kinda tripe."

Looking back, but still embarrassed, I allowed a small smile.

"Yes, sir, I understand that; all the more reason to be embarrassed."

"Umph. Well, don't worry, I'm not gonna kiss ya. Just make sure you stay on your side of the cockpit." He grinned broadly.

The uneasiness broken, we laughed aloud, off intercom, the sound muffled by engine and transmission noise. I could see our crew-chief in the back of the aircraft smile and shake his head. There was an unspoken agreement between enlisted crewmembers and the pilots that allowed the two officers to exchange privileged information without fear it would be repeated. It was one of the many bonding, trust-building comraderies unique to aviation.

"Okay, so given that, you know I'll support your request for extension. However, I gotta tell ya,' we've got some serious roadblocks. First, you and I know you're slated for assignment to Fort Rucker and the Directorate of Evaluation and Standardization. After their last trip here, their Team Chief and I talked. He wants you, I want you, on that traveling DES evaluation team.

You'd be a great asset. Those assignment orders are, by now, being cut at Department of the Army. Short of a war or a national emergency, I don't know if they can be changed. If they were for anywhere else, maybe, but for DES? I kinda doubt it. Also, if they were changed, you probably wouldn't be considered for DES a second time. I know that sounds kinda uppity, but that's the nature of politics at DA Assignments. DES pulled strings to get you, DA jumps through hoops to assign you, then you back out? Leave them hanging?" The colonel's voice trailed off as he shook his head.

"Yes, sir, I know it's a problem," I said lamely.

"Okay. Let's assume we could fix that some way. Well, then, there's the command's policy about extensions. They allow one per soldier. You've had one. You had to extend six months to get the assignment at Eighth Army Standards."

I raised my hand to interject a protest, but the Colonel anticipated me. "I know, the policy wasn't in effect when you extended, but that, I'm afraid, probably won't make any difference. I see second extension requests turned down every week. And these are extensions that we've supported, and on which we've recommended approval, mind you."

This wasn't the analysis I wanted to hear. The "good news" continued.

"Lastly, as commanders, we're supposed to 'counsel' our soldiers before we endorse any extension. We're supposed to explain what impact extensions could have on the folks back home. And specifically, we're talking wives." The Colonel hedged a bit, shifting his weight awkwardly. "Uh, I know you don't have a wife, and Jason, I'm not, repeat, not counseling you, but partner, what about that girl? Dawn, wasn't it? How's this going to affect her? I gotta tell you, in my experience, I've never seen a loved one say, 'Oh great, sweetheart, go ahead and stay another year; I was hoping you would.'"

I had forgotten about the fictional "girl back home." Well, escape was easy enough. I had lied her into existence, I guessed I could lie her out just as well.

"Well, sir, I'm afraid that didn't work out, so I'm free on that front."

The Colonel looked at me in that sixth-sense way he seemed to have and silently shook his head in understanding. Given his reaction, I was certain the word liar was printed on my forehead in capital letters. I'd have to quit hanging around people of quality and character. I felt cheap and soiled.

"Sir, does it make any sense to even try to extend, given all this crap?"

"Jason, there's something important here we haven't touched on, and it impacts the answer to your question."

I could feel this coming; it wasn't going to be easy to answer, and impossible to avoid.

"Yes, sir," I said weakly.

"Well, why do you want to extend? Eighth Army Standards is a great job, and of course," he said with a smile, "you've got a terrific boss. But, Jason, you and I know that DES is the Army's premier assignment for an instructor pilot. You get to make aviation policy worldwide, you get to travel, people look up to you, on and on. You know all that. Why would you risk losing it?" Holding up a hand, he added quickly, "No, don't tell me; I don't want to know. I can guess. And that's all your business, and none of mine. I respect you and trust you to make the right judgments. You're the last guy with whom I'd expect to have a problem. And we don't have a problem. As your friend, I just wanted to surface some things for you to consider. Bottom line? If the reasons to extend outweigh the reasons to decline the most prestigious assignment that'll come your way, then by all means, submit the paperwork and I'll strongly endorse it. But it's a question only you can answer, partner. Whatever you choose, I'll back you."

I responded without hesitation. "Sir, as always, I appreciate your frankness and confidence. I don't ever want to let you down or disappoint you. And I don't believe I am doing either. But, with your permission, I'll start the extension paperwork when we get back."

"Okay, Jason, let's give it a try and see what happens. Like I said, it's great for me. I just hope it's the best thing for you. Now, can I have a coupla aircraft questions? Man, I really studied last night, no kiddin'."

I smiled. "Gee, sir, I don't know, but if pressed, I suppose I could probably dream up a question or two."

The colonel shook his head and laughed at what he'd gotten into.

"You know, sir, I've always been kinda curious about Retreating Blade Stall and how that whole thing works. Sonic compressibility effects and all that. Very confusing. Almost otherworldly. We've got a while, you know, just sittin' here, doing nothing and all. This'd be a great opportunity to straighten me out."

"Jason, I haven't endorsed that paperwork yet, you know. Wanna try for something a little easier, for cryin' out loud?"

"Hey, you asked for it, sir. No guts, no glory."

# Thirty

As February passed, Young and I adopted a routine. Normally, I'd meet her every evening after flight attendant training. A discreet rendezvous point minimized the chances she'd be seen with a barbarian. I'd drive her to Mapo, wait while she talked briefly with her parents, changed from her KAL uniform, and returned to the bottom of the hill. We'd go to dinner, to Yongsan, and perhaps a movie.

Some evenings, weather permitting, we'd stroll about Yongsan's rolling hills, talking about our future and how to manage it, or on darker days, simply hoping we'd have a future. When the weather was bitter, we'd lounge in my quarters, listening to her beloved music, and again, talking about our future. Prior to curfew, I'd drive her home.

On the weekend, we'd spend as much time as possible together. Occasionally, she'd stay the night. I never knew how she explained these weekend absences to her parents. She didn't volunteer the information and when quizzed, was evasive. I gathered she was forced, as she said, "to invent the story of some kind." Lying to her parents troubled her greatly. I concluded she wanted to neither discuss nor think about it.

Time passed. Our relationship evolved, adapting and growing to fit our unique, troubling, wonderful circumstance. We became more tightly bonded. We fell deeper in love.

It was a bright Saturday in early March. I had just met Young for a trip to the countryside. She knew of a seafood restaurant overlooking a series of four lakes about thirty miles northeast of Seoul. A seafood lover, she wanted us to visit, insisting the dinner would be her treat. Before her employment, we'd had a long-running joke that she would buy, but I could pay. Now she was proud to assume the posture of occasional host. I was pleased to indulge her largess.

As we pulled slowly away from her hill, she handed me a map on which she'd traced our route to the lakes in yellow highlighter. I looked down briefly at the map and heard a small noise. I felt no reaction or vibration in the car. I looked up, and to my horror saw an elderly Korean man and his bike on the ground adjacent to the Rocket. I immediately pulled to the curb not more than two feet away.

Young and I stepped out of the car and hurried to the man, who must have been in his sixties. He was dressed in the loose-fitting, traditional Asian clothing favored by many elderly Koreans. He seemed dazed, but not injured. Young stooped beside the old man and spoke in a rapid and concerned voice. Her tone was soft, soothing, and conciliatory. Responding to her, the old man shook his head and began to sit up. Two or three passersby stopped to watch. I began to get nervous.

Young continued to engage the man in quiet conversation. No more than sixty seconds could have lapsed since the collision. Incredibly, however, a small crowd had begun to gather. The colonel's "trouble of any kind" warning again flashed through my mind. I remembered my comment to Hugh that a nickel/dime speeding ticket would be a problem. The ante here was clearly much higher.

Suddenly, an Asian woman who looked to be in her mid-thirties burst through the circle of onlookers. She was very distraught, went directly to the old man and spoke in agitated, rapid-fire Korean, complete with arm waving and gesticulation. The woman's comments seemed to irritate Young who, to this point, had controlled the situation. Unfortunately, thanks primarily to this unknown woman, things were less stable now than just moments before. Whatever infant hopes I had about minimizing this problem vanished with the arrival of the Seoul City Police. How could they have gotten here so quickly, and who called them?

We were tumbling rapidly out of control; no more than three minutes into this melodrama, and the supporting cast included a distraught stranger, a crowd of ten or fifteen people, and now, the police. The only way it could get any worse would be for the Colonel to show up, which at this rate, I expected.

There was much discussion between Young, the police, the angry woman, and to a lesser extent the old man, who sat quietly on the ground, observing. I said nothing, nor was my input solicited. It was a helpless feeling.

I recalled with growing anxiety a briefing I'd received at Yongsan concerning accidents and taxi cabs. The gist of the briefing was in the event of a traffic accident involving a taxi in which you were a passenger, the Army's "unofficial" advice was to put more than the cab-fare on the cab seat and leave, discreetly and quickly. The philosophy in Korea was that the taxi wouldn't have been where it was, and by extension in an accident, had it not been for the passenger. Accordingly, the issue of liability fell to the passenger.

Our current situation was somewhat different, but I imagined that equally bizarre logic applied to elderly Korean men riding rickety bicycles when struck by giant American cars driven by foreign devils. Playing without home-court advantage, I had a growing fear I would lose this game.

Almost simultaneously, the incomprehensible babble of discussion stopped. The players turned and looked at me.

Young nodded toward the older policeman.

"He wants to see your, uh…*unjon myonhojung.*"

"My what?"

Young, slightly agitated, waved her hands back and forth as she tried to find the English word. Frustrated, she repeated what I assumed was the correct Korean phrase, at least twice. I shook my head. She turned and spoke to the younger policeman, who shrugged. Looking back to me, she slowed, took a deep breath, and tried again.

"He wants your small paper that says you can drive the Rockette."

"Oh! Okay. Yeah, got all kinda stuff here." I fished around in the glove box and retrieved every form of ownership, insurance, and United States Army/Korean Status of Forces Agreement papers I could find. I also included my Alabama driver's license. I gave these to the policeman. He turned and spoke briefly with the second policeman. They looked through the papers. The older policeman spoke to Young, who folded her arms at her waist and looked at the ground, nodding her head.

She turned to me and said darkly, "They want you to go to the *kyongch'* also, the uh, police house."

I dropped my chin to my chest, immediately looked up, and began to protest. Young cut me off quickly.

"Do not disagree with this request. Just go with them. You may drive the Rockette. The police house is near here, less perhaps than one minute."

"I don't care how far away it is, Young. I didn't do anything wrong," I said earnestly. "They haven't even asked me any questions. I know this looks bad, but maybe the old guy here is in the wrong. Did you explain all that?"

"Yes, but this person," she said, gesturing toward the woman helping the old man to his feet, "is his daughter and she says you are wrong and struck the man. She says she saw everything." Lowering her voice, Young added, "Jason, I think she wants money."

"Oh, I get it," I said, beginning to understand why the woman was so upset when essentially what we had was a bump between a bicycle and car, both moving at no more than walking speed.

"They are going to visit the, uh, *uisa,*…the doctor. The policeman wants you to wait until this examination is completed, and to write down some details on paper."

"Okay, okay. Let's go," I said, resigned to the bureaucracy, hassle, and delay.

I turned toward the car.

"Jason," Young took my arm, stopping me, "these people don't," she paused, trying to find the right word, "…respect me because of this foreign and Korean thinking. I think they don't believe me, and think worse of me. Please, go with them alone. For now, this is best. I have an idea that might help. It will be okay."

"You're not going?" I asked, shocked and concerned.

"No; for now, I think it is the bad idea. Just go and do what they say. They understand about the language problem and have someone there to help. I will be back to you."

The police had moved to their car but were looking back toward Young and me. She glanced at them and back to me.

"Now you must go!" she concluded urgently, turning me toward the Rocket. She walked to the policeman and apparently explained what she'd told me.

The policeman nodded, got in his car and started the engine. I got in the Rocket. We drove less than a half a mile to what Young called the "police house." The question of the police's timely arrival was more clear. They were, no doubt, simply on the way back to the station and had happened across a crowd gathered around a man on the ground. Just plain old bad luck. Small comfort.

I parked the Rocket in the station lot and followed the two policemen up a set of worn concrete steps and inside the old brick building. The station had four floors; we remained on the first. I passed through a somewhat small main reception area and into a large office. Incredibly for early March, the office was warm; several fans futilely stirred the muggy air. The office floor was covered with well-worn black and beige linoleum squares. There were ten or fifteen old and scarred desks arranged haphazardly around the room. Each desk was occupied, some by uniformed officers, others by what I gathered were officers in "plain clothes." I became the instant object of much staring. Americans were rare-to-nonexistent in Mapo. I may have been the first American inside this police station…a dubious honor.

Through a series of gestures, I concluded I was to sit at a table and fill out police paperwork. Of course, the forms were in Korean. I had to wait for assistance. Eventually a young uniformed police officer approached the table and sat next to me. With a hesitant smile, and in broken English, he explained the forms and how they should be completed. Apparently, this was the person Young said would smooth the Korean-English translation problem. This was not an auspicious start.

The questions and forms proved laborious. I started to become irritated. Unfortunately, Young had reverted to her hesitation to be publicly linked with a foreigner. Damn, I needed her! But rather than come along to help, she had sent me off with the police because she was too shy, or too self-conscious, or simply had surrendered to Fate. While I was apprehensive about the "accident" and its outcome, her abandonment really hurt and troubled me more. I could see we'd have to discuss loyalty, commitment, and trust. If we were to have a future, she'd need to develop these qualities. I was puzzled I'd misread her so badly, but clearly, I had. When I needed her most, she'd let me down.

I slowly worked my way through the questions, my answers obviously in English. An hour passed. Irritated, I now didn't give a damn if they could understand my responses or not.

I began to think I should call the Colonel, or at least Hugh, as the police were apparently serious about making a federal crime of this incident. The military has an unwritten rule: your boss would rather hear bad news from you than from someone outside the "family." I couldn't wait much longer to call Yongsan. For all I knew, the police had already done so. I continued to steam and hurt simultaneously.

I resolved that when the paperwork was done, I'd call the Colonel. That could be my excuse. "Hey, sir, I was doing this paperwork and it was the first chance I've had to call." Sounded reasonable. I had credibility. He'd buy it.

I'd been fumbling with the goddamn papers and suffering stares for nearly two hours. The station, typical of a police precinct anywhere probably, sustained a constant rumbling undercurrent of activity and hubbub. Engrossed in my problems and the paperwork before me, I became only slowly aware of a growing stillness. Finally, distracted by the quiet, I looked up.

All the policemen in the room were standing, either behind their desks or where they had stopped in transit to some task. They were facing the doorway, some with a polite bow, others awkwardly. I looked toward the door. There stood a tall, thin, elderly Korean man with a wispy black and gray beard. Dressed in his country's loose and flowing traditional silk clothing, he looked calm, almost regal, and stood in sharp contrast to the harried policemen in their Western attire. Composed and self-assured, he projected strength and quiet authority, but there was also an air of compassion and grace about him. He stood in the doorway, silent and expressionless. Whoever the man was, he commanded the attention and respect of the police officers.

As I watched in amazement, from behind him, with deference toward and obvious affection for him, stepped Kwang Young!

# Thirty-One

I was stunned! Absolutely stunned. The man had to be Young's father. Jesus, this was where she'd been? God, I'd misjudged her yet again! A wave of guilt and anguish passed over me. Loyalty. Commitment. Trust. The self-righteous words boomeranged to me, cutting through my heart like three dull razors. The discussion I'd planned was still in order, but clearly it was I who needed the lessons. I shook my head in self-reproach. Where was my much valued character? Young had it in aces, I, not at all. She was peerless.

Standing beside her father, Young bowed and motioned slowly with her right arm and hand, palm up, toward the senior policeman.

Without acknowledging her, the old man stepped into the room and toward the policeman in charge. He looked only at the policeman, his face still without expression.

The policeman moved forward, stopping about three feet from the older man and, significantly, bowed first, moderately deep.

Young's father returned the bow, but only half as deep. He spoke, his voice soft but commanding.

The policeman spoke sharply, but not harshly, over his shoulder and the other officers returned to their activities, ignoring the two men at the room's center. The room's transformation was amazing, like turning a switch off and back on. The noise and commotion resumed about the small island of calm that was the policeman, Young, and her father.

I sat about eight feet from, and directly to the left of the trio. Young stood on her father's right, but remained discreetly behind him. Her father spoke again, and the policeman responded deferentially and at length. There were several exchanges of this nature; short, apparent interrogatories from Young's father, more lengthy responses from the policemen.

At one point, Mr. Lee looked to his immediate right, toward, but not at his daughter. He spoke briefly. Young stepped forward, hands clasped below her waist and, incredibly, responded with head down, looking directly at the floor. Then, still looking at the floor, she respectfully resumed her position behind and to her father's right.

I was shocked. Amazed. This was a side of the spunky, show-off, try anything, almost tomboyish woman I never dreamed existed. I'm sure I gaped. In our intense and wonderful relationship, it was the one image of her I recalled most clearly. It was an incredible sight, completely out of character for Young. At least, to the extent I knew her character.

Young's father raised his left arm slightly and gestured toward, but did not look at me. He spoke for perhaps thirty seconds, his longest monologue. The policeman made a comment, and I recognized the Korean word "yes" repeated twice. The older man bowed slightly, the policeman bowed in response, not so deeply this time. The discussion was apparently over.

Young's father turned to his left, toward me. To this point, he had neither looked at, nor directly acknowledged me. I stood. He stopped in front of me and caught my gaze. I had felt this sensation before. Instantly, I knew where Young had acquired the fierce, penetrating eyes she so infrequently, but effectively used. Again, I felt them, the Lee family eyes, their laser-like intensity directly on my heart. Not hostile, but examining. It was discomforting, as if my life's secrets were being sorted and sifted through; the more important ones held to the light and slowly read by a dispassionate evaluator.

I noticed apprehension on Young's face. I recalled our conversation about how carefully we would organize, arrange, practice, and manage my first meeting with her father. Unfortunately, our discussions had never included jailhouse protocol. I could tell she was afraid I would do something idiotic to unbalance her father's magic, and mortify her. No chance. I played it straight.

Her father continued to regard me, his face neutral and without judgment. Spontaneously, I did the only thing I could remember from our discussions that did not include language. I bowed, deeply, as I had seen the policeman do and as Young had taught me. It felt odd. I heard my memory's voice, *"It's just something we don't do in the States."* When I looked back, the laser was turned off. His face had warmed, no smile, just warmed.

Without acknowledgment, he turned to the doorway and almost regally moved to and through it. Young, trailing after, looked at me sideways and winked, again the street-wise New York City kid. All trace of Madame Butterfly had vanished—so long as her father wasn't looking.

I had the fleeting insight that the elder Lee was not a man easily fooled. I also sensed he loved his daughter deeply and would patiently indulge her many not-so-clever-as-she-thought antics and adventures without comment or correction.

With Mr. Lee's departure, the precinct atmosphere quickly returned to normal.

I passed my hand through my hair and almost laughed. Fate had surely won this round. Despite our plans to orchestrate and carefully script my first meeting with Young's father, Fate had decided otherwise, intervening to ensure we'd meet only after I'd managed to land myself in the Mapo "police house," under virtual arrest and charged with vehicular assault of an elderly Korean. Few scenarios could have been more bizarre or less favorable. I sighed deeply. Fate, it appeared, was a formidable opponent.

# Thirty-Two

I sat behind the table, unsure what to do. Most certainly, something had happened on my behalf, but exactly what and its impact were unclear. The senior policeman approached me. I again stood. He picked up the papers over which I had so long and arduously labored. Slowly tearing the forms in half, he tossed them deliberately into the nearest trash can. Smiling at me with friendly exasperation, he gestured to the doorway. I was apparently free to go.

I wasn't sure how to react, so I chose something safe and thanked him in my best Korean, offered my hand, which was accepted, and left the station. Outside, Young was leaning, arms folded, against the Rocket, waiting. She was a welcome sight. I had several questions.

"God! What was all that? Was that your father?"

"Yes. That was my father. I love him very much," she said warmly.

"What happened? What'd he say to the policeman? Where'd he go? What'd you tell him? Why'd you get him? What'd he say about me? Did you see those guys react when he came in? Wow, what was that about?"

Young waved her hands left and right in a "slow down" gesture. I had lost her, but she understood the thrust of my questions.

"My father is a little bit famous in Mapo. It is a long time now, but during the war, he was very, very brave, and sacrificed himself several times. He was, uh…recognized, yes? By the government after the war, and became known for his actions."

"Like a hero, you mean?"

"Yes, I think the English is hero. He has the.…" She gestured in a circular motion across her chest. "Colored cloth items the solders wear here."

"Ribbons? Medals? Decorations?" I suggested.

"I suppose, I do not know the English for these items. But they are for his actions in the war. He was, and you can see is still, well known for this. But even more, really, after the war; he was for some years a leader in the Mapo District, not the same exactly, but like you call a mayor. He spoke for the people at the Seoul city meetings, and once, in the National Assembly on Yoi-do. He was admired, I think. Last, he is *Youngkamneem,* uh, how do you say…an older man, and is respected for this."

"You never said anything about any of this before, only that he doesn't work."

"Well, the war was many years ago. He never speaks of it. Also, he no longer leads the Mapo District people, and rarely speaks of that. So, these things don't seem important for him." She shrugged. "He no longer works. It is correct."

"Well, I'll tell you what," I said, impressed. "Those policemen damn sure knew who he was."

"Yes, I hoped they might, particularly the older policemen."

"Why did you ask him to come?"

"Well, as I said, the policemen did not think so good of me because I am with the foreign barbarian."

I winced at the phrase, but she meant no insult, just a factual description.

"The daughter of the old man said he was hurt and it was your fault, and, so…I don't know. I thought my father could help. We went first to the…*pyong-won.* The place with doctors. I do not know this English."

"Hospital."

"Yes, perhaps this is correct, hospital. The old man was not hurt. Only when his daughter first arrived? Then she suggested the hospital, and talked about the money for doctors. This is when I began to think she only wanted to get money from an American. My father asked to speak with the man alone. When he finished, there was no longer a problem. The man and daughter went away. There was a small doctor charge, but my father paid."

"Christ, your father had to pay their bill?"

"Yes, it was not so much."

"Let's go to your house. I'll thank him properly and reimbur…repay the money."

"Oh, no." Young looked at me in amazement. "This would be a great insult." She shook her head and began again. "Jason, to begin, my father knew of you because of my mother. This jail situation is not how you should meet. Let this circumstance, uh, cool before you see him again. He must have time to consider these things. Next, the doctor charge is his gift to you. And me also. To repay this is like returning a gift. It cannot be done. Perhaps in the future you can give him a small gift. He likes the tobacco very much. But not now. This is not the good idea."

"Oh, okay." I kicked gently at the Rocket's front tire and, smiling, asked, "Did he come willingly? Did you have to beg, like Pocahontas, to save the foreign barbarian?" I grinned stupidly, enjoying how the disaster had turned around.

"What is the Pocahontas?" Young asked, mystified.

"Never mind. What was his reaction when you said you needed him?"

Young shrugged. "He came."

"Did you explain I was in trouble?"

"No, not at first. I just said I need him to help me with the police. As we went down the hill, I told him the story. He said we should go to the *pyongwon* first, that's why it was so long to reach you. Then we came here. He asked the policeman why you were here and what happened. The policeman explained. My father said he spoke with the bicycle man, and that he was not hurt and is gone home. My father said he would like for you to be free. The policeman said yes, this is possible."

"Wow."

"Yes, it is a great honor for you, this request, and an honor for my father that the policeman agrees."

"One last question. What did you say, you know, when your father turned to you?"

"Um, my father asked me to tell the policeman about you. I said you were a good and honest barbarian who did not see the old man and would never hurt a Korean person. I said I thought you were kind and liked the Korean culture and people."

I laughed at Young's dispassionate choice of words.

"One more last question. Did your father say anything about me after he left the station?"

"Well…yes."

"And? What was it?"

Young hesitated, sighed, and began slowly. "He asked me if I loved you," she said, looking at the ground.

"Man, you Lees come right to the point, don't you?"

"What is 'right to the point'?"

"Sorry, I'll explain later. What did you say?" I asked, my ego puffed, anticipating and hungry for the answer.

"I said yes." She raised her chin in that aloof and proud manner I had seen before.

"I bet he liked that little tidbit."

Young ignored my sarcasm. "He said he thought you had a warm heart, and he was glad for that."

"All right, that's great!" I added enthusiastically. "Anything else?"

She hesitated.

"Come on, you can tell me," I said, wriggling, trying to be cute.

She sighed.

"Come on, you can tell me."

"He said, he was afraid your heart was also like, uh...." She searched for the correct word, but couldn't find it. I was in suspense. She turned and placed her hand on the car. "Like this," she said somberly. "What is the word for this?"

I looked at her, suddenly chilled, and whispered, "Glass."

# Thirty-Three

"The Accident," as it became known, was several weeks behind us. In the interim, I had actually been invited to Young's home to meet her family. Prior to that first visit, I felt like Daniel stepping into the lion's den. A thousand cultural, social, and parental pitfalls awaited. I was apprehensive.

Young was hardly reassuring. All the way up the hill she pranced nervously at my side, issuing cultural tips and etiquette advice. I had never seen her so on edge. Having witnessed my public idiocy on multiple occasions, I'm sure she was afraid I had more insanity planned, and would gleefully engage in some form of unpredictable social transgression.

Of course, it all went well. I watched my manners and did not tease. During this and all my visits, Young's family proved polite, considerate, gentle and so far as I could tell, did not refer to me in the third person or as a barbarian.

Young's mother was charming and gracious. It was clear that these characteristics, so endearing and evident in Young, had come directly from her mother. She always greeted me warmly and made me feel very much at ease. Young's home had no furniture of the Western variety, such as couches and chairs. We sat instead in the Asian fashion, on the floor, propped on pillows. Mrs. Lee fussed over me, always bringing the best pillows and making a great but sincere show of plumping and fluffing them. Regardless of the length of my visit, she would ensure I was treated to hot tea and sweet rice cakes. I would, of course, protest and wave my hands, indicating the trouble was too great for so lowly a guest. She would coo something comforting in Korean, ignore my protestations, and continue to fuss. It was all quite embarrassing. I genuinely liked Mrs. Lee, and she seemed to like me. If she feared for her daughter because of my influence, it never showed.

Her brother and sister were exactly as Young had described them. Her brother, sixteen and silly, laughed at everything, was very curious, and constantly wriggled. He was either not as comfortable with—or as accomplished in—English as his older sister, because he seldom spoke it. This was somewhat odd, because he clearly understood the things I said with little, and usually no, translation. Like his sister, he could be direct and normally asked pointed but friendly questions. He had a deep well of interests from which he constantly drew, asking, through Young, about me, the States, cars, the Army, flying, rock and roll, girls, my impressions of Korea, the other countries I'd visited, war in general and Vietnam specifically, and what in the world I might possibly *ever* find attractive about Young. He seemed like any teenager brother anywhere.

The youngest Lee was a smaller version of her big sister. Photo comparison with Young at the same age showed two girls who could have been twins, but for the fact they were born sixteen years apart. Speaking no English, she was quiet around me, but I sensed she had a reserved nature no matter the circumstance. Her smile was winning and she used it frequently. Her growing charm was readily apparent. This wasn't a surprise.

Young's father was reserved but friendly. His family obviously loved and respected him. His voice was quiet and arresting. He spoke infrequently. If he was curious about my background, what I did, or my intentions toward his daughter, he didn't ask. Perhaps he got this information from Young. More likely, he was wise enough to know the important answers, and could roughly guess the future based on his experience with the past. He possessed a natural, gentle grace. His presence was comfortable and commanding. After meeting Mr. Lee, it was clear where Young had acquired these same characteristics. He had a charismatic quality that was difficult to define, but easy to recognize. I could readily understand why soldiers would follow him in combat, and the public vote for him in politics. He was easy to be near, and though we probably didn't speak five paragraphs to one another the entire time I knew him, I liked and respected Mr. Lee. Apparently, despite the circumstances of our initial meeting—and my obvious designs on his daughter—he bore me no ill will.

Young confirmed I was well enough liked, but added that her parents were concerned for us. She was never too specific on this point; I concluded the central issues were cultural differences and geographic distance. Feeling this was some kind of debate or effort to persuade her one way or the other, I pressed my interests in response. I reminded her she was more West than East, and in the Jet Age, distance was conquered in a matter of hours. I hoped for at least a stalemate.

Sustaining the impact of this point-counterpoint debate must have been difficult for Young. The people she most dearly loved were engaged in a tug-of-war. Standing on opposite sides of a sharply drawn north-south line, they pulled her with increasing intensity East and West.

# Thirty-Four

It was just past noon on a bright, high-sky Saturday in early April. Lounging on the bed, half-dozing, half-reading Hemingway's *A Farewell To Arms*, I was distracted by a light tapping at my door.

"Jason? It's Al."

"Yeah?" I hollered, answering loudly enough to be heard in the hallway.

"Phone. It's for 'Mr. Fitzgerald, please.'" Al raised his voice an octave or so, imitating a woman.

"Okay. Thanks." I was expecting Young's call; this had to be it.

I closed the book and placed it on the nightstand, stood, stretched, picked up my blue cotton jacket, and shuffled to the lounge. Entering, I gave a communal greeting to the Lizards, who—in unison, of course—looked up. Some grunted a return greeting; others were silent, but made various gestures of acknowledgement. Again, in unison, they looked back to the TV which spilled a ten-year-old *Mission Impossible* rerun across the lounge.

The telephone receiver was lying on the end table adjacent to the lamp. I picked it up.

"Hello?"

Young's small voice responded.

"Hello, Jason, it is me." Typical of her manner, she came directly to the point. "Shall we meet today?"

I thought it was an odd question; we always "met" on the weekend. Perhaps it was the phrasing.

"Of course. I've been waiting for your call."

"Very well, under my hill at one o'clock?"

Question or statement, my requirements were the same, and so, with a smile, I agreed and headed for the Rocket.

\* \* \*

I drove through the main Yongsan gate and into Seoul's motoring madness.

Zipping expertly in and out of traffic, I maneuvered to the far right lane, pleased with my ability to "out-taxi" the taxis. Even so, a faded beige cab whizzed past, horn blaring, blue smoke hanging in its wake. I was appropriately admonished and humbled.

Korean motoring was a crazy and frenetic experience. I was convinced that Asian and Western driving philosophies and techniques were mutually exclusive and absolutely incompatible. As a defensive measure, I'd abandoned my safe and sane stateside driving habits in favor of the frenzied madness practiced on the packed Seoul streets. It was a classic study in evolutionary behavior: adapt or die!

There were literally thousands of cars, taxis, motorbikes and buses jammed into downtown and suburban Seoul. It was commonplace to see these vehicles buzzing about like a swarm of angry bees, each in a full-speed rush to reach the next stoplight. Watching this phenomena, I'd concluded there were only two speeds practiced in Korean driving: full throttle and full stop. The transition between the two wasn't a gentle declination, as rational intuition suggests, but a gut-wrenching, brake-pedal-stomping, precipitous and immediate fall to zero. Naturally, acceleration presented the opposite scenario.

It seemed logical that, for safety's sake, this full-speed travel required clear communication of intent. To this end, no self-respecting Korean driver would be without a fully functional horn. Horns were sounded for any reason and under any circumstance. Honking communicated many messages, had many subtleties, and was an integral part of daily traffic-life in noisy Seoul. The classic gasoline engine operating sequence of: intake, compression, power, and exhaust was altered in Korea. The mutated formula include the original four elements and a fifth, honking. No honking, no "motorvatin'," to paraphrase Chuck Berry.

In addition to the many inscrutable, idiosyncratic driving techniques, Asian motoring was also possessed of special Driving Rules unknown in the West. My everlasting first-day-Korean-driving memory was learning the Korean Right-of-Way Rule—actual version as opposed to the official, test answer version.

In Korea, if your car's bumper extended beyond the bumper of an adjacent car, even if by inches, you had the right of way. Period. No equivocation. No exceptions. Additionally, the Korean right-of-way was taken, not yielded. Accordingly, there was much minute jostling and maneuvering at stoplights. Lines painted on the street to mark traffic lanes were ignored as drivers schemed to nose ahead of adjacent cars. Streets intended for three lanes of cars typically held six or more of the tiny Korean-made autos. It reminded me of a herd of cattle squeezing through a corral's small gate.

A particularly vexing rule was the Nighttime Intersection Rule. During darkness, a car's headlights must be turned off when stopped at a traffic light. I was never able to understand this protocol. It just seemed nuts. So, to protest, when stopped at a red light, I kept my headlamps on. Inevitably, mine were the only lights shining. Eventually, the stoplight would change to green, and in unison, all headlights would illuminate and off we'd go, zigzagging crazily to our respective destinations. Because I refused to comply with local nighttime practices, I was surely vilified by my Asian counterparts.

However, the most incredible convention I observed was the Sidewalk Rule. I saw this rule in action on several occasions, but could never summon the courage to exercise it myself. I learned this procedure first-hand from the backseat of a Seoul taxi.

My cab was trapped in a stalled knot of vehicles near Itaewon. The driver became agitated, snarled some brusque Korean and impatiently maneuvered the little blue taxi to the street's far right side. Displaying panache and initiative, he boldly took the taxi up and over the curb, directly onto the sidewalk!

With grim determination, he maneuvered carefully past storefronts and through pedestrians. Honking occasionally and waving constantly, he drove slowly along the walkway till clear of the choke point, about seventy yards. He then returned the taxi to the street and we were again on our way.

During this adventure, I sat flabbergasted, mouth agape, hands gripping the driver's headrest. Apparently, however, I was the only one so affected. Neither the stalled drivers nor the displaced shoppers seemed particularly upset—or more interestingly, surprised.

History records a potpourri of fruitless searches: the quest for the Holy Grail, Diogenes's search for an honest man, and the resting place of Amelia Earhart are just three. Another could easily be The Search for a Courteous and Rational Korean Driver. During my eighteen months of Korean driving, I never encountered even one. In the interest of balance, though, perhaps the reverse was true as well. As I did not understand Asian drivers, I imagine they never understood me. No doubt they thought I was, at the least, crazy. Nonetheless, we all survived.

The familiar green sign announcing Mapo in white block letters caught my attention and I joined the traffic roundabout. I circled a time or two, all the while drifting toward the outside of the orbiting cars. I managed to reach the circuit's far right side and Young's street simultaneously. Feeling very much a part of the insanity, I pressed the gas pedal fully to the floor, and like all the other drivers, hoped for the best.

The ever-responsive Rocket darted away from the roundabout's circling, buzzing, honking traffic and somehow emerged safely onto the quiet, tree-lined tranquility of Young's street. The transformation was amazing; it was like passing through another dimension, away from constant discontinuity and into a sedate, genteel world of order and serenity.

Arriving about five minutes early, I pulled adjacent to the sidewalk near the foot of Young's hill, shut down the engine, and waited. One o'clock slipped by, then one-ten. Young was not normally late. It was one-fifteen when she turned the corner and half-ran, half-walked, in that graceful way some women can, toward the Rocket. She opened the car door, sat down, smiled in her disarming fashion, draped her jacket over her jeans and nodded.

"Okay. I regret to be tardy."

Her eclectic choice of "tardy" cause me to smile. My heart warmed.

"It's okay, princess. What kept you?"

"Well," she answered, drawing the word out, "I was…thinking. But perhaps these things we can discuss later," she said seriously.

I thought it was, for her, an odd response, but I didn't press the issue.

"Yes, 'these things we can discuss later,'" I mimicked with a deepening and teasing voice.

She smiled distantly.

Sensing she was somehow out of rhythm, I asked more gently, "Where'd you want to go, pal?"

Looking through the windscreen, she pulled her shoulders close to her neck, held them there briefly, then, with a sigh, relaxed. With wistful pathos, she replied, "Somewhere to find laughter."

I thought it was a beautifully phrased but odd request. Normally she created laughter for us both.

# Thirty-Five

Young suggested we visit the zoo; surely, laughter awaited us there. We left Mapo and drove into the heart of downtown Seoul. Tucked away in one of the capital's few green spots was the City Zoo, small, old, immaculate, and famous throughout Asia. Given our afternoon arrival, the zoo's tiny parking area was long since full. We passed it by and turned left at the nearest side street, then left again onto what can only be described as an expanded alleyway.

These smaller "streets" were actually typical for Korea. Narrow, angular, crowded, and without sidewalks, they were more than functional for ox carts, motorbikes and the tiny Korean taxis, but barely adequate for foreign-devil cars like the Rocket. After twenty minutes of slow searching and ignoring pedestrian stares, we found a tight-fit parking place between a butcher's shop and a laundry. Young had to slide across the seat to exit as she was unable to swing open her door without hitting a concrete wall.

As we walked away, Young looked over her shoulder and commented that the bulky Western car occupied two of the small Korean parking spots. Oddly, this factually accurate pronouncement irritated me and I asked with an edge if she'd preferred that we walk downtown? Recognizing pettiness, she shrugged and let the tacky rejoinder evaporate without comment.

We picked our way through the maze of alleyways and small streets littered with noisy street vendors, hawking every imaginable ware and edible, and lined with tiny, one-room shops. Shortly, we reached a busy boulevard, beyond which lay the zoo. I took Young's hand, and we jogged to the far sidewalk where we turned right toward the admission kiosk.

Aware there was no further excuse to hold hands, I began to release her. Responding, she not only allowed me to keep her hand, but reached across her waist and, pulling me closer, held my arm as well. I felt remorseful for snapping at her, privileged to be with her, and vaguely wary of her public affection.

We walked beside the zoo's thick, dull yellow stucco wall, adjacent to which grew old maple trees. Large branches spread overhead, intertwining to provide a green, protective canopy. Here and there, sunlight slipped between the wide leaves, dappling the walkway and splashing pedestrians with momentary warmth. I said the pattern reminded me of Army camouflage. Young said it looked like the spots on a "child deer."

The fifteen foot wall served as barrier, boundary, and the back of several cages, placing the animals just a few feet from the sidewalk. Such proximity accentuated the numerous, universal zoo smells, most noticeably freshly cut hay and that deep, musty aroma common to large mammals. But also, hiding in the background, was the smell of roasted peanuts, popcorn, and burned cotton candy. The effect was a wonderful mixture, disparate but homogeneous, youthful but older than memory.

With the animals so close, we were privy to all their discussions. Parrots squawked, elephants trumpeted, monkeys chattered, and the big cats growled. The exotic sounds drifted over the wall and wafted to us, some shy and demure, others gregarious and challenging. Each speaker had ideas to surface, arguments to settle and secrets to share. We heard all that was said. We agreed never to tell. As the ever practical Young observed, "Who would believe this kind of thing?" Still, we felt a moral imperative to keep faith with our new confidants.

We reached the kiosk, purchased our tickets and, for an extra five hundred *won*, about one U.S. dollar, a zoo grounds map. Passing through the turnstiles, I noticed Young seemed brighter, more in character.

Almost childlike, she demanded we visit the elephants first. So, we went to see the elephants. She chattered to them in Korean. A large male with long, curving, parchment-yellow tusks seemed to notice her and lumbered near the bars, expecting, I imagine, to get food. Young leaned closer, raising her right arm, apparently hoping to pet the beast. However, more quickly than she could react, the pachyderm flicked out its trunk and lightly brushed her face.

She pulled back in howls of embarrassment, horror, and laughter. She hopped quickly in small circles, brushing her face with both hands and speaking Korean faster than the human ear could absorb. After two or three turns, she stopped and looked at me with shock and amazement.

"It kissed me! Disgusting." Wiping her mouth with her sleeve, she flashed me a wicked grin and added softly, "It is nearly so bad as kissing you."

Public or no, this insult was too much. I grabbed her about the waist and began to tickle, a torture rendering her incapable of coherent thought or action. Laughing, she broke free and began to run, begging me to stop. I, of course, ignored her pleas and remained in full pursuit. We must have presented quite a spectacle to the reserved Koreans. Finally, fatigue, stares and her sense of public deportment proved stronger than my tickle-threats. Taking sanctuary on one side of a picnic table, she stopped and leaned forward, hands against the table-top.

"Okay! Stop. Truce, truce!" she cried breathlessly. "You can be the North Korea; I am the South. Let us have the truce. It is acceptable?" she asked, panting through a smile.

"Maybe. But first, you gotta take it back. Take it back and uh, say…'I, Kwang Young, kiss like an elephant. But please take me back anyway.'"

"And if I do not?" she asked indignantly, standing upright and folding her arms.

"I will eventually catch you, and you know I can, and you know what will happen when I do," I threatened, wiggling and wriggling my fingers menacingly in the air.

"This is not the truce, this is uh, how do you say about the mail of some kind?"

"Ah, blackmail. No, my dear, in this world of ugly power politics, this is not blackmail, but negotiation."

"Uh?"

"Just say what I told you."

She rattled off more incomprehensible Korean, her form of refuge when in need of a cheap victory. "Very well, I said it."

"No, no, no! No way! Unn-uh. Nope. It's gotta be in English there, Ace."

"Humph, okay. Very well." She folded both arms at chest height, stuck her chin in the air and, twisting her penance to suit herself, said, "I am pleased to take you back, even if you kiss Kwang Young like an elephant."

I laughed loudly, rolling my head back. To challenge her on this phrasing would only engender more riposte and evasive discussion, the goal of which was to wear me down and out, something she could easily do. Accordingly, I concluded this was as close as I would get to capitulation and so laughingly accepted her terms.

"Okay. Close enough. Truce." Simply and easily, we had found laughter.

We used our zoo map to locate various exhibits. However, after a while, map reading and navigation became tedious and we simply wandered the tree lined brick paths scattered randomly throughout the old zoo. Approaching the lake, I initiated what had become our game of quotation-matching, a kind of one-upmanship that she regularly won. Under the circumstances, one of our favorite Simon and Garfunkel songs seemed appropriate. I looked casually toward her and began singing quietly, as if without forethought, though I'd run through the lines as best I could in advance. Had she known, Young would have called this last-second preparation "dishonest."

*"Somethin' tells me*
It's all happening at the zoo."

Tilting her head, Young glanced at me with a sly sideways smile. Always ready for a quotation challenge, she easily picked up the thread:

*"I do believe it,*
*I do believe it's true."*

Now my turn, the game tougher; and as usual, in over my head, I strained to remember the animals and their characteristics, finally managing the respectable:

*"The monkeys stand for honesty,*
*Giraffes are insincere,*
*The elephants are kindly, but they're dumb."*

Self-satisfied and relieved, I bowed extravagantly toward Young, as if yielding her the stage. Kwang Young, always the private showoff and irritatingly quotation-quick, supplied her lines without hesitation:

*"Orangutans are skeptical*
*Of changes in their cages,*
*And the zookeeper is very fond of rum."*

I joined her for the last passage, the beat accelerating. However, she, as always, led the way, with me stumbling to catch up:

*"Zebras are reactionaries,*
*Antelopes are missionaries,*
*Pigeons plot in secrecy,*
*And hamsters turn on frequently,*
*At the zoo....*
*At the zoo....*
*At the zoo...."*

We faded to laughter, teenage girl-style giggles, and uncharacteristically for so public a place, a warm hug that rotated us gently left and right. It was one of those rare and golden lifetime moments, remembered years later with joyful regret. A taste of pleasure, fresh, pure and absolutely satisfying. Nothing in my life since has felt quite so good, and in retrospect, quite so painful. We were genuinely, and to the exclusion of all else, absorbed in one another.

I relaxed my arms to release her. Young, however, kept her arms tightly about my neck. She shuddered. It took a moment, but finally I realized her laughter had turned quietly to tears.

Alarmed, I pulled her arms from my neck. "Hey! Hey! Princess, what's this? You okay? What's wrong? What is it?"

She wiped a tear from her cheek and, looking self-consciously left and right, stepped away from our embrace.

"This is due to the troubling circumstance," she managed between large breaths.

"Well, what is it, princess?"

She nodded toward a picnic table and benches near the lake.

"Let us go there."

We sat side by side on the bench, knees touching, backs to the table. After a moment, her tears abated. She sat silently, bent slightly forward, forearms on her thighs, head down, fingers slowly shredding a paper napkin into thin strips. She allowed my hand to trace small circles on her back. I wanted to pull "the troubling circumstance" from her in one huge, cathartic purging. However, I knew this to be futile. So, I waited—anxiously.

Looking at the ground before her, she began slowly, distractedly.

"There is nothing to help us." She shook her head slowly. "We are 'past hope, past cure, past help.'" It sounded like a quotation, but I couldn't place it. She rested her head against my shoulder and began to cry.

I tried to think what might be so profoundly troubling to her. I wondered if her boyfriend had made a reappearance and again been belligerent or hatefully cruel. Given his history, I concluded he was capable of cruelty and retribution. But that didn't seem quite right. She'd dealt with him before without tears, and certainly without loss of hope.

Then it struck me. It had to be her parents; while they liked me, they were very much traditional Koreans and, I was sure, did not approve of our relationship. Perhaps she'd been forbidden to see me. Her earlier tardiness was probably the residue of a disagreement and the unspecified subject of our "things to be discussed later."

The thought was especially chilling because Young, as her culture required, was truly obedient. If they'd issued an edict, naming me *persona non grata*, she'd be torn trying to follow it. Dangerously, and now it appeared, foolishly, we'd sidestepped this parental permission and the related family responsibility issue. I was afraid, if forced, Young would choose her ancient obligations, not our newly grown relationship.

It looked as if a reckoning was at last upon us. I waited in silence, my heart rate accelerating exponentially, my mouth dry. I was frightened and felt totally helpless. Defeating her parents would be a daunting, perhaps impossible task.

She regained her composure and continued, "I discovered the correct word in my English dictionary, pregnant. It means—"

I sat bolt upright. "Good Christ, Young! I know what it means!" I whispered fiercely, looking surreptitiously about like a thief. "What are you saying? What.... Are you telling me you're goddamn pregnant?"

"Yes, this is correct."

"Holy shit!" Panic fell directly on me. I closed my eyes, slumped back against the picnic table and rubbed my forehead.

"Oh, Jason, I am very distressed."

"Yeah, well," I said, fumbling for stability. "I…I…I can imagine that you are. I hope you are, for Christ's sake! Shit! Are you sure? Goddamn it, Kwang Young, we talked about this! Are you sure? You said it 'was not the problem.' Remember that? 'Was. Not. The. Problem.' Just like that. That's what you said. Exactly. Word for word. 'Not the problem.'"

She remained silent and motionless.

"Shit." I punched the bench seat between us, scraping my knuckles. I glanced away without seeing, but turned immediately back to confront her.

"Well, it appears to be quite the goddamn problem now, doesn't it? Yes?" I added sarcastically in a vicious, cheap shot mimic.

She didn't respond, but looked away over the water.

"Any other little surprises?"

She looked down and began to fold and refold the tattered napkin.

"Jesus." I took a deep breath and shook my head.

On the lake, a couple in a blue rowboat paddled inexpertly about, splashing water and turning in inadvertent circles. The wind carried their distant, muffled laughter to the beach, leaving a wake of rippled water. A group of swans drifted with majestic unconcern near a clump of tall reeds, acting very much like the lake's resident royalty. From somewhere behind us, the shrill, joyful laughter of children edged into my consciousness. I calmed a fraction more and kicked at the dirt.

"How did you let this happen, Young?"

"It is the standard biology reaction for some women who practice intercourse," she said, looking up, her face sincere, open, and honest.

Even balanced on the edge of scarlet panic and consuming fright, I had to smile—though briefly. My anger faded further.

Seeing this, Young brightened, relaxed a bit and took my hand. I took a deep breath, regrouped, and tried to right our foundering verbal ship.

"Young, look-it." I smiled nervously and patted her hand. "I don't mean how did it happen literally…biologically. I meant, how did it happen in terms of, uh, protection? You said you were taking the Pill, for Christ's sake. Remember?"

"Yes, well, I didn't like that pill so much…." She shrugged. "I stopped."

"Stopped," I repeated flatly, my irritation growing.

"Yes," she said defensively, just a touch of "high nose" in her manner.

"For how long?" I asked, quietly incredulous.

She shrugged again, sighed, and squinted into the distance. "I do not recall exactly; some time now."

I released her hand. "And when 'exactly' were you going to tell me?"

Young squirmed, staring at the ground. She knew this was a key point she'd fortuitously "overlooked." Instead of responding directly, she evaded. "You would only want to use those…other items."

"Condoms," I provided in a flat, rather too loud voice, the word and a sharp head-bob concurrent.

She flinched, embarrassed. Looking briefly about, she grunted in acknowledgment, refusing to pronounce the word. Then, quickly, she added, "We tried those things. I don't like them, either." She looked at the sky, lips pursed, and ran her hand from front to back through her silky hair, sunlight bouncing off the short, black waves.

Befuddled by her sense of logic and quixotic, sole-source decision making, and facing an issue I assumed was not an issue, I could only expel a large breath. After a moment, I tried again to rally and gather my composure. Deeply ingrained organization and problem-solving skills began to surface.

"Okay. Okay," I said, motioning with palms toward the ground in a "calm down" gesture. "How we got here doesn't matter. It's—it's, uh, what we do now that counts."

"Yes," she asked, "what can we do?" Her tone was equal parts fear, panic, and pain. "This is so difficult. I am very, very distressed! What can we do?" Her voice fractured, tears again nearby, an uncontrollable vicious neighbor. She reached for and grasped my forearm.

Her sense of helplessness and fear was contagious. I was so accustomed to following her lead, I did so again. Unfortunately, she was fully engulfed in panic. A second wave swept over me and I joined her, mainlining the terror; it coursed through my body, quick, certain, unyielding, leaving an infection of cowardice.

I leaned away from her. This was too much. I didn't deserve this…this…disaster. This wasn't my fault! I had it planned. She knew. She knew the plan. Agreed to the plan. She said it wasn't a problem. We'd agreed. She'd agreed. All she needed to do was stick to the goddamn agreement. But no, she'd dug up that Fate crap again. Koreans! Shit.

"What can we do?" She sounded foggy and far away.

This wasn't my fault. I bent forward, placing my head in my hands. I didn't want to think of the wolves that must be upon her. I, I was cut and bleeding and now…now they were stalking me! Circling the camp's perimeter, just beyond the firelight, heard but unseen, they were committed, unmerciful terrorists. Their attack would come. They enjoyed the waiting, savored the stench of fear. When they attacked, it would be vicious, fierce and final. And she'd caused it! She'd brought them. It was her fault! I couldn't help her. Maybe myself. Maybe I could save myself…but not her. I turned away.

I heard my name, as if called from a distance. A tiny groan escaped her and, again, my name, but more distant still, fading. Jagged slivers of glass flew at me. More blood, but different, sobering. This was all wrong. Wasn't this the woman

I loved? Surely, I could find the courage to stand with her against beasts I'd helped summon. Must she always lead? Could she never, never lean on me? What did fault matter now? Confusion and shame joined terror and panic.

A sense that I should be reassuring and strong passed over me, but still irrational, I shrugged it off. Resilient, it touched me again. Surely, I could find something medicinal to say. There must be some small, healing thing even I could do. I rubbed my forehead but couldn't think coherently. Was I equal to her call? Would I actually allow her to fall because I was frozen, frightened? How many times would I doubt her, fail her? She'd never abandoned or denied me. Never. Not after The Accident, not to the policeman in Seoul, not to the culture, not to her parents, not for KAL, never. Disgust and self-loathing crept upon me. I couldn't push them aside. I began to stabilize.

The lake, invisible only moments before, oozed into focus. I felt her grip slacken. The symbolism spurred me further. I sat up. Think! She needed me. A few more seconds would be too late; we would suffer irreparable damage. I turned. Her eyes were fired with fright and fear; they were absolutely piercing, beseeching. But catastrophically, it wasn't only the pregnancy. Now she sensed my vacillation, could smell my cowardice, and most damning, felt my abandonment. She desperately needed me in that purest, primal way. She was sinking. The tempest was in full fury. The final wave upon us. I grasped at a last chance.

"I know you're distressed, princess. I'm sorry." Taking her hand again, I slowed, both to calm and orient myself and to ensure her panic hadn't overcome her English. I continued without a plan, just talking.

"I love you very much, Young. I'll stay with you through this trouble, and any more of any kind that might come, ever. You can always lean against my shoulder. I'll protect you, always. You're the most important thing in my life. You'll never be alone. Unless you send me away, I will never leave you. Do you understand and believe these things?"

She didn't answer, but began again to cry.

I was too late; my abandonment too obvious. I had failed her. I wanted to conjure Merlin's magic, and like Arthur, pull Excalibur not from cold, unyielding stone, but from Young's fragile and wounded heart. But I was no hero, no future king. I was too weak, too flawed. I'd tried too late to comfort, too late to stand by her; my silent hesitation, my self-preservation denial, my emotional infidelity hadn't slipped past unnoticed. I'd tried to save myself and allowed her to fall. I'd abandoned her. For lovers, it was an unforgivable sin, indelibly scratching and inevitably cracking the all too tenuous, temporal, and brittle glass of lover's trust.

But I had, again, misread her. Placing her arms about my neck, she leaned to me and whispered—so…tenderly. Her words drifted to me, each syllable float-ing bright, clear, and slowly sparkling, as if strained *adagio* through a prism.

"Oh, Jason.… I love you dearly. I will hold you in my heart, always…forev-er."

My throat burned, my chest tightened, my vision blurred. I placed my arms about her. I'd received a gift, knowingly given, I did not earn and certainly did not deserve. The conscious acceptance of a flawed heart—what truer measure of love? Quietly, we moved to a different, higher place. No matter our future or my weakness, we had crossed, at least momentarily, into Camelot.

That April afternoon, Young and I became centered, defined, singular. My commitment to stand by her against life's ravages and her pledge to set aside a place for me in her heart were our final and strongest binding. We would again trade angry words. We would face other tragedies. We would most certainly shed many more bitter, hopeless tears. But the keystone was firmly set. I would never again be tempted to abandon her and, to the end, I know in that painful, sixth sense way, she kept her promise to hold me in her heart, always.

# Thirty-Six

We returned to Yongsan in the late afternoon, emotionally exhausted, drained, and most certainly frightened of our uncertain future. Surprisingly, we napped, using sleep, I suppose, as a refuge where we could temporarily lose our troubles. Young, upon waking, said she felt better and called sleep "nature's silent nurse." It sounded like one of her Shakespeare references, but she didn't elaborate.

Darkness drifted about us, its intensity increasing. The stereo, normally lit and singing, was dark and mute, testament to our anguish. I sat on the bed, pillows propped against my back, legs draped over the edge. Young lay on her side, head on my lap, facing me. I ran my hand slowly through her hair, massaged the base of her neck, then began the sequence again. She seemed to welcome this tenderness. I felt her relax as the tension receded.

Despite the circumstance, we were comfortable and pleased to be with one another. She seemed somewhat more at peace. Sharing her secret had released her burden, bringing again that gentle graciousness I so rarely saw in anyone else, and so loved for her to drape about me. I hoped I could bring her some measure of comfort and stability. Perhaps this time I could be the leader. Perhaps I could guide her safely to the jungle's edge. She surely deserved that small gift.

She was the first genuinely good and decent person in my life. Loving, honest, patient, gentle and selfless, she richly deserved life's good things. My skin of comfort was flayed and stripped away to see the condition Hamlet described as, *"the winds of heaven visit her face too roughly."*

For my role in her anguish, I was awash in growing guilt and sorrow. I wanted to absorb her hurt, fear and pain. In what was my greatest failing, I allowed her to carry theses burdens alone. I was appropriately diminished for the unforgivable transgression and left with an ugly, jagged scar, its ache infinite and timeless.

The Korean evening deepened into night. I looked down at Young and shook my head ruefully. My gaze drifted toward the nightstand and fell upon the dog-eared copy of *A Farewell To Arms* I'd put there what seemed like years ago.

I unwillingly thought of Hemingway's dreary assessment of our place in the world; our chances in The Struggle. How did it read? I tried to recall. Something like: *"The world breaks people and this sometimes makes them better."*

No, that wasn't it, too upbeat. No, this passage was pure melancholy and somber darkness. It seemed to fit our situation perfectly.

Reaching across the napping Young, I switched the lamp to its lowest setting, picked up the paperback and flipped the pages, trying to find the line. Finally, regretfully, inevitably, it surfaced, bleakly brilliant:

*"The world breaks everyone, and afterward many are strong at the broken places."*

Okay, we were hurt and frightened, but apparently not broken. I was surprisingly, but temporarily, heartened.

*"…But those that will not break, it kills. It kills the very good, and the very gentle, and the very brave, impartially. If you are none of these you can be sure it will kill you too, but there will be no special hurry."*

No! Hemingway was wrong. Had to be. He died a lonely drunk by his own hand. This gives him perception? Insight? Acumen? Surely not. Young was the essence of gentle goodness. Her reward couldn't be metaphoric death or some twilight half-life. Surely the recompense for quality of character and absolute gentleness wasn't a back-alley mugging by life's executioners. I slipped further into darkness.

I could more readily understand and accept the passage as it applied to me. I was certainly neither good, gentle, nor brave. Still, I was frightened to think my future was death delivered in its worst form: slowly, methodically, without attention to the task, not important enough for the killers to be in any "special hurry."

Yet, this end seemed fitting and proper. My only intent had surprisingly become to love, protect and care for this harmless person. But in this sole and singularly simple task, I had not only failed, but in a malignant and vicious irony had become the very instrument of failure and catastrophic destruction. I ruefully recalled Robert Oppenheimer's self-assessment as the first atomic bomb erupted before him: *"Now, I am become death, destroyer of worlds."*

Could this pathetic quagmire get any thicker? I tossed Hemingway and his morose idiocy across the room. The fluttering pages and subsequent klunk against the opposite wall stirred the half-sleeping Young.

"Jason? What this is?"

I put both hands to my face and rubbed my eyes.

"This is anger and fear and guilt and hopelessness and shame. And probably some others I can't think of just now."

Young considered this comment for a moment.

"Jason, I know these kinds of things, these feelings. I have thought of them for some time before you knew of the baby. They are real, yes. But they are really, uh, shadows of the problem, and not useful. They make the problem difficult to find, not simple to answer."

She placed her hand on my shirt pocket and, forming a small fist, gathered the light blue denim cloth. The force of her intensity tugged me slightly forward

"These feelings come without call, but you must make them go away. Fate has put this question before us. I do not know if it is penalty or, uh, challenge. In the end it makes no difference, yes? But we, sweetheart, you and I, Jason, must answer this question. The answer will be difficult. We may not want the answer. But to begin, to start, you must put these other things away. You can do this, yes?"

Of course, intellectually, I knew she was correct. But emotionally, her guidance would be difficult to implement. However, I had resolved to provide leadership. Leaders don't turn from, but instead welcome the challenges others won't. Clearly, if I were going to lead, now was the time.

"All right, princess, let's do that. Let's answer the question. Are you ready to talk about this? Or is it too soon?"

"It is too late."

"Yeah. I guess it is. But I meant—"

"I know. Yes," she released her grip, "it is time."

I turned out the light. The darkness was somehow more comfortable. It settled over and hid us.

"How do you feel about this, Young?"

"Well, in a strange way, I think this is a wonderful gift," she answered wistfully.

"Yes, princess, it is." I fought back my Western, male urge to add it was also a nightmare. Perhaps leadership also meant exercising appropriate silence.

"Can you imagine, an Amerasian child?" She smiled. "He would have the best from both cultures. We could teach him both languages, both traditions. He would have a foot in both worlds, not lost, but understanding both. My parents would be proud."

At this last reference, she darkened immediately and placed the back of her hand across her eyes. She mumbled briefly in Korean before continuing. "My parents," she groaned, then was silent for some time. Eventually, she looked up at me.

"How does this make you feel?"

"Well...uh...I don't know, exactly. I've not had very long to think about it. I gotta tell you, I wish we didn't have to solve this." Then I added quickly, "I'm not angry with you, sweetheart; it's just unfortunate right now, and the way it happened is…well, never mind. I just wish we weren't where we are. Again, princess, I'm not angry, or if I am, it's with me…I guess."

Sensing I hardly sounded "leaderly" and strong, I added the defensive, confusing and obvious, "You asked how I felt."

Young looked at me blankly. "This is not the very clear answer, Jason."

I closed my eyes and rubbed my forehead. "Sorry. Maybe I just don't know."

"Yes. I understand this kind of thing." She paused a moment, then continued, apparently trying to make the question more pointed.

"How do you feel about the baby?"

"Well…I guess I'd say it all starts with you. I love you dearly, princess. All I want is for you to be happy. You're the most important thing in my life," I said, repeating my early assertion. "If you're at peace, then so am I. If you're happy, then so am I. The opposite is also true. In terms of the baby specifically, uh…." I paused and looked out into the darkness, again trying to collect and identify my feelings. "It's part of us, part of you. I would love and care for it, as I would for you."

Young didn't respond. I was unsure how to interpret her silence. Perhaps she was looking for a specific or different answer. I hadn't tried to guess what she wanted to hear. Though muddled, I'd answered as truthfully as I could. I hoped I'd addressed her concern, because she didn't seek clarification. We sat quietly in the darkness for several minutes.

"Young, I asked you this before and you didn't answer. Will you marry me?"

She placed her hand on my chest. "Jason, this is a wonderful question. I love you for this question, but it does not now have an answer. No, that is not correct. Perhaps it does, but I do not know the answer. Anyway, is this not a different question? Marry or not marry? We still have our baby to consider."

"No, marriage is a good solution for everything. In the first instance, we solve the question of what's to become of us. Then, of course, this also solves what to do about, uh, Junior," I said brightly, rubbing her stomach and bringing a small smile to her face.

"Yes, it does provide an easy answer. But easy is not always, not normally, best. I believe we need to consider these things apart, different. Each has its own good things and…distractions?"

"Disadvantages?"

"Yes, dis-ad-van-tages. The solution seems the same for both, but the questions are quite different. One answer is not always correct for two questions."

"Okay, let's consider them independently. First, will you marry me?"

She closed her eyes and sagged. "Jason, the questions should be considered apart. But the most important one is our baby. That is the first question. The one we need to answer now. Others can follow."

Clearly, she wasn't going to be pushed on the marriage issue, although to me it was an eminently workable and logical solution. However, I relented.

"Okay."

Despite my readiness to focus and continue, awkwardness sat down beside us. It stymied our progress. We three sat looking down the same endless, dank tunnel, each wondering which of the very few options we might find lurking in the dark. Who would lead the way? Awkwardness brought no contribution and simply stared, first at us, then down the path. Young seemed oddly reticent and hesitant to move. At last, trying to lead, I began our journey.

"So, what are our possible actions?"

"Yes," she said evasively, eyes closed. "They are what?"

I squirmed; this was uncomfortable. I started slowly, recognizing danger and feeling clumsy.

"Well, of course, in one solution—and this is only one approach, princess—we have the baby. Then, you—we—put it up for adoption."

"No. This is not acceptable. I could never do this. I could not give my baby away. Also, this idea has another big problem. What more ideas do you have?"

Her rejection was surprisingly quick and clearly final. Normally, she took time to think about, or as she would say, "consider" her position—not so, adoption. And what was this other "big problem?"

I selected what seemed the next logical option. "Okay, then we keep the baby, and—"

"No," she interrupted, a harsh tone to her voice. "This is more of the problem from your first idea. What about KAL? They do not allow this kind of thing; it is clearly there in the contract. I will lose my position without question.

"Then, what of my family? You know very well it is not only a question of the job, but a question of my family's welfare. Yes, I could find another jewelry store kind of work, but I quit that place because the pay was so poor. My family's needs are getting bigger, and also, that job is not acceptable for me. Without a better position, my family is in danger. KAL is very important because it answers all these problems. It is not just a place to work, it is the only way to protect my family. This is the most important thing. Only I can do this. I must do this. I will do this. I do not care the cost."

Instantly, her Han River Gap comments about sacrifice flashed through my mind. *"Sacrifice for family. Sacrifice for ideas. These things…these are most important. These ideas define the Korean people. It is something you must understand, to know us."*

She'd frightened me. Though her thinking was logical and wholly consistent with the concerns and convictions she'd expressed in our first Itaewon meeting, it was coldly calculating and surprisingly dispassionate. Would she apply this robotic logic to us? I pushed the thought aside and tried to focus on one crisis at a time.

Clearly, she was focused, much more so than I. I wondered if she had thought this problem through and was simply going along as I surfaced ideas. She normally led discussions. I thought it odd she'd deferred to me. Did she have a solution? Was she, as usual, waiting for me to arrive at the same place? I began to think so. But I trusted her without question or qualification; if she thought this approach best, then it was.

Nonetheless, I was deep in emotional quicksand. I felt my next sentence would be a blunder, but there appeared to be no other path. In its most basic form, the problem had only two solutions. One was eliminated. From the tunnel's darkness, I could see our too-few options materializing into something dreadful. I tried to be innocuous, avoiding the word.

"Well…uh, princess…think about what you're saying."

Her eyes flashed at me, lasers at full intensity. I felt ashamed, unworthy.

"I know very well what I am saying," she shot back quickly, anger in her voice. Then, more quietly and with regret, she added, "I know very well." A second later, she took my hand in hers, kissed it, and began to cry. Through tears she whispered, "Oh, Jason, is it not clear to you? Do you really not see this? Fate has taken from us the gift of choice. We are trapped."

I fumbled about ineptly, my hopes of bringing leadership, comfort, and stability revealed as a cheap sham. Finally, I responded with the utterly inadequate, "Well, yeah…I guess." I lapsed to senseless, stupid silence.

The room was fully soaked in night's cold and bitter darkness. Stray shards of harsh hallway light lay brutally fluorescent at the door's foot, trying to crawl into our conscience. We were quiet for what seemed a long time. Cowardly, I ceded my false leadership, stepping away from the difficulty ahead. Eventually, Young, always the lioness, moved us with remorseful courage to the final, evil, but inevitable answer.

"There is a hospital that does this kind of thing; I telephoned them. They will see me Tuesday night. Can you drive me there?"

"Of course, princess. But let's talk about—"

She placed her graceful fingers lightly against my lips, aborting my words. She moved her head slowly, left and right, eyes closed; tears lay like bright jewels on her cheeks. When she spoke, there was a profound and final sadness in her voice I'd never before heard, and would hear only once more. She looked up at me, her dark, powerful eyes red and weary.

"Jason, we can talk until morning, and the next, and the next, and the next. This…this sad circumstance will never change because of talk. Talk will not help us find a…a…a clean solution." She paused, and after a moment, again closed her eyes. Almost inaudibly, she said, "Fate. It has not heart or conscience. I hope it also has not memory."

# Thirty-Seven

The hospital. Tuesday night. Late, dark, wet, cold, merciless.

I waited in the car, frightened, apprehensive, guilty, helpless.

Finally, Young returned. She sat silently beside me. Face drawn. Eyes red. Defeated. Slowly, she lowered her forehead to my shoulder. A wounded angel, lost, not fallen. After a long moment, she kissed my cheek, lightly...so...lightly.

We embraced.

We anguished.

We wept.

We forgave one another.

We whispered, "I love you."

We never again spoke of that night.

# PART FOUR

*I'm a-gonna tell ya how it's gonna be,*
*You're gonna give your love to me.*
*Love to last more than one day,*
*Love is lovin' not fade away.*

—*Not Fade Away,*
Buddy Holly

# Thirty-Eight

The nearly-May sunshine was bright but cool. The lake breeze was almost too fresh. No matter how earnestly we tried to conjure the warmth of mid-August, it remained very late April. We had driven north along the main highway from Seoul, the same highway marking the edge of the Papa-73 prohibited area. From an earthbound perspective, the road didn't look so dangerous; it yielded no sense of deadly demarcation. Instead, our passage was flanked by simple, jumbled humanity; dilapidated, multi-room shops and their joyless workers who, ignoring our passage, were dispiritedly fixated on grinding out a day-to-day existence.

Farther north, the small shops became small farms, which became rocky, isolated countryside. About twenty miles from the city limits, another, smaller road intercepted our progress. We turned west, and followed its meandering lead through the newly greening mountain valleys, and deep into the Korean heartland.

The surrounding mountains gave birth to brooks and rivulets, flowing toward the lowlands, joining streams, becoming larger, diverging, becoming smaller. Some rare few reached the Han, but most simply disappeared, melting into the absorbent earth. Occasionally, some persistent, fortunate streams found their way to the same terminus: a canyon, a quarry, a terrain depression. At these places, the water rested and nature created a blessing, a jewel—a lake.

We were most surely the year's first picnickers at a large mountain lake, one of several water sources for thirsty Seoul. As winter grudgingly crawled north toward Manchuria, warmer temperatures and more moderate weather filled the void. Primal genes in me began to awaken and I increasingly whined about missing Alabama's great bass fishing. Young, always happy to please and no doubt tiring of my lament, had surprised me with poles and a Saturday trip to this lake where—supposedly—one could find fish of the best kind. Not bass, or halibut, or trout, but fish willing to be caught.

We sat side by side on a ledge of flat, gray rocks near the water's edge, fishing poles in hand, waiting for action. Earlier, Young had grimaced and looked away when I baited her hook. She'd recoiled in a blur of flailing arms and a scramble of long legs, throwing hot Korean on me when I tried to wipe the worm guts from my fingers on her arm. I thought it was all great fun; oddly, she did not.

Eventually, we managed to bait our hooks and put them in the water. Young's reaction and her subsequent manner suggested she actually hoped to not catch a fish, as doing so would generate another series of unpleasant encounters with nature's slimier side. Clearly, the metropolitan Mapo girl had no prior fishing experience, and from her reactions thus far, wouldn't seek another. Any future we might have would apparently feature me as a fishing soloist. Nevertheless, I couldn't resist the urge to instruct.

"Now, you know what to do if a fish bites, right?"

"Uh, yes. I pull the stick up." With both hands in a death grip about the pole's handle, she gestured dramatically, pulling hard enough to separate the imaginary fish from its dentures. "And turn this, uh, wheel." She fumbled at the reel, creating a snag and nearly dropping the pole into the clear, cold water.

"Well, uh, yeah." I reached over and picked briefly at the snarled line. The reel freewheeled. "It comes naturally; you'll do fine."

She smiled in a hopelessly lost way. I was struck by the impression she secretly hoped to avoid any fish encounter that didn't involve a waiter and a dinner plate.

"This is like the Alabama fish hunting?"

I smiled at the image of hunting fish. "Well, princess, it's not exactly the same, but it's a great substitute and you were great for thinking of it." I leaned in and kissed her lightly. We were isolated, so she didn't resist or become obsessed with who might be watching. Rather, she smiled in a small, pleased way; happy, I imagine, with her gift.

The sun climbed higher and the temperature warmed pleasantly. The earlier chilling breeze was now absent, resting beyond our senses. Our bobbers, floating hypnotically on the water, soon produced that universal, mesmerizing effect known to all fishermen. We fished in silence. Time shuffled pleasantly past.

Suddenly, my bobber bounced once, twice, a third time. I nudged Young, and nodded toward the water. She looked at the red and white ball wide-eyed, entranced. I reached for my pole and slowly, the way an alert fisherman will, picked it up. The bobber remained quiet. I waited another minute, slowly taking slack from the line, each click of the reel clearly discernible and louder than the one before. However, taut line or not, still nothing. Finally, suspecting the worst, I reeled in my hook. Stripped clean. I smirked ruefully, explained what had happened, re-baited my hook, casually tossed my line in the water, and proceeded to drown another worm.

Time slowed again, but Young, as she could do seemingly at will, pushed me without warning to light-speed.

"Jason?"

"Yeah, pal?" I answered distractedly.

"Before me, what did you do?"

Immediately, she had my full attention. I had wondered when this question would surface; even so, I wasn't prepared to answer. I wasn't exactly ashamed of my Itaewon adventures, but neither was I particularly proud of them. Certainly, I didn't want to go into detail with Young. I feigned misunderstanding.

"Why, I was lost, princess. I just didn't know it."

"No, Jason," she said patiently, "I mean, what did you do for your, uh, empty time? Now, we are together at all chances. But before me, where did you go? What did you do?"

"Oh, didn't do much. Just stuff. You know, nothing special." Attempting to change the subject, I tried, "Say, wanna check your hook? You can lead a fish to water, but you can't make it bite." I smiled in a goofy, nervous way and began to reach for her pole. My witticism was absolutely lost on her, but my failure to be forthcoming was not.

"Do you not want to answer this question?"

"What question?"

Young extended her lower lip over her upper and looked across the water. She was becoming irritated with my not so subtle evasiveness. Like her, though, she did not snap at me, raise her voice, or become petulant. After pausing to either gather her thoughts or compose herself—or both, she attacked the problem in the typical family-Lee manner: directly, giving no quarter, smashing ambiguity, allowing me no escape route.

"Jason, do not act that you do not understand. You know very well the question I am asking. You understand this very clearly. If you do not want to answer this question, please say this and I will not ask again, but do not play the acting. This is not polite."

Defeated, I expelled a large breath.

"Well, princess, I guess I did what all the GI's do: I worked on the Rocket, wrote letters home, watched TV with the Lizards, went to the gym, played some ball, went to the movies, went to the Officer's club, read, went on a couple USO tours, shopped," and, saving the worst for last, tried to slip in Itaewon's seedier aspects unnoticed, "and occasionally went to the clubs with Hugh."

Young knew of, but had never met, Hugh. I hoped she would conclude cruising the clubs under Hugh's "adult supervision" was more innocent and acceptable than prowling Itaewon like some lone tomcat.

She was, of course, immediately curious about only one item in my intentionally overlong and camouflaged list, the Itaewon clubs.

"Do you know all these clubs?" she asked in amazement.

"God, Young, of course I don't know 'em *all*. Guy'd go broke goin' to all of 'em. I only went to a couple." Then, sensing that fewer clubs would mitigate my Itaewon sins, I mistakenly volunteered, "Mostly one, really; The Statue."

Young sat back slightly and tilted her head in a questioning gesture. "What kind of name is this, Statue? Statue is the large metal or stone object, a uh, solid picture of something, yes? Like the Han Warriors?"

Anxious to show my knowledge of Korean culture, and seeing an opportunity to imbue The Statue and my visits there with something akin to redeeming value, I responded, "Well, yes. In this case, the reference is to Admiral Yi."

I paused, waiting for some approving comment, some acknowledgment of my cultural acumen. However, she remained very much like the Admiral's statue, silent, observant, indifferent, unimpressed, waiting.

Committed, I continued with this obviously losing gambit.

"The Admiral's statue is in the roundabout between Itaewon district and Yongsan compound. The club is directly behind the statue. So, they chose that name, Statue. Good marketing, I'd say."

Young didn't understand "marketing," but wasn't dissuaded from lunging ahead with increasingly pointed questions.

"What is inside this Statue?

"Well, you know. What you'd expect, tables, chairs, like that."

"Is there music?"

"Yes."

"Is it loud?"

"Depends on the club."

"Are we not talking of The Statue, yes?"

"Then, yes. Uh, no. God! Quit it with the double-negative positives, or whatever those things are, will you?"

"Yes or no?"

"Yes, we're talking of Statue, and no, not so loud."

"Is there the dancing?"

"Yes."

"Did you play dance?"

"Couple times."

"Better than you play ski, uh?"

I took the high road and ignored this cut.

Young ignored my ignore. "Who?"

"Who what?"

"What persons did you play the dance? Not Hugh, I think."

"Uh, no, not Hugh."

"Who?"

"Some people who work there."

"Women?"

"Women what?"

"This persons that 'work there,' they are the women, yes?"

"Yeah. But the guy that plays the records is, well, a guy, and so is the bartender...and the cook."

"These women, do you also talk to them?"

"Sure. Except their English isn't as good as yours."

My suck-up compliment was ignored.

"So, this is why you were pleased with my poor English. What you heard before was not so good, so I am different."

"Yes, Kwang Young, you are indeed different."

"Did you make the dates with these Statue women?"

"No."

"Did you kiss these women?"

"Young! No."

"Did they kiss you?"

"No!"

"Did you touch them?"

"I just said we danced."

"Did you touch them, like me?"

"Of course not."

"I do not believe this."

"It's true. I never did any of those kinds of things, princess."

"Umph. Very well, I want to see this Statue."

"Well, we've driven by it a thousand times."

"Jason, you know very clearly what I mean. I want to visit this place, to see what it is like. I have never been in this kind of place before. I want to go."

"Princess, it's what we just talked about. Nothing really to see, a dark room, some tables and chairs, music. Lotta GI's and Korean women. Not exactly your type of Korean woman, I might add."

"Exactly so. I want to see."

The discussion was finished, the decision made. All that remained was for me to accept the edict and coordinate its occurrence. I groaned inwardly. Christ, the elegant, publicly shy, and always gentle Kwang Young at the Statue. What a nightmare.

I kicked at her pole, shaking the line and disturbing the bobber. Talk about a fish out of water. She'd see a bunch of not so shy—or gentle—GI's mauling the

Hostesses, watch the Pillow Girls operate, talk one-on-one with Hugh, who'd do everything he could to embarrass me, and…

Suddenly, the worst case struck me: she'd meet Spiderwoman! My chin fell to my chest. The idea of mixing a dash of Spiderwoman with a snippet of Young was too much. How best to alleviate the impending disaster? My mind spun quickly, generating and discarding solutions. As usual, in any dealing with Young, I was too slow.

"When can we go?"

Thinking as quickly as I could under the intensity of her laser gaze, I could only surface Hugh's upcoming going-away dinner as a solution. With attention focused on past success, future challenges, and current good-byes, perhaps it would present my best opportunity for distraction and damage control.

"Well, Hugh's going home soon and we're gonna have dinner and a coupl'a drinks at the Statue, just he and I, to celebrate and sorta say goodbye. You're welcome to come to that. I know he'd love to meet you."

"This is the normal Statue night?"

"Well, yeah, mostly normal.

"What is 'mostly normal'?"

"Okay, okay. Not mostly normal, just plain, everyday, no qualifiers, vanilla normal. Okay? Christ, let's not pick nits."

"Do not be mean."

"Sorry."

"Very well, this is the date. I will see this place; it should be fun."

"Fun" would not have been my descriptor, but little matter, the issue was settled. Exasperated, I rubbed my face with both hands. After a moment, I looked up across the water toward the far horizon. The day was becoming even more beautiful. Summer was indeed approaching, not fast enough—or, in that maddening Asian sense Young so much loved of at least two simultaneous and opposite meanings for everything—perhaps too fast.

I dropped my gaze to the bobbers. An evil smile came to my lips. Perhaps justice existed after all.

"Young?"

"Yes?"

I nodded toward the water.

"Princess, look at the bobber." I watched with increasing pleasure as her expression turned from self-satisfaction to a small but apparently increasing form of panic.

"Better pick up your 'stick,' pal. You got a fish on the line."

# Thirty-Nine

April's spring blossomed into May, and the first petals of "glorious summer." Young completed flight attendant training and began serving as a KAL crew member. There was a formal graduation ceremony to which I was invited in spirit, but not in flesh. Young downplayed the event; still it was clear she was proud and pleased to have received her KAL wings.

Young's KAL life began with a thirty-day probationary period, during which her flight assignments were "local," meaning either within Korea or to Japan. Local flights rarely entailed overnight stops, so we saw one another almost daily. Our routine was to meet in the evening on a side street near Kimpo airport. I'd drive her to Mapo, where we'd share dinner and the day's news at our favorite neighborhood restaurant. Fully salaried, Young frequently insisted that she buy our dinners. I suggested this was unnecessary, but she contended it was what she wanted. As usual, I deferred.

Increasingly, our dinner discussions turned from the problems of future, culture, and parents, to center more and more on things KAL. Specifically, on her greatly anticipated assignment to KAL's international routes. She seemed in the grip of a newly-discovered wanderlust. It was understandable; the international destinations were glamorous, and until now she'd rarely been outside of Seoul, and never outside of Korea.

Still, I was less concerned about where she flew than with what we were to become. I was able to steer her easily enough back to "us," but inevitably, she'd wander to dreamy talk of Europe and Hawaii. I was mildly disturbed that she was apparently more concerned with KAL than me. I wanted to be the center of her attention; the excitement in her future. I hid selfish irritation whenever she spoke a little too enthusiastically about Paris, London, Rome, Honolulu, or LA.

Of course, her comments simply mirrored her changes. She had acquired professional skills and sustained life experiences that circumstance and culture denied the average Korean women. She had graciously accepted the absolute joy of hard-earned individual success, and grittily survived private tragedy. Wielding a growing version of her father's self-assurance, she had committed to a foreigner, stepping outside society's boundary, risking discrimination, scorn, and her newly-found livelihood. She was conscious of the risk, but was powerful and confident enough to peacefully ignore it. She continued to venture where she pleased, when, and with whom. I admired her strength, but felt inadequate in comparison. In a secret way of which I was ashamed, I was jealous.

I was also sad. I missed the quiet salesgirl from the jewelry shop. The shy girl who either could not or would not acknowledge my business card. I recalled her immediate retreat behind formal dialogue when the Korean couple entered the store. I remembered our Itaewon shopping trip and her shocked reaction to my Dragon Valley ski proposal. I thought of her culture-crash when I suggested we adopt a first name basis. I smiled at her dumbstruck reaction after stumbling upon the Lizards late one rainy November Saturday. I remembered she was scandalized when I asked to walk her home, in full view of her neighbors and family.

Other memories fell softly to me, but I laid them gently down. The innocent girl with whom I'd started this journey had faded. Materializing was a confident, professional young woman, independent and capable.

Her transformation was heartening, saddening and frightening. Wonderfully, she was beginning to bloom and flower, an extraordinary and remarkable woman, passing forward into summer. But in this passage, her springtime had kept something pure and familiar. That's the sadly cruel nature of growth—an involuntary exchange of the lesser comfort and familiarity we are, for the greater unknown we're to become.

But more darkly and selfishly, her transformation was frightening. She had discovered and embraced self-sufficiency. While I needed her desperately, she loved me desperately. These are very different halves of the same emotional whole.

As April drifted away, I reluctantly acknowledged a lonely and helpless truth: Young was slipping from me. Perhaps beyond my power to recall. The quotation she'd read—what seemed like a thousand years ago—was proving more prophesy than passage.

*"There lives within the very flame of love,*
*A kind of wick or snuff that will abate it."*

We had lived, still lived, within love's flame. Tempered by it, Young had grown, flowered and developed certainty, confidence, and power. A passive witness, I hadn't flowered, but rather followed. I had merely watched, unable to match her changes. As a result, we, as an entity, were weakened. Our lives had imperceptibly shifted, the centerlines no longer exactly, mathematically, concurrent. Our light was more dim, the fog more thick, the path less obvious.

We were becoming the residue of love's abated flame: elusive, dissipating smoke, drifting higher from our source, losing contact, our heart's beat stronger in echo than origin. There was a growing darkness in which I began to stumble and fall. But, as she had done on so many previous occasions, it seemed my lovely, omniscient, indefatigable Young would be unable or, inconceivably…unwilling to rescue me.

# Forty

Hugh laughed quietly, almost to himself, but in a calculated way, just loud enough for me to hear. I ignored him. Never easily dissuaded, Hugh continued chuckling, ominously adding the gesture of hands rubbed gleefully together. I ignored him. Realizing I would not rise to the bait, he elected to use a more direct, less elegant, frontal assault.

"Yes, yes. Finally, the much protected and sheltered Miss Lee and the vagabond reprobate Mr. Stevens will, at last, meet."

We sauntered past the gate guard, out of Yongsan's protective arms, and turned right into the lighthearted evil of Itaewon's warm, early May evening. Ahead of us stood Admiral Yi, and behind him, our destination and my Waterloo, The Statue.

Desperate, and desperate not to show it, I said as casually as possible, "Yeah, should be quite a night." Knowing I shouldn't, but, like an addict, unable to pass on the opportunity, I added, "So, out of respect, try not to embarrass yourself, okay? You've only got a week left; try to exercise a little class for a change."

This, of course, was the opening for which Hugh had been maneuvering.

"Why, Jason, I'm crushed." He turned to look at me, stiffening, slowing his pace, and moving his right hand to his heart. "To think of the time we've spent together, and on the occasion of our last, uh, social function, you disclose your true feelings, to wit: I'm classless!" He sighed heavily and placed the back of his hand on his forehead. "Oh, heavy burden. Lucky I'm not the vengeful type or I'd have to brief-up the virginal Miss Lee—she is a virgin, right?—on some of your less reputable Itaewon adventures. Like the time—"

"See! There! Right goddamn there. That is exactly the kinda shit I'm talkin' about," I complained, fully enmeshed in Hugh's obvious web. "You think this is funny, but I don't know how Young'll react to all this new and seedy stuff. It's bad enough without your embellishments or exaggerations."

"But the stuff about you'd be true, my man. No embellishment, no exaggeration. Of course, you've nothing to fear. I just *know* you've shared all your background with her." Hugh leaned toward me and, lowering his voice, said in a knowing, leering, smarmy way, "True love would do that, you know."

Hugh had me under the point of his sarcasm-spear. As usual, he intended to see me suffer before releasing the pressure. He looked skyward, face contorted in false concentration, as if trying to recall a difficult equation or a long quotation.

"Let's see…." His voice trailed off momentarily, then, "Oh! She'd probably be interested in the time you were carried, literally, by a pair of Military Police to the compound, too drunk to walk, and dumped on the front step of your quarters—where, as I recall, you spent the night." Hugh wrinkled his brow, feigning deep concentration. "Wasn't that the night you lost your ID card? Did you ever find that thing, or do you s'pose it's made its way to North Korea by now?"

He shrugged as if it made little matter, then drove relentlessly on.

"Oh, yeah. Then, there's the time you haggled selling price with one Korean 'Lady-of-Night,' finally getting her to agree to, uh…in light of your concern for 'class,' let's just call it 'oral gratification,' for how much? A quarter, as I recall? Quite the accomplishment! You are a skilled negotiator, young man. Of course, in the good lady's defense, it was nearly curfew, and business musta been slow that night. So, hey, a quarter's better'n nothin'."

A gaggle of six teenaged Korean girls dressed in their school uniforms of navy blue blazers and blue-green plaid skirts came giggling toward us. A storm of incomprehensible language swirled about them. Hugh and I loved to tease, and we made a show of grandly yielding the sidewalk. Sir Walter Raleigh could not have been more chivalrous or courtly. The tittering increased as the group hurried past, holding hands in the Asian custom and very much embarrassed. Looking after them, I smiled and waved. More giggles. I turned back to Hugh.

"I couldn't have given more perfect examples of embellishment and exaggeration. Most—no, all—of your recitation is patent crap! First, I wasn't drunk. I twisted my ankle playin' ball that afternoon and later—because it was hurt—slipped down the last couple of steps at The Statue, makin' it worse. Yes, I couldn't walk. And yes, the MP's had to cart me home, but not because I was drunk. And no, I did not sleep outside my quarters. All of which you know.

"Point the second: my ID card. I lost it at the gym the same day I hurt my ankle. No, it did not show up in North Korea, North Vietnam, or North Carolina. It showed up in the Personnel Office a couple days later, turned in by another gym-rat GI who found it under the rollaway bleachers. Again, all of which you know.

"Third and last, about the uh…'young woman' in question."

"*Young*?" Hugh responded with astonishment.

"Yeah, she was about your age."

"Oh, yeah, she *was* rather youthful."

"So, about the young woman." I cleared my throat. "Well, yeah, there was such an event. But it was in response to a bet from you, of course, that I couldn't do it!" I added hastily. "No money…or bodily fluids…were exchanged…and you know that too!

"So, come on, Hugh," I said despairingly, "don't even kid about that stuff. Young's English is great, but she sometimes takes things literally and doesn't always catch nuance or teasing. If you act serious, she'll believe you, especially since this is the first time you've met. Koreans are a lot more formal than us, so just…just don't. Okay?"

"Would I cause trouble?" Hugh raised his arms to waist level, palms up in an almost religious gesture of supplication. He continued with mock hurt, "Talk about paranoid. You'd think a guy could have some fun at his own goin' away doin's, but apparently not."

"Hugh, you can have plenty of fun, just be careful about what you say to Young, okay? Please? The Statue's the last place I want to take her, but she won't be dissuaded. This is killin' me, you gotta help me out here."

"Okay, okay. What a killjoy. This love crap's turned you into a real grandma."

"Fine. Guilty. Mea culpa. Bring my shawl and rocker. Just be nice for a change. Okay? I'm worried about you and Spiderwoman," I confessed. "If I can just get you two to behave, I may survive the night."

Hugh grinned and slapped me lightly on the shoulder. "It'll be okay, bud, don't worry. I'll take care of you. When she gonna be here?"

"Not sure. She's flying a charter of business guys back from Tokyo, so there's no set schedule. Dunno when her flight's gettin' in. She's gonna change clothes at Kimpo and take a taxi here. Then, after what I hope is a very short visit, I'm takin' her back to Mapo…if you and Spiderwoman haven't poisoned the water and she's still speaking to me."

Hugh shook his head as if he couldn't understand why I'd care what she saw or how she reacted. After twenty-plus years of marriage, these kinds of concerns and adventures were a mystery to him.

We reached the curb opposite The Statue and watched the small Korean-made cars zip by, most belching either blue or black smoke. After a minute, there was a break in the traffic flow and we jogged across the wide, circular intersection to the safety of the far sidewalk. Stepping to the curb, I finally asked the last key question.

"Does Spiderwoman know Young's coming, or who she is?"

Hugh turned his head to me slowly, like the demonically possessed little girl in *The Exorcist*, and with the same twisted and evil smile said, "Oh yeah, you bet."

# Forty-One

I pulled open the heavy green door and bowed deeply, waving Hugh into The Statue. Affecting a haughty manner, he brushed by like some Middle-East potentate, metaphoric robes flowing after. Stopping inside the doorway at the staircase's upper landing, he turned, stood at attention, and extended his arm, bidding me enter. I stepped into the harsh yellow light of a single, dangling, naked lightbulb.

Taking my lead from Hugh, I, too, stood erect, and slipped my arm through his at the elbow. We puffed up our chests and, like the two rogues from Kipling's *The Man Who Would Be King*, descended the stairway arm-in-arm, lock-step, loudly singing an old army marching song....

"I don't know but I've been told,
Eskimo girls are mighty cold,
Sound off!

One, two.
Sound off!
Three, four.
Rack 'em on dow-own.
One, two, three, four,
One, two,

THREE!! FOUR!!"

Our voices preceded us, reaching and filling the approaching club. We arrived at the last step and the arched-doorway threshold simultaneously with our final shouted, "Three! Four!"

Glancing about the club's semi-darkness, I found it a temporary photograph, its subjects frozen in place: three couples immobile on the dance floor; one Hostess midway between her guests and the bar; a man with his hand outstretched for the latrine door, his head turned toward the club entrance; the bartender looking over his shoulder, his hand on a whiskey bottle; the record-playing DJ gawking from his tiny, dimly lit booth; GI's and Korean women at the small, circular tables turned toward the doorway. All eyes were on Hugh and me. The only sound was Simon and Garfunkel's melancholy, *The Boxer*, playing quietly in the background. The well-worn record's random pops and repetitious ticks were clearly audible. I was quite pleased; we had, it seemed, captured the attention of Statue staff and guests.

Naturally, Spiderwoman was the first to recover. She materialized from nowhere in a blur of too-tight jeans and a low-cut blouse, her long black hair flowing with a life of its own. She ripped through the photograph and toward Hugh and me, her normal vulgarity loud in the near-quiet. Stopping inches from us, she dove in, distinct breaks punctuating her words.

"Wha da fuck dis?" she demanded. "You drunk aw' ready? Only seben, Christ sake! First you long time no come, den you come drunk? Piss me off, GI!"

"Again, my delightful Miss Pak, I take umbrage."

"Wha?" Spiderwoman raised her heavily painted eyebrows. Not understanding, her instinct was to attack. She began to lecture with irritation, a waving finger complete with long, hooked nail punctuated the air.

"Wa' you talk 'bout? It no rain. 'Side, you inside. No need umbellage."

Spiderwoman drew closer, stale cigarette smoke heavily about her. She lowered her voice and spoke confidentially to me. Apparently Hugh was exempt, or not worthy of advice.

"You sick, boy. You need something dat cherry-girl not give." Spiderwoman's eyes flicked quickly behind me as if looking for someone, a passing trace of what seemed embarrassment colored her face.

I was surprised we had surfaced Young so quickly, and doubly surprised that she seemed to engender irritation. I was also a little offended at the second reference to Young's virginity in less than ten minutes. However, not wanting to show Spiderwoman she'd scored points, I tried for a riposte with sexual overtones, as she would have expected in "the old days."

"No, no. Quite the contrary, Miss Pak. Mr. Stevens and I are in fine fiddle and kiddle, and we're ready to diddle."

Leering, Hugh extended his hand toward Spiderwoman's breast, but had it slapped back at mid-reach. Not that a GI had never mauled Spiderwoman; it was, after all, part of the job—but the mauling was to be on her terms, and done with discretion. His approach satisfied none of these criteria, and his rebuke was deservedly quick and accurate.

Hugh and I chortled and chuckled moronically at my senseless sexual rhyme and Spiderwoman's defensive reflexes. Miss Pak shook her head in exasperation, grabbed us both by an arm, and pulled/pushed us to a seated position at the nearest empty booth.

"Here. You dink you sit here one goddamn minute no trouble I get back, no sweat?" she asked with sarcasm.

"No sweat!" Hugh replied with gusto, slapping the tabletop loudly.

Spiderwoman "hrrumphed," and bustled back toward the dance floor and the bar. Noticing we were still the center of attention, she called to no one in particular at her usual jet-engine volume, "Okay, okay, everybody see drunk, stupid GI befo'. Go on, go on, eat, dance, drink." Then, seeing the fellow still standing frozen by the latrine, she tossed him a loud laser. "Or pee, Christ sake!"

The club erupted in laughter. The embarrassed man immediately disappeared behind the swinging latrine door.

With Spiderwoman again in control, the Statue assumed its normal ambiance. Hugh's going-home party was off to an auspicious start. The evening's fun had just begun.

# Forty-Two

Our dinner was tasty and filling: spicy *kimchee*, hot *bul-go-gi*, brown rice mixed with barley, some kind of fried beans served in a clear hot-sauce, and plenty of potent Korean beer before, during, and following the meal. As Hugh observed, "It ain't a party without beer."

After "seating" us, Spiderwoman played aloof, dropping by only occasionally, and then withdrawn and grumpy. We tried to kibitz with her, but she had little to say in response and was uncharacteristically sullen. We concluded she was angry to lose Hugh to rotation home, and me to Kwang Young.

Our dinner completed, Hugh and I chatted with unaccustomed seriousness over drinks about what we'd accomplished in the past year and what lay ahead. Hugh was also returning to Fort Rucker. Since he'd come to Eighth Army Standards from DES, he had requested and received orders back to the Directorate.

While we'd be reunited at Fort Rucker, it would be different. We'd see one another at the office and the flight line, but that would be about it. The camaraderie we knew in Korea was born of dependence on one another, isolation, and the inconvenience of expatriate living. In the states, Hugh had a wife and family. His bar-hopping time wouldn't just diminish, it would disappear. His interest in and obligation to weekend domestic chores would again surface. Inevitably, we'd lose the close and common touch we'd discovered at Yongsan. We understood and accepted this, but it dampened our mood nonetheless.

Part of any Army farewell gathering is gift-giving; sometimes two gifts—one serious, one a gag. I had a gag gift and had decided to present it at The Statue, rather than at Hugh's formal farewell party at the Officer's Club with Colonel Barth. The evening's surprising solemnity had nudged us to the edge of depression. I knew my gift would lighten the mood, and since it was a bit "unusual," I wanted to present it before Kwang Young arrived. Now seemed a good time to try for a few laughs.

I quaffed the last of my beer, and assuming an official, in-charge posture, stood, albeit somewhat wobbly, at our table. I tapped my beer glass rapidly with the handle of a dinner knife, and in a loud and commanding military voice declared, "Attention To Orders!"

The time-honored military awards phrase bounced around the club, breaking the low murmur. At its pronouncement, some of the GI's, knowing Hugh and recognizing the game, played along, standing quickly to attention, their chairs making a loud scraping sound as they rubbed across the concrete floor; then, silence.

I looked about, allowing the moment to grow. Satisfied I had milked the situation for all it was worth, I continued in a loud voice.

"In timely recognition of his long and arduous service in the preservation of Korean liberty, yea, on the very borders of Freedom's Frontier...."

In a lowered, sarcastic voice, and to the accompaniment of general snickering, I added, "And somewhat south of said frontier." Then again loudly, "And for risking his considerable reputation as an intrepid aviator...."

All the non-aviation, infantry soldiers booed lustily at this reference in a cheap and typically tacky demonstration of their obvious professional jealousy. I ignored their gauche behavior.

"And as a confirmed and unrepentant drunkard and general ne'er-do-well. And for risking all these things with disregard for his personal safety by repeatedly placing himself in the path of oncoming, terminal velocity, high-speed, low-drag gin bottles—"

Someone near the back wall hooted drunkenly, "Gin, the milk of life!" I laughed along with the crowd. The occasion seemed to be gathering steam.

I didn't see her, but was told that about this time a tall Asian woman with short wavy hair, dressed in dark gray wool slacks and a pearl-gray silk blouse, stepped into the arched stairway entrance, stopped, and looked about. The woman later said I wasn't difficult to find, both standing and talking...loudly. However, immersed in benign ignorance and with the serene stupidity of the unknowing, I continued boldly.

"And lastly, for offending nearly every Korean woman with whom he has come into contact...."

My fingers made quotation marks during the word "contact." The gesture and image brought much loud whooping and many vulgarities from the crowded club. Even the sullen Spiderwoman smiled.

"I present to Hugh Stevens an award, both practical, and in'DICK'ative of his wasted Korean year." I reached below the table and with great ceremony produced an "award" I'd had specially made and delivered to The Statue. Spiderwoman was part of the conspiracy. Her role was to ensure we were seated at the same table where the gift was secreted.

The award was mounted on a piece of dark, stained plywood about eighteen inches square. A foot-long white balloon was clipped, deflated, to the board's center. Immediately above the balloon was a small, circular wire mesh, festooned with ribbons in red, blue, and white, colors from the American and Korean flags. Attached to the plaque, below the dangling balloon, was a small, engraved brass plate, which I read aloud:

*"AWARD OF THE CONDOM"*
French Tickler, Jumbo Class
You'll never fill it up, and it doubles as a rain cap.
(Sorry, it's the smallest they had. Try gluing it on.)
Best always,
Jason

The GI's broke into applause and loud, rowdy laughter. After a moment, the crowd began to chant, "Speech! Speech! Speech!"

Hugh, never at a loss, and considering himself a comic wrongly assigned the life of an Army aviator, rose, bowed majestically, accepted the plaque and gave me a bear hug.

Embarrassed, I sat down.

"Thank you...." Hugh raised his arms to garner the group's attention. "Very much...really. Thanks." The crowd quieted. He spoke only a few words, but they proved key.

"Thanks, but you know, I'm not a very smart guy. No sir, not very smart at all."

Out of the quiet someone hollered, "Got that shit right!" More raucous, wet laughter.

Hugh again quieted the room and continued with a smile.

"So, I need help. I gotta ask Jason here to do as any good instructor pilot would...demonstrate the use of this thing." Hugh sat abruptly, a smirk on his face.

The room erupted with various blurry chants and epitaphs: "Jason! Jason!" And, "Yeah Fitzgerald, show us how it's done." And, of course, the venerable, "You ain't got a hair on your ass if you don't, fly boy."

Hugh looked at me, smiled guilelessly, shrugged, and handed me the plaque. I hesitated a moment, took a deep drink of Hugh's beer, and with determination and new-found courage, stood to great applause, profanity and derisive laughter.

Warming to—no, totally absorbed in—the moment, I smiled broadly, and at the top of my voice yelled over the crowd noise, "As we all know, proper operation of the M1-A1 army issue condom requires lubrication!" With that, I

poured the remainder of Hugh's beer over my head. Not satisfied I was sufficiently lubricated, I also scooped up some butter from the table and rubbed it
across my forehead. I snatched the balloon from the plaque and, with a flourish,
pulled it over my head as far as my ears, sort of ski cap fashion. There was great
applause, loud laughter, whistling, hooting, and other responses best left
unchronicled.

Solicitous of attention, I stepped onto the empty dance floor. The deflated,
elongated white balloon flopped over my left ear; beer dripped from the tip of
my nose. I raised both arms, boxing champion fashion and nodded in affirmation that yes, I was indeed deserving of this adulation.

The applause became rhythmic, the expectations elevated. The DJ played
"The Stripper." The crowd hooted and the old/new cry of, "Take it off," came
rushing toward me from its most recent birthplace near the club's corner.
Mini-spotlights illuminated me; light gray cigarette smoke wafting laterally in
the tight beams of light. I was The Statue's ignorant, happy focus.

The music grew louder. In response, I shuffled about the dance floor in a dis-
mal imitation of a two dollar stripper. I unbuttoned my shirt. The crowd became
louder, their oaths more vulgar. In the heady, spinning, irrational maelstrom of
booze, light, music, noise, and anticipation, I became further emboldened,
grinding and undulating—but my gyrations would entertain this tough Roman
audience only so long.

To avoid the lions, I tried to think of how to complete the "Condom Use
Theme." I quickly struck upon the obvious: simulate an ejaculation! But how?
Spitting milk came immediately to mind. Incredibly, I managed to decide this
absolutely disgusting idea was divinely inspired. I was vaguely aware that actually getting milk might be a problem, but the debauched concept, in and of itself,
was relatively Newtonian.

Before I could act on my depraved plan, the onlookers generously began to
throw money. The crowd's enthusiasm swept me away. I scrambled about trying
to catch the coins, chasing after them as they skittered across the wooden dance
floor and dropping to hands and knees as the coins rolled under tables and
chairs. Spurred on by the lusty crowd, my pursuit was constant and diligent. No
coin would go unsalvaged; they were, after all, Spanish doubloons and pieces of
eight! The crowd cheered my antics. Dignity and self-respect became undefined,
esoteric concepts with no practical use, like the oddly named imaginary numbers
in calculus, or the equally Byzantine black holes of space.

Attempting to extricate myself from beneath a table, I banged my head and
swore loudly, repeatedly, and skillfully. As I stumbled to my feet, the table's occupants applauded, cheered, and patted my back. I held up one U.S. quarter and
bowed in acknowledgement. Rubbing my head and kissing my new-found

wealth, I turned unsteadily back to the dance floor.

I managed four wobbling steps that veered without command toward the club's entry area. Stumbling toward the doorway, I became aware of a quiet presence. I tilted my head and squinted. Slowly, the apparition came into focus.

Standing before me was a tall, elegant Asian woman dressed in gray. Her head was tilted to the left and she wore an expression that was equal parts bewilderment, surprise, and shock. We stared at one another through the raucous din. At last, the woman leaned toward me and, over the crowd's exaltations, inquired, "This is the *normal* Statue night?"

# Forty-Three

The club had lost its collective, rowdy focus. Predominating was the normal, dispersed undertone, a murmur filled with the exchange of secret, passion-soaked bartering. Drowsy background music drifted quietly about the hazy half-light, unnoticed and ignored.

My crisis of embarrassment had passed. An unexpected angel had rescued me. My deliverance occurred quickly and surgically. Young and I stood facing one another on the dance floor. I fumbled for a restorative rejoinder to Young's question. None came immediately to hand.

Miraculously, however, I was saved by Spiderwoman's nimble emergence from the mist of noise and light. She moved quickly to us. She ignored me, but spoke directly to Young. Interestingly, she didn't speak Korean, but her unique bar-girl brand of semi-English. Distractedly, I wondered if Young would understand.

"You Miss Lee?" asked Spiderwoman deferentially, eyes slightly downcast, hands before her at her waist.

Young, recovering her wits, looked slowly from me to Spiderwoman, her head movement preceding her gaze.

I pictured her mental gears shifting, haltingly at first, then with gathering fluidity as she assessed this new source of unbidden humanity. She focused on Spiderwoman, but expressionless, detached, like the first time she looked at me in the jewelry store.

Spiderwoman bowed, relatively deeply. This gesture seem to awaken the unfailingly polite Young, who replied quietly in Korean and returned the bow—to my surprise, equally deep.

Spiderwoman spoke again, this time in Korean. She made a graceful, sweeping gesture, indicated our table. Young nodded and responded with three Korean syllables. She and Spiderwoman turned and walked from the dance floor. I, ignored during this sequence, stood momentarily alone; then, gathering my wits, trailed quickly behind. Tagging along after the women, I buttoned and tucked in my shirt, brushed the dirt from my knees and generally put my clothing to rights. Restoring my dignity would require somewhat more effort.

Catching up as we reached our table, I nodded my head several times and rubbed my hands together as if greatly anticipating what was to follow.

"Okay. Okay. Good," I said, a little too casually. "So. Young. You've met Miss Pak. Uh...good, good. Uh, this," I said, placing my hand on Hugh's shoulder, "This is, uh, my friend Hugh Stevens. Hugh, Young. Young, Hugh. Hugh, Young. Young, well, anyway...."

Hugh rose and extended his hand. "Hi, Miss Lee, I've heard a lotta nice things about you. I'm glad we could finally meet."

I'd never seen Hugh so polite! Things were looking up.

"Thank you, sir." Young shook Hugh's hand and bowed slightly. "Jason has spoken many times of you, and always with great respect and deference."

Her reply sounded more like practiced phrase-book than spontaneous Young, especially the "deference" comment. That word was new, and unfortunately pronounced dee-fur-ence. I wondered if she had prepared. It would be both like and unlike her to do so. Of course, that was her Asian nature, simultaneous point and counterpoint.

Hugh, showing unusual graciousness, smiled, but ignored the pronunciation snafu.

"Well, I should imagine that he would. After all, I taught him everything he knows."

We all laughed, save Spiderwoman. Young noticed this and immediately translated. Spiderwoman grinned, shook her head in the negative and waved dismissively at Hugh. The tension seemed broken.

As we sat, Hugh grinned at me with glee but said nothing. I wondered what the joke might be. He had behaved appropriately, so far. Then I noticed Spiderwoman had an equally silly grin. What was going on? Had I missed something? Young, sitting next to me and across from Spiderwoman, looked at me for a long moment, bemused. She leaned to me and whispered, "Can you now take off your...hat? You look like the man chicken, only with a white, uh, crown."

I snatched the oversized balloon from my head. A small dribble of trapped beer rolled down my face. More laughter. My mind whirled about, trying again to construct a plausible explanation for my behavior and appearance. Unlike my milk-spitting genius which I managed to conjure in two micro-seconds, nothing explanatory or redemptive surfaced.

Fortunately, Spiderwoman intervened, initiating innocuous, diversionary conversation. Serendipity or scheme, the effect was the same; I was, at least for now, safe.

"Miss Lee, it hona you come Statue. Jason come here all time, but now, na so much."

Young closed her eyes about halfway and leaned forward in a seated bow.

"Thank you. Jason explained the club, but I wanted to see. I had not before been to a similar place."

"Shit," Spiderwoman shrugged, "all club same-same. Maybe some mo' noise. Some mo' dark. All same bullshit. I know, I work many club. Miss Lee, wa you do work, eh?"

Interestingly, Young hesitated a moment, then said, "I work at the airline."

Spiderwoman looked confused. Young spoke a single Korean word, presumably "airline" or something similar. The impact was immediate.

"Ohhh, vely nice. Vely nice. Wa you do?" Spiderwoman asked breathlessly.

I could tell Young was uncomfortable with this line of questioning but felt bound by courtesy to respond. She began slowly, a trait she exercised when "shaping the truth," Asian fashion—not quite accurate, not quite wrong.

I smiled inwardly. I loved her dearly at times like these. She was so puzzling, complex, and beguiling.

She looked about the club, her face lightly troubled. The Hostesses were carrying trays of drinks between the tables and the bar, all the while bantering with the GI's. Young, her face again calm, looked back to Spiderwoman. Her answer was brilliant and its nature did not surprise; it demonstrated her gracious character perfectly.

"Well, like you, I am a waitress."

Spiderwoman's face lit up. She smiled and put a hand over her mouth, a habit of the Korean young and unsophisticated when surprised or laughing.

"Like me! No shit? You job like me?"

Young leaned forward in a bow of acknowledgment. "Yes, this is true, we have the same work. Except, you are more fortunate in one or two ways. I must serve the Japanese. You see the Americans. I must travel. You stay always near your family. These things are much better I think, yes?"

Spiderwoman, apparently lost in the English and seeking clarification, spoke in heavy, guttural Korean, making an occasional spitting sound.

Young responded, her light voice crafting Korean that floated, soft and pastel.

Spiderwoman smiled and shook her head in understanding.

Young, having successfully discounted her job and put Spiderwoman at ease, asked, "How long have you worked here?"

It seemed a natural enough question. Again, Miss Pak was moved, but not positively as before. This time, she seemed a mixture of loss, remorse, sadness and embarrassment. She waved at the air with mostly wrist movement.

"Oh, long time. Five year maybe." She looked away toward the dance floor, blew cigarette smoke in the air at a forty-five degree angle, picked a piece of tobacco from her tongue, and regarded the tiny speck momentarily as it rested on the tip of her long, garish red nail. Finally, she looked back toward Young and said in a flat, rough voice, "Long time."

Young apparently missed the change in Spiderwoman's demeanor, because she smiled and pursued the issue. "Oh, good, you like the club, this work."

Leaning forward, Spiderwoman looked suddenly older, worn, almost frightening. She repeated the fragments, her voice part incredulity, part frustration, part sarcasm.

"Da club? Dis work?" She sat back in the booth, shook her head, and turning to Hugh and me, said, "Solly, GI, English too hard. We do Kolea talk. I know dis polite problem, but no can do mo' English. Okay? You not mad maybe, eh? Is okay?"

"Not a problem, Miss Pak, have at it."

And so, Spiderwoman and Young, women at the extreme opposite ends of the cultural spectrum, had a long and surprisingly earnest conversation. I couldn't imagine what ground they might have in common. It seemed questionable they even spoke the same language, listening to their very different inflections and intonations. Nevertheless, they talked exclusively to one another for nearly fifteen minutes. Occasionally, I would catch Young's compassionate, warm laughter lapping around us, quiet and gentle. Other times, Spiderwoman's loud, rough guffaws echoed from the adjacent wall before dropping roughly to the table.

I ruefully noted our group was divided along gender, racial, and linguistic lines. I wondered if this was a small preview of what might await Young and me in the States. It was disturbing. I pushed the discomfort away.

Hugh and I, excluded from the secrets passing between the women, continued our earlier conversation, trying to remain positive. Finally, the two women fell silent. Spiderwoman leaned back in the booth. The sudden quiet and movement broke my conversation with Hugh. Perhaps twenty quietly reflective seconds passed. Hushed murmurs buzzed past us from other tables. I recalled Thoreau's observation, "Silence is the universal refuge." I wondered about the difference between our groups. Why was ours in need of refuge while others seemed unencumbered, apparently feeling no need for protection, comfort, or shelter?

Without warning, Spiderwoman slugged Hugh on the shoulder and banished the silence, announcing, "I go otha table. Too long here. Be back."

She pushed the stubby remainder of her cigarette into the heart of a blue plastic ashtray, simultaneously blowing smoke from the corner of her mouth. She rose and started to turn away, but abruptly stopped and fixed Hugh and me with a hard, chilling glance.

"You be nice Miss Lee, goddamn it, she numba one. You assholes sometime. I know. Be nice!" she enjoined without shame or embarrassment. She raised a waving finger, complete with menacing long nail. "You no wan' me kick you butt, eh?" Disdaining a response, she smiled protectively at Young, shot Hugh and me a second dirty look, turned and left the table, her waist-length black hair swishing freely in her seductive wake.

Hugh and I glanced at one another and broke into laughter. Young smiled in sympathy but looked lost, probably not understanding the pidgin English, vulgarities or threat. I elected to skip clarification. After a moment, Hugh and I calmed.

"Mr. Hugh, you are going home, yes?"

"That's right, Miss Lee, less than a week now." He smiled, pleased at the idea.

"Did you find my country, uh, pleasant?

I shrank in my seat. Hugh hadn't been happy with an assignment to Korea this late in his career, nor was he pleased to be separated from his wife and family for a year. Young's unsuspecting question would surely test his promise to "behave."

"Well, I didn't much get away from Yongsan, but yeah, Korea's okay." Nodding his head, he added, "I know you and Jason traveled a lot."

"Yes, we have been many places. He is the fun person to travel with." Young looked at me a moment, then added tenderly, "He is the good person to be with."

Hugh, not much given to tenderness, grunted. "Yeah, I guess. Say, did you know about the time—"

"Sooooo, Hugh, maybe we could talk about, uh, something else? ...Anything else."

"Oh, come on, don't be modest. I just wanted to share some of my favorite Jason stories. I'm not gonna be here much longer and, well, I just wanted Miss Lee to know the Jason I know."

"Yeah, well, she knows the Jason she knows, and she don't need to know any other Jason, if *you* know what I mean...*Hugh*."

"Nonsense. I'll bet you've been much too humble."

Before I could say more, Hugh began. I slumped.

"So, Miss Lee, did you know that Jason used to do repair work at the home for Korean old people, here in Itaewon?"

Young made no response, so Hugh continued as if she had said, "Gosh, I didn't know that, tell me more."

"Yeah, the Army has a program that tries to, you know, reach out to the locals. The Army coordinates and the soldiers volunteer and do the work. Keeps 'em busy and builds good will all at once. Anyway, the old people's home is pretty old itself, and not all that well built to begin with, and in constant need of somethin' or other. So, there was Jason. Signed up to help. Worked on the weekend. Hauled supplies in the Rocket. Did a lot of good stuff over there."

Of the two, I didn't know if this story, or the Carried-Home-Too-Drunk-To-Walk lie was the more embarrassing. At least this one was true, and as a bonus involved neither too much alcohol nor fallen women.

"Yes, I know of this; Miss Pak said this kind of thing."

"Oh, really?" I blurted. "I didn't know she knew anything about it. What else did Miss Pak say?"

"Only good things about you and Mr. Hugh. She said some of the Americans are not so courtesy. But you are always funny and kind, giving the extra money. A tax, yes?"

"Tip, princess."

"She said you never asked her to go anywhere or do anything with her—uh, how do you say, 'have the sex,' yes?"

I cringed. "Christ, Young, keep it down, will ya?"

Hugh laughed—surprised, I imagined, at Young's direct manner.

"She said you touched her sometimes...."

My chin dropped to my chest. I thought, *Oh Lord, here it comes.*

"...But only in an accident way, or when it was the dancing, or somehow acceptable for Miss Pak. She liked this about you."

I wasn't exactly sure if this generally positive description of my Hostess-groping, relayed by the woman I wanted to impress and marry, was good or bad. Surely, it was more of a problem than not. I pulled at my shirt collar as if suddenly attacked by oppressive heat. There was general quiet around the table.

"Well." I cleared my throat and reached for the remainder of my beer. "Miss Pak is certainly free with information about her guests," I complained testily.

"Yes. But Jason, we spoke also of Miss Pak. She, too, has had the difficult life."

"Yeah? Who ain't?" asked Hugh rhetorically, a trace of bitterness in his voice.

"Miss Pak is probably not the unusual story for the woman in her job. She was in love with the American soldier. He said the same to her. There would be the marriage. Of course, this did not happen. Of course, Miss Pak was left with the pregnant. This is an old and too common history, I think."

This was also news to Hugh and me. Spiderwoman had never mentioned an American boyfriend, lover, fiancé, or child of any variety. This information, of course, begged an obvious question. A second Amerasian child's life sat before us. I was not in the least curious to learn its fate. Christ, why had Young even mentioned this? Direct manner is one thing, poor judgment quite another.

I glanced none too casually about, hoping to spot God lounging somewhere in The Statue. Surely, His rescue skills were the equal of Spiderwoman's. Certainly, He could manage a small miracle and help change the subject. However, as has been my sad and frequent experience, God was nowhere to be found, apparently busy with other miracles in other places.

Unlike me, Hugh had no abortion baggage, no constant, faithful, apparent lifetime demon chewing contentedly on his heart. Unaware of "our situation," he didn't let the obvious evaporate, but rather asked the logical follow-up.

"Did she, uh, have the baby?"

Young lowered her head, simultaneously stretching her neck laterally in a kind of nervous release.

"Yes."

"Well, she didn't have to," Hugh volunteered bluntly.

Silence.

Hugh sipped his beer, simultaneously scanning the table. "Well, she didn't," he said defensively. "It's 1979, there are ways to solve these kinds of problems that are better for everyone."

Still, more silence.

Apparently, he felt the need to further justify his position. "Look, you can't tell me that an illegitimate Amerasian baby, abandoned by its father, a baby that won't be accepted in this culture and will never get a chance in the other, is better off struggling though a lifetime of bias and poverty—and that's what it will be, make no mistake—than, well…than not. The choice to have that baby dooms it and Spiderwoman…and you both know it."

Silence.

I studied my worn and scratched beer glass as if it were a valuable antique I planned to purchase, should it pass my detailed examination.

Finally Young said, "These points are correct, Mr. Hugh. I am sorry this is so, but you are correct in a technology way. But men and woman who play near this fire do not think of technology. They think only of the fire's pleasing heat. But someday…someday they learn the difference between heat and burning. These people—these, uh, players—they hold the dragon's tail; they know this, they understand, but they do not say this. They are foolish and think Fate will pass them, or—or not notice, or have, uh, how do you say? The mercy, yes?"

Young paused momentarily, looking past Hugh, seeing perhaps her personal demon.

"I know Fate very well. It is the bright flame and cold fire. It never warms, but always burns. Fate never passes silently. Fate never sleeps. Fate never forgives. And the center thing? The most important thing? Fate has no heart. Did Miss

Pak choose poorly, Mr. Hugh?" Young shook her head regretfully. "Perhaps...."
Her voice trailed off and she sagged a bit.

I was about to try some soothing non-sequitur, but Young hadn't yet finished. Looking at the tabletop, she continued, almost in a soliloquy.

"Perhaps, Mr. Hugh, perhaps Miss Pak did not have the gift of choice. If this
is so, then her decision is not good or bad, but only what she could do. Perhaps
she could only follow her path. Is it that this is true for us all, yes? We only follow what is set out? We think we have choice. We appear to choose. But really,
we have no choice. This, I think, is so. Living is like a play that is funny, but in
a dark, mean way. Hiding in the crowd, Fate watches the actors. Fate knows the
next scene, the next words, the next action. The actors smile, but never laugh.
Fate laughs, but never smiles."

# Forty-Four

The Rocket rested quietly at the base of Young's hill. The large American car was, by now, a familiar part of the Mapo landscape and seldom drew second looks. The Yongsan-to-Mapo circuit had been completed so many times, it seemed the old green Mercury could make the trip without human intervention, like cows ambling to their night barn.

Inside the Rocket's darkness, Young and I sat silently. Discomfort and indecision washed around me, edging higher, an incoming tide. I had begged us out of The Statue early, ten-thirty or so, shortly after Young's Fate comments. We'd made our way to the Rocket and then to Mapo with minimal conversation. Despite her reticence, I sensed she wasn't angry. Rather, she seemed to be synthesizing her experience, digesting what she'd learned.

And what, exactly, had she learned? She'd discovered I was a "Hostess groper." She knew I was given to public displays of idiocy, so my stripper routine wasn't a real surprise, more like reinforcement. She'd also learned about Spiderwoman and peeked first-hand at a class of women she surely knew existed, but with whom she'd never interacted. She'd seen and experienced The Statue and been exposed to a wide variety of mostly drunk GI's. She'd finally met Hugh, who'd unknowingly escorted her to a seat adjacent to our personal tragedy. This collage of events embodied virtually all my fishing-day fears.

I was tired, stressed, and could smell stale beer seeping from beneath my jacket. I rubbed my forehead. Beer sticky, butter slick. I passed a hand through my hair; clumped together, bound by dried beer. I wanted an aspirin, shower, sleep, and for God to write a letter of absolution, exonerating me for the previous four hours' behavior. However, having previously failed to rescue me by performing the simple miracle of changing the subject, I imagined a full-blown letter was well beyond God's interest, and probably capabilities.

With only myself to depend on, I closed my eyes and tried to concentrate. I wanted to move us, to lift us out of this uncomfortable, unhealthily quiet and foggy valley; but I simply couldn't construct a plan. I became increasingly frustrated and unaccountably, illogically angry with everyone and everything. This experiment, this episode, this quasi-disaster had the ring of a dubious daily-double: a bad idea, poorly done. Intuition warned that Young and I had been wounded.

"This Statue club is the sad place. Why did you go there?"

"Well, Young, it's not sad if you're not looking for sadness," I snapped. "If you go to hear music, and drink, and touch women and be touched, and talk to your friends, and tease the Hostesses, then...then it's not so sad."

Young looked at me, expressionless, and in the fashion common to her and familiar to me, did not immediately respond. She seemed to consider and mull my comments. "Yes, I suppose this is correct. Still, something there is heavy and wrong."

"Yeah? Well, I guess I'm just not a very smart guy. I don't see the 'heavy and wrong' things quite so clearly as some. Maybe I'm part of the weight and, uh, 'wrongs.'"

"Well, I suppose this is possible. But I see this was the poor question." Young rubbed her eyes, then looked away, squinting through the Rocket's semi-clean side window. "Still, angry or not, The Statue is not the happy place."

"Again, Young, it all depends on how you look at it. It never seemed sad to me, still doesn't...much. And I'm not angry, by the way."

"Yes, well...The Statue is supposed to hide its nature from the Americans. Miss Pak said she is never to speak of problems, only the light and happy things. Also, you see, or maybe do not see, things from a different perceptive. Perhaps this is the Eastern-western vision question? They are different, yes?" She reached through the darkness and placed her hand lightly on my knee. A peace gesture.

I smiled despite my frustration and irritability. "Perspective, princess. Different perspective. Uh, yeah, I hope the answer's that simple. I just never noticed."

I stopped and thought a moment, and again became unaccountably angry. I wasn't smart enough, tuned-in enough to accept Young's proffered peace.

"No, it's more than perspective. It's not a sad place, not to me, not to the other GI's. Spiderwoman and the others always make you feel welcome. They always laugh and smile; the music's quiet; the food's good; my friends are there, laughing and joking. I can't be responsible for how the Hostesses feel, for what life's brought them, or for what they cover up. If it weren't for The Statue, they probably wouldn't have a job at all, huh? Or be prostitutes. To me, I just never saw a sad aspect there, and you know what? I don't want to see it. It's just more goddamn problems I can neither control nor influence. They don't specifically affect me, and I just get bogged down and feel bad if I try to solve 'em when there are no solutions; certainly, none I can put in place. Christ. I got my own problems. The Statue is a refuge. I didn't ask for 'em to open it up. I didn't tell 'em to cater to Americans. I didn't ask to come to Korea, but I'm here and there's nothing to be done about it…except wait for June."

In the intervening silence, I replayed my outburst and immediately regretted it. But I was angry, and too youthfully stubborn to apologize.

"You are sorry to be in Korea?" Young's manner was direct as usual, but uncharacteristically cold.

Shit! How'd I maneuvered myself into this mess? How'd I gotten from The Statue to regret about being in Korea? Goddamn it! "Look, Young, I never said that. I just said—"

"You are sorry to be in Korea?"

"Well, I'm trying to answer, for Christ's sake!" I snapped. "Give me a chance, will you? This isn't a trial."

"No, not the trial. But it is the simple question, Jason. Not so many chances are necessary. I think yes or no is an acceptable, easy answer, yes?"

I'd never seen Young sarcastically angry. Instinct told me this was dangerous. I needed to regain my composure. The next few minutes, or for that matter, next few words could do real damage. This had gotten completely out of hand. I breathed deeply and tried again.

"Princess, if I hadn't come to Korea, we'd never have met. How could that be good? You're the most important thing in my life, the most important person in my life. Of course, I'm glad I came to Korea."

Young shook her head in silent understanding, but her manner was aloof.

"It is late. I must go."

"Princess, don't go. Not angry. You're never angry. This is all wrong, and frightening. I'm sorry if I hurt you. I didn't mean to. Tell me it'll be okay."

Young sagged; the formal, detached air about her dissipated.

"Jason, I cannot tell you this kind of thing. You know very well we have the very big and dangerous relation." She paused. "I can tell you I love you. But 'okay'? This I cannot say."

Rubbing her face with both hands in a gesture of weary, resigned exasperation, she said, "We are so…lost. I am not certain where we are, or where we go. We seem frozen. We cannot move to the front, uh, forward? We cannot move back. We move only in the same small place. It is like a, uh, riddle, yes? How can two things be good and bad at once? To love you, it is the most wonderful, and the most worst thing."

Young slumped in the seat, rested her head on the seat back, and closed her eyes. After a moment she asked, "Do you know the story *A Tale of Two Cities*, by the English man, Dickinson?"

"Dickens. Yeah, I know it."

"Um, Dickens. The beginning. It is like us, 'the best of times, the worst of times.' Tonight was not our best time. I hope it is our worst time…but think it is not."

"I don't know, princess. I just don't want you to be angry with me," I said, still upset and nervous. "The Statue's not worth that. The Statue's only a place, not an event, not a morality play, uh, not a moral lesson. It's a bar, for Christ's sake."

"The Statue is…what it is. For you, a bar. For Miss Pak, a job. For me, sadness. We all see it in our own way. Perhaps each view is correct. But no matter, I shall not again go there. It was an idea of fun that in some way did not work."

Young sat up, gathering herself to leave. Then, apparently sensing the need to freshen our bond, she paused, leaned forward and kissed me lightly. She placed her hand against my cheek, rested her forehead against mine, and moving still closer, embraced me.

We held one another tenderly. I began to calm. Through the darkness, I felt her soothing compassion, like an exotic lotion, seep coolly into my emotional crevices, sealing the cracks, healing the wounds.

After some time, she released me, sighed, opened the door, and stepped to the sidewalk. Closing the door, she stooped and leaned against the window's frame, much like that sunny day in downtown Seoul after returning from KAL. This time, however, her arms were empty; she wore no smile; there would be no rescue. For a moment, she looked at me quietly, blankly, then smiled, but from only one corner of her mouth.

I looked away, down the sleeping, dimly lit Mapo street, composing my goodbye, constructing our next meeting time and place. I turned back to the window; it was dark and empty.

Young was gone.

# Forty-Five

The animated women were still three blocks distant, hurrying along the side-walk that paralleled Kimpo's seemingly endless chain-link fence. Backlit by the faintly pinkish halogen ramp and hangar lights, the women were initially a single dark splotch. As the group moved quickly toward me, six individual silhou-ettes materialized. They would be dressed alike, and despite the darkness and distance, I knew the detail of their clothing: navy blue, knee-length pleated skirts, a matching waist-length jacket with silver wings above a black name tag, a white cotton blouse, and black, low-heeled shoes; the flight attendant uniforms of Korean Airlines.

The group reached a street intersection and divided, going different directions, waving to one another, some giving a kind of semi-bow, head and upper body bent slightly forward. Through the mid-May darkness I heard their brightly cheerful, rhythmic Korean language farewells. Another block, another inter-section, a last division, more goodbyes.

One woman, somewhat taller, almost lanky, and in a subtle, indefinable way more graceful than the others, walked on alone toward, and finally to, a shabby, green, American car. Looking about with apparent indifference, the woman stopped, opened the car's rear door, and without watching, casually tossed a blue and white KAL kit bag onto the back seat. She seemed to know where and how it would come to rest, weeks of repetition and routine breeding this comfortable familiarity.

A closed door, two steps, and quickly, she was beside me. She leaned to me, placed her left hand lightly on my right shoulder and kissed my cheek. A warm and pleasant sensation. She sat back about a foot or so, still close; then, tilting her head as if about to ask a question, instead whispered, "Hello."

I smiled, winked, patted her knee, and said quietly, "Hi, princess."

Despite our trials, we were bonding. Our difficulties and pleasantries were agents of change, drawing us closer, winding the twine tightly, narrowing our cultural gap and personal differences to a thin, shallow fissure.

"Well, you're awfully brave tonight. Public kissing?"

"Actually, no. It is dark. No one could see. And you know very well my colleagues do not walk in this direction."

"And lucky for you. Imagine the scandal. Lee Kwang Young, the perfect KAL employee, publicly linked to an American barbarian."

She smiled, and with feigned shock, hand over her heart said, "Yes, imagine. But if I saw them? Then I would call *Saram sallyo! Saram Sallyo!* 'Help, Help! Captured by the foreign devil!'"

"What? Just like that? You'd turn me in so quickly? You no longer find me attractive?" I grinned wolfishly and placed my hand on her thigh. "I find you attractive."

"No, you are not attractive," she teased. "Also, the nice Korean girls? They do not visit with the American Army barbarians. I am the nice Korean girl, so, it must be I am here by the capture."

"Yes, you are nice," I whispered, leaning closer.

"Exactly so." Taking my hand, she deliberately removed it from her mid-thigh and placed it on the steering wheel. Looking toward me with a pleased but embarrassed smile, she asked, "Have you forgotten the directions to Mapo?" Her hand waved in the darkness, a combined gesture of get-back -behind-the-wheel-and-let's-go.

"All right, all right." Duly chastised, I reluctantly started the engine, switched on the headlights, accelerated the Rocket—Korean driver fashion—into the always maniacal traffic, and began to follow our familiar route from Kimpo to the base of Young's Mapo hill.

"So, how was your visit to Tokyo?"

She stretched, arms full length before her, fingers locked, and said through an embarrassed yawn, "Fine." She shook her head quickly, as if tossing off weariness. "The airport at Narita is new and modern, but so far distant from Tokyo." Emphasis on "so far." "In Western miles, about forty, I think. The trip from downtown to the airport is longer than the flight from Narita to Kimpo, and if you are riding the taxi? More expensive!"

"Did you have to take a taxi?"

"Nearly. The KAL crew bus was late in the traffic, so we had to share a JAL bus with the Japanese flight crew."

"Were the Japanese flight attendants courteous to you?" I asked, baiting her, knowing the answer, but mischievously wanting to get a rise from the always composed Young.

She glanced at me, the oncoming headlights partially illuminating the irritation on her face. "Of course not. They always look the other way and play high-nose when you ask a question about where is something, or how to do anything, like the flight-crew procedure for Narita Customs. So, now, we decided to not ask them. Also, if they ask us a question about Kimpo, then we will give them the wrong information."

I chuckled at the latest escalation in the war between the two airlines' flight attendants. Young's smile was devilish. I could see there was more, and clearly, she wanted me to ask. I gladly played along.

"There's more?"

With a large grin, she smoothed a pleat in her skirt and said proudly, "Well. At Narita, we were getting out of the bus, yes? Our suitcase and baggage are in a line on the sidewalk. When I went to get my bag? My foot pushes over the JAL crew case. The wind runs the papers across the parking lot. I played it was the accident, saying: 'Oh, I'm so sorry.' 'Oh, how clumsy.' 'Oh, I am a stupid cow.' 'My mistake.' 'Please, forgive me.' Bowing and humble. Like the ignorant Korean country girl. My colleagues thought this was very good."

I had no trouble believing this; Young could be impish, and if provoked, mischievous, to the detriment of her victim.

"God, Young, is that polite?" I smiled, picturing the arrogant Japanese running helter-skelter about a wind-blown parking lot, trying to retrieve their diplomatic and flight crew paperwork.

"No, of course it is not polite, but they are the Japanese, so, they deserve this kind of activity."

"Young, Young, Young," I repeated ruefully, shaking my head, "remind me never to get on your bad side."

"Don't worry," she laughed and waved her hand dismissively. "There is no empty place on my bad side, too many Japanese there now."

I turned the Rocket left off the main east-west road paralleling the Han River and onto the Songsan bridge, which led from southern Seoul, across the Han, and directly to Mapo.

"Jason, I have news and an idea."

"Yeah? What 'cha got, pal?"

"Friday, my assignment will be to Cheju-do. My crew will stay overnight and return on Saturday. Would you like to make this trip? You could see me work on an actual fight. After all, you know the English phrases as well as I."

"Better," I mumbled.

Young missed my exact words, but was sufficiently convinced of an insult that I was pinched on the shoulder, a particularly favorite form of punishment. However, she didn't break her chain of thought or discourse to berate, but simply continued.

"Afterward, we could meet in secret and play tourist on the island."

"Sure, I'd love to. Sounds like fun," I said, rubbing my upper arm. Then, more warily, I added, "But isn't it kind of dangerous?"

"Um, a little. Of course, I would play like I did not know you on the airplane, or at the airport, or at the hotel." She looked at me in that sweetly serious way of hers and lectured, "And you must do the same. No games, it would not be the funny."

I considered her observation a moment and surfaced a question that had recently begun to trouble me. "Young, what do you suppose KAL would do if they knew about us?"

She rubbed her forehead. "Well…I do not know. There is no, uh, law prohibit this kind of thing in the contract of course, but still…you know very well our culture. They would, I think, find some reason to release me."

"Naturally, princess, I want to go, but aren't you taking a big chance with this trip?"

"Yes, well, I take the big chance with you every day." She looked past me into the late evening darkness, somber and somewhat troubled. "Jason, dear, I cannot explain us. We have so many of the problems, you know this very well. I do not understand how we could even begin. Or how we continue. Or how we will end. But even with these things, I cannot let you go." She shook her head and looked down. "This is my weak character. This is Fate."

Though melancholy wasn't a large part of her nature, nor obvious to those who didn't know her well, I'd come to discover this unique joyful-sorrow lived quietly, but constantly, in her heart. I shared and understood the emotion. We were happy to have a clear vision of life's potentials, but saddened to understand they were inevitably flawed, little more than false promises. Perhaps this odd view of the world was one of the elements that bound us so tightly. Perhaps it was the key element, strong enough for us to ignore race, culture, and practicalities.

"I am afraid for us. I try not to think of the future, but…still, it is there, will always be there." She breathed deeply, looked up, and closing the door on unwanted truths, added, "Even so, Fate will solve this problem." With this pronouncement, she dismissed the issue, sweeping it under our emotional carpet, hidden, to be dealt with subsequently, sometime, some way, somehow, apparently by the unknown and uncontrollable forces of Fate. "But for now, you must make the promise. No games."

Comfortably deferring to her leadership, I abandoned my aviator tendency to analyze and plan for all possible nooks and crannies of all possible contingencies, and returned to the proposed Cheju-do trip.

"Sure. Agreed. I understand. I'll be good, really. No games. Will we stay at the same place?"

"I think so, yes. KAL has the new resort hotel in Cheju city. We will stay there. You can telephone KAL and get a ticket and a room at one time. Mine is already uh...scheduled, as part of the crew."

"You've got this all figured out," I said, somewhat surprised.

"This is not so difficult." Young laughed in the bemused way she so often affected when dealing with me about almost anything. She had become a master at managing me. This wasn't manipulation, but loving compensation. She understood my weaknesses and foibles. She steered us easily around these potholes, nudging, suggesting, hinting, anticipating, and waiting for me to catch on and up. She did these things so well, I normally didn't recognize her magic at work. In this matter of the reservation, knowing I couldn't remember any administrative detail more than two minutes, she handed me a scrap of paper and recited my instructions.

"This is the KAL reservation telephone number. They speak English. The flight is number 1702. The day is next Friday. The time is eight a.m. I wrote this," she explained patiently, "so even you cannot forget or make the mistake." Her growing smile was undiminished by the darkness. "You can do this, yes?"

I, again captive to her charm, mimicked, "I can do this, yes."

# Forty-Six

The fully loaded jetliner accelerated down the Kimpo runway, gathering momentum, pointed directly into the still rising sun. Initially, I felt a bumping sensation which increased with aircraft speed as we rolled over the concrete runway's asphalt expansion joints. At about seventy miles per hour, the wings started to produce lift and the 727 began to get "light on the gear." After a moment, the nose wheel lifted off, then the mains. The bumping sensation disappeared. The pilot applied aft pressure to the flight controls. The nose pitched up about fifteen degrees above the horizon. There was a combined whir and hum of electric motors and hydraulic pumps, followed by a reassuring "thump" as the landing gear was tucked firmly away in the fuselage. KAL Flight 1702 was airborne, destination—Cheju-do.

Young was the flight crew's junior attendant and made only one announcement. From our study time together, I was familiar with all the standard KAL instructions and most of the cabin procedures. I listened closely to her recitation about snack service. It was without error. I was very proud.

Once we reached altitude, Young and another attendant busied themselves with the service cart, rolling it down the aisle, asking passenger drink preference, then serving the beverage of choice along with a small sweet roll and a napkin prominently emblazoned with the KAL logo. The Seoul to Cheju-do en route time was about seventy minutes. The plane was full. The cabin crew worked quickly.

As planned, Young ignored me. Though she passed by my aisle seat several times, she made no acknowledging expression or gesture. There was no "inadvertent" small stagger, her hip brushing lightly against my shoulder. I was just another passenger. She was professionally cool and detached. It was discomforting to know she could varnish over and seal out the warmth between us with such seeming indifference. Even though this had all been arranged in advance, it was surprisingly hurtful.

Reflecting, I reclined my seat and thought that given slightly different circumstances, I could be on this flight and actually not know her at all. What if

I'd not gone into Seoul that day? I rarely did. What if the light hadn't changed to red, stopping me and bringing the little jewelry shop to my attention? What if I'd not ventured inside? I nearly didn't. What if I'd not challenged her to read, or left my business card? What if she'd been offended by my Western manner, hadn't telephoned, or had been disappointed by our Heavenly Gate meeting and simply vanished?

If I wanted to get ridiculous, I could extrapolate this "what if" thinking exponentially to the nth degree. What if her parents, or mine, had never met, or I'd never joined the Army? What if there had been no Korean War, or if America had shunned the UN's call to defend Korea? Certainly, then, we'd have never met.

It was amazing. There were literally years filled with millions of coincidences and circumstances, some tiny, others geo-political and world shaping that directly, specifically affected us. The absence of just one event, any event, would have derailed us. Rather, it certainly seemed we'd long been on a predetermined, intersecting course.

But how wide was the path? How deep? How long? How enduring the intersection? Would we simply pass through one another on our way to something or someone else? Were we the end, or simply another coincidence or circumstance in an as yet undisclosed grand plan? Why had we been tossed together? What was our destiny? Our fate? What would evaporate? What would remain? What would it mean?

I sighed and shook my head. This was much too philosophical, too metaphysical, too intellectual. Young would enjoy this obtuse reasoning. She could spend hours running about in the abstract, examining the various permutations and combinations as her Asian mind patiently constructed, thought through, and deconstructed a million what-ifs. But things like this, things with no clear, definable answers just gave me a headache.

To ease the metaphoric pain, I envisioned Young next to me in bed—a circumstance in which she was generally somewhat more attentive and we normally didn't much worry about philosophy. I smiled wickedly at the image, then remembered my promise to "be good." If she saw the passenger in seat 8C with a no-apparent-reason goofy smile, she would know its origin. My infraction would be noted and subsequent punishment extracted. Quickly, I erased the picture and tried to appear serious. Best to busy myself in chores.

I cast about in my flight bag and picked up the Cheju-do guidebook Young had given me. My assignment was to "find tourist things we could play." I opened the book and was immediately impressed. As recently as 1975, no less than *Newsweek* magazine named Cheju-do one of the world's top ten undiscovered and unspoiled tourist destinations. According to the book, *Newsweek* called

Cheju-do the "Island of the Gods." The article extolled the island's sports attractions such as hiking, fishing, golfing, horseback riding, hunting, and swimming. Newsweek also found much to praise about the friendly nature of the people, the abundant and tasty seafood, and the miles of unspoiled, white sandy beaches. The book indicated the *Asian Wall Street Journal* referred to Cheju-do as Bali. The Korean Tourist Bureau called it "Korea's Hawaii." This place was gonna be okay.

I scanned Cheju-do's geography and learned it was situated about one hundred miles south of the Korean mainland at the confluence of the East China and Yellow Seas. For most of the summer, the island is warmed by the Kuroshio Current and accompanying warm air masses that drift north from the Philippines. To be geologically correct, Cheju-do is, in fact, the top of the extinct Halla-San Volcano. The volcano rises sixty-four hundred feet above the surrounding sea and, surprisingly, is Korea's highest mountain. Halla-San's height, mixed with rising warm, moist, ocean air, produces a shrouding mist at the mountain's top, lending it an aura of mystery.

According to the book, the island's main industries were fishing and farming. On the tropic coast, oranges, pineapples and other citrus fruits grew readily. Staples grew inland. The facts and figures were beginning to run together when a man's voice stated flatly, "You must see the women divers of Cheju-do."

I turned to the Korean man seated next to me, a short fellow, about forty-five, and balding. He wore a white short-sleeved shirt, open at the neck, gray slacks, and large, black-rimmed glasses, through which he squinted and blinked. He looked like Asia's version of Mr. Peepers.

Apparently, I didn't smile or make an encouraging gesture, as the man introduced himself with deprecation and explanation.

"Forgive me, please. I am Mr. Che. I noticed your book, and since you are the foreigner, I thought perhaps this is your first trip to Cheju-do. I have been there many times and, well, just wanted to help." He began to turn away, back to his magazine.

Recovering my manners, I said in my best Young-taught Korean, "Thank you very much, Mr. Che. I appreciate your concern." Then, in English, and with a grin at my upcoming wit added, "You're right, I am a foreigner. And I've never been to Cheju-do."

Mr. Che looked at me with what I took to be new respect. He was clearly surprised by my faultless Korean. Of course, the two sentence phrase, and a few others similar to it, were the full extent of my Korean language skills. I thought fleetingly of Dragon Valley and the predicament my stock-phrases had engendered with the "ski-rental-man."

Thinking I should take the initiative to ensure English usage, I inquired with a winning smile, "What takes you to Cheju-do so frequently?"

Reflexively looking about as if to check for eavesdroppers, Mr. Che replied with a smile and lowered voice. "I work for KAL…Security Branch."

My smile was frozen in place; somewhat idiotically, I'm sure. Had Young and I been somehow "fingered" and the apparently random seating just a clever ruse to catch us "in the act"? Emotionally spinning, I almost missed Mr. Che's next comments.

"KAL employees get the free air ticket passes and room discounts at the hotel. So, I like to go when I can."

"Welllll, imagine that…KAL Security," I repeated dumbly, nodding my head, insipid grin still in place. If this guy was any kind of a detective, he'd have the cuffs on me in short order. In the last ten seconds, I imagined I'd demonstrated every incriminating characteristic a guilty man can exhibit.

Before Mr. Che could arrest me, a lightly accented voice from my right asked, "Pardon me, sir, would you like juice, a soft drink, or coffee?"

Had I not been strapped in, I know I would have jumped directly out of the seat. I turned quickly and gawked. It was, of course, Kwang Young, KAL employee. She stood directly adjacent to her personal American barbarian who, by coincidence, was chatting up the KAL detective charged with ferreting out all such illegal liaisons. Like Shakespeare's tragedies, the major characters were gathered in the same scene, a sure harbinger of impending disaster.

I almost moaned in response to Young's question, but managed the enlightened, "Uh, drink?"

Young, seldom flustered, and no doubt wanting to kick me, replied dispassionately, "Yes, sir, we have juice, soft drinks, or coffee." Knowing her acerbic wit, I was sure she would have preferred, "Yes, sir, drink. You know, liquid refreshment, generally taken by mouth to stave off death from, oh, dehydration, for example."

Still fishing for composure, I stammered, "Coffee?"

Young chose to accept my questioning response as an answer and poured me coffee. Then, though she clearly knew I was a cream and sugar guy, asked, "Cream or sugar, sir?"

The question was actually risky, as in my demented state I could have easily said, "You know I take both, Young." However, I sputtered, "Uh, yeah, thanks."

Young supplied these items, serviced the rest of my row and moved away, escaping toward the aft cabin.

Mr. Che turned in his seat to watch her walk away and winking at me, said, "Younger and more, uh, cuter every day, eh?" Then, offhandedly, he added, "Of course, she's more your age."

This had to be the bait. The vicious hook was surely resting inside the innocuous, universally male comments. However, I was slowly gathering my wits, and wouldn't bite. "Younger" every day, indeed. Cheap pun artist. Maybe he'd better stick to arresting people. Two could play this game. I stalled.

"Security Branch? What do you secure?" A poor attempt at gallows humor. I felt a light sweat-sheen at the back of my neck. God, give me the ski-rental-guy and our three stooges routine any day.

Mr. Che, however, was gracious and laughed politely. "Well, I don't really 'secure' anything, I work in the Security Branch Accounting Department, checking travel reports and claims for money, that sort of thing. Boring, really."

Only decorum prevented me from laughing out loud. Mr. Che never knew how close I came to kissing him. God love the little guy; he was a pencil-pushing, rear echelon-dwelling, no combat experienced, white sock-wearing, pocket protector-having, document reviewing, number crunching, green eye-shaded, back-office bureaucrat!

I eased back in my seat and smiled. Mr. Che was one hundred percent Mr. Peepers; zero percent Elliot Ness. At least for now, there'd be no illicit relationship arrests.

# Forty-Seven

The aircraft droned on, comfortable in its flight profile. The cabin was quiet, passengers satiated, flight attendants resting. Mr. Che proved a knowledgeable and friendly traveling companion. He regaled me with accounting debit and credit "war stories" I didn't understand, and tidbits about Cheju-do that were most informative. He was a ten-year KAL employee and used his free passes to visit the island about twice a year.

I specifically asked Mr. Che about the "diving women" he'd mentioned earlier. I'd never heard of them. Of course, a week earlier, I'd never heard of Cheju-do. He showed me a section about them in the guidebook, explaining they were called *Haenyo*, and for thousands of years, symbolic of the island. The women free-dive to the sea bottom for as long as four minutes, bringing to the surface plants and occasionally oysters, both of which are sold to restaurants. Through my dining experiences with Young, I'd learned seaweed, when dried to a brittle consistency, tastes very much like potato chips. The oysters are prized as aphrodisiacs.

The women dive year-round, despite winter water temperatures in the mid-thirties. Interestingly, *Haenyo* range from teenagers to grandmothers in their sixties. The book explained that the women dove in black, shiny wetsuits complete with hoods, fins and masks. However, this concession to dive-clothing technology was recent. For hundreds of years, *Haenyo* wore skimpy white diving shifts. Mr. Che said, somewhat disdainfully, that there was an old law that actually prohibited men from looking at the divers when dressed in their traditional white, revealing attire. I decided the *Haenyo* was a "tourist thing we could play" and turned the page corner down.

Mr. Che recommended other Cheju-do sites, and within fifteen minutes, my guidebook was dog-eared in multiple places. I'd compiled a list that was sure to impress Young. I would try to parley this into big points, explaining how diligently I had worked to construct such a complete and comprehensive inventory of Cheju-do tourist sites. I'd probably—no, definitely—not give the knowledgeable Mr. Che any credit. He'd understand.

After some general pleasantries, Mr. Che revealed he was a lifelong bachelor, but had plans to retain a matchmaking or marriage company.

"This is normally done by the parents, but I am well past this age. So, I must do this myself," he said, looking at the seat back in front of him.

"We don't have arranged marriages in the States."

"Well, this is not arranged. It is, uh…purchased."

It seemed an odd distinction, but I didn't pursue the seemingly fine language point.

Surprising me, Mr. Che inquired pointedly, "Do you have the Korean girl-friend?"

It was an interesting question. I could play it safe and lie, or I could flirt with danger a bit and talk about the pre-KAL Young. I felt adventurous.

"Well…."

As I was about to describe Young, I saw her in the forward cabin. I remembered our discussion of KAL cultural prejudices and my resultant promise. I decided cheap thrills were not worth putting her in jeopardy, even a little. Mr. Che, though very friendly and apparently very Western, was after all, a KAL employee. I shifted gears and changed lanes.

"Well, no. No Korean girlfriend. No girlfriend of any kind."

"Then, you should consider this. The Korean woman is very humble, obedient, and trained to please the husbands. As I am older, I think I make the mistake not getting one before."

I thought perhaps it was again the language barrier, but he made it sound somehow brutal.

Mr. Che took out a small notepad and an address book from his traveling case. He tore out a page from the notepad. Consulting the small book, he wrote a phone number on the paper and handed it to me.

"This is the marriage arrangement company. They can find the suitable woman for every kind of man. You should try this."

"But Mr. Che, I don't want to get married."

"Who say marry? You do not have to marry the girl. You can send back if she does not please you. So, just try; if not so good, or if you don't really want to begin, no difference. Send back. This is not the problem."

I smiled, a mixture of embarrassment and politeness, and thanked Mr. Che for his "thoughtfulness." Clearly, some Korean men did not hold their women in much esteem, viewing them as humble and obedient commodities, existing for pleasure and service. The marriage company reduced romance to something akin to shopping for a new lounge chair. Try it. Don't like it? Bring it back. It seemed Mr. Che's apparently harmless language distinction between "arranged" and "purchased" wasn't a charming disconnect at all.

Fingering Mr. Che's note, I leaned back in my seat and tried to imagine Young "obedient and humble." The image nearly made me laugh aloud. Young could be described in many, many ways; those two adjectives, however, would never fit. Mr. Che made me realize that I treated her the way most Asian men would not. I wondered if her interest in me was fueled by my obvious Western deference to, and open affection for her. If so, was that bad? Was I just a simple and unique curiosity? Before I could reach a conclusion, Mr. Che's voice brought me back aboard KAL 1702.

"This company? They have some woman who can speak English," he observed reassuringly.

Intrigued, I asked, "Really? Where do they, uh, get these women?"

Mr. Che shrugged. "Mostly from the country farms where girls are worthless. Some are from the fishing village where they are almost worthless; others from the city, with the poor family." After a short pause, he added knowledgeably, "It is usually the city girls with the English. They bring the most money for the family."

"You mean this marriage company buys these women from their families and matches them with men? For a price? Sells them?" I tried to not sound unsophisticated, flabbergasted, or Western. "Do the women have…have right of refusal?" I stammered, unsuccessfully hiding my surprise.

"Yes, the company sell them. They buy them. It is profitable: a low purchase price, a high sell price. This is the good business."

Spoken from the soul of an accountant.

"Refusal? Uh, this word means no? You mean the woman can say no? Uh, no sale?"

I nodded.

Mr. Che's head rolled back against the seat and he laughed loudly.

"No. No 'refusal,'" he said derisively. "They are only the woman. If there is not having this service, then what could they do?"

What could they do indeed? Korean society was male dominated and had been for hundreds, probably thousands of years. Korean women worked in labor trades, or jobs nobody wanted, or stayed at home, or became…prostitutes, I supposed. Lord knows I'd seen plenty of prostitutes in Itaewon.

I recalled my earlier assessment of Mr. Che: "apparently very Western." I was glad I'd rethought my veiled disclosure about Young. While most Korean women were functionally in the Middle Ages, or worse, Young was educated, independent, and working in a prestigious job. I was again struck by the fortunate confluence of circumstance that afforded her the opportunity to seek and secure her KAL position; and more darkly, how quickly it could all be lost.

We'd have to be especially careful. What had Young said only last week? *"You know my culture, they would find some reason to release me.*" Should she lose her job, Young wouldn't, of course, be sold into bondage, but certainly, she'd never again be in a position to so dramatically frame her life's future for success. She was nearly across the threshold, only a few more steps. I vowed to help her through success's doorway, no matter the cost.

Mr. Che reclined his seat, catching my attention. I shook my head imperceptibly as his words worked again through my mind: *"What could they do? They are only women."* Mr. Che was a product of his culture, and to the extent cultural bias mitigates the "soft crimes" of intolerance and prejudice, technically innocent. But on a larger scale, as a citizen of the world he, as do we all, carried the joyous burden of basic humanity, whose responsibilities and consequences can never be abdicated, ignored, or excused.

I was not qualified, or indeed fit, to act as either jury or judge, but it seemed abundantly clear that Mr. Che was neither the righteous Elliot Ness nor the hapless Mr. Peepers, but rather, an antebellum plantation owner—trading in and treading on the human spirit.

# Forty-Eight

We were winded after the first mile. Halla-San, so calm, peaceful, and majestic from the comfort of our hotel, was proving an implacable topographical match for our aerobic fitness. The guidebook described Halla-San's Orimok hiking trail as wide, well marked, and the shortest route to the top. Unfortunately, the book didn't indicate it was also the steepest route to the top.

We started well enough. After check in, we met in the prearranged spot, a small tea house about two blocks from the hotel. Young reviewed the list of guidebook spots I'd catalogued; was, as I'd hoped, impressed, and picked two to visit. Feeling athletic and adventurous, we rented bikes, and encountered no difficulty in locating or reaching our first destination, Dragon Head Rock, in the Cheju city harbor a mile or so north of our KAL hotel.

Unlike Dragon Valley, where skis were my master, biking and I had a long and happy history, so Young and I were on equal skill terms. Nevertheless, blessed with coordination and stamina, and tirelessly competitive, Young pedaled ahead, proudly reaching the waterfront area first. She was not loath to point out our arrival sequence.

The guidebook explained that, in antiquity, a young, willful dragon, disobeying its parents, descended from Halla-San's sacred fire. Upon reaching the ocean, the dragon stepped into the chilling water and was turned immediately to stone, forever frozen in place. After a few minutes of gawking at a black rock formation that, from a distance, looked vaguely like a dragon's head with a flared mane—if indeed dragons have manes—we got back on our bikes and, leaving the willful beast to its fate, pedaled away from the harbor and toward the city limits.

We biked south from Cheju city, toward Halla-San mountain and our second destination, translated as "White Deer Lake," in the volcano's crater. The sun was warm on our shoulders, the morning's gray ocean fog having quietly yielded to a high blue sky. The city's buildings and traffic fell quickly behind us and soon we were alone, side by side, on a flat country road that wound through a narrowing, deepening valley.

Here, the island was almost alpine. Meadows, lightly dusted with bright yellow flowers, spread from the roadside to the base of encroaching hills. As we biked, the hills moved still closer to the roadway, eventually becoming mountains with a clear tree-line demarcation between the lower greenery and the higher, rock-strewn, barren tops. The road's pitch increased slightly, and we exerted more effort to sustain the same cycling speed. Finally, we reached the Orimok trailhead on Halla-San's northwest slope. We secured our bikes near a sign that Young said read "White Deer Lake, 10 Kilometers" and began our hike up the mountain.

At the four kilometer mark, we came upon a rough-hewn log bench in a small clearing. We gladly sat down to rest. Clearly, our hike to the lake wasn't going to be as simple as we'd thought. In a complicating adjunct, it was now mid-afternoon; to reach the top and descend again before dark would be a questionable achievement.

We were discussing our options given the horizontal and vertical distance, our fitness, and the time constraints when we heard a bell, or more accurately, several bells. Young raised her head quickly, eyes wide, turned to look up the trail and simultaneously placed her hand on my arm in a gesture for silence.

"Do you hear this?" she asked, still looking up the mountain.

"Uh, yeah. Sounds like bells, lot of little ones," I wheezed, rubbing my calves, more fatigued and sore than I wanted to admit. "You know, Young, if you're too tired to make the climb, it's okay, I'll understand."

She ignored the insult, raised her hand to silence me, and tilted her head, listening to the bells. They became louder as whatever they were, or it was, approached from the pathway—opposite our direction of travel, now very close.

Through the tree line about twenty feet distant materialized what appeared to be a woman, strangely dressed, even for Korea. She wore flowing, cream-colored robes of utilitarian cotton. Around her neck were draped four colored sashes, white, green, red and black. Each sash was marked with oddly-shaped symbols. About her waist was a hemp belt. A cloth pouch hung from her left side, a leather pouch from her right. Interestingly, small bells were sewn everywhere across her garment: sleeves, bosom, skirt, everywhere. She couldn't move without ringing. A small, square black hat was seated squarely on what appeared to be her completely shaved head.

To my surprise, Young rose, bowed relatively deeply, and spoke deferentially in Korean. The strangely attired woman stopped, raised her right hand palm outward, and responded to what I gathered was Young's greeting. Young and the woman conversed for perhaps another two minutes. During this time, I was ignored, at least in gesture, and probably in word as well. Eventually there was a pause.

"Young, what's going on? Who is this, uh, person? Is there a problem?"

Softly distracted and without forethought, Young placed the fingertips of her left hand lightly on my chest in that ancient, subliminal way bonded lovers do.

"I am sorry. No, no problem. Jason, this is a kind of priest. She is correctly called a *Mudang*, or, only here on Cheju-do, a *Shimbang*."

"What religion?" I asked, taking in her odd dress and hiding my skepticism as best I could.

"This is the Shaman religion."

"Never heard of it," I said flatly.

"This religion is the oldest in my country, but is now not so…popular as in old times. It was born here, on Cheju-do. Halla-San is where the gods live and, to the Shaman people, a holy place. There are many temples on this mountain."

Seeing I wasn't impressed, Young apparently decided more background would be beneficial.

"Shaman is not the standard Western religion, you know. This religion is very old, perhaps one thousand years before Christ. It is a religion that believes in many gods, not just one. It also believes that every living thing has a spirit. The priests do, uh, how do you say, ceremonies, yes? They speak with the spirit world. The ceremonies do many things. They can change events here, in this world. Help the sick, bring better rice and farming, make the fishing improve, see and report what will happen in the future."

"'See and report what will happen,'" I repeated with sarcastic incredulity. I rolled my eyes and shook my head.

With a trace of irritation, Young responded. "Do not all religions speak with spirits in some way? Do not all religions try to change, control, or know the future? This is no different. Do not be so quick to, uh, dispose of this religion because you do not know it…and it is Eastern."

"Uh, I think you mean dismiss."

Young normally accepted any and all grammar help gracefully, but she answered with the edge still on her voice.

"Yes, dismiss is exactly what I mean. But no matter if it is dispose or dismiss, it is the same idea. You know this very well."

"Okay, okay, princess. I'm sorry; don't be upset. I didn't mean to slur anyone's religion. It just seems, well, different, that's all."

Young didn't respond. Careful not to offend, I cast about for a way to ask if she seriously believed in what sounded to me like the religious counterpart of "snake-oil" medicine at best, or voodoo at worst.

"Uh, I didn't know you were interested in, what did ya call it…? Shaman, Shamanism?"

"Well, I am primarily the Buddhist, as you know, but perhaps the Buddhist does not know all the correct answers. It is not the problem to believe in more than one kind of thing."

I nodded my head in understanding, even though I didn't. I'd found Asians generally, and Young specifically, rarely had concrete philosophical positions. Young's dual-religion posture was typically amorphous and classically Asian. She could comfortably believe in a primary religion of type X, and a secondary religion of type Y. In the event type X was short on some critical account, type Y could compensate. If X and Y were at odds on a given issue, Asians simply ignored the disconnect, or more preferably, more elegantly, rationalized it, explaining there was no conflict, only a "misunderstanding" or "misinterpretation" of key points, and further meditation would bridge the apparent rift.

To the complex and intricate Eastern mind, there was no inconsistency in this X does and does not equal Y logic. Quite the contrary, they seemed to think it prudent to address all possibilities. I called this conveniently wide Asian view of the world "lateral thinking." Young was never enamored of the phrase. I rather liked it.

I looked again at the woman's odd attire and asked, "Are those her normal clothes, or her 'ceremony' clothes?"

"Both. This is the clothing for the Shimbang. Each, I think, is a little different, but it is something like this for all the priests."

"I see. Why bells?"

"They call to the spirit world. The four cloth strips, here?" Young motioned about her neck. "These items are for the major times in life. White is to be born, green is life, red is love, and black is death. The symbols on them all mean different things, and during the ceremony the priest can read them with small, uh, sticks she keeps in the cloth bag." Young gestured to the pouch hanging from the woman's hemp belt.

At this point, the priest, who had been standing quietly, turned and joined me on the bench. She looked at me with interest for a few moments and then spoke to Young at length. Young glanced at me several times during the discourse and her subsequent rejoinder. The longer the priest spoke, the more subdued Young became. At one point, she looked at the priest in surprise and spoke in a questioning tone. The priest responded with a shrug and Young again became subdued. Eventually, Young nodded in affirmation, acknowledging a comment or question.

The Shimbang stood, took the red and black sashes from about her neck and walked to the center of the clearing. She turned to Young and apparently asked a question. Young again looked surprised, tilted her head, gave a nervous laugh, and placing her hand near her throat, responded. The Shimbang returned the black sash to her neck and lay the red sash on the ground.

The priest fished about in her pouch and pulled out a handful of colorfully painted sticks, each about four inches long and half the diameter of a pencil. She placed these on the far left end of the red sash. From the leather pouch on her right side, she produced a handful of shredded and shaved dried material that looked like a combination of tobacco, wood chips, dried moss, and brown, broken leaves. She piled this matter in a heap on the ground near the sash. Reaching beneath her robes, she brought out a handful of fine white powder which she sprinkled over the pile of dried material. She sat back on her haunches, turned, and looked expectantly at Young.

Young turned to me and asked, "Do you have the Korean money?"

"Yes, princess, I do."

I had the clear sense we were shortly to be separated from some of our cash by this charlatan-character who'd leaped directly from Huckleberry Finn's Mississippi River banks to land center stage in our lives.

"Please give me ten thousand *won*."

"Ten thousand *won*!"

"Yes, this is correct. We have this much?"

"Yeah, '*we*' do," I replied, sarcastically emphasizing "we." "But '*we*' won't for long if you're about to do what I think."

"Jason, this is the good purchase. Do not be the…how do you say? Skin wad? Remember, 'I buy, you pay.'" Young turned her palm up and wriggled those long, elegant fingers.

I laughed loudly at her crisscrossed idiom, received another pinch, sighed, dug in my pocket and pulled out the Korean equivalent of about twenty dollars. I handed the bills to Young who, in turn, gave them to the Shimbang.

"Uh, what's our ten thousand *won* going to buy?" I ventured, trying to keep the sarcasm from my voice.

Young looked at me sideways, trying to read my tone and manner. I smiled brightly. I doubted this fooled her, but otherwise occupied, she made no critical comment.

"The Shimbang asked about us. She knew we are, uh, lovers. She said this is the problem, but would ask the spirit world to help us and to tell us our fate."

This was too much. I wanted to snatch the money from our supposed priest. Young, however, would have been horrified. More importantly, this "service" was obviously something she wanted. Always willing to follow her lead and unable to resist her wishes, I restrained myself.

"Well, great! I hope this helps; not much else has." Sarcasm was again only inches away.

Young said nothing, but shot me a searching glance. I tried to look guiltless.

The Shimbang knelt before the red cloth. A match materialized in her hand.

She lit the pile of white powered and dried mixture, which didn't burn but smoldered, producing a grayish white smoke. Oddly, the smoke didn't rise, but began to spread laterally with surprising speed, filling our small clearing.

The Shimbang began to chant, a low-in-the-throat, mournful groan. After a moment, she also began to sway gently, simultaneously moving her hands left and right across the skirt of her robes, causing the small bells to sound. She continued this chanting and swaying for some time. Eventually, she picked up the eight or nine small painted sticks and rubbed them between her hands with moderate vigor. After a few seconds of this, she allowed the sticks to fall on the sash. Simultaneously, she stopped all sound and movement.

The trail and clearing were extraordinarily quiet. I heard, almost too loudly, a popping and hissing sound from the smoldering pile. The flame was no more than two inches tall, but burned constantly and with great vigor in an odd, aqua-blue color. The smoke lay about the clearing, its fragrance dusting the leaves and branches. The smell wasn't acrid as I'd expected, but sweet and sticky, a kind of pine trace to it. The mountain air turned humid and slightly heavy.

My palms were damp and clammy. I was suddenly thirsty. Our three person world took on a slow-motion quality. A flying insect buzzed nearby my face, sounding very loud and angry. I was unable to brush it away. I wondered why it was mad and wanted to ask, but couldn't quite form the words. I looked sluggishly to Young who was kneeling opposite the Shimbang, the red sash a wounded, bleeding earth between them. Young sat rigidly, her lips open, eyes wide in what seemed part trance, part concentration, part fascination.

The small painted sticks had landed akimbo and askew, but interestingly, most pointed to the cloth's various symbols. The Shimbang removed two sticks that pointed to nothing and returned them to her pouch. She sat perfectly still and silent, apparently reading the symbols. An indeterminate amount of time passed.

Eventually, the Shimbang looked at Young and began to speak. Her voice sounded thick and slow, like a record played at too slow a speed. Young's rapt attention was focused on the priest, who motioned frequently to the sticks and cloth before her. Occasionally, she gestured slowly to me. As the priest spoke, Young placed the fingers of one hand over her mouth and lowered her head, nodding. Finally, the Shimbang fell silent. We sat quietly.

The afternoon seemed to cool quickly, the air again was alpine crisp, having lost its sudden, drowsy humidity. The clearing was smoke-free. Young was still in her kneeling posture, looking at the ground. The priest had returned the sticks to her pouch, hung the red sash around her neck, placed loose dirt on the smoldering pile, extinguishing it, and was again seated on the bench beside me.

I had somehow not actually noticed her *do* any of these things. Nonetheless,

I knew she'd done them all. Gathering my inexplicably absent wits, I asked the immobile and transfixed Young, "You okay, princess?"

My voice seemed to catch her attention, break her reverie. She looked at me, a growing focus on her face.

"Uh, yes. Okay."

The foggy sense of a few moments earlier was rapidly receding, replaced by my Western skepticism. "So, what did the spirit world say? Is our fate changed?"

Young didn't immediately respond, but slowly looked first at the priest, then to me. She answered, her voice dense, stripped of its usual light, lilting quality.

"It is not so clear a yes or no answer. The Shimbang told a story."

"A story," I responded flatly.

"Yes, normally answers to this, uh, ceremony are in a story. The Shimbang discovers the story, then tells what it means."

"Okay, a story. What's it about?"

Young extended her lower lip, took a deep breath and, with increasing clarity in her voice, explained.

"Our story is short, simple and old. Our story is about love, devotion, foolishness and death. There is a lost raven. The raven wanders, looking for its home. One day, it sees an injured fox. The raven flies to the fox. The fox is not far from its home, but cannot move. The fox will die without food and water. The raven understands this, and because it has the good and pure heart, brings the fox these things every day. During this time, the raven stays in a tree near the fox, watching and to be the help. The injured fox slowly heals. One day, the raven brings food for the fox. The fox—now, uh, not broken, healthy—rises and kills the raven."

"Christ! What kinda story's that, and what's it got to do with us, or Fate?"

Young sighed and looked out across the valley, now slowly filling with remorseful shadow. "Jason, it is the nature of the fox to hunt and kill birds. It is not the nature of birds to care for the fox. The raven tried to change its nature, change its fate. The, uh, how do you say? Motive? Was most pure and honest, but that is not important. The raven acted against its nature, against its fate. This foolishness brought death."

"Look, Young, princess, it's a, uh, cute story. But I don't get it." Looking at the immobile Shimbang, I asked, "Can we get our twenty bucks back?"

Young ignored my sarcasm. "Sweetheart, we, our circumstance, our life, is like this raven and fox, and like them, it is our nature to be different. We can try to change this. We have the good and wonderful reason to change this. We may even succeed for a time. But over time, our nature, our fate, our future, cannot be changed. It will always be what it is. We will always be what we are. Our fate is there now, waiting. If we believe we can change it, our foolishness will kill us."

I rubbed my face in exasperation. One of the many things I dearly loved about Young was her multi-faceted and unpredictable nature. But watching her bright and educated mind succumb to this elementary school hocus-pocus began to irritate me. Ravens and foxes, for Christ's sake! It sounded like a bad job of stealing something out of Thornton Burgess's *Old Mother West Wind* stories.

I looked up and raised both hands in a stop gesture. "Okay. Fine. We have the unsolicited, but fully paid for, opinion of one Shaman 'priest.'" I placed heavy sarcasm on priest. "Great. Terrific. Now, I suggest—"

I was about to launch into a further diatribe when Young interrupted in that quietly tender but powerful way she could assume.

"No, Jason, this is not her opinion. She does not have the opinion. She only…reports."

"Reports?"

"Yes, reports. This story, this report. This is not the opinion. This is the future."

# Forty-Nine

The 727 rolled slowly left, establishing a fifteen degree bank angle. The aircraft's pointed nose swept leisurely across the horizon. Shafts of golden evening sunlight rotated through the small passenger windows, falling like sequential spotlights throughout the cabin. The wings leveled. The engine noise decreased. Immediately, the horizon began to climb in the window. We were aligned on extended final for Kimpo, and descending.

The hydraulics whirred powerfully as the landing gear lowered. My seat rocked slightly when the gear reached the fully extended position and locked reassuringly into place. The whine of high-powered electric motors announced wing flap extension. The aircraft slowed. A combination of flight control and throttle adjustments compensated for the changing aerodynamic forces. We maintained a constant, descending approach angle.

The aircraft passed peacefully through a scattered cloud layer at about two thousand feet and continued descending, bumped through some light turbulence at about five hundred feet, and finally reached a point five feet above the runway centerline. Simultaneously, the throttles were reduced and aft pressure was applied to the flight controls. The two actions coordinated to affect a smooth touchdown. Rudder pedal pressure and counter pressure assured the airplane's giant wheels would be aligned in the direction of roll at touchdown. I heard and felt the mains touch. There was a sharp squeal, a gentle bounce and a second, more subdued squeal. The aircraft balanced delicately, nose high on the big tires; then, reacting to deceleration and the loss of lift, the nose gear began to drift lower. Finally, full runway contact. I felt the aviator's rush of relief with the feel of rubber wedded to concrete. We were on rollout to the nearest "speed permitting" taxi-way. KAL's flight 1704, Cheju-do to Seoul, was "destination-termination—Kimpo Airport."

I looked into the forward cabin area. Young, having completed all her pre- and post-landing duties, was strapped into the rearward facing crew seat mounted on the most forward cabin bulkhead. To my surprise, she was looking directly at me. She turned up the corner of her mouth and closed one eye slowly in a kind of semi-wink only I would notice. An acknowledgment. It felt good. I sat back in my seat and waited for the aircraft to taxi clear of the runway and to the arrival gate. I slipped back to the previous day's adventures.

After our Shimbang escapade, Young and I hiked another two kilometers up the Orimok trail, but the day's surprisingly late hour turned us back before we reached White Deer Lake. I couldn't understand where the time had gone. I recalled we'd discussed the potential of an evening return, but only as a remote contingency. Then, suddenly, a chunk of our day had simply disappeared. It was puzzling. It didn't seem we'd spent that much time with the Shimbang. Nonetheless, it was nearly five when, three quarters of the way up the mountain, we decided to turn back.

We reached our bikes at dusk. The return ride to Cheju city was mostly downhill, less arduous, a quicker trip. As darkness settled around us, the night sounds came alive; crickets chirped, owls cooed, and from a nearby lake or wetland, the haunting call of a loon drifted plaintively through the early summer evening.

A quarter moon lit the night. Unfortunately, the bikes had no lighting, not even reflectors. Ever the safety conscious aviator, I was concerned about our visibility on the nighttime country roads. Young, consistently carefree, discounted my worry and correctly pointed out that we'd probably be in more danger on Cheju's city lighted streets. I laughingly agreed, knowing the habits of Korean drivers.

After much weaving and dodging of the late evening city traffic, we finally arrived at the rental shop, returned our bikes, ate dinner at an obscure restaurant describe by Young as "too humble for any KAL crew," and began strolling back to the hotel. About five minutes from the hotel, Young stopped, and pulling me along, stepped into the shadowy doorway of a closed shop.

"We should go back single."

I smiled inwardly at her unintended pun. "Okay." I nuzzled her neck and whispered, "Can I see you tonight?"

Emboldened, I'm sure, by the concealing darkness, Young placed her hand on my face and rested her cheek on my chest.

"Sweetheart, I have the roommate. It will be difficult to say where am I all today, impossible to say for all night, or even part of the night."

I sighed.

In a small voice, sounding almost guilty, she said, "Tell me you understand."

I hugged her gently, turning us slightly left and right.

"Of course, princess, I understand. It won't always be so difficult. We won't always have to sneak around. But you're right, for now, we can't take chances. Even this is really too much." I relaxed my arms to release her, but she held me a moment more.

"I love you, Jason."

"I love you, too, princess."

"Jason?"

"Yes?"

Young looked at the ground and scratched about with the toe of her shoe. "Do you believe this story of the Shimbang?"

"No, princess, I don't. I think she's just a woman who could easily see we were in love, guessed at our problems, and put on a good show, complete with a little story she's probably used a hundred times before. No. I don't believe a word of it and neither should you. No one can see the future, princess. Not even the Shaman Shimbang of Cheju-do, 'Island of the Gods.'"

Young didn't respond, but again placed her cheek against my chest. After a moment she asked, "Do you think we can change our fate?"

I sighed and, exasperated, closed my eyes. She could be tirelessly dogged about Fate.

"Young, I don't know. I'm not sure I even believe in Fate." While I loved her without qualification, this Fate business was trying. It was late and I was sticky and tired. I didn't want to go down this foggy Fate path again.

I was frantically biting off sharp comments when she again spoke in that lilting way, her voice full with pathos.

"Never mind, I guess it really does not matter. If we try, then it was supposed to be. If we do not try, that too was our fate."

I remained silent, hoping her observation was rhetorical.

"Jason, there is one more thing I do not understand."

"What, princess?"

"The Shimbang said my question about our future was not the one to ask, that our future makes no difference to me. What does this mean, I asked, but she makes only the motion with her shoulder. Then, said zeros and seven are the bad kind of thing. What does this mean? Why does it make no difference for me? Why not you also…or us? And why?"

"Young, I don't know. I don't know what any of it means. Does it matter? Really? It's all a game anyway. She's not right or wrong, it's just a game. Forget about it, princess."

Young leaned to her right and rested against the doorjamb. The moonlight illuminated her skin, highlighting its smooth texture and creamy tone. I was again struck by her simple beauty. She looked up at me.

"You know, the Shimbang was—in one way, at least—correct."

"How's that?"

"We do not, cannot, control our future."

"Oh?"

"Umm." Slumping a bit, she looked over my shoulder toward Juliet's "inconstant moon." "Our future, it controls us."

# Fifty

June arrived, my last month. The Cheju-do trip was nearly two weeks distant. With my Korean tour draining rapidly away, Young and I became increasingly anxious about our cloudy and indeterminate future. My extension request, submitted after the flight with Colonel Barth to the 117th Aviation Company, had been disapproved. Shortly, I would leave for Alabama. My limited options were exhausted. Consistent with our history, all the emotionally corrosive choices and decisions had passed me by. Unfairly, but inevitably, our future fell to Young and choices only she could make.

Young remained fatalistic and accepting about what lay ahead or what might come. I, in contrast, searched relentlessly for metaphoric buttons or dials that, if properly manipulated, would produce the desired results. With frantic enthusiasm, I drew up diverse scenarios. If we did thus-and-so, then fairy tales resulted and we "lived happily ever after." Conversely, if we pushed the wrong buttons, or the correct buttons in the wrong sequence, tragedy ensued and we never saw one another again.

Young was generally reticent during my wild machinations, refusing to expend emotional energy or intellectual capital on events she viewed as unmanageable, no matter how clever or Machiavellian the scheme.

One evening, we were engaged in yet another one-sided what-if-we-try-this "discussion" when Young casually mentioned her parents had invited me to visit. Of course, I'd been to her small, Korean-style apartment many times. But her parents' "invitation" made this seem more like a formal audience, complete with agenda, rather than an evening's casual pleasantries. Nonetheless, the visit was set for the following weekend.

\* \* \*

I pulled the Rocket out of Mapo's Friday evening traffic and parked at the base of Young's hill, where I found her waiting.

"Hi, princess," I said, closing the car door behind me. "How are you?"

"Fine, thank you," she answered with her customary smile.

This was public, so, no hugs, no cheek-pecks, and certainly no kissing. Hand-holding was a gray area where I, as usual, followed her lead; sometimes it was yes, but generally, no. Today was no. We began to trudge up the hill. Typical of her nature, Young came directly to the point.

"I think my mother and father want to talk with us about our future."

"Oh, really? What an interesting topic. Wish we woulda thought to do that. Hey, maybe they know something we don't, 'cause we can't seem to figure it out." I laughed sarcastically. "Hope they don't wanna know what we got planned."

Young didn't respond to this blunt and indelicate assessment of our troubles. "What do you think they'll say?"

"It is difficult to know. We have not talked about this meeting, so I am not certain."

"What do you think?" Without waiting for an answer, I continued to the worst case—this, typical of my nature. "What if they forbid us to see one another, or marry?"

Surprisingly, Young winced. It was a mannerism I hadn't previously seen from her.

"Jason, do not ask me this question. They love me and they like you too much to make this kind of request."

I kicked lazily at a child's marble lying lost in a pencil-width concrete crack. It skidded colorfully against the base of a stone wall and, with gathering momentum, rolled unchecked down the pathway.

"Hope so," I mumbled morosely.

Young looked at me with an appraising sideways glance, her intuition at work.

"Are you well?" she asked solicitously.

My testy answers reflected my mood. I would need to keep my emotions in check. In Asia, good manners and politeness are important, nearly above all else; they could even redeem a barbarian. The last thing I wanted was to insult her parents, cause anyone a loss of face, or prove myself unworthy.

"Yeah, princess, I'm okay. I apologize; I'm just a little edgy. Maybe it's because our time's getting so short. Maybe I'm scared. Maybe it's due to phases of the moon, or international interest rates, or…I don't know," I answered, shaking my head.

During the previous few weeks, I'd become increasingly concerned about us. Our future seemed uncontrollable, and this bothered me greatly. I was unable to concentrate, slept poorly, was constantly nervous, and had actually begun to lose weight.

"Umm," was all she said, but her tone and manner made it clear she understood and sympathized. Despite the public setting, she took my hand, squeezed it compassionately, pulled it close to her side, and smiled.

Immediately, I felt better. How could she always invoke just the right magic? Shoulder the burden just when needed most? More reason to love her. More reason to fret.

Near the top of the hill, we turned left onto a smaller concrete walkway perhaps ten feet wide. Her family's apartment was on the right, about thirty feet from the corner. In the classic Korean style, her home was single story with a reddish-orange tiled roof, corners turned upward. Following Asian tradition, a concrete wall approximately ten feet tall surrounded her home. We stepped through a dark green metal door in the wall and into a small rectangular, open air, brick courtyard. Two other families shared the little quadrant. Their apartments, on our left and right, faced a tiny but perfectly groomed and colorful flower garden centered in the courtyard.

We crossed the fifteen feet to Young's apartment. Passing through a sliding wooden door, we stepped into a small entry area that served as a combination reception room, foyer, hallway and front porch. The area was covered, but not heated. A small one-person kitchen and larder was to our left. The living areas were to the right, a toilet area directly in front of us. As is the Asian custom for older style dwellings, the apartment had no shower or bath facilities. Bathing was done communally, sometimes gender segregated, sometimes not, at a local bathhouse, the *Mogyokt'ang*.

We removed our shoes, again, common practice in Korea, and placed them in the entry area. Young slid open a door to the living area. We stepped into a small, irregularly shaped room in which she, I, her brother and sister had talked and laughed during previous visits. There was no Western-style furniture in this room, or elsewhere in the apartment. Large pillows replaced chairs. Guests and hosts simply sat cross-legged on the floor. Sleeping was much the same. Thicker padded mats replaced pillows. Normally, Young's parents slept in this room.

The floors were covered in light gray linoleum and heated by brick-lined tunnels or flues. Warm air from *ondol* stoves, usually located in the kitchen, passed through the flues, through the floor, and warmed the room. *Ondol* was simply charcoal pressed into black cylinders, generally about eighteen inches long and eight inches in diameter. The cylinders were placed in specially shaped stoves, lit and allowed to burn slowly, needing replacement about once every four to six hours.

The *ondol* cooking and heating system had been in use about fifteen hundred years, was inexpensive and worked reasonably well, but was exceedingly dangerous. The burning charcoal produces a poisonous, odorless, colorless gas. The flues and stoves were by no means airtight, so exhaust leaks were common. As a precaution, each heated room had to be vented; normally, a window or door was "cracked" slightly to allow fresh air flow. Newly-arrived soldiers were briefed about the *ondol* danger, in the event they spent a night outside their American compound, which used Western heating methods. GIs who lived "on the economy" were specifically prohibited from renting quarters with *ondol* systems. Even with precautions and awareness, a handful of deaths were attributed annually to insufficient ventilation in *ondol*-heated buildings. Inevitably, at least one of these deaths would be an American serviceman.

Young picked up a bright blue pillow lying beneath the window, plumped it, and placed it in one of two black-lacquered mother-of-pearl upright chests. These small apartments generally didn't include the luxury of closets, so chests and trunks served as storage areas for clothes, pillows, blankets, sleeping mats and the like. Turning toward me, she shrugged in a kind of fatalistic way and crossed to a sliding, wooden-framed, paper door. She slid the door open and we stepped though, me first, she following, into what would be the living room in a Western house.

The room was slightly larger than the one we'd just left, and rectangular. The only Western concession was a portable television sitting on a small table against the wall to the left. Standing against the longer wall opposite the door was a large wardrobe. Constructed of light-colored wood, the wardrobe contained a variety of articles that had no other home, such as magazines, board games, desk items and, of course, cushions. A table with legs about eighteen inches long stood in the corner. It was used for various activities including game playing, eating, and study.

Young's parents stood in the room's center, dressed in Korea's traditional clothing, the *hanbok*. Young wore this attire during some KAL flights and had explained it in detail.

Her mother's *hanbok* featured a white, billowy, floor-length strapless skirt or dress; the *chïma*, a kind of wrapping, secured it beneath the arms. She wore a short vest, the *chogori*, over her *chïma*. The green *chogori* was tied at the front with a large bow, the wide yellow ribbon-tails falling to the knee.

Young's father, also traditionally dressed, wore a loose, light blue, square-bottom shirt over which he wore a dark blue vest, the *chokki*. His baggy pantaloons, *paji*, were gray and tied at the ankle. His *magoja*, or waistcoat, was white.

The material of both *hanboks* appeared to be silk. Clearly, her parents were dressed for the occasion. Young and I were underdressed in jeans. I wore a Cincinnati Reds T-shirt. Another *faux pas*. Young, at least, had upgraded to a denim blouse.

Young bowed deeply. A devotee of polite behavior, I realized I should do the same and half a second later also bowed. Bowing to her parents, in her home, seemed perfectly natural. Her parents returned the bow and gestured for us to sit on thick black pillows. Mrs. Lee immediately left the room but quickly returned with *nok ch'a* and *yakbap*, green tea and sweet rice cakes. As usual, she fussed over me and spoke Korean soothingly, in quiet and comforting tones. She had an absolute genius for this and I immediately began to lose my edginess. Tea was poured and we sat without conversation, slurping in the Asian fashion.

While Young's propensity, and apparently her father's as well, was to speak directly to the point, it was more typically Korean to sidle up to the actual topic. This was true socially and in business. Koreans considered it an art to comfortably postpone the central issue with skillful small talk. The Lee family did not have this particular cultural trait in abundance. Fidgeting in place, it was all they could manage to sip their tea in silence.

After the minimum of quiet had been observed, Young's father spoke, his voice soft and commanding. Unusual for him, he spoke at some length. While he talked, his wife sat quietly beside him and looked at the floor. Young, sitting adjacent to me and opposite her father, did the same, but occasionally glanced at Mr. Lee and on several occasions murmured "umm," as if in acknowledgment or agreement. When her father stopped speaking, Young bowed slightly, and turned to me.

"My father said he loves me very much. He said my mother also loves me very much. He said that, for them, the most important thing is that I am well and happy. He said they also want this for my brother and small sister. He said that he and my mother have made their lives and are happy. He wants his children to also do this."

I nodded, but didn't look at her parents. My peripheral vision caught them watching me appraisingly. I hoped my reaction was appropriate.

Young turned back to her father and nodded. He spoke, again at some length. The two women maintained the same posture as earlier, eyes downcast, listening. He finished speaking. Young turned to me.

"My parents said to tell you they like you very much and think you are the kind and good man. You are the first American they know. They hope all the Americans are like you."

I smiled, bowed slightly and in my best Young-tutored Korean said, "Thank you very much," to which her parents responded "You're welcome," in English.

I looked up with considerable surprise. They smiled broadly. We all laughed, a good, honest sound with no language ambiguity; the tension eased considerably. Apparently, Young had been tutoring them as well. It occurred to me that after sixty plus years, these were probably their first English words.

The laughter drifted away through the open window and into the Korean evening. Young smiled and continued, "My parents said they know that you love me, and...." she blushed beautifully, "that I love you. My father said they know this feeling is not something they can change...or should. We must find our own way about this point. But my father wants to know, please, what is it are we going to do about our future?"

It was an eminently fair question. The family absolutely depended on Young for survival, this was clear. If that support was going to change, even a little, they had the right to know. It was not only Young's future at issue, but theirs as well. This equation had many variables. Though it was a rational and simple question, I had no idea how to answer. They watched me carefully. I tried to keep my face calm and expressionless, Asian style.

I glanced at Young, hoping she would once again save me, but she looked directly at the floor before her. Apparently she either couldn't, or wouldn't, step in, though she clearly knew my—our—quandary. On impulse, I decided not to be vague or clever, but to tell the truth as I knew it was and hoped it would be. If things worked out, we'd be exercising that truth soon enough; if not, it wouldn't matter.

"Tell them I love and honor you deeply. Tell them your happiness is my only thought, exactly the same as they want for you. I will do anything to make this so. Tell them I tried to stay in Korea, but my request was disapproved. I don't know for certain where our future lies, but tell them I want to marry you and take you to Alabama."

Young was again blushing, something she didn't ordinarily do. She spoke to her parents who made no interim acknowledgment, but continued to listen. When she finished, her father nodded his head slowly in understanding and regarded me. A very small, warm smile ran across his face; then, he again became expressionless.

We sat in silence for a moment or two. It wasn't an awkward place; more like we were all attempting to sort out exactly what had been said, what it meant, and how next to proceed.

Mr. Lee spoke. This time, at about the halfway point, Young shifted her gaze from the floor before her to her father. Still later, I noticed Young lick her lips, upper first, then lower, then a kind of blotting them together. This was a mannerism she affected when nervous or concerned. Mr. Lee finished speaking. Young didn't immediately respond but looked to her mother, whose face, as always, was filled with warmth. Young bowed slightly to her parents and turned to me.

"My parents said that while they are old, they have not forgotten this young and in love feeling. My father said they are still in love today." She smiled wistfully at this. "He said it is different from years ago, but it is still love. He said if

I am fortunate, Fate has this kind of love for me." She stopped momentarily and sighed, dropping her gaze to the floor. "My parents said they do not want me to go from Korea."

My heart stopped, but I forced myself to remain expressionless; an emotional reaction would be considered very bad manners.

"They said they are concerned about how to pay the house money, and food, and…well, all those kind of everyday things. They are concerned that my brother could not finish the university. They are concerned about to, uh, pay the doctor as they get older. They are concerned about my small sister and who would care for her if they cannot. They are concerned about me in America and the different culture things. They are concerned to not see me if I go so far away. They said they have these and other worries." She stopped again and looked at her parents, eyes wide and moist.

Her father slowly closed his eyes and nodded, as if encouraging her to continue.

My heart had now reversed itself and was beating at twice its normal rate.

"My parents said these things are important, but concern only the family and not my happiness. They said again that my happiness was most important. My father said if this means I must go with you and they would lose me, they would make this sacrifice and honor this choice. This choice is one you and I must make. No matter what we choose, they will accept. But the choice is only ours. They cannot help us, but will not stop us."

I immediately thought of Young's impassioned plea at the Han River Gap.

"*Sacrifice for country. Sacrifice for family. Sacrifice for ideas. These ideas…this kind of feeling describes the Korean people. It is something you must understand to know us. To really know me.*"

It was becoming clear that either Young, her parents or I would soon have the opportunity to meet and intimately embrace this idea of sacrifice. With numbing distraction, I wondered which of us it would be.

# Fifty-One

We sat in our Mapo café, very much in love, early June floating about us. Time was rushing away, its speed, as my economics professor used to say, "increasing at an increasing rate." Before us on the table lay my KAL airplane ticket to the States and my orders for Fort Rucker, Alabama. The unyielding papers specified I would leave Korea in three days. We weren't depressed, exactly, but we were very concerned.

We had discussed how to continue our relationship since Dragon Valley, some six months ago. The issue was a sad apparition, always hovering nearby. What had Young said about sadness during that first visit to my quarters? *"A deep cut, always with us. Sometimes hidden, sometimes ignored. But, always present, there, in shadow."* Despite the agonizing, we were no closer to exorcising this shadowy spirit now than months before. Was it possible there was no good answer? I refused to accept this; we'd simply not yet come across it.

"Young, look-it, we'll find our way through this."

She glanced at me, eyes large and sad, but said nothing.

"You know I want to marry you." I pushed the salt shaker aimlessly about the gray Formica tabletop. "This is probably the only case of a GI rejected by a Korean," I added sarcastically.

Young shot me a sideways glance, irritation and hurt on her face. "Jason, this is not correct. You know this. I am not rejecting. Only, I must make sure all my questions here, in Korea, are answered before I choose anything or go anywhere."

"I know, princess. I know. I'm sorry, I didn't mean to hurt you. It was a bad joke."

She again fell silent, and looking down at her mostly uneaten dinner, herded bits of rice and barley aimlessly across the plate with wooden chopsticks.

"Say," I offered brightly, "do you remember our first meeting?"

She looked up, smiling. "Yes, of course."

"Do you know what?"

"Umm, what?"

"I didn't know your name when I left your shop, and you didn't say anything encouraging, so I forgot all about you. When you called? That first time? I didn't know who you were. Did you know that?"

"Yes, I remember you were confused. So, I wonder, uh, 'What kind of person can forget me so soon? Is this low character common for the American people?'"

"Yes." I grinned. "Now you know. The lowest of character."

She smiled slowly and shook her head.

"So, why did you call? Why'd you contact a 'foreign barbarian'?"

Young slumped in her chair, looked appraisingly at the ceiling and slipped both hands into the front pockets of her jeans.

"Ummm. This is the good question. I do not really know. Lots of small reasons, I suppose, and perhaps one, uh, odd one."

She paused, looking at me as if deciding whether or not to continue. After a moment, she began deliberately.

"You were funny. You had a warm smile. You made me laugh. I liked that you, almost, knew *Richard III*. You seemed a little helpless. You were, oh, just different; a foreigner, yes, but this was interesting, also. I do not know. I just felt something…honest and comfortable about you. Intuition," she added pointedly, recalling her earlier struggle with the word.

She paused and looked through the shop's small window as if gathering her thoughts, then quickly back to me with a wicked, hungry smile.

"And maybe," she leaned close, giggled, and added in a whisper, "you were a little bit cute." Under the table, out of sight, she rubbed her foot against my leg.

I grinned widely, ego hugely inflated, a victim once again of her sweet charm and easy graciousness.

"What's odd about all that? Especially the last part? I am, after all, 'cute.'"

"Well, nothing actually. But the odd reason is," she paused, leaned back in her chair, then continued slowly, "when I finished reading? It was like something, uh, walked past us I could…feel. It was warm, and frightening, and quick, but it was there. I still do not know what this was."

"Yeah, I remember. Very strange. It was like we were somehow…touched, actually, literally by the words."

"Um."

We paused; each, I suppose, reliving our first moments. But we were too serious. I tried to brighten the mood.

"Will you miss the Lizards?"

She laughed. "Yes. But the Lizards will be okay, if the TV is working."

"Yeah."

There was a bit of an awkward pause.

"When I get back to the States and get an address, I'll write and let you know what it is right away. My phone number, too, so if you need me, I'll be just a phone call away."

"Yes, just a phone call," she echoed quietly, looking quickly away through the window and into the Mapo darkness.

"Hey, I'll take some pictures, too. You can see what you're missing. Do you want a big or small yard?"

Still looking away, fingering the gold chain at her throat, she asked distractedly, "What is a 'yard'?"

"Uh, it's like a courtyard, only with grass all around the house."

She turned quickly toward me, placed her hand on mine, and almost blurted, "Oh, Jason, what if I cannot come to Alabama?"

"Young, don't even think that."

"But what if it is the circumstance?" she pressed.

I squeezed her hand.

"I'm telling you, princess, we will figure a way to make this happen."

The old woman who owned the café appeared at the table and spoke to Young who, sitting up quickly, looked at her watch in surprise and responded briefly in Korean. She raised her wristwatch for me to see.

"Look, it is nearly eleven forty. We must go!"

"Oh. Yeah. Okay."

Young paid our bill and we left the restaurant. The street, as always at this hour, was deserted. I turned left toward the hill and the concrete pathway. Young, however, with a different destination in mind, turned right. Realizing she was not alongside, I stopped and turned to find her. She was walking to the Rocket.

"Yongsan is too far to walk, and not in that direction," she called over her shoulder. "We must ride the Rockette. Hurry."

# PART FIVE

*Tears, Idle Tears, I know not what they mean.*
*Tears from the depth of some divine despair.*

—*Tears Idle Tears,*
Alfred Lord Tennyson

# Fifty-Two

Our last evening began warm, pleasant and silly. Young and I were "under the hill," leaning against the Rocket, our mood unexpectedly light and easy. We'd made several trips up and down the concrete pathway, refusing to say our final farewell. When reaching her courtyard door, we'd say goodbye; then, Young would say, "Okay, I will walk you down." At the bottom, we'd exchange another goodbye, followed immediately by my, "Okay, I'll walk you up." This silliness continued for some time. It burned our regretful energy; it deferred our sorrow; it did not delay curfew. Finally, Time, our immutable opponent, intervened. Curfew began to take form and, with dispassionate malevolence, accelerate toward us.

"Okay." I gestured with my wristwatch. "Last time," I admonished. "I'll walk you up. And you're gonna stay up, okay?"

A nod, but different, somber; then she murmured, "Very well."

We moved away from the Rocket and toward the concrete path. After a step or two, Young stopped and turned, looking back at the old green car. She walked to it and, smiling wistfully, placed her hand on the hood.

"This is warm. It is like the car has life." She moved her hand in small circles. "It is part of us, you know. The Rockette gave us many opportunities together. The many trips home, the Han Warriors, Suwon, KAL examinations, The Accident, the short winter drives, the Zoo, trips to and from Kimpo. He even did not work at the correct chance." She smiled bashfully at the Rocket's failure to start that frigid night we returned from Dragon Valley. "He has been the good and true, silent friend. I will miss him."

She patted the fender and turned away, her fingertips lingering on the metal. With her right hand, she reached for my arm. She leaned against me, placing both hands just above my elbow. Together, we began our last walk up Young's familiar hill.

"So, it won't be long before I'll be back. My new job's got lots of travel; Korea's always one of the destinations. I don't know when the next trip here is, but soon, not more than a year for sure. Shoot, we'll have this all ironed out before then for sure. Anyway, we'll write every week, okay? No weaseling, every week. That's doable, not too much, not too little."

"Umm," she mumbled. Since the meeting with her parents, Young had become unaccountably more somber. I tried again to cheer her.

"Come on, princess, things will work out. You'll like Alabama, and after that, we'll probably be assigned to Germany. Remember, you said we'd visit Montmartre? And Sacred Heart. Well, they're just next door in France. We can get there, no problem."

"No, Jason. You said we could meet there."

"Okay, okay. Doesn't matter who said what, it's gonna happen. That's the point."

Young didn't share my optimism, and only nodded half-heartedly.

We walked along the narrow concrete path. Protecting us from the darkness, the accommodating moon busily lit the way, painting mimicking shadows at our side. Young continued funereally, head down, watching our dark friends as they moved in sympathetic synchronization.

"Come on, Young, it's gonna be all right. I love you. We'll get this straight. We just need some more time. We'll write to one another. You know our future's together; it's just how we get there, that's all. This is just a little delay, a little bump in the road."

"Jason, I know you think this is the future and that we can, uh, manage what will happen to us. But I believe our fate and circumstances have their own course. I am afraid they are on a different path than your idea."

This was the first time I'd heard Young so positively negative. I began to taste the fear of loss and, with increasing desperation, tried to dismiss it.

"Young, don't be silly. This problem, this 'circumstance,' can be solved. We've talked endlessly about this. We can't just quit, roll over and die. This Fate's-in-charge business is nuts! We love each other. We can win this battle."

A weary sigh slipped through her lips. Then, as if to a child who understands but will not accept, she said, "My dear, dear Jason, yes, we have talked about this endlessly, and yes, it is our central difference. There is not a 'battle' to win. There is not 'solving' to discover. There are only problems and circumstance. The different cultures and my family are problems. Big problems. In the end, these things will…tear, uh, cut us. I think we cannot change this circumstance."

Young stopped. I turned toward her. Pain was suddenly on her face. She looked briefly left and right, apparently without seeing, gathering her thoughts. Looking back to me, she continued earnestly.

"Sweetheart, not all dreams are true. Not all journeys find the destination, some are lost. But surely, all journeys end. It is not so important where we journey, but how." Pausing momentarily, she added, "And most, uh, remarkable for us? That we, from different worlds thousands of miles away, so different, could find each other and travel at all. These warm things, these are the most important."

"Young, I don't like the sound of this. Stop it; you're scaring me. You make it sound like I'm losing you."

"Do not be frightened." She placed her hand lightly on my cheek; her voice broke. "We will always be together. But perhaps, dear, it will be in a different way."

My heart was beating quickly. "Wha, what do you mean? What are you saying?"

"Jason, it is more and more clear. Our lives are on different paths." She took her hand from my cheek, looked at the ground, and in a small voice, said, "This, I think, is our fate." She paused again, and raising her head to look at me, said, "You know this very well. You do."

"No! Stop it. No. I don't know anything of the kind. What I do know 'very well' is that the future's not set. We can call it 'battles' or 'journeys' or 'solutions' or any name you like, but what happens tomorrow is a function of what we do today."

Slipping my hands from hers, I placed them on her shoulders and with desperation rising in my voice, said, "There's nothing mysterious about this, princess. There is no great, universal, master plan. We're not pawns. We're the choices we make. We're the choices we will make. I make the choice to love you. Somehow, we're gonna be together. Period. That's how it's gonna be."

She responded quietly, "Dear, this is my precise point. You make a choice, yes. But me? I cannot choose. This is stolen from me. Fate has taken my choice. Like Miss Pak, it only seems I have the choice."

There was a long pause, mine from frustration and fright, hers apparently from a sense of what to say, how to explain. She sighed deeply.

"Truly, you love me, Jason. I know this very well. Of course...." Placing her hand lightly on my forearm, her grip increased as she spoke. "...I love you. Fate has allowed this gift." A painful strain surfaced in her voice. "But this is not all we need for happiness." She paused again. "I know very well you think of me as Western, and in many ways I am. But I am also very Korean. The more I think about this, the more I understand. I feel the country. I cannot change my nature. Do you remember the Shimbang's story? It is not the nature of the bird to care for the fox."

I was too frightened to react with my customary disdain to any Shimbang reference.

"I hear the Eastern voice clearly. I should have listened more carefully when it first called. I am afraid I am more East than West. This is difficult to explain, dear, try to understand."

But I didn't understand. I simply looked at her with the growing realization that we were reaching some kind of climax. Incredibly, instantly, after months of coy, evasive hiding, our future was upon us in a blitzkrieg, furious lightning, unconcerned for effect or aftermath. After so much agonizing, so much writhing, so much planning, a most dreadful and frightening future was coalescing before me at supersonic speeds. My emotional brakes were fully engaged—and completely ineffective.

"Jason, think of my 'choice.'" She used the word with soft derision. "Can you imagine yourself here, in Seoul, forever? All your culture things far away. All the things you know since a child, gone." She moved both hands in a kind of rolling motion as if to emphasize each point. "You are looking different than other people, talking different, worried about your family, unable to see your family, unable to work an acceptable job; even the food, land, and weather, different. These are the things you are asking, but I must answer. These things have nothing to do with love, or not love. They are small, normal, everyday things. But they have power to kill us. In time, Jason, they would. What kind of choice this is?"

She looked directly at me with those dark, expressive eyes. I heard for only the second time that deep-running, sorrowful tenor.

"Oh, Jason, I love you too much for that kind of thing. Fate has chosen an end for us. You see this. But we can choose when…and how." She clasped my forearm. "Jason, let it be today, now, the hurt soft with love; not tomorrow, with anger and distance between us."

I was numb. I couldn't believe what I'd heard. We'd discussed this possibility before, many times, as one of the endless scenarios I'd dreamed up, but I refused to accept it might be the actual solution. Regaining my senses, I shook my head and started to interrupt, but Young wasn't finished.

Placing a finger on my lips, she continued, her words burning acidic as they settled over me, "Jason, I must stay in my world, with my culture. I cannot change my nature. You love me, I know. Do not ask me to say no to my nature."

Pausing, she closed her eyes and gently bit her lower lip.

"But it is not only the culture. It is also my family. They will let me go but, you know very well, I cannot go. You know this. They say this because they love me. But they need me. You know this is so. I need them. I must protect and care for them. Who else can do this? Only I can do this. I cannot abandon them…I cannot." Her voice fractured. "I must release you, Jason. And you…you must let me go."

We looked at one another, her desperate pronouncement lingering loudly in the dark silence. Speechless, I shook my head. This was too sudden.

Intellectually, I understood her reasoning, but emotionally…emotionally I simply could not let her go! She was too much a part of me, too…deeply tangled around me. I couldn't do this. I wasn't strong enough. I needed her too much. I couldn't let her go.

Recognizing I needed a final push, she took a deep breath, looked directly in my eyes, placed her right hand over my heart, and gave a last tender nudge.

"Jason, I cannot do this alone. It is not possible. Be Asian. Make this sacrifice. Give me this gift, and…and I will forever keep it. Remember my promise? 'I will hold you in my heart, always,' Jason; you will never be far from me. We will be together. You can do this, yes? You can do this! Do not make me ask again, please. I cannot." Tears flowed rapidly down her cheeks. "I cannot." She wept with a hopeless passion, Saint Jude touching her heart.

I was terrified and lost, but at the edge of understanding. Across the border lay a dark epiphany. Culture and circumstance, a hydra even love couldn't slay. After so much convoluted, distorted agony, so much machination, so many Machiavellian schemes, it was really simple and quite straightforward: she would not, could not leave Korea nor abandon her family. The question of who had what choice seemed almost academic. Nothing would change our apparently predetermined future.

My heart was torn. My thoughts speeded out of control. The worst scenario realized? Denial fell over me. This could not be! Our best times our only times? No! Movies don't end like this! There's always a solution! We had come too far, suffered too much, found too much; had too much before us to see our future in past tense. This could not be the end. We cannot die here! There must be an escape.

The sound of Young's tears called me. Her anguish brought me back to our dim path. Even through this, I couldn't abide her wrenching sorrow. I would do anything to comfort her. I surrendered.

At that moment, my life began to change. Slowly, the joyful white water calmed to dark. The steady, quiet rains began. A black mist shrouded Camelot. Excalibur slipped from me. Inevitable Death, silent and relentless, lurked.

Reading my defeat, Young placed both hands lightly on my chest. I slid my arms about her familiar waist. With her fingers maintaining contact, she gingerly leaned backward, her lovely weight suspended against my arms. Eyes closed, lips slightly parted, tears glistening, she lifted her face to the night sky, a gesture of hopelessness and grief, as if releasing her spirit.

In protective desperation, I pulled her gently to me. Resigned and forlorn, she placed her arms about my neck, resting first her forehead, then her cheek against my chest…weeping. I felt the warm issue of her sorrow soak and stain my skin.

We maintained this posture, gently swaying, our joint-life spilling away. Our heartbeat, imperceptible, at the edge of silence, dark and eternal. Death's impatient vapor waiting.

Young whispered haltingly in my ear, her breath wet, heavy and labored. "Oh, Jason…Jason." She squeezed me tightly, paused, then called for the final time upon *Hamlet*. "'This…this is the poison of deep grief.'"

As we sometimes did, she wanted me to complete the passage. But I was helpless, in accelerating free-fall through the shimmering, burning boundary of tears.

With the grace and compassion it seemed only she possessed, Young gentled me a moment, her fingertips against my cheek, her head on my chest. I calmed briefly, and stumbled through the words.

"'When sorrows come…they come not, single spies…but in battalions.'"

We wept.

Death's gentle handmaiden, Mercy, at last stilled our heart.

It was finished.

The vapor enclosed us.

We were lost.

# Fifty-Three

I leaned forward, straining against my seatbelt, wiped condensation from the window and tried to find Mapo through the gray, layered clouds. The city lay under a thin, tattered overcast. Only Nam San's Seoul Tower rose above the ragged cloud-tops.

The aircraft continued to climb through the early evening rain. Seoul receded, smaller and smaller. The left wing began to rise. I willed it down, but the 747 was uncooperative and rolled into a climbing right turn toward Los Angeles and an alien world. Without warning, my window filled with wispy gray, as if a shade had been pulled, a curtain closed, or a connection lost. Korea vanished. Vanished so quickly and completely that it might never have been there. My new, old life had begun again.

I closed my eyes, slumped, and let my head rest against the seat back. The previous eighteen hours were the most difficult of my life. My sense of loss was raw. Reality was overwhelming. I was alone. Part of me was missing. My best friend was gone. I wouldn't see her in the evening, or the following day, or the weekend, or ever. I could no longer seek her counsel, rest in the warmth of her tenderness, or share her life. The gift and balm of her presence had been irreversibly excised, cruelly and without sedation.

"You are Mr. Fitzgerald, yes?"

With a start, I sat upright, recognizing the syntax. Adjacent to my seat stood an attractive Asian woman dressed in a colorful white and blue *hanbok*. Her KAL name tag read "Miss Park."

I nodded. "Yes, that's right."

"In a moment, we will reach cruising altitude. Then, you can please come with me to your seat in first class."

I smiled ruefully. "Sure, be glad to go to first class, but there's some kinda mistake." Reaching inside my jacket, I said, "My ticket's for coach."

From the folds of her *chogori*, Miss Park produced a yellow strip of paper that looked as if it had been torn from a teletype machine. Her lips moved silently as she read the text. She looked at the armrest to confirm the seat number, then refocused on me.

"You are Mr. Jason Fitzgerald, yes?"

"None other."

"There is no mistake," she said with authority. "I am the Senior Flight Attendant, Miss Park. You are our guest today, sir. We have a first class seat for you." She gestured with the yellow paper. "This MSC is from KAL Flight Operations at Kimpo. It is different from your ticket."

"What's MSC?"

"Uh, Manifest Seating Change." Miss Park looked at the paper. "It is from a KAL person, uh...LKY. Do you know the LKY person?"

I looked at the cabin floor. "Yes." I paused, fighting the catch in my voice. "Yes, Miss Park. I know LKY."

"Good."

There was an audible drop in engine noise as the throttles were adjusted from climb-power to cruise settings. The aircraft pitched slightly nose down and the jetliner leveled off.

Miss Park nodded. "You may come now."

I gathered my carry-on baggage and we walked toward the forward cabin, climbed the circular staircase, and stepped into the half empty first class section. I was escorted to an empty row and a wide, tan leather seat adjacent to a window. Miss Park motioned to another attendant who walked quickly to us. Miss Park spoke briefly. The woman glanced at me knowingly and acknowledged her instructions with a short bow.

"Sir, this is Miss Kim, she will assist you." Miss Park smiled briefly and disappeared down the staircase.

Miss Kim looked at me kindly and bowed.

"*Annyong hashimnikka*, Mr. Fitzgerald. *Ch'oum poepgesumnida. Mannase pan'-gapsumnida.*"

I smiled at the challenge of untangling the simple greeting and responded, "*Ne annyong hashimnikka*, Miss Kim. *Chal chinaesumnida. Kamsahmnida.*"

"Very good, sir. Miss Lee said you would know these things and I must do the examination."

"You know Miss Lee!"

"Yes, very well; we did the KAL training together. She came to Kimpo this morning, early, and we spoke of you. I have orders." Miss Kim straightened slightly and, with a serious expression, said, "I am to certain you have the quiet and happy flight." Giggling lightly, she looked back to me. "Miss Lee said she will know if this is not so and will...how do you say, getting back?"

"Uh, get even? Get revenge?"

"Exactly. This is the phrase, 'get revenge.' So, please Mr. Fitzgerald, you can give me the good report, yes?"

I laughed. "No problem, Miss Kim, consider it done."

We exchanged a few more pleasantries, after which Miss Kim excused herself. Young had worked her magic one last time. I actually felt better.

The aircraft continued eastbound, away from the setting sun. Darkness seeped into the cabin. My fellow passengers quietly settled in for the long trans-Pacific flight. I snapped off the seat light and rested my head against the airplane's small, cold window. I'd had almost no sleep for at least twenty-four hours. My head ached. My eyes were red and tired. I was physically exhausted and emotionally drained. I closed my eyes and forced my mind to stop. Eventually, I nodded off.

I slept fitfully, waking briefly about midnight and again shortly after four. I dozed off and on, finally waking about six. I rubbed my eyes and looked through the window. The horizon had begun to brighten, dimming the stars. The cloudless morning sky was calm; the ocean's surface pool-table flat.

In the approaching dawn, the world was cleanly and simply divided. Below the horizon, the dusky ocean spread laterally into the limitless dark. In counterpoint, the sky was painted in slowly kaleidoscoping colors; vibrant streaks of fiery red that melted to orange, cooled to yellow, and solidified as daylight.

Miss Kim materialized in a rustle of silk. Like a redeeming angel, she brought coffee and a steaming hot hand-towel.

"Bless you, Miss Kim; I really need this."

"*Ch'onmaneyo.* Can I do anything for you, Mr. Fitzgerald?"

"No. Not unless you can turn the airplane around and go back."

She bowed playfully. "Always your humble servant, I will try this, but cannot say for certain it will be acceptable."

There was a moment of awkward silence. Miss Kim looked quickly about the dim cabin at the still sleeping travelers, then reached in the pocket of her *hanbok* and withdrew a single white envelope. She leaned toward me.

"Miss Lee instructed I give you this in the morning," she whispered. "She said to say this is from the first day she knew for certain."

Surprised, I took the envelope and nodded, not trusting my voice.

Miss Kim bowed and disappeared.

*The first day she knew for certain.* Anxiously, I turned on my small overhead seat light, worked my finger under the sealed flap, and tore open the envelope. Inside was a photograph. I held it under the light. It was the picture I'd taken of Young standing adjacent to the Seoul Warriors, high above the bright Han River that warm November day, so recently, so long ago. On the reverse side, she'd neatly written the most lovely words, a reminder, a pledge:

*Remember my promise.*
*I will hold you in my heart, <u>always</u>.*
*You will never be far from me.*
*We will be together.*
*Y.*

I held the photograph tightly, swallowed the lump in my throat, and looked again through the window. The sun rested stoically on the horizon. The morning was calm, its dramatic birth complete, the intense, defining colors faded to memory. But the morning's essence, its...heart, its promise...the sweet, sustaining promise remained. No matter my fate or hers, the unbroken promise would linger with us, and one day be fulfilled.

# PART SIX
## Astoria, Oregon
## December 13, 1998

*But if this world keeps right on turnin',*
*For the better or the worse,*
*An' all he ever gets is older and around.*
*From the rockin' of the cradle,*
*To the rollin' of the hearse,*
*The goin' up was worth the comin' down.*

—*The Pilgrim: Chapter 33,*
Kris Kristofferson

# Epilogue

Saunders closed the manuscript, leaned back in the chair, removed his glasses, and looked with wistful melancholy at his old friend. Wilson lay peacefully immobile, silhouetted in moonlight against the large bedroom window.

The rain had stopped, replaced by a relentless coastal wind that pushed through the frosty night, petulantly rattling the old, single-pane window and moaning past the cedar gables. The fireplace hearth was dark, flames turned to embers, warmth forced aside by the Pacific Northwest cold and December damp.

The muffled and distant sound of clock chimes drifted slowly up the worn staircase, down the narrow hallway, and into the bedroom. Saunders squinted at his watch. Late, too late. He looked regretfully at Wilson, and with a chill, recalled Hamlet's warning, *"'Tis now the very witching time of night."* The dawn would arrive soon enough. Shortly, the old house would be filled with sheriffs, attorneys, coroners, and other officious bureaucrats of reckoning, each indifferently determined to find and record cause and effect. For now, peace and dignity were well served by silence and solitude.

The old photograph lay near Wilson's cold fingertips, face up on the blue woolen blanket. Saunders reached for the picture and lifted it to the dim lamplight. The youthful woman's warmly serious gaze seemed to track him. He thought it a pleasant, comfortable sensation. He looked again at the frail, silent man; then, back to the woman. Surely, she was smiling now.

With a sigh, he slipped the picture into his shirt pocket. Standing, he switched off the lamp, walked across the squeaking wooden floor to the doorway, turned, and looked back through the fading darkness toward the bed.

He leaned wearily against the door-post and massaged his forehead. With a sigh, he thought of young hearts, alight with innocence and so dangerously unaware of the dark wolves. He thought of sacrifice and its painful, ennobling cost. He thought of physical separation and emotional connectivity. He thought of twenty-year promises, bound hearts, and reality's brutal zeal to crush both. He closed his eyes and saw Young the way he remembered her best, standing high above the Han, forever bathed in November's warm, brilliant sunlight. He looked regretfully at Wilson, lying washed in December's cold, final moonlight. Where were they now?

The wind again bullied the window. Stirred from his reverie, Saunders reached for the heavy door and pulled it slowly toward him. A brass hinge groaned. The room began to disappear. The oak frame creaked. The door's edge rubbed stubbornly against the jamb, but continued to close. There was a frustrated metallic sound as the old latching mechanism tried vainly to seat, its long separated pieces searching for one another. He gently tugged and turned the knob. Immediately, there was the audible snap of two matching parts, parts machined to fit only one another, clicking firmly into place. Finally, the door was closed, the lock engaged, the journey complete, and Young's sweet, sustaining promise...fulfilled.

Born in Indiana and raised in Ohio, GALEN KINDLEY is now a "naturalized citizen" of the Great Pacific Northwest. He lives quietly—and on his best behavior–in a small town about forty miles east of Seattle with his pesky and manic Welsh Terrier, Kris.

He began college in the fall of 1967, but the disaster ended about a year later when the University of Cincinnati asked him rather bluntly to leave and never return. Based on his grades and class attendance, this was an eminently fair request. Galen rationalized his predicament saying, "The world probably didn't need another math major." Apparently, the world agreed.

The United States Army, however, wasn't so picky. Galen joined that august group in late 1968, graduating from Helicopter Pilot flight training in November, 1969. Since he'd been very good all year long, and it was just before Christmas, Santa rewarded him with an assignment to the 190th Assault Helicopter Company in Viet Nam. Higher authority eventually decided that a year of combat experience was more than sufficient, and mercifully sent him to Fort Rucker, Alabama as an instructor pilot, where he learned flying with students was more dangerous than flying in Viet Nam! During the course of the next nineteen years, he spent time in Korea, Germany, and another "tour" at Fort Rucker. His assignments dealt exclusively with flying and instructing. He retired from the Army in December, 1988 after four years at Fort Lewis, Washington.

During his Army time he doggedly pursed a college degree, finally eking out the last credit hour requirements in late 1988. In December, he graduated with a bachelor of arts and a double major in Information Systems Management and Accounting--in the event you're doing the math, that would be 20 plus years to obtain a four-year degree.

Galen essentially "fell into" his writing career. Many of the flying positions he held also required writing. As an instructor pilot he discovered verbal skills--a close cousin to the written word--were vitally important. His auditor position requires clear and precise writing to communicate sometimes contentious audit results. Over time, he began to appreciate that word choice and sequence was more than a matter of happenstance. The more he wrote, the more he enjoyed it. His tour in Korea sparked an interest in Asia and led him to combine his growing interest in writing with his fascination for things Asian. The result? "Hearts of the Morning Calm."

Visit his website at
www.HeartsoftheMorningCalm.com